GW01453045

One Million Project
FANTASY ANTHOLOGY

40 fantastic short tales
Compiled by
Jason Greenfield

Fantasy – Science Fiction
Fantasy Supernatural

DARK INK PRESS

Index: Genre – Title – Author

Copyright

Dedication

This book is dedicated to 3 groups of people: The dozens of contributors (writers, promotional artists, media, admin, tech) who gave of their time and skills to help a good cause, the charities and activists who spend every day trying to make the world a better place by helping others and finally, you the reader, who bought this collection and have helped contribute towards raising ONE MILLION POUNDS and making this a globally known cause. Thank you all. Jason.

Acknowledgments

Our story writers – 40 wonderful writers whose names you'll find in the index and at the head of each story. Our cover designers/artists - you'll find their names at the end of each story.

COMPILING EDITOR - JASON GREENFIELD

OMP: FANTASY PROJECT MANAGER - LINN NEILSON

OMP: FANTASY EDITOR - SHARON RHOADS

MAIN COVER DESIGNS - D.J. MEYERS

MAIN COVER LOGO DESIGN - CLAUDIA MURRAY

FORMATTING AND IMAGE EDITING - DECLAN CONNER

PUBLISHER - OMP PUBLISHING: WITH ASSISTANCE FROM KATE ANDERSON & DARK INK PRESS

Introduction

Welcome to the OMP, a project very dear to my heart and years in the making. Before you lies a journey into 40 varied and fantastic stories by 40 different writers including myself. Hopefully you will be thoroughly entertained as well as gain the satisfaction of knowing your money is going to a good cause.

The collection you see before you was born out of two separate notions of mine that didn't seem very workable on their own. Firstly, having written several novels, I wanted to do a collection of stories but even when I had the idea of adding other writers to it, it seemed like it didn't have much chance of standing out among the millions of other EBooks and print books on Amazon and elsewhere.

My second notion was a deep desire to do something to help people; having watched programs on the homeless, and experienced the agonies of a relative contracting cancer (my mother - now many years in remission thankfully) these were the two areas of charity that I wanted to raise money and awareness for.

However I had no idea, how I, a mere writer, could ever be in a position to do anything significant.

Then suddenly a synapse sparked in my head and it all made perfect sense! What if I could combine my short story collection with the charity issue - now I have a hook for one and a vehicle to raise money for the other! Ideas came fast and furious ... I would build up a network of creative people (and promotions/media folk) - writers to contribute the stories and artists to do covers. The primary goal would be to raise money for our chosen charities and as a secondary goal, the work of the creative people within would have exposure to a large audience. Many more ideas and strategies have come of this since then and hopefully there will be huge global word of mouth to make this project a success.

It's called the ONE MILLION PROJECT as that is an aspirational figure - raising £1,000,000 (and hopefully more) and so far we have four anthologies debuting in early 2018 with more books and other projects within the OMP brand to follow.

100% of the profits of this collection are going to charity so I really hope that you will give the wonderful, generous and talented people who have given their time, skills and effort for free, a look and check out their other projects - all our writers can be found via their personal bio and links at the end of their stories. Please support them and if you like the collections (see links at end for the other OMP anthologies) please tell all your friends to download and help spread the word.

NOTE: OMP Fantasy presents a variety of different genres - Fantasy, Sci-Fi and Supernatural Fantasy. Stories are of differing lengths (with a few writers choosing to do multiple mini stories so in fact there's more than 40 overall!) - While standardizing the look of the collections, I've tried to keep the individual characteristics and style of the writer intact where I can.

Now without further ado, I present 40 great stories

Enjoy.

Jason Greenfield.

Dragon

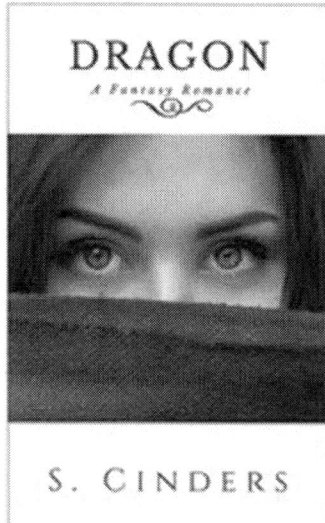

S. Cinders

Rachel has lived her entire life knowing that she has never been enough. The final straw occurs when her longtime boyfriend leaves her for another man at work. Seeking solace, Rachel goes to the one place that she has always found peace, the woods. And from there she slips into another dimension and she learns what the truly important things in life are.

I work with special needs children with emotional disabilities by day and scramble about typing stories on my laptop at night. Writing is so much more than a hobby to me, I would consider it therapy if you will. I adore 'happily every afters' and finding the good in others. I am all too aware of the realities of life, but I can't help but think that deep down everyone has something redeeming about them. Sometimes we just need to keep on digging.

Chapter 1

Asingle drop of water teetered on the edge of his drenched black strands. His deeply tanned skin had already taken a reddish hue, and I knew that we had minutes or even seconds before the beast would awake. His eyes flashed yellow and then turned a deep jade color. All right before they landed on me and then fire blazed from his throat.

His head reared up, and scarlet scales replaced where flesh had been moments earlier. Those reddened scales looked to be almost metal in appearance. But how could they grace his body so tightly? And at times they appeared to be almost black. My mind was reeling. Even though I had just witnessed the event, I still couldn't fathom that a man had just turned into a beast.

Dragon's weren't real; they couldn't be.

"Who sent you here?" His velvet voice was as deep as the ocean.

I shook my head in fear. "No one."

He growled low in his throat, and black smoke erupted from his nostrils. "We don't get humankind in our realm. Who sent you here?"

My heart was pounding, and I wasn't sure if I was getting enough air inside of my lungs. "I was walking." There began to be dark spots in the corners of my vision, I tried to blink them away. "I was…"

The next thing I knew I was laying on a large pile of straw. The dragon was nowhere to be seen, and I said a silent prayer because I knew that it all had to have been a horrible dream. But I was wide awake now, and everything could go back to how it should be.

And then it hit me—I didn't really have anything to go back to—not anymore.

My boyfriend Thomas had left me for a partner at his firm. His name is Stephen. I have always liked Stephen and even had him over for dinner several times. Apparently, I didn't like him as well as Thomas did.

What kind of fool loses her boyfriend to another man?

When Thomas came back to the apartment to pick up the rest of his things I wanted to make sure that I wasn't there. So, instead, I drove out to Kettering Forest. I have always loved hiking here. The rivers and trails are unparalleled.

But looking around myself, it seems that I have stumbled into some type of cave. The light was getting dim, and I knew that I would have a very difficult time seeing my way back down the trail. I felt in my back pocket for my phone.

2

But it wasn't there.

Don't panic.

"Woman!"

Panic!

I couldn't help the scream that escaped my lips.

"Argh! Stop! Woman, stop that!"

The Dragon pushed a talon over my mouth. It was sharp, but he was very careful not to slice my skin. I was breathing heavily and had gained a small measure of control.

"I am going to let go," he warned, "I do not want you to scream again."

I nodded slowly.

His talon was surprisingly cool against my warm skin.

The moment it left my skin I took a deep breath to steady myself. "I thought you weren't real," I stammered.

He tossed his large head back and made a gargling noise. Was he going to roast me? I curled into a little ball, but that only seemed to make him louder, and it was then that it dawned on me.

The dragon was laughing—at me.

"You are most amusing," he smiled at me, and his large razor-sharp teeth glinted in the remaining light.

"It is getting late, I will need to get back to my car."

He cocked his large head to his side, "What is a car?"

Is he for real?

"You know, a car? An automobile? My Honda Accord gets great gas mileage on the highway, almost paid off?"

He looked confused. "I do not know the terms of which you speak."

"For transportation. A large metal vehicle?" I didn't know any other way to describe it.

If a dragon could shrug his shoulders, this one did. "It has been quite some time since I have had interaction with a human. Perhaps these cars as you say are new."

Was he for real?

"When was the last time you spoke with a human? Because I am pretty sure cars have been around for hundred years."

He nodded. "That explains it. I haven't spoken with man for at least two hundred."

Now I knew that I was either dreaming or dead. These things just didn't happen to me. Dragons didn't exist, and they certainly didn't live for hundreds of years.

"Am I dead?"

The gargling again.

"I'm not kidding."

He rolled onto his back, and I wondered for a brief moment if it hurt those spiky scales that stood up.

"Listen, Dragon…"

"Daemon," he interrupted me.

"Excuse me?" I asked.

"My name is Daemon," he replied again with a toothy smile.

"Rachel," I replied hesitantly, "Rachel Moore."

"Moore what?" he asked.

"More nothing," I said angrily, "that is just my last name."

"Seems cruel to name a child more. You are more than enough Rachel."

"Oh, good Lord." I rolled my eyes. "Never mind, it's getting dark, are there lights in this cave?"

Daemon looked surprised. "Dragons can see in the dark, I am sorry I had forgotten about your weak human eyes."

I gave him a less than happy glance. "You are too kind."

Chapter 2

"There is no way in hell I am climbing on your back." I looked at Daemon in horror.

"Rachel, if I am to try and help you find your car you will need to guide me. How can you do that from the ground?" Daemon asked patiently.

I hated how calm and rational he sounded.

And that he was calm and rational.

"What if I fall off?" I mumbled.

He started to smile. "I will not allow you to fall off."

I looked at him incredulously. "Are you telling me that you have feeling on the top of your scales?"

Daemon looked mortally offended. "Do you have feeling in your back?"

"Of course, I do!"

"Then why would you assume that I do not?" His nose was emitting tiny spirals of black smoke showing his ire.

I shrugged. "They don't look very soft."

Daemon sighed. "When I covered your mouth with my talon did I hurt you?"

4

I shook my head. "No, you were very careful."

"Rachel, I have been a dragon for a very long time. I know how to protect a newborn babe, I am more than certain I can carry and coddle a full-grown woman."

Now I was feeling a little sheepish, it was getting late, and I knew that without Daemon's ability to see in the dark I would be completely lost.

"I am sorry," I ducked my head. "You are right. I am overreacting."

"Rachel, come here."

Daemon was so much larger than I was. At full height, I would say between ten or eleven feet tall. To my five-foot-three, he was more than double my size.

"Do not be afraid of me, little one," he tipped my chin up with his talon. "Please touch my scales. See for yourself, I will not harm you."

I could feel a tremendous heat coming off him. I tentatively stretched my hand out to touch his arm. The moment that I touched his red scales my hand sealed itself to him. I cried out as fire erupted around my arm.

"Daemon!" I screamed, "What is happening?"

"Rachel." Daemon was looking at me with astonishment. "This cannot be!"

The fire was racing up my arm. Burning, scalding me to the point where I didn't know if I would still have skin left on my body. I wanted to die. The pain was so intense.

I knew that I was screaming, and that Daemon was trying to calm me down, but no matter what I did I could not remove my hand from his arm.

"Hold on, Rachel," he pleaded, "I didn't know! Honestly!"

I was starting to feel incredibly heavy. The pain was so intense. Death seemed preferable.

Why had all these things happened to me?

Is this how my life was to end?

"Rachel, you are going to make it, little one," Daemon's voice seemed further off now.

My breathing was shallower. And the heat, it was so hot. The fire building, roiling up from the depths of my gut. I was going to vomit. I needed to some air but couldn't get my breath.

The heat.

The fire.

Suddenly, I opened my mouth, and a great ball of fire erupted from my mouth.

I almost fell flat on my face, having no energy after.

"Bloody hell, Rachel!" Daemon laughed. "New Dragons aren't able to breathe fire for weeks!"

Why was he telling me this?

I felt so sick. Stumbling to the side, I realized that Daemon didn't seem quite so big as he steadied me. And then I noticed that I could see quite clearly around me even though night had most certainly fallen.

I whipped my head around and smacked myself in the face with a golden tail.

To my extreme horror—the tail belonged to me.

"You made me a dragon?" I screamed.

My voice had taken a much deeper, guttural tone. My arms were replaced with golden scales, and I had a long sharp tail. I knew that Daemon had fierce looking wings on his back and reached back hesitantly to see if I possessed the same.

A sharp pain pierced through me as I tugged on them—permanently attached.

"What did you do?" I raged at him.

Daemon looked confused. "I did nothing. It was all you."

"What are you talking about?" I cried.

"Rachel, I have no idea why you were placed in the human world. If you were raised here in Tarletha as you should have been, you would have changed with your first womanly flow. Dragons are not creatures that are meant to live alone. They have soul mates, and I have waited centuries to find mine."

I didn't like the sound of this, "How do you know if someone is your soul mate?"

"When you touch, you will feel the burn of love's fire. Ours burned so brightly it forced you to turn." He looked at me hesitantly. "But let's not worry about that right now. Rachel. Who were your parents? How did you end up in the human world?"

"I was adopted as a baby," I said, quietly, "My parents were older, and they passed a few years back. I don't have any other close family. I was dating Thomas, but he left—it doesn't matter."

Daemon frowned. "He left you?"

I huffed, and spirals of black smoke appeared. "For another man. You may have gotten a bad bargain for a soul mate, Daemon."

He looked at me savagely. "Don't ever say that, Rachel. That man is a fool. Most men are, but he is the greatest of them all. I don't blame him for loving another. But I don't see how anyone could walk away from you."

I didn't realize that I was crying until he wrapped me in his arms, our scales clashing and clanking together as he rocked me back and forth.

I am not sure how long we stood there. He held me tightly, and I cried out all the hurt and frustration of rejection and starting new.

When I pulled back, I realized something had drastically changed. Daemon's long black hair brushed his tan shoulders. He had some type of tribal tattoo that made up most of his right shoulder and arm. I have never seen a man with such an impeccable body. Washboard abs that I desperately wanted to lick every nook and cranny.

He was wearing leather breeches and boots. But his eyes, those jade eyes, they were the same as the dragon.

My dragon.

"Daemon?" I whispered.

"It is me, Rachel." He smiled, and I melted.

Chapter 3

Three weeks later

"You are getting so much better!" Daemon shouted as I stumbled back to my feet.

I was terrible at flying. I could burn things with my fire, spear things with my talons, grasp things in my claws, but damn it, I was crap at flying.

"You know that is not true," I grumbled, extending my wings back out again.

"But you keep getting up again, and that is half the battle."

I rolled my eyes at him. Daemon hadn't said anything more about being my soul mate, but he was certainly growing on me. He was quick to make sure that I was comfortable. That I had enough to eat, or that I was warm enough. Daemon was funny and liked to laugh, there were so many things to like about him.

I worried that maybe I was falling too far too fast.

Daemon had sent a message to the head council that his soulmate had been found. I had no idea that they were even organized enough to have a council.

He told me not to worry. It was only protocol. But I couldn't help the tiny niggling of fear that sat at the back of my mind. I wouldn't leave him even if they tried to force me.

The truth was that for the first time in my life I was happy.

And that was worth fighting for.

"Come on, Rach, try again!"

I grunted, "You are a task master, Daemon!"

But I concentrated hard and started to flap my giant wings. I felt the familiar tugging and whooshing of air as it circulated around me.

"Stop thinking Rachel," Daemon admonished. "Just feel, let your wings feel the air. They will know when it is time."

"My wings don't have a brain, Dummy," I replied,

Daemon laughed. "Just try it my way for once!"

I huffed, "Just once!"

Letting go of everything I continued to flap my wings letting them feel the air around me. Bit by bit, I could feel the air stir my golden scales. This was different, slowly I opened my eyes.

Daemon was watching me, "Come!"

That was the only thing he said, and when he took to the air, I followed. I couldn't miss his bright scarlet scales zipping and zapping through the blue sky. He was simply magnificent. I marveled at how perfect he was.

Not only did he keep looking back to make sure that I was alright but he would shout encouragement to me.

"Rachel, beautifully done! Look at you!"

I beamed at his praise. I was doing it. I was flying.

It was euphoric. I had never felt so free.

This was what I was born to do.

Back and forth all through the day, we frolicked among the clouds.

It was utopia.

And then they came.

"Your name is Antabuse. You were abducted as a child. You are the crowned princess of these lands."

I sat there in shock clutching Daemon's hand as they eyed him in disgust.

"You are not required to remain with the peasant."

How could they not see him clearly? Dragon's had excellent sight.

"During the great war, you were abducted and taken to the human realm. Time moves differently there. It has been five hundred years."

I wasn't thirty-four? Or I was both thirty-four and five hundred respectively?

But the most upsetting news of all was when the oldest dragon, one covered in silver scales rasped out, "Royalty does not mate with anything lower than gentry. Daemon is of the lowest social class and not fit to serve as your consort."

That was unacceptable.

You see, for my entire life, I had always been the one to not fit.

My adoptive parents while kind where so much older that they wanted a quiet, respectable child. I had the heart of a dragon, even though I didn't know it. I was constantly disappointing them with my rash outbursts and passionate nature.

In school, they wanted me to become a doctor or a lawyer. I was an artist. I could paint for hours, usually forestry scenes. Not surprising, seeing my true lineage, but once again terribly disappointing.

I started dating Thomas for my parents. If I couldn't be a lawyer, at least I could marry one, I thought. And for once they were content, but secretly in my heart, I knew that it was for them and not for me. I did grow to love him, in my own way.

When my parents died, he was all I had left, and they had been so happy I had chosen him. I now see clearly why it hurt so much. I was grieving the loss of my parents once again.

The only person in my entire life that has ever looked at me and saw me for who I really am is Daemon. He was kind to me before he ever knew I was his mate. One simple touch and he changed my life, my future, indeed my entire world.

He has spent every moment of the last three weeks loving me.

Daemon loves me.

The thought was so overwhelming that I almost stumbled. But the warmth that started burning in my heart confirmed the fact that not only did I know this for a fact, but I loved him in return.

The elderly dragon was still talking, but I completely ignored him.

"Daemon," his red spiked tail was draped over his shoulder, and his eyes were cast down. When he glanced up at me, the pain in his jade eyes was almost more than I could bear. "Daemon, I Rachel, accept thee as my mate. For now, and always."

He was shocked. The other two dragons started yelling and moving toward me, but Daemon quickly flew over to stand in front of me. He was bigger and meaner than the Royal guard that had been sent.

"I Daemon, accept thee, Rachel, as my mate. For now, and always.

I love you, Rachel."

I felt a tear slide down my golden scales, "I love you too, Daemon."

The elderly dragon was furious, "They will denounce you!"

I smiled up into Daemon's eyes, "Let them do what they may. I have found happiness, and plan on having a large rowdy family with this dragon. I don't need crowns or gold. But everyone needs to be loved."

Daemon wrapped her in his arms, "And I will always love you."

The End

God Bless! S. Cinders.

https://www.amazon.com/S.-Cinders/e/B01M6WPKBS

https://www.wattpad.com/user/cinders75

Cover by Author.

Sanctuary

Xanxa Symanah

A story about a fantasy author written by a fantasy writer. Take a brief glimpse into one of the worlds created by Xanxa and witness how the Carpathian gangster families operate. Find out what motivates them and what they will do to protect those they care for. The characters Parsivaal Probyt and Lord Andreas Cesario feature in some of Xanxa's full length novels.

***

"I'll kill her!" the outraged voice yelled, followed by the sound of a computer tablet being thrown against a wall. "How dare she insult me in such a brazen manner!"

"Kill who?" his wife enquired, concerned by her husband's irrational outburst.

"This writer woman!" he growled, gesturing towards the tablet, which now lay in pieces on the floor. "Thinks she can get away with lampooning me in her latest pseudo-Carpathian saga. I'll make sure she never writes another word!"

***

The woman risked a glance over her shoulder, hoping that she had shaken off the cloaked figure who had been pursuing her. Scanning the crowds, she caught sight of the assassin, forcing his way through the mass of people in the square. Taking a deep breath, she broke into another run, the air burning in her lungs as she neared exhaustion.

The little side-street was an unexpected escape route. Taking a deep breath, she turned into it, barely slowing her frantic pace. She had not gone far when she came to a row of shops, the first being an old junk shop bearing the name MISCELLANIUM on a faded sign above the front window.

A bell chimed when she entered the shop. The interior was dark, only lit by a few flickering gas lamps. When her eyes adjusted to the gloom, she stared around at the haphazard arrangement of old furniture, rugs, scientific equipment, books, paintings, ornaments and other artefacts.

Her eyes were drawn to a glass globe on one of the high shelves. Reaching up, she grabbed it, feeling strange energies pulse through her fingers when they made contact with the glass. It glowed in her hand and a soft female voice spoke. "Welcome, Syrene Khylym, enter the Circle and you will find sanctuary. Wind turns green and the Goddess smiles."

She almost dropped the globe in shock. "What?" she exclaimed, glancing around to make sure that no-one else had entered the shop behind her.

The globe repeated its message. She knew that "the Circle" was a reference to the organised crime syndicate known as the Carpathian Way or the Carpathian Movement, but the rest of the message was a total mystery to her.

"You come seeking sanctuary, my dear?" a quavering voice enquired. She turned around to see a tall, thin, elderly man with long, tangled, white hair standing behind the counter at the rear of the shop. She was certain that he had not been there when she had first entered.

"This globe spoke to me" she told him, holding up the artefact to show him. "It knows my name. How can that be?"

"It only speaks to those in need" he remarked, smiling at her. "'Tis the voice of Iraevesh, the Goddess of Justice, offering you sanctuary.

Clearly, you have a story to tell and I would like to hear it."

She sighed heavily and walked over to the counter, still holding the globe. "I'm a writer of fantasy novels. Not a particularly famous one, but I've been moderately successful over the past few years. Two days ago, I received a death threat from one Lord Thanasio Cordotti. He believes that the central character in my latest book is based on him and shows him in an unflattering way. I'd never heard of him until he sent me the death threat, so how could I have written about him?"

"Lord Thanasio Cordotti" the elderly shopkeeper mused, running his fingers through his tangled hair. "I can't say I've ever heard of him either, but I happen to be friends with a Carpathian Spy Master. I feel sure that he will know of Lord Cordotti. I'll contact him."

He closed his eyes and leaned on the counter. A moment later, another man appeared beside him – a small, thin fellow with dark waist-length hair and a droopy moustache. He produced a computer tablet and began typing rapidly, muttering to himself all the while. "Cordotti, aye, Fifth Echelon, Patriarch Lord Thanasio, three brothers, one sister, all involved in the family business of perfume distilling. Unremarkable family, never made the headlines for any reason."

He slid the tablet over to Syrene. She scanned the database entries, paying particular attention to the photographs of Lord Thanasio. He looked to be in his early forties, with light brown hair and a round face. It was not the sort of face which would stand out in a crowd; in fact it was instantly forgettable.

"So Lord Thanasio be sending assassins after ye, eh?" the little Spy Master enquired, looking at her intently.

"Aye" she confirmed, handing the tablet back to him. "The first one broke into my house. I was lucky that I managed to knock him out with my brass door-stop. I was so shaken up that I went to stay with a friend in another part of the city. This morning, I awoke to find my friend dead. Her throat had been cut. I panicked and ran. I had no idea where to go, as I don't know many people in this city. I've only lived here for just over a year. I thought I'd be safe in a public place but the assassin must have been hiding and waiting for me to leave. I've been running and hiding from him all day."

"The Goddess led you here" the elderly man remarked. "She obviously considers you to be important, or else she would not have offered you sanctuary."

"This is all very confusing for me" Syrene admitted. "I mean, I've had critics trashing my novels before. It's all part of the territory for an author, but death threats from a man I've never heard of? And why would a Carpathian Goddess offer me sanctuary from a Carpathian Lord? It doesn't make sense."

"Iraevesh knows what be in yer heart and soul" the little Spy Master spoke, giving her a sly grin. "Besides, it goes against the Carpathian Code of Honour to issue death threats to non-Carpathians. Ye have every right to take action against him."

"What sort of action?" Syrene asked. "The City Watch won't deal with any incidents relating to Carpathians, so there's no point in reporting it to them."

"City Watch be worse than useless" the Spy Master commented with a chuckle. "But there be plenty ye can do. Like taking out a counter-contract on Lord Cordotti, for example. I'd be more than happy to oblige."

Syrene stared at the little man in astonishment. "You'd kill him for me?"

"Aye, of course" he replied, reaching over the counter and patting her arm reassuringly. "Tis no less than he deserves."

"And what would I have to do for you in return? From what I know of Carpathians, your services wouldn't come for free."

The little man stroked his moustache. "I be sure we can work something out. Ye be a writer and we Carpathians always appreciate the power of words. From yer accent, I can tell that ye be Yttrian by birth. Yer command of Varathusian be most excellent for an off-worlder. How many other languages do ye know?"

Blushing at the compliment, Syrene replied "Virian, Malvanian and Varathusian. I was a language major at school. I graduated from the Kashmir Language Academy and I worked as a freelance translator for many years before I started writing novels."

The Spy Master gave a beaming smile. "Then we have a way in for ye" he announced. "Ye come and work for the Inner Circle Alliance as a translator and I'll deal with Lord Cordotti for ye. Ye'll be under our protection in one of our safe houses and ye'll never have to fear an assassin again. Ye'd be able to work on yer novels in peace."

"Sounds too good to be true."

The Spy Master pulled back the cuff of his jacket, displaying the Carpathian brandmark just above his right wrist – a stylised version of a serpent eating its tail. Syrene was familiar with the symbol. She had seen it many times since coming to live in Veretris City. The little man then raised his right hand and used his index finger to trace a circle in the air. "Carpathian honour" he said. "I be Lord Andreas Cesario, Spy Master for the Inner Circle Alliance of the Carpathian Way and tis me pleasure to offer ye sanctuary."

Syrene looked down at the globe in her hands, then back up at the two men standing behind the counter. Her heart beat faster as she replied "I accept."

***

Lord Thanasio Cordotti waited for his chauffeur to open the limousine door. He had an important business meeting to attend and was running late. He hoisted his document case and slid it onto the back seat of the vehicle before getting in.

There was a blur of motion beside him, too fast for his eyes to follow. He let out a low moan as the garrotting wire bit into his neck. He saw his own blood spraying out in front of him before he slumped over on the seat.

The chauffeur grinned and drove away from the Cordotti mansion.

***

Lady Theresa Cordotti blinked away tears. She read the message again. She had returned from a shopping trip to find the scroll tied with red ribbon placed on her dressing table. Red ribbon only meant one thing – a death notice.

"Chimera Obscura to Lady Theresa Cordotti – Sometimes a story is just a story. Words only have power if you pay attention to them. Your husband has paid the price. His story will serve as a cautionary tale. Her stories will continue unabated."

She shook her head and pushed the scroll aside. The message made no sense to her.

***

The bookstore was already crowded when Lady Cordotti arrived there. Syrene Khylym was her favourite author and Lady Cordotti was looking forward to reading her latest novel. Her late husband had never thought much of fantasy novels and had often denounced

15

Syrene Khylym's work as garbage. It was one of the few things which they had disagreed upon during their twenty-year marriage.

She glanced around at the mass of people in the bookstore before joining the queue to have her copy of *Chimera Obscura* signed by Syrene Khylym. Prior to her husband's passing, she would have felt uncomfortable attending a book-signing by this particular author, but a great many things had changed in the last six months. Thanasio had named her as Matriarch in his Will and since then she had done her best to run the family businesses, despite the jealousy and disapproval from her husband's siblings.

She was almost at the front of the queue when she felt a sharp sting at the back of her neck. A hot dizziness came over her in waves and she staggered, clutching at the man in front of her for support. He turned around and shoved her aside, giving her a disdainful look.

A security guard came to her rescue a few moments later. "Tis the heat in here, I expect" he remarked, helping her up. "I'll find ye somewhere nice and quiet to lay down. I'll also make sure ye don't miss out on the book-signing. Tis Lady Theresa Cordotti, right?"

She nodded weakly and allowed him to escort her away from the queue.

"What was all that about?" Syrene enquired, having witnessed the incident.

"Poor woman was overcome by the heat" Andreas explained, leaning in close so that no-one else could overhear their conversation. "She'll be fine in a while. I'll take good care of her, so don't worry."

***

Once Syrene had resumed her book-signing, Andreas excused himself and hastened to the security office, where his colleague was waiting.

"Job done as instructed" the man stated, inclining his head and tracing a circle in the air with the index finger of his right hand. "What should I do with the body?"

"Burn it" Andreas ordered. "The remaining members of the Cordotti family will be far too busy arguing over who gets to be Patriarch or Matriarch to be bothered with filing a missing persons report on her. At least our dear Syrene will be safe now."

"Ye believe that Lady Cordotti was going to kill Syrene?" the colleague questioned.

Andreas held up a perfume bottle. "I know so. Y'see, many of those in the perfume trade also know about poisons. Lady Cordotti planned to give this to Syrene as a gift. Payback for what we did to her husband."

***

The book-signing was over. Syrene put down her pen and went to the security office to collect her personal belongings. She could not help noticing the perfume bottle on the desk. She picked it up.

"Don't!" Andreas warned, but it was too late.

A sickly sweet fragrance filled the air, causing Syrene to choke. "That's got to be the most disgusting perfume I've ever smelled!" she exclaimed, putting the bottle back down on the desk.

Andreas stared at her, his heart pounding while he waited for the poison to take effect. "Ye be alright, me dear?" he enquired, taking her by the arm to steady her.

"Aye, I just need to get some air" she replied, managing a small smile.

"I'd best come with ye" he offered, sighing with relief and guiding her out of the security office.

Outside, Syrene took in deep breaths to rid herself of the cloying smell of the perfume. It had been a good day, better than she had expected.

The End

You can find Xanxa's work at these places:

https://www.amazon.co.uk/Xanxa-Symanah/e/B00S3TRL3E/ref=sr_ntt_srch_lnk_1?qid=1506037760&sr=8-1&follow-button-add=B00S3TRL3E_author&

https://www.amazon.com/Xanxa-Symanah/e/B00S3TRL3E/ref=sr_ntt_srch_lnk_1?qid=1506037663&sr=8-1

https://virianchronicler.blogspot.com.br/

Cover by Author.

Mythlands: The Beginning

Jason Greenfield

Author's Foreword

The Mythical Creatures and The Mythlands they inhabit were born sort of by accident. I had joined a writing site called WriteOn (now sadly closed as of March 22nd 2017) and had been encouraged to join in their weekend writing challenges as a way of meeting and interacting with people - I did so religiously, doing at least one challenge prompt every weekend, starting off with mostly one-off shorts and gradually developing ongoing characters and concepts.

The weekend challenge stories (and later writing challenges such as Story Cubes and others) were roughly 500-1500 worders with prompt words (or picture dice, cards etc) and a line such as 'Imagine you were waiting in a queue -' Prompt word could be 'Impatient.

One weekend I received the following prompt from a STORY CUBES challenge and wrote what was intended to be a one-off story:

Dice Roll – FIRE, FAIRY, TORTOISE and my story description for

NEPOTISM was –

The CEO of MCI receives Ariel's report into the Arson Investigation at one of the Corporation's eateries. Is it as he feared - that the fire was caused by an old friend's negligence?

And that 532 word story was it for the idea ... except it wasn't. I had an idea for more Mythical Creatures but it would only work if I got certain words as a prompt for the next weekend challenge. I needed either cat or owl, but what were the chances!!??

It turns out that was the week of the Super Bowl, so from a prompt of 'Superb Owl,' and the instruction - In 500 words, imagine what happens when a character encounters a superb owl, came a 572 word story (I use the word count as more of a guide than an absolute limit) entitled WHAT A HOOT! It took place within the same continuity of The Mythlands, with some vague connections to the first story, but using different characters.

By this time I was receiving comments and interest in the Mythical Creatures so I decided to write one more ... just one more (I swear it!) tale, albeit a bit longer. I called it THE HEIST and used the Story Cubes picture dice roll of Feb 7th 2016 to put together a slightly longer tale of 1053 words in three short parts. Dice Roll – RAT, APPLE, CACTUS.

That was it and while the ending could have been expanded on, I left it as a bit of a morality tale - after all only a perfect prompt the following week could inspire me enough to ... I think you know where I'm going with this ...

The Prompt – Unrequited.

The Challenge - In 500 words, tell a story in which love is unrequited.

So I added a fourth and final part ... until the fifth part. After that I gave up and decided to give into the inspiration and requests for more HEIST. To date I have done over 100 (small) parts and turned this into a sprawling fantasy adventure with ... well everything. Those small flash fiction parts are now mini chapters in a planned THREE (big) PART epic. I am almost finished with Part Two and together with a spin off (Convention of Cats) that fits in between two Heist chapters (with story points that play into The Heist) and a companion series called Mythical Origins (with mostly one-off more personal stories about Mythland inhabitants and the Mythlands itself), I am way on my way to producing George RR Martin amounts of material and hopefully a concept that will see print in it's own discrete collections. (It's already serialized in Volumes 2-4 - 5 due soon - of my Amazon published BITE SIZE STORIES, along with all my other flash fiction) and maybe even animation or film and other media.

But for now please enjoy the first two mini stories and first 4 scenes of The Heist which form a closed and complete story ... until, ya know ... the next bit!

***

Nepotism

Arson Investigation

There was a knock at the door.

'Come.'

Mrs. Tiggywinkle stuck her head around the frame. 'Sorry to disturb you Sir, but Ariel is here for her 2 o 'clock.'

'Ah, excellent. Send her in.'

A moment later a tiny six inch figure flitted past Mrs Tiggywinkle's furry head and alighted on the CEO's desk.

The Chief Exec continued writing for a moment, then slowly and deliberately removed his reading glasses and replaced them with the special magnifiers. They made his sparkling brown eyes stand out, as if many times enlarged. With a wave of his gnarled right hand, the old boy indicated that Ariel should seat herself on a tiny chair set up on the top of the desk, especially for Fairy visitors.

'Good ... afternoon, Ariel. Have you ... completed your ... investigation of the ... site?'

Ariel took a moment to adjust her amplifier and then her voice boomed around the luxuriously appointed office.

Seeing the CEO wince, she held up a tiny hand in apology and re-adjusted to get the right volume and eliminate the feedback and echo.

'It's mixed news I bring thee Master Chairman.'

The old fellow blinked and waved a slow hand to show that she should continue. These Fey had a penchant for dramatic pauses and although the CEO of Mythical Creatures Interdimensional was a cautious and thorough sort, much given to careful deliberation and the opposite of hasty, he preferred others impart their information at a measured but not over drawn out pace.

Ariel acknowledged this and withdrew her specially designed

21

tablet, to upload the full report to his system. In the meantime she knew the Chief would want the general details, painful as they might be for him to hear.

'While mine own investigations found no hint of deliberation, nor malice cruelly intended in regards to the fire, tis my unfortunate duty to inform thee Master, that negligence be the cause.'

The CEO sighed. 'Go on.'

'Tis the fault of the Manager … safety checks were rushed and hurried. Standards neglected I fear.'

'The kitchens … I … assume.'

Ariel nodded. 'Aye, tis so. Master O'Hare, though known to be a congenial host and well beloved figure to the patrons, cared only, t'would seem, to mingle with the dinner crowds and bask in their attentions, tis told. His neglect of the workings of the establishment, be well known. I have in mine possession, affidavits from the cook and wait staff. The Easter Bunny was fair furious, as he had reminded Master O'Hare of these safety measures time and time anon.'

The Chief sighed heavily. 'Then I have no choice … but to reassign him … to a position less likely … to do harm.'

Ariel frowned. 'Master, I know you and he go back, but the creature is a pernicious loon. I recommend dismissal.'

The CEO called for Mrs. Tiggywinkle and began to slowly, agonizingly stand. As his PA helped him into his shell, The Tortoise reflected on Ariel's words. He SHOULD sack his old friend, but ever since he'd won their race, he'd felt responsible.

No, reassignment it would have to be … somewhere where the Hare couldn't cause any damage!

What a Hoot

Welcome to the Land of the Mythical Creatures

There is a land. A place in space and time that is attached to the greater Mythlands of legend.

In the Mythlands, heroes and legends dwell … epic adventures are re-told and added to, on a frequent basis. In the section of which I speak, however, the inhabitants prefer to live a quieter life, content to bask in past glories. Their fables and tales are mostly told and now these creatures seek only to enjoy eternity and the simple company of their peers.

This is the land of the Mythical Creatures, although that description itself is a slight misnomer. Most hail from fables or fairy tales ... the literature and legend of the mortal realm. There are few men or even humanoids in this quiet, green covered area, where the sun always shines (well, mostly. The odd spot of rain is good for the crops) and the sky is usually a pleasant blue.

Today, a member of the board of Mythical Creatures Interdimensional, is enjoying a break from the rat race. He has come to the lake-house he shares with his partner, to relax and renew.

Idyll

The Pussycat woke up to the smell of coffee and breakfast.

He yawned and stretched out in a languid fashion. Then he rolled onto his side and his arm sought ...

'Oh!' he exclaimed as he realized he was alone. A note scented of lavender lay on the pillow. 'Back soon, my love,' it read.

'Now where could the silly old duffer be?' murmured the Pussycat.

'Perhaps the Farmer's Market? But why didn't he wait? We had planned to go together ... I do hope he doesn't forget the marrows and squash and ... why am I talking to myself!'

The Pussycat decided he needed his coffee and so he descended to the ground floor of their idyllic cottage. A fresh pot of Brazilian roast awaited him on the stove and a note on the fridge told him breakfast was within.

A cold collation of meats and cheeses with lovingly arranged melon slices intersected with berries had been prepared. The Pussycat was pleased but sad at the same time, for he would have loved to have breakfasted with his partner of all these decades, especially as today was their ...

He was struck by a thought! 'I hope the Tortoise hasn't called him to the office! I shall be very cross if that's the case!'

But after all, there was no reason why the old duffer wouldn't have let him know if it were so and ... hullo!

'Why, he's left his glasses on the kitchen table! He can't have gone far, for without them he can hardly see far at all!'

But then came a shout from outside.

'Aha, he's back, but why at the back instead of the front!' declared the Pussycat to himself.

Resolving to see, he exited out of the patio door and saw ...

'Surprise!!' shouted his tawny partner, spreading a wingspan to the lake.

Upon the water sat something that had not been there before ... a boat! A beautiful pea green boat!

'Did I get the colour right?' his love asked, anxiously ruffling his feathers.

The Pussycat felt tears come to his eyes as he handed over the glasses. 'See for yourself you superb Owl, you! It's perfect. Every detail is as I remember! What a hoot!'

The Owl smiled. 'Happy Anniversary,' he told the Pussycat and they hugged.

The Heist: trickster, World Tree and Vegas Baby!

In the Mythlands, there exist certain places which are echoes of the mortal world. These places have become so legendary that they are duplicated elsewhere. One such place is Las Vegas ... but our story doesn't start there, nor does it start in the Realm of the Mythical Creatures, although one of our fur covered friends does play a prominent role.

No, let us start our tale some few hundred leagues from the borders of the domain of the Mythical Creatures and some distance from Myth Vegas.

Trickster

The Sign of Fafnir, an Inn on the outskirts of the City of Asgard.

'Ah, thy tale of woe rings most familiar, for I too am an outsider, even among my own people.' The hooded man signalled for two more flagons of ale. 'But pray continue my lop eared friend.'

The Hare was already well on the way to becoming severely inebriated. 'He's supposed to be my best friend, but all he does is treat me like a child! It wasn't my fault the place burnt down ... s'not as if I deliberately started the fire! Faulty wiring they said ... not up to code ... and just because I was managing the joint I'm supposed to be ... hic .... reshponshible!'

'A terrible injustice,' commiserated the gaunt, dark haired God.

'What brings thee to fair Asgard?'

The Hare burped. 'Ahhhh. Sorry. Yeah, so good ol Tortoise ... condescending bald green wrinkled ... where wash I? Oh yeah, he says not to worry, sends me to manage one of his casinos in Vegas ... the Lucky Cactus. After the trauma of it, I'm expected to get straight back to work!! No Sir, says I ... vacation first. So good ol Tort says he'd prefer I went straight there, but screw that and screw him. Jess … did I tell you about Jess?'

'Aye, a most voluptuous redheaded beauty ye said.'

'Yeah. I met her last month … she sings - classy, nightclub stuff, ya know. Anyway, she agreed to come with and sing in the Sunshine Lounge, but first she had this gig in Asgard and what the hey … I've never been.'

His companion signalled for more ale as the Hare finished his seventh flagon. 'My new friend, I am concerned for thee.'

'What! Why?'

'Such a woman … hast thou the coin to impress her?'

'Uh … I will once I'm there. Damn Tortoise won't give me an advance and all my money's in my car … lemme tell ya, she loves that car … red, 1958 cherry red convertible. In the mortal realm it's called a Thunderbird.'

'Thou wilst still need monies methinks, friend Hare. Mayhaps I can help thee, for just the other morn, a friend asked if I knew a stout fellow who wished to make easy coin. All thou needs do is take an item with thee across the border and keep it until my friend can collect. Tis a golden antiquity. No doubt thou hast questions …'

'How much? My share I mean.'

The green eyed man smiled and wrote down a sum.

The Hare's eyes widened. 'Loki, my man, you have yourself a deal!'

World Tree

And so several days later, the Hare, having been assured he was merely a courier for an item, which he would keep, so Loki and his friends could avoid an unjust tax imposed by the cruel and unreasonable authorities, found himself parked by the trunk of a huge tree.

Jessica sat in the car filing her nails. 'How much longer baby?' she inquired of our 'hero.'

The Hare looked at his watch. 'Loki said half past the hour.'

'And you're sure this is on the up n up?'

The Hare looked at her, with impatience tempered only for the way she made him feel when he checked out her smoking hot bod in that figure hugging red evening dress.

'Babe, I already told you. Loki's friend Ida … or something. The sculptress. She works in gold and centuries ago she made him this apple as a gift.'

'The one the giant Eagle stole?'

'Yeah, apparently it was some joke his brother, the Thunder God played on him. The Eagle swooped down and stole the golden apple and took it to the top of the tree.'

'That tree? It's supposed to go up hundreds of miles isn't it!?'

'Yeah and down hundreds from here too ... if not thousands. Anyway the Eagle lives at the top and he kept the apple. Loki finally got permission from his old man to recover it, but apparently there's some antiquities tax ... 40%. So he's doing it on the quiet. His contact's the last one anyone will suspect ... a messenger guy who goes between the top and the bottom. The plan is to blame the theft on this huge dragon who lives at the bottom. It's perfect .. the Eagle and the Dragon hate each other, see?'

'Ok .... I ... ewwwww, a giant rat!!!'

The Hare glanced upwards.

'Ho!' shouted the creature. 'Be thee O'Hare?' I am Ratatoskr and ... ah apologies my lady for mine appearance. Originally a squirrel I be, but by the fancies of the mortal imaginings and confusion about mine name, I have morphed into the seeming of a rodent and ...'

'Whatever buddy. We're on a schedule here. Do you have the apple?'

'Aye,' answered the messenger of the world tree and threw it down.

The Hare leaped aside and with some difficulty heaved the football sized golden apple into the back seat. Then they were off.

Vegas Baby

10 hours later as they hit the desert, the Hare was still feeling jubilant. They'd gotten away with it ... good for nothing screw up, am I, Tortoise, he thought as he raced along and took another slug at his bottle of JD.

'Slow down baby!' squealed Jessica.

The Hare's mood was broken and he turned towards her with irritation before ...

***

Crawling from the wreckage, the Hare looked around for Jessica

'Ohmigod, ohmigod.'

26

He frantically tried to give her CPR ... no pulse, NO PULSE!
Ohmigod. Ohmigod.

The Hare was crying ... panicking ... overwrought. He acted by instinct ... dialling the Tortoise's number. His buddy ... his good old buddy. The Tortoise ... the good old, fantastic Tortoise, would fix everything!

The Heist: Unrequited

In the few hours it had taken the MCI corporate helicopter to reach the desert east of Myth Vegas, the Hare had calmed down a lot.

Now, standing, sweating by the hole he'd dug with his bare paws and having dragged poor Jessica to the edge, he was now reconsidering his options.

What was the Tortoise going to do anyway? Grease a few palms to have this declared an accident ... it WAS an accident. One he was capable of sorting himself without that damned interfering wrinkled bald old ... no, fair's fair, even if he'd buried Jessica and nobody ever connected him to her disappearance, he still had to walk close to 40 miles to Vegas. He didn't fancy that ... the least old Tort could do was give him a lift.

In a way this was all the Tortoise's fault! If his so called friend hadn't continually made him feel like a worthless screw-up, he would never have felt the need to prove the green salad tosser wrong! He would never have let himself be talked into smuggling a stolen golden apple out of the land of Asgard ... why would he, if the damned Tortoise had given him some seed money for the new job!

So it stood to reason that, having been put in a position he would never have gotten into if not for his old 'friend', he, The Hare would not have been so jubilant about getting one over on old Tort.

Therefore he would not have been racing his Thunderbird while downing a bottle of Jack Daniels - he would not have crashed and Jessica would still be alive ... if not for the Tortoise.

The chopper was coming in to land and surprise, surprise, old Tort had come in person to gloat!

With his bodyguard, Papa Bear behind, holding up an umbrella, the Tortoise slowly emerged from the helicopter wearing a white suit and panama hat. He was leaning heavily on his stick.

'Hare ... my friend ... are you ...' he faltered, his voice, heavy with emotion.

The Hare glared. 'Fine. You took your time ... I've dug a grave.

Don't need your help ...' he batted the air as something flitted by his ears.

'Loon!' screamed Ariel as she landed on Jessica's ample bosom. 'Addle pated sap wit! The lass still has the spark of life within her!!'

Moments later the fey unleashed a fiery burst of energy and jump-started Jessica's heart. With a cough and a splutter, the lovely redhead sat up. It took her all of a moment to ascertain her situation ... the hole, the wrecked car ... the insipid expression of relief on the Hare's face as he ...'

'Jess!! Baby!! You're alive!!'

His joy turned to pain as Jessica punched him dead on the nose.

'You unbelievable asshole!!'

She stalked off towards the chopper.

The Hare took a moment to recover and then looked at the Tortoise angrily. 'I could have saved her and made myself look a hero ... but you and your damn fairy had to interfere. GO TO HELL!!!' He loped off towards the chopper, leaving The Tortoise standing there, an expression of pain on his face.

Ariel alighted on his shoulder. 'Master Chairman, once again the beast proves unworthy. Why, I beseech thee, tell me ... why dost thou not let the wretch fare for himself?'

The Tortoise's huge brown eyes were moist as his gaze followed the Hare to the chopper, where he was being prevented from boarding by the expedient of Jessica's heel in his face.

'He's my friend,' said the Tortoise sadly.

Author's Afterword

As previously mentioned, that was going to be the wrap, but then I decided to write more and it turned into a sprawling fantasy epic - the likes of which you'll never have seen before! I realised I'd left The Hare in a good and bad place. A bad place because he wasn't exactly coming across as sympathetic but a good place because as a 'hero's journey' goes, having the protagonist start so low down, was going to be a helluva adventure (and great fodder for a writer) to get him to a place where he maintained character and personality while still growing as a character to become a (flawed) hero. I was pretty pleased with how that all developed and I hope you'll be interested in reading the whole story when its done!

As an extra, here are a few entries from the character profiles that will accompany each book in the trilogy - I can guarantee you a cast of thousands from the known and beloved to many obscure characters from myth, legend, literature, fairytales, folklore, pop culture, film, cartoon, comics and even a few Internet memes!

***

The Tortoise

The story of The Tortoise and The Hare originated between 2600 and 2700 years ago as part of Aesop's Fables (number 226 in the Perry Index). The story persisted throughout the ages but was most popularized in the 19th and 20th centuries.

In the present day, The Tortoise has been Chairman/Chief Executive Officer of Mythical Creatures Interdimensional since the Mythlands came into being some seven decades ago. This was mainly due to The Tortoise taking charge and leading the structuring of a new society following the chaos when many characters suddenly appeared together in the new composite world. MCI is the ruling body of the Domain of the Mythical Creatures and The Tortoise it's benevolent leader.

The Tortoise is a wise and just leader who has dedicated his life to serving his people and maintaining peace and stability within the realms. He is looked upon as an equal and much respected by the rulers of other realms in The Mythlands, such as King Babar, Queen Ozma and the Godheads (The rulers of the godly pantheons - Odin, Zeus, Osiris etc).

His one weakness is his sense of responsibility for his old friend The Hare.

In appearance and personality, The Tortoise is slow of speech and body, but quick of mind and intelligence. He is ancient looking, bent over and walks (on two legs) with the aid of a stick. He is about 4.5 feet tall and is an anthropomorphic animal or Upright. He is dressed in his shell but sometimes wears suits - most often a cream suit with a panama hat. He has big brown soulful eyes and speaks in slow and measured tones. His voice is somewhere between Winston Churchill and JFK.

The Hare. See above for original source.

On arrival in the Mythlands circa 1946, The Hare has drifted from place to place, searching for meaning to his existence and usually from one 'get rich quick' scheme to another. He has travelled the Mythlands extensively and being a social creature, has met and befriended many characters. The Hare is quite well liked but not taken too seriously as he is quick to act, quick to get bored and generally lacks follow through. While not the brightest of creatures, Hare is not unintelligent but he rarely bothers to think things through and beyond a certain animal cunning that he has used to mixed effect in his schemes, he lives in and for the moment.

Hare seems to exemplify qualities that are both independent and interdependent. He is extremely susceptible to cultural influences and while charming and charismatic himself, can fall prey to trickery from others who possess those traits. Flattery can be used to damaging effect against The Hare and appealing to his immense ego often blinds him against manipulation. In his own mind, The Hare is a rugged individualist, leader of men and trend setter - he is very influenced by the fashions and culture of the times and his appearance throughout the decades reflects this. From his zoot suits of the 1940's to his long haired, leather jacketed easy rider image of the 1960's through to the present, The Hare probably has one of the most extensive wardrobes in The Mythlands. These days he tends to go for skinny jeans with heavy metal logo emblazoned t-shirts and retro 80's style light jackets with rolled up sleeves and dark shades and DM boots or gaudy, bright trainers with flashing neon strips.

As one of the many creatures without a defined name and back-story, The Hare has adopted a faux Irish background in recent years and the alias of O'Hare, in order to give himself cultural roots ... and because he thought it was cool.

The Hare has a complicated relationship with his oldest friend The Tortoise - he will take money and jobs from his friend but resent him at the same time, often imagining Tortoise's kindness to be born of a desire to control and act superior. In recent years Hare was given a position at MCI, first as the host/manager of a trendy restaurant (which burned down due to his neglecting safety regs) and then the plum job of Entertainments Executive (complete with a seat on the board) and Manager of the Lucky Cactus Casino/Resort in Myth Vegas.

Among his many good friends he counts The Golden Goose, Mr Toad, Pegasus and a fair few of his fellow rabbits, anthropomorphic or otherwise. Hare has been a bit of a womanizer and ladies man for most of his existence but that began to change when he met Jessica Bunny. Although their relationship got off to a rocky start, Jessica makes The Hare want to be a better man and he genuinely tries to change his ways for her and for himself because of her.

In appearance The Hare is a tall, skinny rabbit man - a bit over 6 foot tall, with what could be described as a near 'heroin chic' frame. His fur is a white grey in colour but not from age - he's always been this colour. Unlike The Tortoise, Hare looks young and fresh faced and bursting with energy - his natural athletic abilities, speed and climbing skills are almost uncanny and he has been known to bare hand climb up mountains and huge trees at a rapid pace and in a forest he can swing and jump from tree to tree in a Tarzan-like fashion.

Ariel the Fairy (Ariel Tempestbourne) –

Ariel is a Fey/Fairy of roughly six inches in height. She originates from Shakespeare's play The Tempest (circa 1610). Perhaps due to mortal misconceptions, she identifies as Elizabethan and often expresses a fondness for those times and 'Good Queen Bess.' Her speech patterns remain strictly 16th century and she refuses to modernize them. Ariel has a fiery temper and is quick to anger. However her other traits include extreme loyalty and a sense of justice. She faithfully serves The Tortoise as his chief investigator and is partnered to her good friend, MCI Security Chief, Big Bruin (formerly Papa Bear). They often play Good Bear, bad Fairy in interrogation scenarios. Ariel has wings and can fly - she presumably has other fairy powers. She is slim, blonde and attractive, but her looks are often marred by her seemingly permanent scowl.

The Owl and The Pussycat

Both characters originate in a 'nonsense poem' from Edward Lear's 1871 book 'Nonsense Songs, Stories, Botany and Alphabets.' The tale of these two anthropomorphic animals has grown popular with many retellings. In the Mythlands it's revealed that both characters are male and have been in a loving gay relationship for over seven decades.

The Owl is a senior member of the board at MCI, responsible, among other duties for trade delegations with other lands. He recently opened negotiations at the Cair Paravel summit with isolationist Narnia.

In appearance he is about five and a half feet tall, blocky with tawny feathering and green eyes, usually wearing business apparel, a bow tie and horn rimmed glasses.

The Pussycat's occupation (if he has one) is so far unrevealed. He

31

is a bit taller than his partner and slim with black fur. They are both uprights who walk on two legs and wear clothes.

Loki - The son of giants, adopted son of Odin and adoptive brother of Thor is part of the Asgardian Pantheon of Gods from Norse mythology. He is known as the Trickster and alternatively the God of Mischief and the God of Evil. All gods including Loki will be based on their mythological descriptions with slight tweaks. Loki and other Gods of Asgard and other Pantheons like Olympus talk in a faux Shakespearean patois based loosely on the versions from Marvel Comics.

Loki is clever, conniving and manipulative. As one of the Heist's foremost antagonists, he sets events into motion and manipulates characters like The Hare.

Jessica Bunny –

Character loosely based on a well known femme fatale from an 80's movie. Jessica is a stunning and voluptuous redhead with two failed marriages behind her. Formerly married to Mr. Rabbit and Mr. Bunny and then involved with The Hare, it's a standing joke that Jessica has a certain type. She is human and roughly 5'8 to 5'10 in height. On finding herself in the Mythlands sometime in the late 1990's, Jessica has survived on her wits and charm. She has taken classes in the University of Domain City under teachers such as Professor Chicken-Licken, and briefly adventured with two of her classmates Goldie and Lara, before becoming a touring night club singer. Jessica is intelligent, sophisticated and has a keen sense of survival and a stylish Noir attitude. She is an expert shot and can handle herself in a fight. Her major weakness is bad choice in men (mostly anthropomorphic rabbits).

Big Bruin –

Formerly known as Papa Bear, Bruin first appeared in a tale by Robert Southey published in 1837 (A collection entitled The Doctor). This tale predated the more famous version that included Goldilocks. In fact Southey was not the original creator and used an old verbal tale, which he had been telling since 1813 but whose origin predated that.

When his family arrived in The Mythlands, Papa Bear and the others reinvented themselves and as Big Bruin, he rose to become MCI's Chief of Security and established a close friendship and professional partnership with Ariel the Fairy.

Unlike many anthropomorphic bears, Bruin looks like a huge grizzly bear but mostly walks upright on two legs. He wears a shirt and waistcoat with shoulder holster with a fedora hat and occasionally a jacket, but rarely trousers or footwear unless at a formal event. Bruin has a 1940's noir detective style and considers himself a cop first and foremost. He is loyal to the Tortoise and would take a bullet for him.

Bruin has a close relationship with his wife and his son, the now grown Baby Bear who despite being almost as big as his father is called Little Bear.

Little Bear –

(see Big Bruin for origins) formerly Baby Bear, LB's hero is his father and he has followed in Bruin's footsteps and now works as Head of Security for MCI at their Myth Vegas Casino/Resort, The Lucky Cactus. LB is slightly smaller and slimmer than his father with light brown/black fur as opposed to the dark black of Bruin. He usually wears a tuxedo and has made it his mission to look after the interests of his boss, The Hare and ensure the smooth running of the Casino. LB is highly professional, well liked and respected by his team and those who know him.

The Butcher, The Baker and The Candlestick Maker –

These characters have their origins in the nursery rhyme 'Rub a Dub Dub,' published in the second volume of James Hook's Christmas Box (1798). Minor characters in the Heist, they are revealed to have become part of Little Bear's Casino security team in Myth Vegas.

The Three Billy Goats Gruff

Originating in a Norwegian fairy tale of unknown date origin, the tale of the goats was first collected between 1841 and 1844 by Peter Christian Asbjornsen and Jorgen Moe in their book Norske Folkeeventyr. In the Mythlands the three are brothers and work security under Little Bear in Myth Vegas.

Various dead humans who have been reborn in The Mythlands after reaching legendary status –

Includes Frankie, Sammy, Deano, Marilyn, Amy, the recently arrived David and others.

Mr Toad

First appearing in Kenneth Grahame's The Wind in the Willows published in 1908, Toad is a major character in The Heist. He is not much different from his traditional portrayal but has expanded the scope of his experiences since finding himself in The Mythlands. Toad Hall is now located in the south of the Domain, not too far north of the Magic Forrest (spelling deliberate).

Toad is a bit over 4 foot tall, good hearted, kind and loyal to a fault, he still retains some of his more negative characteristics such as vanity and ego. The latter traits give him a good deal in common with his good friend The Hare. Toad is not unintelligent but his trusting nature and general outlook (blinkered point of view, obsessions with new crazes and simplistic way of looking at things) sometimes make him appear foolish and naïve.

He is often underestimated and can occasionally display rare flashes of insight.

He is also a canny businessman and one of the wealthiest individuals in the Mythlands as well as being a major shareholder at MCI which entitles him to a seat on the board.

Since arriving in the Mythlands at its beginnings, Toad has fought his boredom by using his vast wealth to travel the length and breadth of the land (including being a regular high roller in Myth Vegas) and has met many of it's denizens. He counts kings, queens and people of influence among his friends and is very close to King Babar of Elephantland.

His weaknesses include being overly trusting and relying on money to solve problems. However he has recently taken on a sensible new valet/butler who looks after his interests and stops him from making mistakes that he would regret.

King Babar

The king of the Elephants first appeared in Histoire de Babar written by Jean de Brunhoff in 1931. He is very similar to his traditional depiction barring later additions that are not in the public domain.

Unlike many of the other MC characters, Babar and his subjects didn't experience such a traumatic upheaval as his entire realm of Elephantland was relocated to the Mythlands and with a few adjustments to new borders, life continued on normally. Babar has since travelled extensively, extending diplomatic relations to most of the other realms and meeting many of their prominent citizens. He is a major shareholder at MCI and a close personal friend of Mr Toad and The Tortoise.

Babar is a kind hearted and pleasant sort who enjoys a happy married life to his beloved Queen Celeste; he mostly resides (foreign trips and high roller excursions to Myth Vegas aside) in his palace in the capital Celesteville with his children and small grandchildren and is ably assisted by councillors such as Pompadour. Physically Babar is well over six foot and though bulky, mostly slim for an elephant but developing a bit of a stomach in recent years.

Elephantland continues to maintain an uneasy truce with their hostile neighbours in Rhinoland.

The End

If you'd like to see more of my work or say hi/comment, you can find me on the following links.

https://www.facebook.com/TheJasonGreenfield/
https://www.facebook.com/ForeverTornByJasonGreenfield/
https://www.facebook.com/TheUnseenManBook/

https://twitter.com/JayGreenfield?lang=en – doubles as OMP Twitter.

https://www.amazon.com/Jason-Greenfield/e/B00CBFLI1W/
https://www.amazon.co.uk/Jason-Greenfield/e/B00CBFLI1W/

And last but not least, you can find more Mythlands info, art and previews here –
https://www.facebook.com/MythicalCreaturesInterdimensional/

Cover by Sally A Barr.

Blinded by Love: Jimmy's Journal

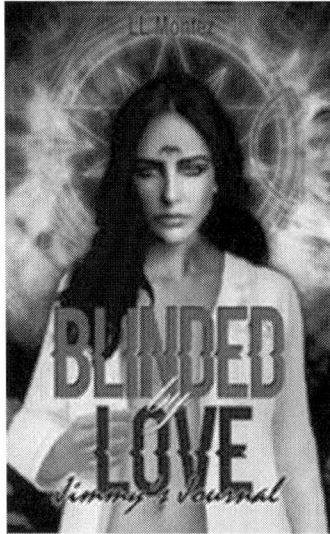

LL Montez

Jimmy McCormak is looking for love in another dimension. Fate strikes him hard the day he stumbles across the work of Dr. Salem Mort—a mysterious woman with the three most beautiful brown eyes he's ever seen. Love-struck and with entirely too much time on his hands, Jimmy sets out to become one of the elite Blinkatari—a group dedicated to the study of opening the third eye. Opening his third eye would grant him access to the Reflect, the elusive ether-world where Dr. Mort currently resides.

Lesser men might be deterred by the ominous nature of the Reflect, but not Jimmy.

Armed with pure intentions, a step-by-step how-to, and all the downloadable audio supplements available, Jimmy is ready to become a Master Blinkatari and prove that love at third sight really does exist.

***

This is the real and true-life attempt by me, James Randall McCormak, to open my third eye. What you're about to read is what happens to me while following the process laid out by Doctors Jingju and Mort, founders of the Institutum Blinkabamus Laxo. This series of steps, as outlined by the guy and lady doctor above, was written after years of observation and practice with many cultures steeped in Penial mythology. It will be me, Jimmy, who attempts to become the first Blinkatari in America. While I've heard of guys doing it and becoming Blinkatari in Jamaica, Tonga, Mexico, France, and other places of voodoo, I will attempt to be the first to achieve this right in the heart of Nebraska. Fuck yeah.

Why would I take the risk of psychic-piercing my own set of hazel peep-holes, resulting in a long, permanent future of darkness?

For love. Duh.

For love, I will attempt to access another dimension.

For love, I will risk the functionality of my original eyes because I heard that if the first attempt fails, so does all chance at seeing another pair of tits again. Literally, you go blind. I've read the forum posts. After Google-translating the practically nonsensical alphabet soup by *polythemustard53*, I figured out that it's something like shooting out your eye with a psychic BB.

Doctor Mort doesn't know me yet. Lucky for me, the Blinkatari only comprise of eight dudes, three being over fifty. My chances of getting real close to her are real good. Maybe we'll meet up in The Reflect. I've seen pictures of her partner, Lorenzo Jingju. The guy is a dweeby bird man--a disproportionately composed human with large and small angles that make me wonder if he was first discovered holed under an opera house. How he managed to get a research partner like Dr. Mort is beyond comprehension. Maybe the answers lie in The Reflect... *whimsical upscale flourish*

I've read their research. While I think Jingju has the largest quantity behind him, Mort describes it with so much potent detail, it feels like I'm seeing the Reflect with sexy, brown-eyed binoculars. She describes it as, and I quote:

A land of decadence beyond eyes and fingers and slip of skin that our senses are blind to. Our cornea in this world are not properly equipped to replicate items of this spectrum as since our birth and development, these images have been blackened and were never called upon to react upon our waking consciousness. The Penial gland, engorged and sensitive to this new palette, will react in languid pulses-

38

-a rhythm similar to the flap of goose wings or to the heartbeat of sperm whales. Our first hearing of these sights will therefore heighten our experience of the Reflect...

(www.blinkinstitute.co.uk)

Just seeing that again, copy and pasting it from the ebook into this document brings a tingle to the middle of my forehead.

I imagine us together. She and I, existing like two perfect beams of light in another dimension. I want to feel her aura wrapped around mine.

Thus, I announce to the world:

I, Jimmy, will open my third eye, therefore gaining access to psychic dimension known as The Reflect.

If you find this journal abandoned suddenly, it means I've probably been sucked into the other side and am most likely gone forever--please tell Caroline McCormick.

Just kidding. Don't tell my mom.

***

The Functions and Five Step Process of Penial BloomMorphology as Studied through Observation, Integration, and Speculation in Sensory-Armed Capacities

Introduction and Step 1 as noted and practiced by Dr. Lorenzo Jingju

Welcome, student, to the published guide on BloomMorphology--or in what might sound more warm and welcoming--opening your third eye, blooming your Penial gland, allowing your in-sight to burgeon. I, Dr. Lorenzo Jingju of the Institutum Blinkabamus Laxo, with my partner in research Dr. Salem Mort, will attempt to outline the simple but strenuous process we took to participating in BloomMorphology.

When desiring to open what most know, in error, as "the sixth chakra", one must be in pursuit of the next dimension. The student must be willing to create and enhance the visibility of dimensions beyond man's reach.

Begin with the following step and proceed cautiously from there.

A word of warning: If you encounter beings from the Reflect, do not engage. Do not lure them to your side. If you have trouble, the hotline number is located in the Help Me *portion of this ebook*

Let us begin.

Step 1: Sit cross-legged on a surface made of squiggled tenticular grips--that of a shag rug would work perfectly. The little arms will

extend and keep your body from entering the Reflect. It is crucial that your corporeal form stay grounded for the majority of our preliminary exercises. It would not bode well if you were to blip out of existence too soon.

Once you have gotten yourself into position, close your eyes tight. Tight enough where you can feel the folds of your lids slouching over. Take your finger and touch the wrinkles your lids make in an upward motion while clamping your lids tighter and tighter. Keep your legs crossed.

Open your mouth. Work your lips into a squared shape, keeping the edges straight and sharp.

With your fingers over your eyes moving in the constant upward fashion, let out a noise from the diaphragm that hums low but moves in an arc over your tongue upon its exit from your body. For a demonstration you can download our audio supplements for $2.99 on iTunes.

Repeat process for one hour through the next three days.

***

Jimmy's Journal on Opening the Third Eye

Day 1:

My eyes are closed tight and they hurt--while they are closed I see a bar forming right across the darkness, like it's making an H on the inside. Or there is a high counter that, in my eyelids, I can't see over, like I'm too short to reach the pie in the center of it. I close them tighter and the bar gets brighter. Is that the Reflect? I wonder if Dr. Mort is already here. I feel a headache coming.

Day 2:

My eyes are closed tight again and they hurt just as much as they did yesterday. The bar is there again. It's not any clearer or less clear than it was. I stared at Dr. Mort's picture on the cover for a while today, hoping that when I closed my eyes, she'd be there.

Nothing. Just the bar. And this fucking headache.

Day 3:

This day started out hesitantly. Burning headache since Day 1 has barely receded. I felt like quitting, but seeing her three beautiful, round, brown eyes piercing through the iPad screen into my bedroom found me scampering to get back to the spot I designated for my "platform to the Reflect".

She wants me to be there. Maybe it's my teetering existence at the border of the Reflect that's sharpening my sense of her, maybe it's this goddamned asshole of a headache, but I feel compelled to keep trying. There's going to come a day when my eye opens and I'll see her in front of me not just in the white lines of my device, but tangible enough to absorb.

When I close them today, the bar is there, but no, wait, no it's not a bar! It's the bottom edge of a box and the other three edges are freshly illuminated. It's so clear, like it's always been there. The longer I stare at the black box, I see that it's a box that's eclipsing another light source. Purple rays are coming out the sides. It's covering this purple light and I'm shutting my eyes tighter to try and make those purple lines strike out harder. Maybe tomorrow.

***

Steps 2 and 3 as noted and performed by Dr. Salem Mort.

After completing Step 1, outlined previously by Dr. Jingju, make sure to pay close attention as the next three steps are crucial and more complicated.

Keep your eyes closed, never open them during this exercise.

Now imagine a wall. This is the wall you must keep up at all times. Never let this wall down. If you do, we will not be held responsible for the debris that float-falls to your third eye. Your gland is sensitive to these items such as dust and ether particles.

Keep your eyes closed. Imagine the wall.

Once you have the wall, focus on one brick. That brick is heavy in your hands, yes the brick has folded into your hands and is no longer stationed in the wall. Don't worry, The Reflect will not notice one missing brick. Hold your brick and let it be cradled in your lap like you are the nest and it is the vulture's rump.

Sway.

Sway back and forth with the brick at your center.

Swing you inverted pendulum, swing.

Jimmy's Journal on Opening the Third Eye
Day 4:

My brick is black, just like the box. Actually I can't tell the difference between the two. When my eyes close, the box is there and the light behind it has gone from purple to white. Shiny. The brick in my hands feels like air. There's no real brick.

I rock around and wobble back and forth. This rocks me and my brick and my box into a place where stars crawl out of the corner of my anti-peripherals. They creep out slow, like real stars when they move over the horizon. My box looked like a horizon once. A bar horizon. The stars are moving over it in jerky shapes. Does being pointy make something a star? The box is fading behind the horizon and the jagged stars are filling the blackness.

Just when I was beginning to feel sick from all the wobbling, I hear, I shit you not, her voice.

Step 3 requires the following materials:

Sandpaper
Water with three drops of green food coloring
One Kleenex
Two gloves of the same hand - preferably left
A piece of scotch tape
A favorite snack high in amino acid

Once you have gathered the afore mentioned items, fold the sandpaper in half and place it directly in the water, the folded edges horizontal. Once the paper has been soaked all the way though, let it dry on the Kleenex.

Eat the snack while the sandpaper dries.

After the sandpaper dries with a green tint, tape it to a place at eye level near your meditation platform.

Stare into the green sandpaper. Stare unblinking for thirty seconds. Close your eyes. Shut them tight for one minute. Open for thirty. Repeat.

After going through the cycle six times, put on one of the gloves. Let the other one drape over your palm with fingers matched to fingers as if mirrored. Put that gloved hand against the wall where your paper is taped. Touch the wall. Touch the other hand against the wall and think that this glove in your hand is not your own.

With hand on wall, watch the paper for three minutes. No blinking. Close your eyes.
Open the door. There I'll be, on the other side.

***

Jimmy's Journal on Opening the Third Eye

Day 6:

When I close my eyes, I hear her voice in the jagged lines of the stars. I thought she was calling me over to her, asking me to come forward. I smell something sweet on the hand that touches the wall touching the glove. Our hands touch loudly. I can feel her and we're close.

There's another smell there, but it's one I'm not familiar with. The strange shadow sounds like rot.

Step 4 as noted and performed by Dr. Lorenzo Jingju.

Congratulations! You've made it to Step 4. If you have come this far, your dedication to the practice of BloomMorphology as perfected by the Blinkatari is indeed an incredible one. Only one step follows this. In my humble opinion, after years of research and intensive study of the fine art of BloomMorphology, this is the most crucial step that must be performed correctly.

Return to your green paper that should be dried and shriveled around the edges. Take the sandpaper and close your eyes. Rub the paper gently over your cheek until you feel the itch as it cuts its way to the inside of your mouth.

Like that, yes.

Let the grit crumble down the skin. Keep your eyes closed. Feel the abrasive in your cheek chipping its way outside, shredding your inside-mouth.

When you close your eyes, look at your wall. Check each brick. The one you held previously should have been replaced exactly where you found it. The Reflect will note this change. You wouldn't want anything bad to happen, would you, you little shit?

***

Jimmy's Journal on Opening the Third Eye

Day 7:

I don't see the box anymore because it's coming out of my mouth past my molars.

That smell has gotten more and more pungent and when my eyes are closed and when the sandpaper is scratching my face, I can see the smell coming out from the wall. Smells like piss, or like the color maroon, or like guns cocking. It doesn't feel like Dr. Mort. What it feels like is the blunt edges of a NO TRESPASSING sign.

But what's the point of paying sixty bucks for this ebook if they don't want to let anyone in?

Step 5 as noted and performed by Dr. Salem Mort.

Most of you will not make it to Step 5. You don't have the wherewithall. You don't have the gumption or the huevos. You won't make it because your mind is pudding. You are weak and that is normal. The member of the Institutum Blinkabamus Laxo must have great strength in mind and eye or else he will remain closed to The Reflect and never board the transit.

If you have made it, the final step will bring in a light so bright, you'll wish you were learning to close your third eye shut with a staple-gun. Just know that the light you've seen so far, the light that is behind, is only the edges of the light that you will expose when your lid flies open. Many who have tried to perform BloomMorphology have been blinded and their eye(s) permanently destroyed. Be cautious.

The final step is to return to the sandpaper that has been rubbed raw.

Stare at your paper, the more skin flecks, the more productive this meeting will be.

Look at your square.

Close your eyes.

Look at your square.

Touch your eyes, the middle of your finger hitting the pupil behind the shades.

With your left thumb, press in the center of your forehead where your Penial gland rests behind flaps of paltry skin that have hampered your true Vision. Press hard, bending your thumb. Take the thumb of your free right hand and, directly across from where your left thumb is pressing on the back of your head, press going forward in the other direction. We are going to pop it open like a pimple.

Jimmy's Journal on Opening the Third Eye

Day 8:

The box is there and I don't want to watch the wall anymore because it has my face crudely painted on it. I place my thumbs in the exact spot and ectoplasmic goo unfurls from my cheek-hole in curly smoke that's the color of string cheese. I feel it blinking under my thumb. In the box, the blackness fades. It opens. The box is opening. I hear her voice again, Dr. Mort is here with me and I just want to tell her, it was for her. I did this for her. Because she is brave and so am I and we can live in The Reflect. I'll brush her hair back away from her eye so we can speak without lips.

Open faster, open harder. Open like Chinese New Year.

In the box, when it disappears, the light shines white. I see nothing but the expansive brightness that stretches through The Reflect like the sun punches through cigarette burn holes in thick curtains. But I don't know if these are galaxies even though they look like planets.

I can't see the planets like I did before.

The box appears in the distance and rushes for me, getting bigger and bigger. It stops in front of me where my mouth is open at the cheek and puffing ringlets.

It considers me. The smell is back, like it wanted to be the first to greet me. The box is not Dr. Mort, but she's here somewhere.

The lid clicks and opens. Inside the box is a mouth opened wide and chomping. The white teeth are framed by perfect white gums in sick fish color. They open lipless and scream at me, yelling silent things. They snap shut without the snap. I can't open my eyes. My real eyes, the ones I closed. I hope that they are still there.

The mouth works up and down up and down. Where's my wall? I must have either passed through it to the other side or it turned to wax paper because this thing wasn't supposed to get through.

It bites the air. It masticates. It drools.

My thumbs are numb from pressing my head. My head is numb from being pressed by thumbs. My eyes are sore from watching the mouth. My eyes are still closed.

My left thumb is sore from being bitten like a nipple.

I open my eyes.

The room looks normal.

The sandpaper and stickless tape fall off the wall and lay on the floor.

I close my eyes again to test it. The mouth greets me in The Reflect with a wide display of Chiclet teeth.

My legs have fallen asleep. I don't know how much time has passed here on the floor. There is a bump in the middle of my forehead.

When I scramble to the mirror and throw back my hair, I see it there. In the place where I expected my third eye to open with the same brightness as its hazel partners, is a bump made of tiny Tic-Tac teeth, opening and closing without speaking.

Dr. Mort? What happened?

Jimmy's Journal on Opening the Third Eye

Day 40 or something like that:

I haven't opened this document because I've been a little scared to look back and see where I went wrong. The mouth now appears whenever I sleep. I dream of it and pace around the gateway of The Reflect, hoping they'll let me through.

The fourth orifice, as I've learned it's called, is some kind of misunderstood, natural phenomenon. I have yet to discover a group or institute dedicated to it. The most information the Internet has been able to provide is that it was a punishment in some cultures.

I wanted to be assured I was really there in The Reflect, that I heard and felt Dr. Mort and hoped that she was just as aware of me. I reached out to the Institutum Blinkabamus Laxo two weeks ago and received this email yesterday.

Dear James,

We are sorry that you are experiencing difficulty with our program. Dr. Mort and I have discussed your issue at length and are unsure of where the error occurred.

We regret to be of so little assistance. Maybe next time, when you attempt to steal another man's partner, you'll consider all the possible repercussions.

Sincerely,

Dr. Lorenzo Jingju
Master Blinkatari
Co-Founder of the
Institutum Blinkabamus Laxo

The End

LL Montez can be found at these links:

https://www.wattpad.com/user/LLMontez

Twitter: https://twitter.com/LLMontez

Cover by Faera Lane.

The Silver Warrior

Adrian G. Hilder

Adrian G Hilder was born in 1970 in Lincolnshire, UK to an English father and a Scottish mother and grew up as a child of the Royal Air Force. Moving house every few years with his parents (and later on brother) was the norm and began when he was four months old.

Adrian has lived on several RAF bases in the UK and Germany, and there was a time when he had spent more of his life in Germany than he had the UK.

His early years in continental Europe meant many family holidays immersed in the bewitching beauty of Bavaria, the Swiss and Austrian Alps. These locations inspire some settings and even events in his stories.

Today, Adrian lives in Hampshire, UK with his wife and three boys just a few miles from where Jane Austen wrote many of her works. As a teenager, Adrian had two great passions: computer programming and fantasy stories.

In October 2013, having worked in the IT industry since 1991, Adrian decided the time to realize his long-held ambition to write a fantasy story was long overdue. His debut story, The General's Legacy, is the result of combining everything he has learned about creating fast paced dramatic stories, combined with what his imagination has been brewing for over twenty-eight years.

Early-autumn in the year of the Church of the Sun, 1852; 7 days before the last Battle of Beldon Valley.

If God had written in the dawn sky over the port city of Halimouth "This way lies adventure worthy of song," Quain could hardly have been more eager to make landfall. And yet, another part of his mind he never allowed a voice knew the shadows of blood, pain, and death were already upon him. If he allowed that part of his mind to speak the shadows grew darker and multiplied in number. The General of Valendo had called. The sport of battle was near.

The ship nudged into dock and mooring ropes hauled it to a halt. Quain made a clicking sound with his tongue, and without pulling on the reins, a white stallion loaded like a pack mule followed him over the gangplank. As he walked Quain scanned the crowd. The dearth of men in evidence he expected. Women and older children wore the work clothes and began unloading ships in on the morning tide. Foreigners were absent too — no tanned Ruberans or black faces from Carvail. Quain surmised they saw no sense in trading with a kingdom expected to fall.

Quain caught a glint of earrings and gold teeth. With a glance, he counted five men leaning against a shop front with their tattooed arms crossed. Each wore a cutlass stuck through their belt. They turned to look at him. Quain grinned up at his horse.

'We need every man we can get, Clarence,' he whispered to his horse as he moved to its flanks. He flipped over a waxed leather cover revealing polished plate armour netted to the saddle. Reaching behind a bronze sword hilt, he pulled out a water skin and drank. With his head back and staring down his nose, he watched the tattooed pirates watching him. What were they doing ashore?

Replacing the water skin and leather cover, Quain led the horse away from the dock and up Halimouth's cobbled alleys. Quain had contemplated wearing his armour on the boat to save time, but sunk by metal and drowning at sea was a stupid fate to tempt. Besides, the blacksmith to whom he tossed a silver coin would be glad of the extra service he could offer.

'Once again you are needed to dress me for battle, Amadeus.'

'As you wish sir,' Amadeus led the horse into his yard and peeled off the leather cover. 'Is this armour for battle or for show sir?' Amadeus wore a dubious frown.

Quain grinned. 'Both, of course.'

'No manner of metal I know shines like a mirror and still turns a blade.'

'It's our very own Valendo steel. Polished by hand with a little enchantment for extra shine.'

Amadeus' eyebrows arched, then he shrugged, pulled loose the netting and unloaded the armour.

'Your boys not here to help?' asked Quain.

'My boys are now men gone north with the army two days ago,' Amadeus raised the gambeson before his critical eye then held it out. Quain slid his arms into the padded jacket and secured buckles on the front while the blacksmith turned to fetch the breastplate.

'But they're just boys.'

'You were barely more than a boy first time you came here. They're grown up now.'

A grin replaced a frown on Quain's face. 'I was at least twenty.'

'Still a boy to my eye. Now you're a man yet to know the wisdom of middle age.'

'Boys like me never grow up,' Quain winked. 'We just get grey and wrinkly someday.'

Amadeus slicked a lock of black and grey hair across his bald head and lifted the breast plate. Quain stood while Amadeus secured buckles and fitted the remaining armour parts at his own methodical pace.

'Now I feel like I'm in my second home,' said Quain.

'I thought armour and the battlefield were your only home. Unless you count the whore's tent.'

Quain smiled again. 'I haven't told you, have I? Some things do change... even for me. I'm married now.'

Amadeus' eyes went wide, and for a moment his jaw hung slack. 'You found a redhead of simple mind and needs to marry?'

'No, quite the opposite. She's blonde. And clever. And a mage.'

'A what?'

'A mage. You know — intelligent people who can use magic.'

'And she married you!' the blacksmith laughed. 'Thought you wanted to score yourself a redhead to complete the full set.'

'Before we began courting—'

'You? Courting?'

'I know. Like I said, things change. She caught me leaving one of the Queen of Emiria's Handmaiden's bed chamber. She managed to smile in a way that combined amusement, disappointment, and disapproval all at the same time. I suddenly felt sad and unworthy. Like I'd lost something precious I needed to feel complete.'

'You? Sad?'

'Only the once in this lifetime, Amadeus.'

'I see you have new armour, but your shield is the same,' he said pointing to a vivid blue shield with a yellow sun emblem hanging behind the saddle. 'You've changed your sword too.' The blacksmith reached for the bronze hilt.

'Don't touch it!'

Amadeus flinched at Quain's outburst. 'You almost look *afraid* I will touch it.'

'It's complicated. You might not be strong enough,' Quain looked Amadeus in the eye, any hint of humour gone. 'Then I'd have to kill you.'

'I've been handling swords since you were a child.'

'Sorry, Amadeus. Not like this one you haven't.'

'What kind of trouble have you found for yourself now, young sir?'

'Well, that's the point, Amadeus. I found trouble before it found me — as the general tells me I should.'

'Whatever that's supposed to mean.'

'Always see trouble coming, so you are prepared.'

'Now you are prepared for the battlefield once more.'

'A battlefield that's still three days ride away. I can't be late. It wouldn't do to miss the adventure.'

'Sun's blessings go with you, sir.'

Quain mounted his horse and gave Amadeus a wave with his gauntleted hand. Then he rode up the cobbled road and out of the city into a land of forests and rolling hills.

***

Spling! It was the sound of a bird dropping striking the arm of Quain's armour. Mid-way between a splat and a ping — must be a spling. Looping the reigns around one thumb, he raised his palms and eyes to the twilight sky and offered thanks to God for this gift from the heavens. He lifted his visor and inspected the chalk-white deposit on the shining armour. Then he looked all around his saddle and down the horses' flanks as if he expected to find some forgotten rag he might use to buff off the offending muck. A futile pursuit, he knew. He'd packed every item of his scant luggage into the saddle bags himself and never thought to prepare for this.

'Should've hired myself a squire,' he muttered to Clarence, rubbing the bird dropping with his gauntleted hand only to succeed in spreading the mess. The horse stopped in its tracks.

'Stand and deliver,' said a voice conversationally.

Quain stopped rubbing and looked up.

'I think that's what a highway man is supposed to say. I don't know for sure. I'm not practiced at robbing from something that isn't afloat at sea.'

A tattooed pirate stood in the center of the road with a longsword leveled at Clarence.

'I refuse,' said Quain. 'Say, you haven't got an old rag on you, have you?'

'A what?'

'A rag. Bird mess you see,' said Quain pointing. 'Really like to clean it off and look my best before I go up in front of the soldiers later.'

The pirate cackled. 'Just what I took you for. Some popinjay of a nobles' son arrived on the boat from Ephire looking for glory while real soldiers die around you. I think I shall call you the Silver Warrior. You look just like your mother's best silver tea service done up like that.'

Quain beamed. 'Say, I like that! *Silver Warrior.* I never thought of asking a pirate to give me a sobriquet. Think of a song. A song with Silver Warrior in the lyrics. Not some coarse sea shanty — a proper song like a bard would make up.'

'I only make up songs when I'm drunk on rum with a whore on my lap.'

'Maybe later then. After the battle. We'll get drunk and make up the song.'

'After this battle, you'll be stripped naked and left on the roadside, or dead.'

53

'I wasn't talking about this battle,' said Quain. 'I'm talking about the battle I'm rapidly running late for, while I sit here and speak to you. I need more soldiers. Sweet longsword. Excellent for cutting through armour. Where'd you get it?'

'It's mine.'

'Don't believe you. You and your shipmates had a cutlass each this morning.'

'I bought it.'

'There won't be a sword of any kind in the kingdom that's not in the hands of a soldier right now. And soldiers are armed with short swords. Who gave you the sword?'

'I stole it from the last fop like you that came riding up this road.'

'Impossible! There is no other fop just like me,' Quain grinned, holding his hands open. 'I'm unique.'

'Uniquely in trouble, I would say, since you know I'm not alone.'

Quain frowned and scratched at the palm of his left gauntlet. 'Sure you don't have a rag of some kind? I've got bird muck on my gauntlet now.' He held his hand up, palm facing the pirate for inspection.

'Don't be worried about bird muck pretty boy. We'll clean it up before we sell your armour.'

'Pretty boy?' Quain feigned disgust. 'Handsome — dashing maybe. But pretty? No one has called me that before. Oh, and here are your friends.'

Four more pirates rustled from the forest and flanked Quain's horse. Like their apparent leader, they also held longswords.

'Not much of a trap fellas. I could just ride off,' said Quain.

'Try it. Ever been hit in the back with a crossbow bolt at short range?' a pirate on Quain's left asked rhetorically.

'More of you then?'

The lead pirate shot a dark look at the new arrival who'd spoken. 'Off the horse, pretty boy,' the pirate growled. 'Time to strip.'

'I suppose you'll be wanting my shield too?'

The pirate nodded. Quain grasped the shield handle and released it from a strap that had secured it to the saddle. Buckling the shield to his left arm, he winked at the lead pirate. 'Patience, ugly boy.'

'You aren't doing yourself any favours with the insults.'

'I thought you should know that most women don't find a man with earlobes stretched halfway down his neck by a pair of huge gold earrings — that look quite ridiculous by the way — at all attractive.'

'Maybe I don't care if a woman finds me attractive or not, pretty boy. I take her anyway!' The pirate pointed his sword at Quain.

Quain stared down at the blade and examined the hilt — leather wrapped grey steel. He arched his eyebrows then looked the pirate square in his brown eyes.

'Off the horse pretty boy,' growled the pirate.

Quain shrugged beneath his armour, slid his leg over the saddle then tumbled to the ground with one foot still stuck in the stirrups. He hung there like a chicken picked up by one leg. The pirates exchanged looks and laughed as they gathered around him.

Quain shook his foot free of the stirrup, held out his hand and addressed the lead pirate. 'I lack a squire to assist me. Perhaps you would pull me up.'

The pirate switched the longsword to his left hand then appeared to think better of helping. 'Get up!' he yelled.

Quain rolled over and got to his feet. 'Those are women's earrings,' Quain squinted at the lead pirate and looked closer. 'Now I see them up close, they're definitely earrings for women.'

Moths to a flame — the pirates all stared at their leader's earrings.

It was enough.

A tooth led a spray of blood blowing out of the nearest pirate's mouth as the edge of Quain's shield smashed into his jaw. The pirate's eyes all turned Quain's way in wonder. A longsword let out a metallic song as it hit the ground, the next pirate crying in pain when Quain's shield edge struck his hand. A third pirate raised his sword in time to ward off the blows from the fallen longsword now in Quain's hand.

Quain raised his shield, deflected a strike from the pirate with the fractured jaw and the lead pirate backed off. 'You fight dirty like a pirate,' he grinned mirthlessly, but Quain never saw it.

The fourth pirate parried two blows before Quain slapped him across the temples with the flat of his blade sending him into a place of darkness and dreams.

Four pirates remained standing now. One with a cracked jaw unsteady on his feet, one sword-less, a third showing fear in his eyes and the leader. They all backed off and spread around Quain who had Clarence at his back. The white warhorse stood impassive as a castle wall.

'A dirty pirate you say? I'm a pretty boy popinjay, remember? I may live in a lord's castle, but my father was a woodsman — a trapper scratching out a living selling furs and game. But you're quite right. A noble man he was.'

'Game's over,' said the lead pirate. 'There are four of us, and we won't be falling for any more of your tricks. Strip off the armour… pretty boy.'

Quain slapped his visor down. 'You'll have to come and get it.'

It was just a glance — a momentary look at the other three pirates to order an attack. Quain's blade swept in before the words came out. The pirate replied, slashing at Quain as if it were a light cutlass and not the solid weight of a longsword he wielded. Quain brushed aside the blows with his shield, turned in and burst his opponent's nose with his fist. The pirate staggered back, earrings swinging. The remaining pair of pirates still armed set upon Quain, raining blows down on his shield and sword. Quain side stepped around them, so one of his opponents always fouled the reach of the other. A flicker of steel, the flat of a blade and another pirate toppled with a battered ear. The remaining pirate backed off, reassessing his chances.

'A superb display of swordsmanship Lieutenant General Quain Marln.' The voice was new, came from behind Quain and had a distinct accent that put a strong rolling characteristic "r" in the word "superb."

Quain faced his shield off to the pirate and turned to face the new arrival. 'And there you are,' said Quain in an even tone.

'You pretend you expected to see me. No one sees me coming.' The man pointed a heavy crossbow at Quain's chest. It was loaded. Belted at his waist was another of the longswords. Dressed from head to toe in brown leather the man looked nothing like a regular soldier.

'I never saw you. I saw your tells,' said Quain.

'I am careful. You saw nothing,' the man sneered.

Quain held up the longsword by the blade. 'Valendo longswords are fashioned with wire wrapped hilts. The sea mongrels you hired carry these longswords with leather wrapped grips — the Nearhon way.' Quain looked around at the pirates. 'Oh yes, you're the stooges of a Nearhon scout. It's treason fellas.'

'Drop the sword lieutenant general. And then do as you have been instructed. Remove the armour so we can have a long and unpleasant conversation about your army. Or will you force me to shoot you? This crossbow bolt will pierce your armour and your heart. I am an excellent shot.'

The pirates looked on like a herd of startled deer. Quain winked at them and made clicking noises with his tongue. Clarence's ears pricked up and then the horse began to turn around on the spot. Quain suddenly tossed the longsword at the Nearhon scout who caught it between his chest and the crossbow. Grasping the bronze hilt of his sword it rasped free of the scabbard buckled at Clarence's now exposed flank. Quain ducked, and a crossbow bolt ricocheted off his angled shield. Three strides closed the distance with the Nearhon scout. Quain swept his blade down and cleaved the crossbow from the scout's grasp. As if the blade weighed no more than a knife, Quain stepped in and drew the sword through a backhanded swing. A splash of blood. A crimson line in the scout's neck yawned open, and his head toppled and fell to the ground. Like a drunk too exhausted to try and get home the body sank to its knees then fell.

Quain turned his gaze on the pirates, his sword blade pointing straight up. A jewel in the cross guard shone like a tiny sun in the evening twilight.

'Lieutenant General Quain Marl?' said the lead pirate with the smashed nose.

Quain nodded, then grinned. 'Except I'm still liking that Silver Warrior idea.'

'The general's right-hand man?'

'Oh no. I'm his left-hand man. The general's right-hand man has little patience and absolutely no sense of humour. If you'd tried to ambush him, you'd be a greasy pile of burning flesh or a cloud of ash drifting on this delightful evening breeze by now. So, is it to be execution or conscription?'

'What?' said the lead pirate.

'You aided the enemy of the kingdom in a time of war. That's treason. Conscription into the general's army is getting off lightly and giving you a chance to redeem your worthless souls. Valendo needs every man it can get in the coming battle.'

'Conscription?' The pirate with the bloody ear laughed. 'You and what press gang?'

Quain's grin was almost evil. 'I am the press gang.'

'We don't have to stand for this. Let's get him.' The pirate with the bloody ear raised his sword.

'Bran, you idiot! We couldn't best him before he drew that enchanted blade,' said the lead pirate with the smashed nose.

'I wouldn't bother to run. Clarence is faster than any of you sea mongrels. You can try and steal and ride him if you want. It'll be funny to watch you try.'

The pirate with the blooded ear gave Quain a calculating look that lasted many heartbeats. Then his shoulders sagged, and he offered his sword.

'Keep the sword. You'll need it soon enough. Now, start marching north. Haliford is only a few miles, and we'll make it before dark if you're fit enough.'

The downed pirate groaned and rose to his feet. Quain returned his sword to its scabbard, and the yellow jewel went dark. He walked to the headless corpse and leaned over it. 'Sorry, no time for a burial.' Quain rubbed the bird muck off his armour and gauntlet on the Nearhon scout's leather garb. Then he inspected the face of his shield and sighed. The ricocheting crossbow bolt had left a groove of bare metal in the blue painted surface. Mounting his horse, he prompted the animal into a trot with a few clicks of his tongue and followed the pirates.

'Now we need that song for the march,' Quain called ahead. 'More fun with a whole army, but pirates are used to singing. I'm sure I can count on you. I need a song about the Silver Warrior. Something catchy. I want the army singing it when we get to Beldon Valley. Better make it good fellas. Remember it's me that decides where you will be positioned on the battlefield when the real fighting begins.'

The drone of the reluctant singers faded away as they marched north on the woodland road. The sightless eyes in the severed head of the Nearhon scout watched them go.

The End

Connect with Adrian G Hilder at the following link:

https://adrianhilder.com/

Cover by T.E. Bradford.

Under the Monster's Bed

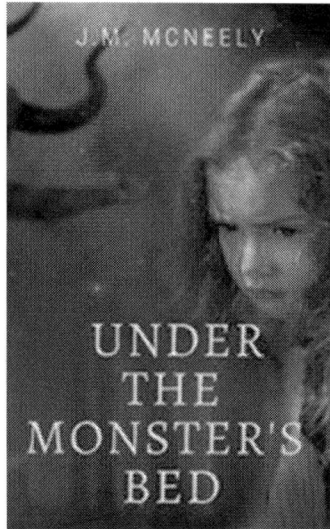

J.M. McNeely

J.M. McNeely writes short stories in all genres assisted by a temperamental cat companion named Griffin who scares away monsters. Both are honored to be a part of OMP

***

She couldn't see it. She couldn't hear it. But that just made it more real.

Everyone knew the monster was under the bed. It was every bit as real as the Tooth Fairy or Santa Claus. In fact, it was even more real. The Tooth Fairy flitted away to the Molar Island after she had collected her prize. The monster was always hiding.

It didn't matter that Emily's bed was really just a lumpy mattress in the corner of her tiny room. The monster could still hide in the tiny space between the mattress and the floor. This just made it scarier. It meant that each night, Emily's head lay just inches from the creature, protected only by the thinnest barrier of springs and foam.

Tonight she thought about how the monster's teeth were just inches from her face. Its wretched stomach was probably grumbling and growling until it got so hungry that it would snapcrunch her whole. Or maybe it would stick her ponytail in a straw and slurp her up. Or maybe it would just start nibbling at her toenails and keep munching until it got to her eyes.

NOOOOOO!

Emily jumped out of bed with a shriek, startling Smokeball, her sleepy grey cat. Smokeball was an napping expert and it took quite a lot to jolt him from his peaceful slumber. He was having a dream where he actually caught that red laser pointer dot and wasn't happy having his hunt abruptly interrupted. It was even worse when Emily jumped out of bed and Smokeball found himself suddenly tossed around in a sea of blankets and stuffed animals.

Emily had already abandoned ship scurrying to the other side of the room and ducking into the closet. A bit risky since everyone knows closets are a monster's second favorite hiding place, but it was the best shelter she could find.

Emily stood there shuddering behind a neat row of hanging shirts providing some cover from the monster's night-vision eyes. She peered out behind her favorite blouse trying to see if her nocturnal enemy had made its move. As usual, the room was deathly silent, Monsters had fearsome roars but they could evoke more terror by sitting silently in wait.

That didn't mean Emily could let her gaze go. Not for a second. Maybe if she stayed hidden, the creature would leave. Certainly there were plenty of other children to scare. Why couldn't the boogey monster go dance somewhere else?

Emily saw that Smokeball had already found a comfortable spot and was back to his slumbers. She didn't know how the cat could sleep so soundly with certain doom just inches away. Emily would not be so blessed. She stayed awake hiding in her closet sanctuary until the first merciful ray of sunlight peered through her window ensuring safety.

***

It was a bleary eyed morning with Emily's parents asking her if she another bad night's sleep. What could she tell them? They'd just lecture her that she was in second grade and far too old to believe in monsters. As she trudged out the door to the bus stop, Emily looked back at Smokeball sleeping on the couch. She wished she was a cat. Then she could sleep during the day and stay awake all night.

School was a blur. She met up with her friends Jayla and Katie. Last year the two coolest girls in school wouldn't even speak to Emily. Emily wasn't rich or popular like them, and had to practically beg to become part of their circle.

Of course, Emily could never tell her two 'best friends' about what lurked under her bed. She was afraid they wouldn't be her best friends anymore. So she just listened to them talk and giggle about things that used to seem so important. Every so often Emily would nod so they would think she was still listening, but the two were so busy chattering that she didn't have to nod much. They certainly didn't seem to care how upset Emily was.

Emily barely made it through class with both eyes open. Rather than sit with her 'best friends' at lunch, Emily made her way to back stairway in the back of the school. It led out to the dumpsters in the alley and no one used it much. She set her phone alarm for an hour and slumped down on one of the steps to get some monster-free slumber.

"Hello," a soft voice interrupted her plans. Emily looked up to see a small girl teetering up at the top of the steps. Emily thought she recognized her from class but couldn't remember her name. This girl might be what you'd describe as mousy, but a mouse scurrying down the hall would catch Emily's attention. This girl was just barely there.

"Do you mind if I sit with you?" the girl whispered. Emily nodded and the girl sat down her plain brown lunch bag that matched the color of her flimsy hair.

"I'm Mary," she said as she stared down into her bag. She pulled out a plain peanut butter sandwich. "Usually no one comes down here."

"Yeah, that's why I'm here," Emily yawned. "I didn't get much sleep."

Mary nodded. "Monsters."

"What?" Emily asked.

"Monsters," Mary repeated. "I'm right, aren't I?"

Emily sighed. She had been too embarrassed to admit her fears to her friends but explaining to a stranger was somehow worse. "What makes you say something crazy like that?"

"I just asked a question," Mary said. "I wasn't trying to be crazy. So, monsters?"

Emily relented. "Yes, monsters. Or just one, I think. I hope there's not more than one."

"There's usually not," Mary replied. "Monsters don't like to share their spaces."

"And what makes you an expert on monsters?" Emily asked.

"I'm not an expert," Mary answered. "I just know stuff."

"So if you know so much stuff, how do I make it go away?" Emily asked.

"Cat," Mary answered. "Monsters hate cats."

"I have a cat," Emily said. "But I still have a monster."

"Yes," Mary nodded. "But the monster hasn't hurt you, has it?"

"Not yet."

"It's because you have a cat. Monsters hate cats," Mary repeated.

"That is ridiculous," Emily said. "You mean to tell me that monsters are afraid of cats because they bite and scratch? My cat just sits there like a lump."

"Cats are stronger and faster than monsters," Mary nodded. "Even lazy ones like yours. But monsters just hate cats. I didn't say they're afraid of them."

"So why do monsters hate cats?"

"They're allergic," Mary said.

"What?" Emily laughed nearly spitting her tuna sandwich out her nose. "You're kidding right?"

"No," Mary said in her deadpan voice. "I was not kidding." No one would accuse Mary of being the class clown.

"You don't even need a real cat," Mary continued. "You could have a stuffed animal cat and the monster would leave you alone because it thinks the cat is real. Monsters aren't very smart."

"Look, I don't just want the monster to leave me alone," Emily said. "I don't want the monster under my bed at all."

"I see," Mary said. "Most people don't, I guess. There is only one way to get rid of it for good then."

Emily sighed. If she wasn't so tired she would just walk away from this nonsense. But instead she just looked at Mary's averted eyes and waited for the answer.

"To make the monster under the bed go away, you have to go under its bed and scare it," Mary answered.

"Uh-huh," Emily sighed. "And how do I go under a monster's bed?"

"You crawl under it," Mary said. "This is how you go under anyone's bed, isn't it?"

Emily rolled her eyes. She didn't know if this girl was being snarky or clueless. Since it's impossible to be snarky when you're clueless, she figured the latter. Emily was a pretty smart seven year-old, after all, but she had to admit she still didn't know how to solve the monster problem.

"Can I come to your house?" Mary asked.

What?" Emily asked. "I'm not supposed to have people at my house without my mom's permission," For once she was glad for her mom's rules because she really didn't want this strange girl over.

"I don't have to go in your house. Just outside it," Mary explained. She put her uneaten sandwich back in her bag and stood up to leave. "I'll meet you in front of the flagpole after school. I'm really glad I can help. Good-bye."

Emily didn't say anything. She really didn't know what to say at this point. At least she wasn't tired anymore.

***

Emily wasn't sure if she was going to meet her odd new acquaintance but there she was standing in front of the flag pole holding her paper lunch bag. The two said nothing until they reached Emily's house. Mary immediately stomped over the grass and ran to the side of the house.

"Hey! You're not supposed to walk on the grass. My mom's gonna kill me!" Emily yelled as she followed Mary who was now hunched over rubbing the dirt. "What are you doing?"

"Get down and help me," Mary answered. She threw a handful of dirt behind her nearly hitting Emily's shoes.

"I am not getting my dress all dirty. My mom is so gonna kill me," Emily said.

"I do not think she will kill you," Mary said. "No wonder you have a monster under your bed. Are you always so afraid that someone is going to kill you? Monsters can smell fear, you know."

"What are you looking for?" Emily asked completely ignoring Mary's last comment.

"Something strange," Mary answered. "Worms."

"Worms are strange," Emily said.

"Two headed worms are," Mary said. "That's how we know we're close to where the monsters live. Aha!"

Emily saw Mary grab a worm from the ground which indeed had two heads. The heads wriggled around Mary's finger; perhaps trying to get her to let it go back to its underground two-headed wormy life. Emily didn't know whether to be grossed out or completely fascinated.

Mary pulled at the worm but it wouldn't budge from the ground. It was as though Mary was embroiled in a tug of war game with the earth.

"Maybe you should leave the creepy worm alone," Emily suggested. "I don't see what worms have to do with monsters anyway. You're never going to pull it out."

"I'm not trying to pull it out," Mary said. "I'm trying to open the trapdoor but it's stuck."

"Trapdoor?" Emily asked. She was wondering why she invited this strange worm-tugging girl to her home.

"Yeah, and this worm's the handle," Mary explained. She pulled harder at the worm and the grass and earth underneath it ripped away like a door in the ground revealing a hole. Upon closer inspection there was a tight spiraling set of concrete stairs that led deep below into the pit.

"After you," Mary gestured.

"Why me?" Emily asked.

"It's your monster," Mary answered. "It would be rude for me to go first."

"No! We're going to tell my mom about this," Emily insisted. "She'll know what to do."

"Has your mom ever seen the monster? Does she believe in monsters?" Mary asked.

"No and no," Emily answered.

"So she's not gonna be able to see any of this," Mary said. "The worm's already started burrowing back into the ground and pretty soon the dirt's gonna cover up this hole. Then we'll have to find another two headed worm which could take days. We were really lucky this time."

"You call this lucky?" Emily asked. "Do we really want to climb down into a hole that's gonna be filled up with dirt?"

"Do you really want to have a monster under your bed?" Mary asked. "He's gonna wonder who bothered his pet worm."

"I'll tell him it was you!" Emily threatened.

"He won't believe you," Mary said. She motioned towards the hole. "After you."

Emily tested the stairs with her foot and they seemed solid. Using her phone to light the way, she slowly descended as Mary followed right behind.

"Be careful," Mary warned. "It's gonna get slimier as we get deeper."

"How deep is it going to get?" Emily asked. "Why are we even doing this? Why are you even here?"

"I don't get much chance to help people," Mary said. "It's hard to help when most people ignore you."

"You call this help?" Emily said. "We're going deep into a cave where there's hungry worms just waiting to eat us, I bet. No. This is crazy. I'm going back up and.....yaaaaa!"

Emily's foot slipped on a patch of slime and she went falling backwards. Mary grabbed the falling girl's arms trying to hold her steady.

"Careful," Mary said. "I warned you that it gets slippery."

Emily gasped looking around for her phone which had been flung from her grasp. Without its light, she was blind in the overwhelming darkness.

"Call me so I can find it," Emily asked Mary.

"Call you with what? I don't have a phone."

"What do you mean you don't have a phone?" Emily demanded. "Who doesn't have a phone? Are you Amish or something?"

"No one ever calls me, so why would I need a phone?" Mary answered. "Just bend down and feel each step. It can't have gone far."

"Ewwww!" Emily screamed as her hand felt the sticky slime growing on the stairs.

"It's harmless," Mary said. "But don't rub in on your clothes. I don't think it washes off."

"I hate this! I hate this!" Emily said.

"Here's your phone," Mary said. "Right under your foot." She pressed the key on the phone and it illuminated their current situation. They were now almost at the bottom of the stairs in a large open cavern. Emily looked back at the claustrophobic staircase they had just descended and wondered how she found the courage to come this far.

"You can rub the slime off on my back if you want," Mary offered as she handed Emily's phone back to her. "I don't really care about my clothes anyway."

"Maybe you should get better clothes," Emily said rubbing the sticky blue stuff off her hands. "Where do we go now?"

"We're right where we want to be," Mary said. "We're under the monster's bed."

"Really?" Emily asked. She shone her phone up at the cavern ceiling. It looked just like you'd expect the roof of a cave to look with rocks and stalactites hanging above. But it also seemed to ripple and shake like it was made of something much more flimsy than earth and stone.

"The monster's tossing and turning on its mattress up there," Mary explained. "I think he's scared because we're down here."

"The monster is up there???" Emily asked. "And it's scared of us?"

"Well, yes," Mary said. "It doesn't know for sure what's down here so it's thinking the worst. You were scared of the monster even though you had never seen it, right? Well, it feels the same way about you. The monster's probably wondering if we have big teeth or poison claws. That kind of thing. It's gonna be up all night worrying if it doesn't go to sleep and have nightmares instead."

"I kind of feel bad," Emily said. "I didn't like it when it was scaring me. So what now? Shouldn't we go tell the monster not to scare me anymore? Or at least see what it looks like?"

"Well, yes. You can just run up that tunnel over there," Mary pointed. "But I don't think that's a good idea. If it sees you, it might not think you're very scary. Then it might eat you."

"But what if the monster isn't scary at all?" Emily asked. "I at least have to see what this thing that has kept me up all night looks like. I'll be really quiet. It won't even see me."

"I don't know if that's such a good idea," Mary said but curiosity had already gotten the better of Emily and she went running up through the tunnel on the other side of the cavern. The tunnel wasn't terribly long but it narrowed quickly, and Emily had to crawl through it. When she emerged she saw what appeared to be an actual bed.

It was much bigger than her bed, but a bed nonetheless. Emily looked around and saw that she was now in a bedroom. It was huge and everything in it was giant sized, but it was pretty much like Emily's own room back home. There were posters up on the walls (except they were all pictures of spiders.) There were dolls on shelves and on the floor (except all the dolls were scowling and they had snakes for hair.) There was a nightlight plugged into the wall (except instead of brightening the room, it cast a cone of darkness.)

So a little creepy, but Emily thought maybe this monster was just like her. She slid out from under the bed to try to get a look at the monster. Most likely it wasn't scary at all.

Wrong! The thing sleeping on the bed had a body as big as her mom's car. And it had scales all over and rows of bat wings all over its back. It had a lashing tail full of spikes. Its head was twice the size of its body and inside was a bottomless pit of a mouth lined with rows and rows of gnashing teeth. Worst of all, it had hundreds of eyes suspended from stalks floating above its gruesome head.

One of the eyes slithered down to where Emily was sitting and stared right at her face.

Emily screamed.

So did the monster. The monster screamed and screamed and screamed. Imagine one hundred giant fingernails scratching one hundred blackboards all at once. The monster's screams sounded much, much worse.

This was the first time the monster had ever screamed in its entire life. Even in its worst nightmares, the monster had never seen a creature so terrifying as this girl in its room. Emily's eyes were sunk into its face like they had been pressed into her skull. She had hair on the top of her head instead of fins and spikes. But scariest of all was that little tiny mouth. You couldn't see when that small mouth and tiny teeth would strike next.

The monster screamed even louder.

Mary, meanwhile had heard this horrendous cacophony and went running to see if Emily was alright. Or still alive. She crawled through the tunnel to see the two embroiled in what looked like a screaming contest. The monster was obviously winning.

"Emily, I think we should leave," Mary suggested. She deliberately averted her eyes from the monster because if she saw what it looked like, she might start screaming too.

For once, Emily wholeheartedly agreed with Mary and she let the girl lead her back under the bed and down through the tunnel.

Unfortunately, one of the eyestalks slithered over to the two girls. The giant eyeball on top of the eyestalk plopped right in front of them effectively blocked their escape route. Then another giant eye swooshed over next to the first. The two eyes were joined by yet another followed by one hovering over the girls staring straight down at them.

"Try not to look scared," Mary advised Emily.

"How do I do that?" Emily asked. "There are giant monster eyes all around us."

"WHO HIDE UNDER GRULAG'S BED?" the monster roared.

The two girls shrieked as even more eyes hovered above them.

"WHY YOU TRY TO SCARE GRULAG? THAT NOT NICE!" the monster roared even louder.

Emily tried to say she was sorry but all she could manage was a whimper which really didn't answer Grulag's question at all.

"G-g-grulag, your monstrousness," Mary stuttered. "We're only here because you were hiding under my f-friend's bed. That wasn't n-nice either."

"GRULAG NOT TRY TO SCARE ANYONE. GRULAG WANTED NICE QUIET PLACE TO HIDE. UNDER BED IS NICE QUIET PLACE."

"You know, I get that," Mary said. "Sometimes I need to go somewhere all alone where it's quiet."

"Me too," Emily agreed.

"BUT YOU NOT GO UNDER GRULAG'S BED FOR QUIET. YOU GO UNDER GRULAG'S BED TO TRY TO SCARE GRULAG. GRULAG NOT LIKE THAT AT ALL!"

The monster gnashed its 45 rows of teeth in its house sized mouth which was even scarier than its screams and roars. Emily tried looking past the eyes surrounding them up the stalks connected to those eyes and up to the monstrous face that was connected to the stalks. She then decided that was a bad idea. She didn't want to look at the monster. The eyes were scary enough.

"Grulag, we're very sorry," Emily said as she stared down at the ground so she wouldn't have to see any of Grulag's scary monster parts.

Mary opened up her paper bag and pulled out the uneaten peanut butter sandwich. She dropped the bag on the ground and held the sandwich up to one of the eyes. "How about a snack to show you how sorry we are. We promise it will taste much better than we would."

Emily nodded her head in agreement.

"DOES SANDWICH HAVE ROCKS AND CENTIPEDES IN IT?" Grulag asked?

"Sorry, they were all out of centipedes today," Mary apologized.

One of the eyes lowered to the ground and Mary's shaking hands set the sandwich on top of the giant eyeball. The eye then flew back over to its owner where it spun around and dropped the morsel in Grulag's massive mouth.

"Good?" Mary asked.

"SANDWICH NEEDS HORSEFLIES, BUT GRULAG LIKE."

"Oh good," Emily said. "So you'll let us go now?"

The eyes blinked and the teeth gnashed. "GRULAG NO LET YOU GO. IF GRULAG LET YOU GO, THEN YOU SNEAK UNDER GRUGAG'S BED TOMORROW AND BITE GRULAG WITH YOUR TINY TEETH. GRULAG HAS TO EAT YOU NOW."

Mary and Emily shuddered as the eyes moved closer barely giving them any room to stand.

"JUMP ON GRULAG'S EYE SO GRULAG CAN CARRY YOU TO MOUTH AND EAT YOU TOO. WHO WILL BE FIRST?"

Emily did not want to be eaten. If there was one thing worse than having a monster under your bed it was being swallowed by one. But Mary, who she barely even knew, had risked everything to help her. It was the least Emily could do to keep her from being the first monster snack.

"Me," Emily raised her hand. One of the eyes touched down on the ground and blinked, letting Emily know she was supposed to climb on it.

"Mary, thank you for helping me," Emily said. "I'm sorry I was kind of rude to you."

"No," Mary said. "Grulag, please don't eat her. Please!"

"GRULAG NOT KNOW WHAT 'PLEASE' MEANS. GRULAG JUST WANTS TO EAT LITTLE TINY MONSTERS SO THEY NO HURT GRULAG ANYMORE."

"We won't. We promise," Emily pleaded but the eyes weren't going anywhere.

"Oh yeah?" Mary said. "Well, we have lots of other tiny monster friends and all I got to do is use my magic monster caller and you're gonna have hundreds of little monsters swarming under your bed like bugs. Like bedbugs!"

"Magic monster caller?" Emily asked?

"Yeah," Mary said. She picked up the paper bag from the ground, blew in it until it was full of air then slammed her hand against it and.......

POP!!!!!

The monster screamed even louder at the sound of the fearsome magic monster caller. Its eyes spun wildly around the room like pool balls.

Mary grabbed Emily's hand and they slid under the bed and through the tunnel down to the cavern. Up above them the rocky ceiling rippled and shook threatening to throw a storm of rocks and stalactites down on the two girls.

"Grulag's pretty upset," Emily said staring up at the ceiling which she now knew to be the bottom of the monster's bed.

"I think we should run," Mary suggested.

"I think that's your best idea ever," Emily agreed.

The two found their way to the narrow stone spiral staircase. As they ran up, dirt flew down in their faces threatening to knock them down the slimy steps. But the two held each other steady as they trudged up the perilous stairs. They held their breath so they wouldn't suck any of the flying dirt into their lungs. Just as they saw a small ray of sunlight, they were pelted by a hailstorm of sharp grass blades.

With a final burst of energy, they held hands and together they lunged up towards the surface. They shot up through the hole then fell down to the ground right in front of Emily's house. They watched as the last grain of dirt covered up the hole. Then the grass flew to the ground and each blade planted itself back into the dirt. It now looked as though nothing had ever happened.

Well, except for the fact that Emily and Mary were both completely covered in dust and mud. But after almost being eaten by a monster that really wasn't so bad.

Mary coughed. "Are you still alive?"

Emily wiped away the dirt caked over her eyes. "Yeah. I think."

"At least the monster won't be bothering you anymore," Mary said.

Emily just nodded. "Thanks. I mean it." She smiled at Mary. "Hey, did you want to hang out tomorrow?"

A wide grin crossed Mary's face and her eyes met Emily's for the first time. She looked so different. She looked so happy. "Really? You want to hang out with me?" Mary asked.

"Well, you're a little strange, but yeah," Emily smiled. "You were really there for me."

"So did you want to meet at the flagpole again after school?" Mary asked

"Sure, but you have to get a phone one of these days." Emily said.

"Okay," Mary said as she slowly got up and shook dust out of her hair. "What do you think of Ghost Dragons?"

"Ghost Dragons?" Emily asked.

Mary nodded. "I'm just trying to think of more adventures for us." She waved and walked away. "See you tomorrow."

"Sure," Emily said as she watched Mary walk away to wherever it was that she lived. "I really hope she was joking about that."

Emily wasn't even thinking about tomorrow. She just wanted a long hot bath to wash the entire day away.

That night, before going to bed, Emily placed two small rocks under her mattress.

"I remember you liked them," Emily spoke to what appeared to be thin air. "Sorry, I don't have any centipedes. They're kind of gross."

From beneath the mattress, a very tiny voice spoke. "grulag love crunchy rocks!" The monster under the bed sounded a lot smaller when you weren't face to face with it. "you bring grulag more rocks tomorrow."

"What was that word I taught you?" Emily asked.

"please," the monster said.

"Good Grulag," Emily smiled. This was quite a day. She had not only survived this adventure, she had made two new friends in the process. Emily curled up with her cat and slept sounder than she ever had in her entire life.

The End

You can find more of J.M's stories at:

https://www.wattpad.com/user/JMMCNEELY

Cover by Susan K. Saltos.

Unicorn Shrine

Chie Hatsume Pamyu

What will Himiko do now that her grandmother has died? Alone and afraid, she must deal with the future she faces.

***

13-year old Himiko Naka was once a girl with two loving parents. Sadly, her parents passed away, so she moved in with her grandmother. After her grandmother died, a repo-man came into the house. He told Himiko that he'd take care of her after he repossessed all of her grandmother's belongings. 'What! He's going to repossess me!', she thought. She packed her belongings, grabbed her backpack and frantically ran away. And the repo-man yelled "Wait!" in a confused tone of voice.

To relieve the grief she had developed after her grandmother died, she tried to remember all of the cartoons that she had seen on TV as she began strolling around a park. The image of Bambi popped up in her mind. 'Maybe I should move into the forest?', the naive girl thought. After Himiko had finished packing up her belongings, she headed off into a nearby forest.

Due to her hunger and her extreme appetite, Himiko began to gather food by picking berries from bushes. However, she accidentally reached very deep into one of the bushes with one of her hands. Via this hand, she could feel the tip of a cold bony object. She grabbed the tip of the object and quickly pulled it out of the bush. To her surprise, the object was a horn. After admiring the horn, Himiko put it into her backpack. She quickly went back to gathering berries.

Full of berries, Himiko decided to look around at the ground. She quickly noticed a trail of hoof-like footprints. She followed the trail slowly and wound up in a cave. Himiko walked around the cave slowly. Suddenly, a shadow approached her. "Oh no! It's a dangerous creature!", she thought. Himiko expected some kind of huge wildcat to come. But to her relief, a horse-like creature with a huge dot mark on its forehead came to her.

"It's a unicorn. Oh my god! Grandma used to tell me unicorn stories! And now they're real!", blurted Himiko. Suddenly, she saw tears dripping from the unicorn's eyes. The creature was badly injured in one of its hind legs. There were marks from some kind of animal trap on it. "Oh you poor thing, you must have accidentally walked into a hunter's trap," she said. So she glued the horn back onto the dot on the unicorn's head. Then after she walked around with the unicorn, she noticed that there was an abandoned shrine nearby. She entered the shrine. "From now on this shall be my new home! Unicorn shrine!"

The End

Connect with Chie Hatsume Pamyu at:

https://www.wattpad.com/user/ChieHatsumePamyu

http://unisuniverse.tumblr.com/

Photo Artist Credit: Yegrinna. https://labrass.deviantart.com/

Cover by Susan K Saltos

Warrior's Blood

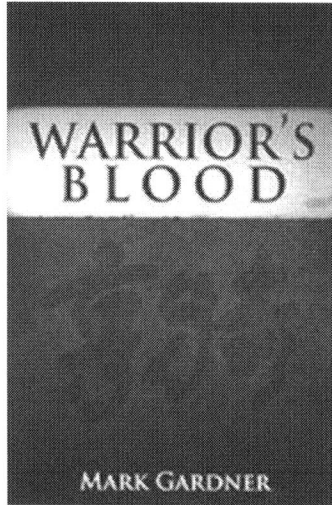

Mark Gardner

Mark Gardner is an author and broadcast professional from Prescott, Arizona. His grandfather introduced him to the alternate history writings of Harry Turtledove at a young age. That started a life-long love affair with speculative fiction. After being fired from a thankless job in retail sales, he began to write his own stories. His first publication was Body Rentals. Since then, he has written 11 books, including War of the Worlds: Retaliation, the superhero series, Sixteen Sunsets Saga, and hard sci-fi collaborative novel, Days Until Home. His books are favorites among fans of Sin City, The Martian, The Punisher, and Firefly. His work is a fast paced, no-nonsense, thrill ride into many genres, including science fiction, superhero, dystopian, and historical fiction. His works are available in nine languages, and he has fans on all seven continents.

Warrior's Blood ended up in my historical fiction novel, Champion Standing. Originally it was a stand-alone story, and when I was editing Champion Standing I was hacking and slashing words out of the story and ended up with a too-low word count. I rewrote

Warrior's Blood and inserted it along with a flash fiction piece I had written to an Internet prompt. Warrior's Blood as a standalone has been in a few charity anthologies.

***

The day's first match ended abruptly when another warrior decapitated a contestant. The ear-shattering chorus of warriors shouting to warn the guardians of heaven that a warrior was coming home was followed by swift action on the part of the Council of Judges to rule in the event. For the first time in the tournament, a warrior was disqualified and discredited for an overt act of aggression. In a short, but poignant ceremony, the warrior was exiled from the island in dishonor and disgrace. It is interesting to note that in what was explained later as having been a strange quirk of coincidence and nothing more, the ship carrying this warrior off the island suffered a catastrophic fire, resulting in the loss of all hands. Of further interest, the entire crew compliment was made up of members of the same clan. While there are those who could consider this action unbecoming of a warrior and a certain act of dishonor, others simply accept the coincidence story and suggest, strongly, that the matter be laid to rest. As there is no court of appeal to either the Council of Judges decision, or that of an inexplicably destroyed ship, calmer minds prevailed and the incident was, for the best part, eventually forgotten.

The second match of the day saw Qiao eliminated in a closely fought battle between two matched opponents. A crowd favorite following his epic match with Liao the previous day, his defeat was a rare enigma, indeed. Seldom did it happen that a competitor was eliminated, and yet still be the recipient of the lion's share of crowd appreciation over the winner of the match. That was the case on this second day of competition, as a strange day of matches continued to unfurl. Qiao, for his part, celebrated long into the night, and long into the week. He dedicated the remainder of his time on Hainan Island to helping prepare Liao for his run at the championship.

When Liao did enter the arena for his first fight of the day, it was over almost before it started.

The two warriors paced each other at first. Round and round they circled, each measuring the other, neither seeming to want to make the first move. Without warning, Liao's opponent saw his opening and charged. Two steps into his charge, the man seemed to slip on an unknown slippery spot on the arena floor, spin several times, and finally land face down on the business end of his Dao. His injury was not life threatening, but it was enough to end his tournament run, and allow Liao an even longer respite with which to prepare for what would prove to be a more challenging second round match.

In all, four more Warriors were eliminated from the tournament during this first round of the second day of competition.

***

As was tradition for time immemorial, there was a break following the second day of competition to allow the competitors a chance to regroup, recover, rest, revitalize and recreate. It was a much-needed time out after the intense drama and physical exertion of the tournament. In was also a time of retaliation from some of the less successful, somewhat dishonorable factions who had been eliminated from competition.

To Liao, little change was called for. The astral landscape preceding the Hainan dawn found him beginning his day with the usual regiment of warm-up exercises and calisthenics. If he was to be successful, there was neither room nor time for a lapse in his routine.

As he had the previous day, Liao made his way to the square where meals were prepared. He selected a similar course as the day before, including extra tea, and once again took his place with the already seated Shui and the Nubian.

"Liao," the older man stood as Liao approached' "you're overdressed. Finish your meal; there is much to be accomplished today." Before Liao could answer, Shui turned and walked off in the direction of their quarters.

Curious, he turned to the Nubian, but before he could ask, she too stood, and spoke briefly before following off in her companion's direction. "Eat, Liao. You're going to need the energy. Ten minutes. Your quarters." And she was gone.

***

Liao returned to find clothing and equipment already laid out on his bed. Beside the clothing was an assortment of hand-blade weapons and a Han survival belt, the type of which he had not seen since he was a much younger man.

Liao immediately determined what Shui had planned for the three of them for the day. They were going on a hunt, and Liao's pulse raced at the prospect. He had questions about the female Nubian accompanying them, but elected to defer to the older man's judgment in the matter. As a matter of course, however, Han women did not ordinarily participate in the hunt. That there was far more to this Nubian than met the eye was something Liao had long since come to understand, yet without knowing exactly what it was that set her aside, or made her of such interest to Shui.

He had already seen the next day's rankings, and once again his first match was the last of the first round, albeit rounds were shortened somewhat due to the loss of competitors. But he had the entire day, much of the night, and a good portion of the next morning to entertain this hunt, and still have time to prepare for his next match, so Liao enthusiastically welcomed the challenge.

The unlikely trio headed southwest into the densest part of the forest surrounding the tournament village, away from the Great China Sea. Shui's intended base camp was a three-hour trek into the woods, giving the hunters more than adequate time to find their camp, engage in the hunt, kill, clean, cook and eat any quarry they could find, and return in time for Liao's next match.

The wilderness area into which the trio traveled was truly a forest primeval. While the Han People were born with an incredible natural sense of direction, it was Shui's familiarity with the area that ultimately kept them from getting hopelessly lost; so dense was the landscape that greeted them. The barely distinguishable path was overgrown with a thick, densely populated growth that resisted the blades used to cut their path through the surrounding jungle, although to say it was simply a jungle was not entirely accurate. The forests were a combination of tropical and old growth flora and fauna. Infrequent breaks in the dense overgrowth revealed towering hardwood trees, the tops of which would have been difficult to see even if the lower level branches and foliage were less compressed. Imported plant-life adapted well, mixing virtually indistinguishably from the native mix. So, too, did the imported wildlife. Herbivores and carnivores lived well with the indigenous creatures. A harmonious agreement between them was reached, neither species, indigenous or imported, dominated the other.

Domesticated species as well as free roaming wild species flourished in this forest, much to the delight both of the permanent population of the island and the frequent visitors. Hunting on

Hainan Island was a favorite pastime among those of the empire who could afford the luxury. Because the industry had so flourished, strict rules of control had been established to protect the island from going the way of other such paradises throughout the Empire. The only weapons allowed during the hunt were the hunter's personal blade, a Han version of a bow and arrow, or spear. This was as much a cultural provision as it was an ecological one. After all, a warrior who could not defeat his prey with such basic weaponry was not truly a hunter. His honor was lacking. Hans understood the more elegant side of the hunt - man against the elements; man against the beast. Additionally, even on Hainan Island, the hunter hunted only what he would take and eat. Hunting for sport was virtually unheard of within the Empire.

It was this world of the hunt that beckoned Liao, Shui, and the female Nubian. They continued their march deeper and deeper into the forest until at last, Shui announced they had reached their destination. From here they would branch out in search of their prey: wild tiger - the ultimate feast for a seasoned warrior. This was the goal Shui had sought for the trio, but especially for Liao. Shui would orchestrate the hunt so Liao would capture the beast, granting him the right to partake of the spoils of the hunt first. More importantly, the taking of the beast in the wild would serve to bolster Liao's confidence for what remained of the competition. Shui knew from experience that from here on out, there were no holds barred in the Hainan Island Dao Tournament. The rules were still there, but with so much on the line, sometimes rules were overlooked in the heat of battle, and in the layers of politics that somehow still managed to find their way into this most prestigious of Han honors.

The three walked silently through a canopy of lush, green overgrowth; Shui taking the lead, followed by the Nubian; Liao at the tail end of their group. They would stop periodically when Shui would point something out along the barely distinguishable trail.

"I have been coming to these woods since I was a child," the older man spoke almost reverently. "My father would take me hunting along this very trail. I killed my first tiger not far from the place where we'll establish our camp."

They continued for another hour, the elder warrior still commenting, directing their attention to this tree, or that rock, or a flower, snake or animal unique to the forest. "Here," he spoke again, "and here alone grow the herbs that are used in the *Warrior's Blood*, but don't look for them, Liao - without the secret of how they are blended, knowing the individual plants is meaningless."

After nearly three hours, Shui finally called the party to a halt. He motioned for Liao and the Nubian to wait while he stepped into what appeared to be an opening in the brush that the two of them had completely missed. A short time later, the old Warrior emerged, a look of satisfaction and contentment clear on his face. "Well, what are you waiting for," he challenged. "We've arrived!" He stepped back, holding open the passage while Liao and the woman passed through, emerging into a battered, overgrown clearing that appeared to be the remains of an old hunters camp.

Shui, firmly in his element, began to establish the camp.

"Liao, scout the surrounding area, but not too far. It is easy to get lost in these woods. Gather kindling and firewood, and while you're out there, scout the area for recent signs of tiger. Unless things have changed greatly since the last time I was here, the area is still a great hunting ground for them.

"Nala, begin setting up the fire circle. It won't be necessary to restore the whole camp - we won't be here that long. Just enough room for a fire; room to cook, eat, rest, and then be on our way. I'll be back in a few minutes. I seem to recall a source of fresh drinking water not far from here."

Shui had not been away long when Liao returned to the clearing, arms burdened by the heavy load of kindling and firewood he carried, his eyes full of fire and excitement.

"If the trails I discovered are any indication, these woods are indeed the perfect place to hunt tiger," he said, excitement barely hidden from his voice. "There are trails everywhere! It will be a glorious hunt!"

"He said you would like it, Liao," the Nubian said over her shoulder.

Liao set the load of firewood near the edge of the clearing, carrying to the pit the Nubian had cleared out only the kindling and enough branches of wood to get the fire going. He helped the Nubian arrange the kindling while she produced a flint and steel. She struck them together several times and a spark ignited the pile of small twigs and dry grasses. As the fire began to smolder, Liao handed her the branches he carried back with him. Beginning with the small ones, she placed them carefully around the small flame, seeking the best possible combination for a good, long lasting fire. If the hunt were both timely and successful, there would be a good bed of coals waiting for Liao when he returned with his catch.

While they finished the fire, Shui returned to the clearing, carrying several skins of fresh water. He hung the skins from pegs he found below the lower branches of one of the trees in the clearing, and motioned for Liao and the Nubian to come over to him. The three of them sat together for several moments, several paces removed from the growing warmth of the fire, before Shui began to speak.

"This place has a great history, Liao. Three generations of my family have hunted here. My clan dies with me, Liao, so I leave you to remember this place." He reached into a pocket hidden within his great cloak and withdrew a folded skin parchment, opened it and handed it to the younger man. Liao showed the Nubian what he had been given, while Shui continued his narrative.

"That map will help you find your way back here. It has been five years since the last time I was here, and the clearing still looks as though no one has discovered it. It can be your secret place as it was once mine, if you like."

He motioned to the Nubian, who silently withdrew a cask of Baijiu from her pack. She passed the bottle first to Shui, who took a long pull before offering the beverage back to Liao and the Nubian. As they both took their drink in turn, he continued.

"This place has been kept as a family secret, passed down from Father to Firstborn Son. My Grandfather passed it to my Father, who in turn passed it on to me. This camp has seen many a hunt, Liao. I have a feeling somehow that this will be my last."

Shui looked off in the distant trees for a moment, took another long pull from the bottle of Baijiu, and went on.

"Promise me that you will show this place to Kaden. Promise me that it will not be forgotten when I die. But promise me nothing now, Liao. Come!"

Shui stood, beckoning the others to do the same.

"The best time for the hunt is before the sun reaches its zenith. If we're to have a successful hunt, and have you back in time for your next match, now is the time for us to set out. You found signs of tiger trail?"

Liao nodded, rising to his feet and extending a hand to help the woman as well.

"Good. Take only your blade. Nala will bring a spear and net, I will offer direction and support. Let us be off now."

81

***

Shui stood by while Liao and the woman, in that order, preceded him into the forest where Liao had seen the tiger trail earlier. While Shui was clearly the leader in all respects of this outing, the actual details of the hunt he left to Liao. It was the younger man, after all, who would do the actual work, and it must of necessity be the younger man who executed the task at hand. To have matters settled in any other fashion would distract from Shui's intended purpose, which was to better prepare Liao for the second half of the Tournament. Naturally, he knew the forest surrounding them better than any of the three members of his party. He had memorized these trails before the Nubian was even born. He knew that tigers, being the creatures of habit and evolution that they were, would follow courses set eons before by instinct. He knew exactly where, when and how Liao would likely find his catch, but he also knew that the younger man must discover these things for himself if the experience were to benefit him at all. To his great pleasure, the younger man did not disappoint him. Liao was proving to be as skilled a hunter and tracker as he had already proven himself to be skilled with his Dao.

The task was neither easy, nor quickly resolved.

Liao, taking point in the expedition quickly slipped into the role Shui laid out for him. He spoke first to the woman. "You will follow behind me until the scent is captured," he instructed. "Then you will watch for my signal. I will inform you where and how to place yourself."

He spoke next to Shui. "You will circle in the opposite direction from which I send the Nubian. We will encircle the beast from three sides, cutting off any escape route. It will be your task to ensure that the beast will keep moving in my direction, once it is flushed."

Shui and the Nubian each in turn signaled their understanding and acceptance of his instructions, and began to fall slightly behind Liao in their passage along the trail.

Liao proved to be an excellent tracker, picking up the tiger trail within minutes of the trio leaving camp.

There are several easily notable signs of tiger trail an experienced tracker will distinguish. First, if the trail is relatively clear of debris, are the actual tracks left by the animal after its passage. A good trail will reveal the footprints of several beasts. The larger the animal, the deeper and larger its print. If the animal is taking a leisurely pace, the print left behind will be deeper than if the animal were running.

Once the trail of prints had been discovered, Liao immediately dropped to his knees, searching and smelling for telltale signs of the passage of the animal. Tigers are by nature highly territorial, and like many other territorial animals; they mark their declared habitat by spraying. There was generally no sign of droppings along a well-traveled trail. Tigers, despite their appearance, were remarkably clean creatures. Not only did they not like their warrens to be full of the odor of their droppings, neither did they care for their territory to be so recognized. It was one thing to declare to other tigers that this was their territory. It was something completely different to announce to other predators who shared their woods, and who might possibly list fresh tiger meat along with their choice of delicacies, the location of their trails, and possibly their warrens, hence, tigers were meticulous in the burying of their droppings, often outside of their own territorial roaming.

Tiger spray was something once learned, no hunter ever forgot. The sweet, musky fragrance left by their passing was easily followed if the passing was recent enough. Liao soon found fresh evidence of a recently passing group of tigers, and set his team to alertness as he formally began the hunt. Motioning the Nubian to his left, and Shui to his right, Liao proceeded along the trail almost crawling upon all fours, not wanting to spook the object of his hunt, so fresh were the signs on the trail. Slowly he crept, barely breathing as he moved closer to his target. Silent as the depth of space, he advanced, increasingly aware as he moved, of the starkly vivid world around him. Liao moved as one with his forest. So subtle were his movements, he barely left evidence that he, too, had followed the trail established by the tiger he sought. The trail was fresh. The scent was strong. The moment was soon at hand. So skillful were his advances that even Shui lost sight of the younger man as he closed in on his quarry.

The forest around them grew silent, almost as if in anticipation of what was about to unfold. Even the insects, whose clicking and chirping was their constant companion, seemed awestruck by the presence of the young hunter, their almost incessant hum of activity softened to a respectful whisper by the careful, stealthy movements below. Time seemed to stand still, as it so often does during life's pivotal moments. A dance, as it were, began to unfold as Liao crept unseen into the clearing where a small pack of tigers had recently passed. All that remained of their pack was the dominant male. The rest of the pack had continued on to the stream where they took their water while he remained behind, almost as if to secure the clearing where they would rest during the heat of the day.

Liao silently motioned to the Nubian and to Shui to begin to close ranks on the beast while he moved ever closer to his prey. The huge cat, which had seemed to this point unaware of the ballet of movement closing in around him, suddenly took notice; sensing for the first time that his world was about to change. It rose quietly from its haunches, the hairs on its back standing, nostrils flaring, eyes darting about the clearing, sensing something, yet not understanding what was about to befall it.

Slowly the circle closed. Quietly the trio slipped closer to the mighty beast now pacing anxiously in an ever-shrinking circle at the center of the clearing. Suddenly, the huge animal reacted. Millennia of evolutionary development and raw, natural instinct narrowed into a focal point that drove the beast to a decision, such that it was for an animal incapable of logical thought or rational action. In an instant of frozen time shorter than the beat of a heart; at the very moment Liao had chosen to enter the clearing, the beast charged the Nubian.

She reacted as any seasoned, skilled hunter would - facing down the aggressor, her spear raised in offensive rather than defensive posture; voice loudly proclaiming that she would not be intimidated by her challenger. From one side, Shui moved quickly to thwart the charge of the beast, hoping only to deflect the huge animal's charge in Liao's direction, or at the least to distract the animal while Liao made his charge. Blade in hand, Liao moved swiftly across the clearing, each determined stride taking him closer to the animal. Shui moved closer, the Nubian's net brandished and flailing wildly at the beast. The woman stood her ground, even advancing a few carefully measured paces in the direction of the beast, spear drawn, ready to mete out the death blow should the animal's charge continue unabated. Liao leapt across the clearing, seeming to take flight as he approached the huge bulk only now turning to recognize the threat to its flank.

The animal pivoted swiftly on its rear legs to face the charging warrior. Seeing the greater danger approaching, it quickly lowered its head and charged the blur of motion that was Liao.

The two met in a violent clash at the center of the clearing, the beast howling its obstinate cry of defiance; the Warrior's battle cry adding to the din. Together the two rolled over and over in the dirt and loose grass of the clearing, each carefully avoiding the deadly tip of the others determination; each struggling to overcome the masterful advance of the other. Round and round went the dance of the determined. Over and over the two massive bulks rolled, neither wanting to yield to the domination of the other. Drizzles of blood began to ooze from each aggressor as the dance for supremacy moved on through stanza after grueling stanza, until finally, after countless tense moments of thunderous noise and agonizing expense of energy, one of the competitors in this finely orchestrated ballet saw his opening, and made the move that would decide the outcome. In a nearly epic feat of Herculean effort, Liao rolled both himself and the beast, turning wildly until he was positioned on the animal's back, legs wrapped tightly around its muscular torso, reached forward with one arm and grabbed the animal's head. With the other arm, the Warrior stretched to his fullest, quickly and deeply drawing his blade across the animal's throat. The huge animal flailed wildly, exerting enormous amounts of energy in what would ultimately be a wasted effort to derail the grasp of the mighty warrior clinging stubbornly to its back.

The beast circled the clearing several times, thrashing wildly in hopes of displacing the increasingly heavy weight on its back. For what seemed to Liao to be a small eternity, the beast continued to rage wildly within the clearing, the Nubian and Shui turning it back to the center whenever it tried to make for the undergrowth. Finally, after great loss of blood, it's energy reserves drained, the mighty animal slowed its rampage. Falling first to its front legs, then to its rear legs, and finally on its side, the proud beast lay at last, panting weakly while life giving blood ebbed from the wound on its neck.

With the speed only a seasoned Warrior and hunter could have developed after years of battle and seasons of the hunt, Liao rolled the beast over onto its back, careful to avoid the still dangerous fangs protruding from the animal's jaw. He raised his knife over his head, and with both hands grasping the handle, plunged the blade deeply into the beast's head. He rose over the beast, placing his foot on the animal's chest, retrieved his blade and shouted the victor's cry while the beast beneath him finally gave up its valiant battle.

Liao then fell to his knees and embraced the fallen animal. Taking its head in his hands, and turning it so that he faced the beast directly, eye to eye, Liao silently closed his own eyes and tipped his head ever so slightly to the dead animal, as if to say, "Today you have fought the good fight. You have fought and died with honor."

The moment passed, Shui and the Nubian joined him in the clearing. Together, they field dressed and skinned the animal and mounted it on the Nubian's spear. Liao and Shui then hoisted the ends of the spear up to their shoulders while the Nubian gathered up the other items they had carried with them into the hunt. In a silence almost as solemn and poignant as those moments just before taking the beast, the trio walked back to the clearing where they made camp. The fire there had burned down to coals perfect for cooking, waiting for their return. The two men set the spitted beast on the rack at either side of the bed of coals and settled in for a well deserved rest while the animal slowly cooked.

At long last, when the meat was ready to be eaten, the three hunters each took their blades, cut off a respectable slice of meat and seated themselves near the fire. As they reaped the pleasure of the hunt, Shui spoke.

"A hunt well done, Liao. I have hunted these woods, as I said, ever since I was a child. Today you bested the largest tiger I have ever seen, and in a fight well fought. I shall sing songs of this hunt around the fires of my old age, and at the tables of great men."

"I have not felt such exhilaration in a very long time," the younger man added. "Even the match victories in this tournament were not as fulfilling as was this hunt. I, too, shall sing songs, but my verses will be to the beast, and to the generosity of a wise man whose love of the hunt brought me to this place."

The three sat in relative silence, each taking more of the meat, each passing around the skin of Baijiu until they were content and filled. The remainder of the beast was wrapped to be carried back with them, to share at the evening meal with whomever should pass their table; the price of dinner being the retelling of the day's tale.

***

The trek back to the village took longer than it had taken to get to the hunting camp because of the additional burden of the beast they carried. Even with the amount the three had eaten, and what was left behind after dressing the animal, its weight was a formidable burden for the two men. They arrived just as people were beginning to straggle into the square for the evening meal, so the possibility that fresh tiger was now on the menu, even if for only a limited number of diners, made for an especially jubilant welcome. That all partakers would also be subject to the story of the hunt was immaterial. Hans were, after all, even better storytellers than they were hunters, and the better the hunt, the better the story. As this had been an especially good hunt, it made for an especially good story, and Shui, Liao and the Nubian were especially good storytellers, although admittedly, Shui and the Nubian far exceeded him in this area. It was not long before their small table attracted a substantial gathering. Even after the meat was long gone, the crowd grew. There had been no tournament matches upon which to build tales this day, so most of the good tales had already been told. The most disinterested of passersby were ready for a fresh, new tale. Stories of battles won in combat were by far the favorite, but a story of battles won during the hunt was the next best thing.

The telling of the tale itself took on almost epic proportions. Shui would begin. Liao and the Nubian would jump in and add what they could when Shui stopped to breath, drink or eat. Normally, the hunter himself would tell the tale, but since Shui and the Nubian had been witness to the defeat of the beast, their perspective, embellished as only a Han can, made the outing a truly remarkable occasion. As the evening grew deeper and darker, as twilight became midnight, the epic proportion of the tale only grew, and with it, Liao's reputation. When the next day's matches finally began, there was not a warrior left alive in the tournament who did not think twice about the prospect of facing him. Some, confident in a way that only Hans can be, looked at the opportunity with great anticipation. Others came carefully to understand that this young first-timer was a force to be reckoned with; that his progress thus far in the tournament was undoubtedly not a fluke, and that he would likely continue to find success. Long after Liao excused himself from the table where now most of the Warriors remaining on Hainan Island were gathered, the story, and his legend, continued to grow.

The End

Connect with Mark Gardner at:

https://www.amazon.com/Mark-Gardner/e/B008LHJVAY/

Cover by Author.

The King's Children

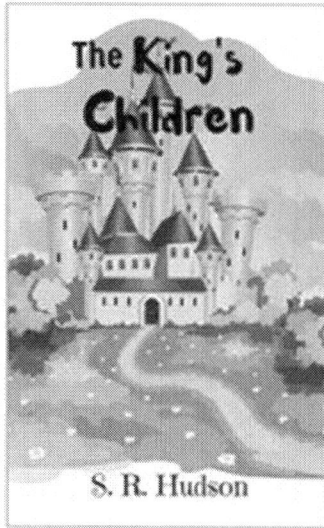

Staci Hudson

The King is sick, and he needs to choose one of his five children to be heir to the throne. He enlists the help of a Fairy Godmother to help him choose. Along the way, the children learn to be careful what you wish for, but one child learns the most important lesson of all.

Staci was inspired to write this short story after her grandmother struggled to get through Staci's fantasy novel. It was her wish to provide something easy her grandmother could read and enjoy.

***

Once upon a time, there lived a noble and wise King. One day, the King became very ill. The King grew worried as each day passed, and he continued to get worse. He made a decision to choose an heir to his throne in case something were to happen to him.

Tradition always stated the eldest child would inherit the throne.

However, the King did not agree with the tradition. He had five children, and he wanted to give each child a fair chance, so he devised a plan and called for the Fairy Godmother.

At first, the Fairy Godmother was difficult to track down. Fairy Godmothers like to keep busy making dreams come true after all. After she agreed to the King's plan, the King called for his five children. George and Victoria were the oldest. Henry was the middle child and always so full of energy. Elizabeth was younger than Henry by two years. Little Diana was the youngest and smallest of the siblings. They filed into his bedchamber in a neat, single file line.

The King said, "My dearest children, I have called the Fairy Godmother here to grant each of you one wish. Today, she shall grant George a wish. She will return tomorrow for Victoria's wish."

George stepped forward, but before he could say a word, the King had one more thing to add.

"Think carefully for what you want, because you only get one wish."

George bowed and then politely said, "Fairy Godmother, I wish to be the richest person in the land."

The Fairy Godmother said to him, "Before I grant your wish, can you please tell me why you chose this out of all the wishes in the world?"

George replied instantly, "Because I believe money could solve all my problems. There would not be a thing I could not buy! I could share with my friends, family, and even the poor."

The Fairy Godmother waved her wand in three circles and with a burst of blue light the wish was granted.

Victoria pointed at her older brother. "George, your clothes are different. And you have many fine gold rings!" Sure enough George's clothes changed to the most expensive and finest silk robes, and gold rings appeared on each of his fingers.

"Check your bedchamber," said The Fairy Godmother. "I'll see you tomorrow. Enjoy your fortune," she said as she disappeared in a puff of pink smoke.

George quickly rushed to his bedchamber with his other brother and three sisters following close behind. His entire bedroom was filled with gold, diamonds, sapphires, rubies, and emeralds. George was overcome with joy as he thought about all the things he could buy with his new fortune.

"Have one of the servants fetch me some parchment and a quill. I wish to write down a list of all the things I want," George told his younger brother, Henry.

After George received his quill and parchment he began to work on his wish list. An hour passed before he decided to take a break. He strolled past his youngest sister, Diana, who was quietly looking out the window.

George called out to her, "Diana, why are you looking out the window? I thought you normally took a nap at this time."

Diana said, "I was watching the big crowd of people. They have been trying to get into the palace to see you."

George rushed down the stairs to the grand hall. He ran through the hall, past all the guards, and to the palace doors. All the servants struggled to keep the doors closed. Suddenly they were knocked down as the doors flung open and a swarm of people rushed up to George.

"Prince George, we have heard of your fortune. You cannot possibly need all of it."

"Yes, Prince George, let us take some of it off your hands."

The people continued to tell George what to do with his fortune. Many begged for some of his riches, while others asked politely.

Regardless, George became very upset. It was his fortune — nobody else's! Only George had the right to decide what he would do with it. He wanted to share, but the people kept asking for more. The baker complained that George gave the seamstress more than him, but the farmer said he needed the most because he had ten kids to feed. George could not take it anymore, so he ran away to his bedroom and locked himself in. For the rest of the afternoon people came to his door, begging for money.

Just when George thought it was finally safe to leave his room, a mean voice spoke to him.

The mean voice said, "Prince George, if you do not hand over your entire fortune to me, I will do terrible things to your family. I have men standing by, ready to kidnap Princess Diana. I will also order my army to attack the Kingdom."

George panicked because he did not want anyone to get hurt, especially his little sister, so he did as he was told. The wicked man had twenty servants carry the fortune out. After the man left, George climbed into his bed and stared at the ceiling. George was miserable and regretted his wish. He realized that riches were not everything, and riches could not solve all his problems.

The next day, the Fairy Godmother returned and greeted an impatient Victoria. She tapped her feet and twirled her fingers through her hair.

The Fairy Godmother smiled. "Good Morning, Victoria. What is your wish?"

"I wish to be the most beautiful in the land because I want everyone to know who I am, and I want everyone to love me," she said with her head held high.

Again, the Fairy Godmother waved her wand in a circle three times, and with a burst of blue light, the wish had been granted.

Elizabeth said, "Wow, sister, you are so beautiful! I've never seen a fairer maiden in all the land."

The other siblings agreed.

The Fairy Godmother waved goodbye. "Take care. See you tomorrow, Henry." And just like before, she disappeared in a plume of pink smoke.

Victoria did not want to waste any time before showing off her new face. She rounded up some servants to escort her around the streets. Everywhere she went people admired her and told her how beautiful she was. Victoria enjoyed all the attention she received. She thought she would never get tired of it.

"Ah, this is the life. Much better than George's silly wish for fortune," she thought.

As she continued her walk, women followed her everywhere she went, demanding to know the secret of her beauty. Men followed her too, often throwing themselves at her feet or showering her with gifts of flowers and chocolates.

Victoria was so happy until the men started fighting over her. Then she became upset and even a little angry. Soon, the fighting turned into more than Victoria could handle. Women yelled at her and accused her of stealing their husbands and boyfriends. She burst into tears and ran as fast as she could back to the palace.

"This isn't what I wanted!" she cried. "I wanted people to admire me and to like me." She sobbed all the way back, and as she reached the doors she nearly ran into a pretty woman standing next to an old wizard.

"Excuse me. I'm sorry for nearly running into you, but I really must get inside. I had a bad day," Victoria said between sobs.

The pretty woman screamed, "How dare you become prettier than me? For years, I have been voted the most beautiful in the Kingdom, but now you are the most beautiful. I will not allow it!" She turned to the wizard and ordered him to use his magic on Victoria.

He scratched his long, white beard, and said sadly, "I'm sorry,

Princess Victoria, but I have to do what she says." A bright flash blinded Victoria. When she opened her eyes, the pretty woman and the wizard were no longer there.

She rushed inside and did not stop until she reached her full-length mirror in her bedchamber. She let out a sigh of relief as she saw that nothing had changed. A small knock on the door caused her to panic.

"W-who is it?" she called out cautiously.

The timid voice of her youngest sister reached her ears.

"It's me, Diana. I saw what happened at the palace doors. Are you all right?"

Victoria smiled. "Yes, I'm fine. In fact, come on in and chat with me a bit." She pulled out a stool for her sister to sit on, and then she reached for a brush to comb her long, brown hair.

Diana listened to Victoria talk about her day like a good little girl. The King had taught Diana to always be quiet and to listen when others are speaking. However, this time Diana had to go against what her father taught her.

"Victoria," she interrupted, "I don't mean to be rude, but... Your hair is falling out."

Victoria looked into the mirror and screamed. Huge chunks of her beautiful hair had fallen out. Soon, she had no hair left. Victoria put her face in her hands and cried.

"I'm ugly!" she yelled.

"I don't think you're ugly," said Diana. "I love you just the way you are and so does Daddy, George, Henry, and Elizabeth."

Victoria stopped crying and said, "You're right. My family will always love me. Thank you, Diana."

As Diana walked out the door, she said, "If you don't like being bald, you could always wear a wig, or you could wear a neat hat. I'm quite fond of hats with feathers in them. It won't be so bad."

The day passed and Victoria thought about her awful day. She picked out a nice purple hat with a bright pink feather and put it on. As she looked at herself in the mirror, she thought about what she learned.

"Looks are not everything. I learned this the hard way," she said to the mirror. The rest of the day and the night went by without incident.

"Good morning, everyone! Are you ready, Henry?" The Fairy Godmother said cheerfully. Henry ran up to her and flexed as he shouted, "I wish to be the strongest in the land. With my strength, nothing can stop me!"

George and Victoria gulped loudly. They both knew nothing good would come from the wish. Elizabeth and Diana watched quietly as the Fairy Godmother waved her wand in three circles. A burst of blue light lit up the room, meaning the wish had been granted.

Henry dashed to the nearest table and picked it up with ease.

"Look, I am the strongest now," he shouted with joy. He ran all over the castle showing off his strength.

"I bet I could lift a horse," Henry said to the servants. He rushed to the palace doors to get outside to the stables, but as he was opening the doors, they ripped off.

"Oops, guess I don't know my own strength," he said with a grin.

He came to the first horse he saw and lifted it easily with just his pinky. All day he showed off his strength. People would crowd around to watch. But soon, his siblings grew tired of watching and each went back inside the palace.

When Henry returned for dinner he looked miserable.

"What's wrong, Henry?" Diana asked.

"Oh, it was fun being super strong at first, but now it's not fun anymore," he said as he plopped down in a chair.

"What happened, brother?" Elizabeth asked.

He sighed. "Today I tried to give someone a high-five, and it sent them flying into a pile of hay. And later, when I was trying to sign autographs for my fans, I kept breaking every quill that was given to me." He let out another long sigh and then finished. "I'm just too strong. It's not fun anymore."

His siblings sat in silence as they watched Henry pick up a fork and bend it accidentally. Then he picked up a glass and it shattered in his hand.

"Don't worry, Henry. I'll feed you," little Diana said timidly.

The other siblings stood up to help Diana with Henry. With the effort of all the siblings they got him fed and only a few dishes were broken.

"Thank you so much, brother and sisters."

The siblings said goodnight to each other and then each headed to their own bedroom.

Henry pulled on his bed sheets and heard a loud ripping sound. Poor Henry ripped his bed sheets in half accidentally. He sighed and crawled into bed and hoped that Elizabeth and Diana would wish for better things. What would those two possibly wish for anyway?

The Fairy Godmother arrived bright and early the next morning.

Elizabeth bowed. "Fairy Godmother, I was going to wish to be the smartest in the land, but wishes like that don't seem to work out. So I decided to wish to be a mind reader. I think it will be the most useful, and I don't see how something could go wrong."

"Very well... a one... a two... a three!" And with a burst of blue light the wish was granted.

"Thank you, Fairy Godmother," Elizabeth called out as she ran outside to test her mind reading ability.

The Fairy Godmother looked at Diana and said with a smile, "You are the last one, my dear. I'll see you tomorrow. Be careful what you wish for." Again, she disappeared in a puff of pink smoke.

It did not take long for Elizabeth to regret her wish. There were so many people around, that all of their thoughts were overwhelming her. She couldn't make sense of anything. And some people thought about mean things that hurt her feelings.

After ten minutes, Elizabeth came back in the palace and said, "This stinks! I wish I never made this wish. It's too noisy with all the thinking going on. Don't people ever stop?"

She sat down at a table with George and Victoria. Henry was standing because he was afraid of breaking the chair.

"I thought for sure that nothing could go wrong with this wish."

Elizabeth continued to complain until Henry said, "Do you need a hug?"

Her eyes opened wide and she let out a scream that echoed through the whole castle. "No, you might break my bones!" she yelled as she dashed up the stairs past Diana.

Henry sighed and walked off. Victoria and George followed Henry while Diana chased after Elizabeth.

"What's wrong, Elizabeth?" Diana whispered to her sister.

"I already know what you're thinking Diana, and yes, I am sad because of the wish. These wishes have caused nothing but trouble. George lost all his fortune, Victoria lost her hair, Henry can't touch anything without it breaking, and I'm about to go crazy!" Elizabeth shouted as she pulled at her ponytail.

"But we still have each other. We'll always have each other," Diana said softly.

"What are you going to wish for, Diana?" Elizabeth asked curiously.

"Oh, it's a secret," Diana said as she winked at her sister. Before Diana left the room, Elizabeth read her mind, but Diana was only thinking about how she wanted her father to get better and how she wanted her siblings to be happy. Elizabeth wondered if Diana would wish for their happiness and good health.

The Fairy Godmother arrived the next morning to be greeted by the four anxious faces of George, Henry, Victoria, and Elizabeth.

"Where is Diana?" The King asked.

"We don't know," replied his four children.

"Here I am. Sorry to keep you waiting. I was just thinking," Diana said cheerfully as she entered the King's bedchamber.

"Are you ready for your wish?" The Fairy Godmother asked.

"Yes, I am," she said politely. "I watched my brothers and sisters make wishes, and I watched them all become sad and upset. I decided, Fairy Godmother, that I do not want a wish."

Everyone gasped at the little girl.

"Are you sure? This is a once in a lifetime opportunity," the Fairy Godmother said.

Diana nodded her head. "Yes, I am sure. I'm going to make my own happiness in life."

"Very well," the Fairy Godmother began, "as a result of your noble and kind actions, I will return your siblings back to normal. Take care, Royal Family!" For the last time, she waved her wand in three circles. When the blue light disappeared, the siblings knew all was right again.

The King called out to his children, "What did you learn from this?"

George spoke first. "I learned that having riches can not solve all your problems, and riches are not everything."

Victoria spoke next. "I learned that being beautiful isn't everything. And after a lot of thinking, I realized that everyone is beautiful on the inside and that is what really matters."

Next, it was Henry's turn.

"I learned that having strength can be super neat, but it can also be bad. I hurt people and broke things without meaning to." Then he turned to Diana. "By watching Diana, I learned that real strength isn't physical strength."

Then Elizabeth spoke. "Father, I learned to be careful what you wish for. I think Diana had the right idea in not making a wish, because mine only made me miserable and cranky."

Lastly, Diana went, "I learned that family is the most important thing, because no matter what bad things might come your way, you will always have your family to stand by you."

The King addressed Diana, "Princess Diana, I hereby declare you the heir to my throne. You have shown you are worthy." Her siblings did not object. Instead they cheered her on. Years went by and the King recovered to everyone's delight. When Princess Diana grew up, she became the best Queen the Kingdom had ever known. Under her rule, the entire Kingdom had become one big happy family.

The End

Staci Hudson can be found at:

https://www.wattpad.com/user/Staci_the_Writer

Cover by T.E. Bradford.

The Perfect Tree

Sarah A Wilson

Editor's Introduction – Sarah Wilson is a long time friend and fellow writer. When I was putting the OMP together I knew I wanted a story by her because of the calibre of her writing. The Perfect Tree didn't disappoint – as an example of a mythological quest story, it's flawless in tone and pacing. In fact I would go so far as to say that if this was put into a re-edited version of the Iliad or any book of ancient Greek myth, it would be indistinguishable to most readers from the originals.

However Sarah's story somehow manages to transcend even this illustrious origin and it strikes me it could also make a wonderful Pixar/animated film that would delight children and adults alike. You can probably tell I have a high opinion of this work but don't take my word for it... start reading and enjoy.

***

Once long ago, when the Ancient Gods still held court atop Mount Olympus, and mankind had not long tamed the field and the beasts therein, there once stood a sacred pomegranate grove, honoured to Aphrodite, Goddess of love, sprung from the blood of her slain mortal consort, Adonis. Within this grove dwelled a nymph and a satyr, custodians of the trees. Their names are lost to time, but their story was not. And neither was their love.

But their union was barren. The only fruit that flourished within that grove was upon the trees that they tended.

Though they prayed to their patron goddess for children, Aphrodite was too busy pursuing her own lustful interests, either mourning the loss of one mortal lover or pursuing a new one, to heed the faithful couple.

It fell to the goddess Demeter, the goddess of the harvest, to hear their plea. She promised them that a child would come to them if they took upon themselves the task she desired.

The lovers agreed, but little did they know that Demeter's offer was not an act of charity, but an act of vengeance. For it was from this same orchard, whence came the fateful fruit, whose ruby seeds the consumption of which, confined the Goddess's beautiful daughter Persephone in the underworld, bringing winter into the world. In bitterness and anger for the loss of her own child, Demeter judged that the couple would never have issue, until they had grown what all the Gods of Olympus had judged to be, the perfect tree.

But the Gods were capricious. Some demanded a tree with silver leaves, some, with golden bark. Some demanded a tree that bore fruit. Others demanded that which bore nuts. Others demanded a tree that had the sweetest blossoms. Some, for a tree with needles as sharp as thorns. Not just amongst themselves were the Gods so changeable. From day to day, each one would change his or her mind on what defined perfection.

So the nymph and satyr toiled. The grove became an orchard, the orchard a wood and the wood became a mighty forest, stretching from the high eyries of the western mountains to the rivers of the eastern valleys, from the heat of the southern sands to the snow and frost of the northern wastes.

And still, the Gods could not agree.

The years passed.

The lovers began to fall into despair.

With each new tree that grew, and was rejected, the love they bore each other began to wane. Doubt and discord entered their hearts. They began to quarrel over the slightest thing and each new day brought not hope, but distance between them.

It came to pass one year, in the height of summer, Demeter looked down from Olympus upon the world of men, and she rejoiced in what she saw. She marvelled how man had tamed the land in her honour, how ripe the wheat, how luscious grew the olive and the apple, how prodigious the flock. She felt a presence nearby and turned to see Lord Zeus, ruler of the gods of Olympus standing beside her.

"What see you, Lady Demeter?"

"My Lord Zeus, what a wondrous sight is the industry of man. See how like the sea, doth undulate the fields of wheat and barley. See how the fruit weighs heavily upon the boughs of the orchards. Is this not a sight for exultation?"

Lord Zeus looked down upon the earth and saw all that Demeter said was true until his eye alighted upon the forest.

"Lady Demeter, consider you not the forest? Where your fields are seas, is this not the ocean? Where only fruits grow in your orchards, what bounty hangs ripe upon the boughs of these trees? What are the ears of corn, compared to the greenest leaf? Where only cattle and sheep roam in the cultivated meadows, all manner of beast and fowl shelter beneath its proud canopy? All the toil of mankind is but little, compared to the toil of two souls in love!"

Now Demeter was angered at this slight. Her pride wounded, she fled Olympus and descended beyond the lands of men, to the underworld realm of the dark God, Hades. She found him sat upon his ebony throne, eyeing her slyly beneath his dark brows, and as if to mock her presence, he plucked a pomegranate from a cornucopia beside him and rolled it idly between the palms of his hands.

"My Lady Demeter, your presence here is a surprise to me. Does your daughter mourn the separation from her dear husband, that you would bring her home to me, whilst the sun still bears its summer warmth upon the land of men?" His words dripped with sarcasm as poison drips from the fangs of the Hydra.

"Persephone is not with me, Lord Hades, nor does she know of my visit to your hallowed halls."

"Then why, gracious Demeter, would the Goddess of Life and Fertility deign to visit me in the here in the land of Death and Decay?"

"I wish from you a boon, my Lord."

Instead of answering her, Lord Hades took an iron knife and sliced into the ripe fruit, the scarlet juice flowing over his hands like sacrificial blood. He took a segment and chewed it thoughtfully as he pondered her request.

"And what form would this boon take?"

"Lord Zeus has insulted me."

Lord Hades took another bite from the fruits, crunching the bittersweet seeds.

"How has he insulted you?"

"By saying that the sprawling chaos of the Great Forest is more beautiful to his eye than all the golden order of my wheat fields. All the blossoms and burgeoning fruits of my orchards are but naught compared with one single leaf from that forest, which I might add, may never have grown at all, if not for my prompting. For this affront I desire the services of the Erinyes, those dark sisters of deepest Tartarus, to assuage my thirst for retribution."

At this request, even the Dark Lord was stunned. The half-eaten fruit fell from his hand, scattering its ruby seeds upon the marble floor. He sat back upon his throne and laughed.

"You wish to unleash the Furies, upon the world of men? For what purpose? To destroy a forest? My lady, are you mad?"

With great a cry of rage that shook the very foundations of the earth, Demeter seemed to fill the chamber with her passion, her eyes burned with such hatred that even Hades, mighty God that he was, cowered before her.

"Do not question my wrath, my Lord! I, who could bring plagues and starvation upon the world of men and fill the underworld to bursting! Never forget, that I have not yet forgiven you for the abduction of my daughter, so do as I request, or you shall be the one that bears the brunt of my aggression!"

Hades fumbled with shaking fingers within the folds of his robe and pulled out a large stone key. He tossed it towards the ferocious Goddess.

"This is the key to the gates of Tartarus. Take it and with it unleash the Furies. Do with them what you will."

Without another word, Demeter turned and left the hall of Hades, leaving the fearful God in her wake.

When Demeter returned to the world above, with the Furies in her train, she came as a great summer storm, darkening the world above. All mankind trembled before the dying of the light.

It was not just mortals that were afraid by the coming of the storm. Persephone had been walking in a meadow, plucking flowers to plait into a crown as a gift for her mother. She saw the darkened sky and felt a great chill in her heart. She knew instantly it was mother's wrath that had prompted this tempest. In a vision, she saw all that had passed, the slight by Zeus, the conversation between Lord Hades, and the release of the Furies from Tartarus. With a feeling of foreboding, she discarded her blooms, and raced towards the heart of the storm, hoping that she could reason with the elder goddess.

On her arrival, she saw with horror, her mother already unleashed the power of the Furies upon the forest. Alecto, first of the three, entered the soil and turned what was fertile to bitterest poison. Leaves turned brown and wilted at her touch. Even the coniferous trees, which shed not their needles even in the harshest of winters, shrivelled and bent before the presence of the evil spirit. Tisiphone, the second of the dark sisters, entered the villages and cities that fringed the forest, piercing the hearts of men and awakening malicious intent within them. Leaving their homes and fields and families, they came upon the forest with their axes, saws, and burning brands of fire, laying waste to acre upon acre of trunk and branch, root and leaf. Bird and beast alike fled before the devastation. Their purpose fulfilled, the two Furies returned to their home in the depths of Tartarus.

Demeter triumphed in the destruction, but every tree that fell only served to fuel her great ire.

Persephone rushed to her mother and tugged at her gown, pleading with her to cease her madness.

"Oh mother, what is it that you do? You, a Goddess of life and bounty now bent on wilful destruction? This act is against all nature!"

Enraptured by her madness, Demeter cast her daughter away from her.

"Treacherous child, it is because of you that the earth trembles before the might of Demeter. Leave now, before you too perish in my wrath!"

"No, mother, I beg of you, please..."

But Demeter would not listen and instead, cast the last of the Furies, Megaera, into the forest. Her task, as the spirit of jealousy, to sunder forever the bond between the two lovers. Persephone followed swiftly afterwards, hoping to catch the malevolent spirit before she wreaked her purpose on the two guardians. As she pursued Megeara, through the burning trees, she sent a brief prayer to Lord Zeus for rain to quench the fires and the hearts of men and to wash the poison from soil and make it wholesome again. The lord of Olympus heard her prayer and sent the Hyades, the nymphs of rain and sorrow, to weep plaintive tears upon the forest. As soon as the first drops fell, the fire began to die away, and the mortals, freed from the power of Tisiphone, dropped their tools and returned bewildered to their homesteads.

Megeara all too soon came across the nymph and the satyr, sleeping within a clearing at the heart of the forest. Between them grew the sapling of a tree so wondrous that even the denizen of Hell paused momentarily to venerate its beauty. Her admiration did not last long as she reminded herself of her purpose. Her form became that of smoke, and as she leaned over the sleeping satyr, he breathed in her wickedness. Waking as if from a nightmare, the satyr cried half in terror, half in rage, trying in vain to fight the malignancy that tore through his mind.

The sleeping nymph woke with a start at his cry and seeing her beloved possessed with anger, his eyes burning with violence. She cowered in fear beside the little sapling as the satyr towered over her.

The satyr in his violent rage tore the sapling from the earth. He raised it above his head as if to strike the cowering nymph, but before he could issue the blow, Persephone caught the satyr by the wrist and unarmed him. The nymph leapt up and fled into the dark depths of the forest.

The Satyr then turned his rage upon the young Goddess, but fearing naught, Persephone pressed her palm upon his breast. At her healing touch, Megaera departed his body and returned to her unhallowed home beneath the world. The satyr collapsed exhausted upon the ground. He saw the sapling lying beside him, broken and already withering. He looked further upon the borders of the forest and saw the destruction that had already had been wreaked there. He placed his head in his hands and wept.

Persephone was stirred with pity for the creature. She reached out and placed her hand under his chin raising his eyes to hers. Though afraid of the presence before him, he lifted his hands to her, soliciting her mercy.

"Oh my Lady, what have I done?"

"This was not your fault, my good satyr. Rather it was a rash act of jealousy by my mother, Demeter."

"My lady, why would your mother, wish to destroy us?"

So, Persephone told the satyr of the vision she had in the meadow. The satyr listened with grievous sorrow in his heart. When he heard that his beloved had fled in terror of him, he prostrated himself upon the earth in lament.

"Where, my lady, has my beloved fled?"

"That, I know not."

"I must go find her." He stood and made as if to run, but Persephone caught him by the arm.

"The nymph fled in fear of you. To follow her would be folly and would only spur her further in her flight. Here is your purpose, my friend. Your task here is to protect the forest and try to undo what has already been inflicted upon it, to help it to heal."

"How can I heal the forest alone?"

Persephone pressed his hand upon the bark of a nearby tree. From beneath his palm sprung a blossoming twig.

"With the love and hope in your heart. Fear not, I will send an emissary in your stead."

The goddess cast her eyes around the clearing, searching for one to send in search of the nymph, but it seemed that all the denizens of the forest, beat of hoof and claw, bird of wing and song, had all departed. Then from the edge of the clearing, the Goddess heard a faint noise. Investigating closer, she found, a hen-pigeon, brooding on her nest in the hollow of a tree.

Stirred by the light of the goddess, the pigeon rose from her nest and fluttered her wings.

"My lady Persephone! I am humbled by your presence! To what do I owe this honour?"

"Mistress Pigeon, I am in need of your help. The nymph, one of the guardians of this forest, has fled in terror, and even I know not where she has gone. Will you be my emissary and seek she that is lost?"

The pigeon gave a look of uncertainty.

"My lady Goddess, would that I could. Alas, I cannot leave. I sit upon my eggs and should I leave them, they would surely perish."

"Where is your mate?"

The pigeon looked sadly towards the path of destruction left in the wake of the Furies.

"My lady, he set at break of day out to find food and has not returned. I fear that he has perished in the devastation."

Persephone was perplexed at what to do until she felt the satyr touch her arm.

"My Lady, if it please you, if I cannot follow the path of my beloved, then at least let me be of use in this case. I will take care of the pigeon's eggs. I solemnly swear in your presence that no harm shall come to them."

With utmost care, he took the nest and placed it on his head, tying it firmly into the tangles of his thick curly hair. Satisfied the Satyr would keep his promise that her eggs would be safe, the pigeon stretched her wings.

"My lady Persephone, whither shall I fly?"

The goddess looked around and then stretched forth her arm.

"Fly, fly, on the backs of the Winds. Trace the breath of Eurus to the valleys of the East, where the sun rises at the dawn. Seek there the nymph and if you find her not, return as swiftly as you came."

The pigeon flew upwards, swooping through the forest almost as fast as the thunderbolt of Zeus. However, she was not the only one to journey to the East, for Demeter had watched from the shadows of the clearing. Her heart still burning for retribution, she became like a mist and fled eastward easily overtaking her daughter's emissary. It was not long before Demeter had found her own agent; a tiger unrivalled in ferocity save for the Goddess herself, lay dozing beside a sheltered pool. She took control of the dreaming beast and in that form waited until the pigeon flew near. When she sighted her quarry, she urged the creature through the undergrowth in pursuit of her oblivious prey.

After a long flight, the pigeon arrived at a great and bounteous valley, unaware that the mother Goddess was on her trail and that she was in great peril. She traced the course of a long and winding river, which ran through the middle of the valley. At long last, she came to the edge of a wide lake. In the middle of the lake was an island and on the island a tree. Carrying across the water from this tree, the pigeon heard a melody, as sweet and harmonious as to break a heart. Often had the pigeon heard the nymph singing such a melody as she worked amongst the glades, and hope rose in her breast. She landed on a nearby branch to listen, little knowing that the tiger was already behind, claws unsheathed, preparing to spring.

At the very last minute, the pigeon took to the wing and swooped towards the island. The tiger landed in the shallows of the lake and retreated with damp fur and even damper enthusiasm. Though tigers are excellent swimmers, and the island was not so far, the lake was deep and rippled with dangerous undercurrents. Demeter retreated from the mind of the tiger and left it slumbering at the edge of the water. Looking out into the depths, she saw the undulating form of a large river serpent. Diving beneath the waves

Demeter took possession of the leviathan. Slinking through the water, the disguised Goddess followed the pigeon to the island. Surfacing briefly, she saw her intended victim alight upon the branch of a tree. The Goddess silently slithered from the water, and hid her reptilian form in the shadows of the nether branches.

The pigeon perched upon the branch of the tree, and looked about her for the source of the song. Alas, she found she was thwarted in her hope, for it was not the nymph who sang so beautifully, but a simple nightingale, sitting upon her nest in a hollow at the side of the trunk.

The pigeon hopped up close to the nest and politely greeted the Nightingale.

"Mistress Nightingale, of voice so sweet, forgive me this interruption, but I have a request of you."

The nightingale ceased her song and turned her olive green head.

"Dear cousin, Pigeon, ask away. What is it that you request of me? Another song perhaps?"

"No, no. My request is of a far more serious nature. The nymph of the Great Forest has fled her home because of the wrath of the Goddess Demeter. I have been sent by Lady Persephone to find her. Perchance you have you seen her pass this way?"

The nightingale drooped her beak and shook her pretty head.

"I am afraid, dear cousin, that I live a solitary life upon my island, seeing no being but myself."

The pigeon ruffled her feathers anxiously. Seeing her distress, the nightingale stretched out a wing to calm her.

"Do not despair so easily, dear cousin! Perhaps one of my many sisters who also nest within this valley has seen her. Give me one moment, and you shall have your answer."

The nightingale flew to the top of the tree and from her orange breast issued a lively refrain, sweet to the ears as honey to the tongue.

From across the water first one nightingale replied, then another, and another, until the whole valley resonated with harmony. The pigeon stood upon the branch enraptured by the sound. Sadly almost as swiftly as it had begun, the song ended. The pigeon turned to the nightingale, but was disheartened to see a look of sorrow on her face.

"I'm so sorry, my dear cousin, but my sisters have confirmed it. The nymph for whom you seek has not been seen in this valley."

The pigeon lowered her head and issued a great sigh.

"If such be the case, then I must return to the Great Forest at once!"

As she stretched her wings in preparation for flight, the nightingale reached to a nearby twig and plucked a golden fruit from the end of it, offering it to the pigeon.

"Wait, before you go, take you this fruit that grows only in this valley and give this to the satyr. When it may be that you find the nymph, and she and the satyr are reunited, this may perhaps help them to grow the perfect tree."

In the shadows below, Demeter saw the nightingale bestow her gift could no longer contain her rage. She lashed the scaly body of the serpent hard against the tree, shuddering it from root to canopy.

The pigeon took the berry in her clawed foot and sprang into the air in alarm.

"What is happening?" she wailed as the branch trembled.

The nightingale peered cautiously beneath the branch just as another impact set the tree swaying.

"A river serpent is attacking the tree! Strange. They usually inhabit the marshes and do not venture so far to the centre of the lake."

The pigeon cautiously glanced over the side of the branch, but when she looked straight into the jade green eyes of the aquatic predator, she saw much more there than mere bestial instinct. The creature snapped its hungry jaws at the startled bird and hurled itself at the tree again. Bark and branches rained down upon its scaly back but did nothing to diminish its raging passion.

"Dear cousin, this is no ordinary serpent! I fear it is a vile machination of Demeter to sway me from my quest. Please, I beg of you, help me please!"

Now, even though the nightingale was a small bird, she was brave, and she would be damned if she let a mindless reptile in the possession of a goddess, destroy her home and threaten her kin. She turned to the pigeon.

"I have an idea to distract the creature. When I give the signal, fly as fast as you can."

"What signal, dear cousin?"

"Don't worry; you'll hear it."

The nightingale hopped down from the branch. Deftly avoiding the snapping jaws of the reptile, she alighted upon the snout and clinging tightly to the scaly flesh, took a deep breath, opened her beak and uttered the most obscene, piercing discord which would have deafened a mere man. Unfortunate then for the vengeful Goddess, that the serpents that populated the rivers of the Eastern valley had far superior hearing. Whilst the creature stumbled, disorientated to the lapping waves to drown the sound that rang in its ears, the pigeon took flight.

She called back to the nightingale as she sped across the water.

"Thank you, dear cousin. May blessings be upon you and may your song never end!"

Halfway across the lake, she glanced behind her to see the river serpent in ardent pursuit. As she neared the shoreline, she saw the tiger still lying asleep at the water's edge. An idea stuck her, but one that could prove fatal if she faltered in its execution. She seized the fruit in her beak and then swooping low, raked her claws along the head and neck of the prone beast, waking it instantly. Seeing her fly low, the serpent leapt from the water like a dart...

...straight at the jaws of the enraged tiger. The surprised feline instinctively bit down hard against the snout of the reptile and shaking its head, flung it whole against a tree, knocking it senseless. The tiger's sharp claws shredded through the armoured skin of the serpent, flaying it to the bone. Demeter tumbled headlong from her stricken host as the victorious predator eviscerated its scaly foe. She glanced furiously at the retreating form of the pigeon as she too glided rapidly from the valley.

When the pigeon arrived back at the clearing at the heart of the forest exhausted from her long flight, Persephone stretched forth her arm and the pigeon alighted on her hand. Almost immediately her weariness left her, and she felt a renewal that even the blessings of sleep could not rival.

Persephone brought the pigeon close to her face.

"Mistress Pigeon, tell me, did you find the nymph in the valleys of the East?"

The pigeon bowed her head and told the goddess of her flight to the lone island and her meeting with the nightingale.

"Alas, Lady Persephone, she could not be found in all the valley. It is certain she did not travel there."

The satyr gave a moan of grief. The pigeon flew down from the hand of the goddess unto his palm.

"Do not despair, my friend. My journey to the East was not entirely unsuccessful. As I was leaving, the nightingale gave me a present to give to you."

She presented her gift to the satyr.

"What is this fruit? I have not seen the like before."

"I know not my friend, but it only grows in the eastern valleys. The nightingale said it will perhaps help you to grow the perfect tree."

"I thank you on behalf of the nightingale, for such a wondrous gift."

The pigeon once more alighted upon the Persephone's outstretched hand. Remembering the attack of the river serpent, the bird tried in vain to warn the goddess how her quest was imperilled.

"My lady I must tell you, whilst in the valley…"

But the goddess would not listen and admonished her feathered messenger.

"No more long stories! The forest may still perish if the nymph is not found!"

The pigeon gave a sigh and bowed her head.

"Whither shall I fly, this time my dear Lady?"

The goddess looked round and stretched forth her hand in a new direction

"Fly, fly, on the backs of the Winds. Trace the breath of Notus to the deserts of the South, where the air burns like fire and the sands sting like the bites of flies. Seek there the nymph and if you find her not, return as swiftly as you came."

Taking to the wing, the pigeon flew almost as fast as the arrow of Apollo, over land and sea, until all she saw under the burning sun was mile upon mile of desolate sand. Exhausted by the heat and her flight she took shelter by a rocky outcrop, which cast its shadow long upon the dune. But the pigeon was mistaken, that the rock would provide her with any kind of asylum, for Demeter had found a new host with which to enact her vengeance. Hidden in a cleft of the rock was a scorpion, strong of claw and virulent of poison. As the pigeon rested, the scorpion scuttled silently out. It paused within inches of the bird, tail held high, poised to strike, when in a spray of sand, the pigeon once more took to the wing, insensible to the threat she had just eluded. Demeter cursed her ill luck, but then, looking upon the shifting sand, she saw another, perhaps more appropriate vessel to house her malice.

As the day began to close, and the heat of the desert abated, the much-fatigued pigeon espied a large clear pool, fringed by date palms laden with immature fruit, and wondrous desert blooms. She alighted amongst the trees and shaking the dust from her feathers, stooped to dip her beak in the cool, fresh waters. As she supped, she noticed a shadow falling over her and looked up to see a great flock of swallows flying down to roost amongst the fronds of the palm trees. One of their number swooped down beside her at the edge of the water. She recognised him as one of her neighbours and friends in the Great Forest.

"Master Swallow, how good it is to see a familiar face in such a place so dry and desolate."

The swallow was much surprised by this meeting.

"Why Madame Pigeon, why came you to this southern land, so far from the forest where both of us were hatched?"

"My dear cousin, I am on a quest to seek the nymph of the Great Forest at the behest of the Goddess Persephone."

She told the swallow of her journey to the East and her meeting with the nightingale and how on her return to the Great Forest, Persephone had sent her to the South. She told him of the threat of Demeter, and how she had narrowly escaped her vehemence. When she finished telling her tale, the swallow looked gravely at his neighbour.

"Alas, my friend I have not seen her of whom you speak. I and my kin have flown many miles across the roaring seas and whispering southern sands we saw no sign of man nor beast in all our long migration."

The pigeon was disappointed by this news, bowed her head and gave a sigh.

"If such be the case, then I must not tarry here. I must return to the Great Forest at once!"

As she prepared for flight, she was disturbed by a sudden splash in the pool behind them. Then another, and another as dates cascaded into the water below. Looking up, both birds were terrified to see a large, venomous viper descending from the overhanging fruit. The snake hissed and bared its vicious fangs. It darted rapidly towards the ground, missing the two birds as they instantly took to the wing. Undeterred, the snake reared for another strike. The swallow called out to his companions,

"Brothers, sisters, swallows all, fly. Beware! Danger! Danger!"

From every palm and bush, a cloud of swallows dived upon the viper, pecking it with their beaks, scratching at it with their claws. The viper defended itself in vain as the multitude of its feathered foe overwhelmed it. The stricken serpent could do little but flee the oasis for the comparative safety of the sands.

The pigeon and the swallow watched as the snake retreated over the dunes.

"That was no ordinary serpent."

"No, Master Swallow. I fear it was another incarnation of Demeter, come to hinder my quest. I must return to the forest and tell Lady Persephone of this threat."

The swallow turned and plucked a hanging yellow flower from a date palm beside him.

"Wait, before you go, take you this bloom that grows only in the desert and give this to the satyr. When it may be that you find the nymph, and she and the satyr are reunited, this may perhaps help them to grow the perfect tree."

The pigeon took the flower in her claw and took to the wing.

"Thank you for your gift!" she called back. "Many blessings fall upon you and your kin. May your wings never grow weary, and your numbers never diminish!"

The pigeon flew through the dark of night, across the desert and the sea. She arrived back at the clearing at the heart of the Forest a few hours after dawn.

Again Persephone stretched forth her arm, and the pigeon alighted on her hand, again her fatigue left her, and strength rushed through her homely body.

"Mistress Pigeon, tell me, did you find the nymph in the deserts of the South?"

The pigeon bowed her head and told the goddess of her meeting with the swallow and how he nor his brethren and seen anything in all the shifting sands.

"Alas, Lady Persephone, she could not be found in all the desert. It is certain she did not travel there."

The satyr cried in sorrow and beat his breast. The pigeon flew down from the hand of the goddess unto his palm.

"Do not despair, my friend. My journey to the South was not entirely unsuccessful. As I was leaving, the swallow granted me this gift to give to you."

She presented the yellow flower to the satyr.

"What is this bloom? I have not seen the like before."

"I know not my friend, but it only grows in the South, beneath the burning desert sun. The swallow said it will perhaps help you to grow the perfect tree."

"I thank you on behalf of the swallow, for such a wondrous gift."

The pigeon once more alighted upon the Persephone's outstretched hand.

Remembering the attack of the viper, the bird tried in vain to warn the goddess how her quest was imperilled.

"My lady, I must tell you, whilst in the desert…"

But the goddess would not listen and admonished her feathered messenger.

"No more long stories! The forest may still perish if the nymph is not found!"

The pigeon gave a sigh and bowed her head.

"Whither shall I fly, this time my dear Lady?"

The goddess looked round and stretched forth her hand in a new direction

"Fly, fly, on the backs of the Wind. Trace the breath of Zephyr to the mountains of the West, where the sun rests at night, and great stone spires raise their mighty heads into the heavens."

Bruised and mortified by her latest defeat, Demeter once more stood concealed at the edge of the clearing. Watching the pigeon take flight, the Goddess was reluctant to follow the bird once more, but for the ceaseless prompting of her anger. Heading westward, she was not far from the clearing, when she found prostrated on the ground, a lone grey wolf, emaciated and half-mad with hunger. She took the withered animal as a host, renewed it with what strength she could spare and bounded through the trees in the pigeon's wake.

Onward the pigeon flew, almost as fast as the sandals of Hermes. After a long flight, she saw the grey stone of the mountains rise high against the tops of the trees, and the sight gave her courage. However, as she approached the foothills on the edge of the forest, she felt a great rush of air behind her. Glancing above she saw a sight to freeze her blood. A great golden eagle, larger even than a man, curved of beak and sharp of talon was bearing down upon her. She flew fast, fast enough to almost burst her little heart, but still, the eagle gained upon her. Swooping down amongst the scarce trees that surrounded the foothills she hoped to lose the eagle amongst the branches, but as she glided low, the wolf who had before been hidden by the branches suddenly leapt up and snapped at the terrified bird. Faced with death both below and above her, the pigeon was in a desperate situation. As she reached the foot of the mountain, she was trapped between the downward spiral of the eagle and the wolf bounding ceaselessly over fallen boulders to reach her. Out of the corner of her eye, she spied a cleft in cliff ahead of her. She circled swiftly in the air and tucking her feet tightly to her chest she turned sideways and plunged headlong into the crack. As she sped through the opening, she heard the wolf's frustrated howl behind her.

The fissure was so narrow, the pigeon feared that she would get stuck, but thankfully she saw light at the end of the cleft and glided towards it. Convinced that there was no way the wolf could have followed her through the rock, the pigeon soared up through the air.

Alas, she had forgotten the eagle could easily have surmounted the cliff.

Without warning, she felt the rasp of scales against her feathers as vast talons curled around her, and everything went dark.

When light returned to the pigeon, she found to her horror, that she was seated in an enormous nest, the foul stench of rotting flesh hanging heavy in the air.

Everywhere she looked lay the bones of the slain, some as small as mice, others larger than a deer. A great shadow blocked her light and glancing upward in absolute terror, she saw the eagle poised to strike, the scimitar of his beak high in the air, ready to bear down upon her.

The pigeon bowed her head in defeat and uttered one last invocation to any deity who would hear it.

"Oh my lady Persephone, I have failed you. May the Gods have mercy upon me!"

On hearing this, the eagle halted, his beak barely inches from the breast of the pigeon. He turned his head, and his vast amber eye peered at her quizzically.

From his beak issued a deep rumbling voice.

"Who are you, humble bird, to invoke the mercy of the Gods?"

Not daring to look into his eye the pigeon bowed as low as she could before this mighty presence.

"My lord Eagle, king of birds, I beg of you let me live, for I am on a sacred mission from my lady Persephone, to find the nymph of the Great Forest."

"Do not be lying to me, little bird, or I will not even leave your bones to ornament my nest!"

The eagle gently nudged his beak under the pigeon to raise her head. He looked deep into her eyes, even to her very soul.

"Yes, indeed. You speak truth. You are a messenger of the Gods. Fool I would be to make a meal of such an errant ambassador considering my own connection to the Lords and Ladies of mighty Olympus!"

The pigeon looked at him quizzically.

"What mean you, my lord?"

"Know you not who I am?"

"Why, a great eagle, my lord!"

"I am much more than a mere eagle," he laughed. "What other common raptor could compare with me, whose bloodline has been favoured by the Lord of Olympus himself?"

The eagle raised himself high and with one vast wing he tapped himself on the breast.

"I am a direct descendant of Aetos Dios, the Eagle of Zeus, his symbol and the bearer of his sacred sceptre. As you say you are on a mission from the Gods themselves, I will no longer hinder you in your quest. Perchance, there is a way, by means of an apology, that I may help you in your mission?"

The pigeon took a deep breath and recounted her story so far, how she was thwarted in her journey to both the East and the South and her meeting with both the nightingale and the swallow. The eagle listened gravely to the end of her tale and bowed his head in thought.

"Alas, my dear messenger, woe betide me to add sorrow on your quest, but the nymph has not travelled this way. My eyes have a vision so powerful, that even from the highest point upon this eyrie I could see an ant crawl beneath a pebble at the foot of the mountains. I have not, nor do I now, see she of whom you seek. What I do see, is a lean, malicious-looking wolf who has not stirred from the rocks below, since I brought you up to this eyrie."

Looking down from the nest, all the pigeon could see was a dark speck barely hidden amongst the grey rocks, but even from her high perch, the pigeon could not help but feel the malevolence emanate from the creature below.

"My lord, what you see is no ordinary wolf!"

The pigeon told the eagle how she had been pursued in her quest by the various guises of Demeter, and how it had only been through the actions of her new found friends that she had escaped.

The eagle listened solemnly to this news and shook his golden head.

"My heart grieves me, that I should live to see an age where the Gods of Olympus should turn against their very natures for so trivial a matter. Little bird, do not fear pursuit from this vile miscreant. I have a plan to help you escape from its vicious intent."

When the eagle had relayed his plan, the pigeon prepared herself for flight. As she stretched her wings, the eagle reached into the branches of his nest and pulled forth from the innermost boughs a shining silver nut and offered it to the pigeon.

"Before you go, take you this nut that grows only on the summits of the highest mountains and take it with you to the Forest. When it may be that you find the nymph, and she and the satyr are reunited, this may perhaps help them to grow the perfect tree."

The pigeon took the nut in her clawed foot and took flight.

"Thank you, my lord eagle! Many blessings fall upon you and may your eyes never grow dim."

Below, the wolf-host watched hungrily as the bird cascaded through the air. As the pigeon dived nearer, the snarling maw hung open like a trap. At the last second, the pigeon tumbled deftly avoided the snapping jaws. She sailed over the wolf's head and back eastward through the forest to the clearing.

Too late did the wolf see the eagle in the pigeon's wake. The mighty talons buried themselves in its wasted frame. With the wolf in his grasp, the eagle spiralled upwards and on reaching a great height, cast the wolf downward, dashing it upon the rocks below.

Demeter fled her expiring host, in a torment of agony, cursing all creatures of feather and beak. She quickly swallowed her rage, as a plan formed within her mind. If the nymph had not fled to the east, the south, or the west, there was only one place that she could have gone; the frozen lands of the north.

Outstripping the very winds, Demeter fled northward over the cold, deep ocean, until she found a barren land of snow and ice. Within this land, Demeter discovered a cave, and sleeping within the cave a colossal beast. The beast stank of spoiled meat and better yet, every breath it exhaled carried traces of the water-sickness. What better host, could the Goddess find, to be the instrument of her retribution? Possessing the diseased mind of the beast, she commanded it to hunt down the nymph and to destroy her.

Meanwhile, the pigeon had arrived back at the clearing and once more alighting on the hand of the young Goddess, and felt the rejuvenation of her holy force.

Persephone brought the pigeon close to her face.

"Mistress Pigeon, tell me, did you find the nymph in the mountains of the West?"

The pigeon bowed her head, and told the goddess of the eagle, how he had pursued her, how at her invocation to the gods he had shown mercy and his sorrow at not having seen the nymph.

"Alas, Lady Persephone, she could not be found amongst all the mountains. It is certain she did not travel there."

The satyr wailed and was about to tear his hair when the pigeon flew down and grasped his fingers with her foot and snapped at him with her beak.

"Master Satyr, please do not rip so at your tresses! Remember it is there that you hold my eggs. Remember your promise to keep them safe!"

The satyr was humbled by this outburst and lowered his head. He held out his hand for the pigeon to alight.

"Do not despair, my friend. My journey to the West was not entirely unsuccessful. As I was leaving, the eagle granted me this gift to give to you."

She presented the silver nut to the satyr.

"What is this nut? I have not seen the like before."

"I know not my friend, but it only grows in the West, at the summits of the highest mountains. The eagle said it will aid you to grow the perfect tree."

The satyr nodded his head, carefully.

"I thank you on behalf of the eagle, for such a wondrous gift."

The pigeon once more alighted upon the Persephone's outstretched hand

"My lady, I must speak warn you of the perils I encountered whilst flying to the mountains..."

But the goddess would not listen and admonished her feathered messenger.

"No more long stories! The forest may still perish if the nymph is not found!"

The pigeon gave a sigh and bowed her head.

"Whither shall I fly, this time my dear Lady?"

"If the nymph cannot be found in the valley of East, the deserts of the South nor the mountains of the West, there is only one direction she could have fled. Fly, you then on the backs of the Winds. Trace the breath of Boreas to North, to the boundaries of the frozen waste, where rolling pines shed not their spiny leaves, and the sky burns with the colours of Iris's wings."

Taking to the wing, the pigeon flew towards the freezing North, almost as swift as the sword of Thanatos. Across the land and she flew until she came upon the open waters of a great northern ocean.

The air was colder than the southern deserts were hot, the sky was permanently grey and icy rain fell constantly in torrent. The further north the pigeon travelled, the worse the storm grew. The raindrops became solid ice, and the pigeon was wracked with pain every time one struck her. At one point, one so large struck her across the beak, she would have nearly plunged down into the water beneath if she had not gathered her senses in time. No longer able to see through the driving deluge, the pigeon sought shelter, amongst the sparse rocks which dotted the northern seas. As the storm battered against her wings, she saw a huge rocky outcrop rising high out of the ocean. She swopped down and found a hollow in the rock, which though draughty, would shelter her from the worst of the tempest.

The pigeon soon found she was not alone in her refuge. As she ruffled her feathers to dry them, a small voice called out behind her.

"Who goes there, disturbing our rest? Be you friend or foe?"

The pigeon turned and saw at the rear of the crevice was a nest and sat upon it, two curious birds. Black and white was their plumage, but their beaks were the colours of a sunset. The pigeon cautiously approached the nest and eyed the two birds curiously.

"Friend, I hope. To whom am I addressing, for I have met many birds, yet of your kind, I have not yet been acquainted."

One of the birds hopped down from the nest.

"We are Puffins, good Mistress, native birds to these northern climes. From your beak and plumage, I see you are a pigeon. I have not seen many of your kin this far north, and those that I have seen have been lost here by storms. I fear they may have perished, but I cannot truly say."

"True, that I have been lost in a storm," replied the pigeon, "But there is purpose to my flight. I have been sent by the goddess Persephone, to find the nymph of the Great Forest."

The pigeon then told the puffins of her adventures so far, all the kindness she had found and the perils she had faced on her long journey.

This time, it was the Puffin upon the nest that spoke.

"Good mistress, take heart! I have seen the lady of whom you seek, whilst I was out hunting for fish. She has fled further north, to the land of The Burning Sky."

My old friend, the Snow Goose, guided her there, not three days ago."

"This is joyful news! Lady Persephone herself told me of such a country, before she sent me north. But please, I am lost upon this endless Ocean. Could either of you guide me to this country?"

The first puffin looked towards its mate, who shook its head most vehemently.

"I'm afraid we cannot, for we sit upon our eggs and when one hunts the other must brood".

The pigeon felt a moment of sorrow for her own eggs, and the loss of her mate.

"Then please, tell me how I can get to the land of The Burning Sky?"

The first Puffin stepped forward and peered through the entrance of the hollow. Outside, the storm had abated, but dark clouds still muddled the sky. He pointed upward with his sable wing.

"Fly high above the clouds, always keeping the sun by your left wing. When the sun sets, look straight ahead of you as darkness falls. Search for the brightest star, near the Bear's tail. When first it shines its light upon the world, it will herald a wave of colours across the sky. It will to you seem like a rainbow has been sewn into the cloak of night. There beneath your wings is the land which you seek. Fly down along the timberlines until you reach the Grand Pine, tallest tree in the land. There in a small cavern in the tangle of the roots, the Snow Goose lays her nest. She will know where to find the nymph. Beware though, the Goose is a proud fowl, prouder than any eagle. She may not speak to you, unless you humble yourself before her."

With a fond farewell, the pigeon left the Puffins on their rocky nest and soared upwards until she was high above the clouds. On she flew, always keeping the sun over her left wing. As the sun sank in the west, the clouds rolled away. Save for the rolling waves, the sea and the firmament seemed as one.

When night fell, it fell absolute; a pitch black pall darker than the halls of Hades. The moon itself seemed shrouded, and the stars were dim. Cold and weary from her long flight, the pigeon began to lose hope as she searched the night sky for any familiar pattern to guide her. Sleep began to claim her, and it was all she could do to stop herself from tumbling towards the waters below. Just as her eyes were closing, the sky erupted in a dazzling brilliance, as the jewel of the night sky, the pole star, cast its radiance upon the world. As it glittered in the ebony darkness, just as the Puffin said, it cast in the wake of its luminance, ribbons of colours which danced across the sky. There beneath the irradiated heavens, the pigeon found the shore of a land blanketed in ice and snow. She glided between the pine trees until she found one that seemed to tower over the others like a mountain towers over a pebble. She alighted amongst a tangle of roots so knotted that even the brave Macedonian would have been reluctant to cleave it. At the heart of the tangle was a nest of woven pine branches, and upon the nest brooded a large, white bird with a neck nearly as long as the Thyrsus of Dionysus. She eyed the pigeon haughtily as she approached and narrowed her dark eyes.

"Who are you, humble bird to seek audience with the Snow Goose?"

The pigeon bowed so low before the nest that her beak scraped against the bare earth.

"Madame, I am but a lowly pigeon, but the request I make of you comes from the Gods themselves. I am an emissary to the goddess Persephone and have been sent to the North, on a grave mission."

The pigeon, still stooped before the goose's eyes, told her story of Demeter's wrath, the flight of the nymph, her unsuccessful journeys to the East, the South and the West, her meeting with the Puffins and finally her journey to the land of The Burning Sky.

The Snow Goose raised herself from her nest.

"Your journey is at an end, messenger of Persephone. Raise your head and look behind you."

The pigeon turned her head, and saw in the shadows, almost hidden under a blanket of pine needle and moulted feathers, a sad, bedraggled figure. Her clothing torn, hair unkempt and feet blistered by her wild flight, she was almost unrecognisable as the nymph of the Great Forest.

The pigeon ambled over to her and lay her grey head on the nymph's lap.

"Oh Mistress, you know not how happy I am to finally find you here!"

"As I am to see you, my dear friend. Tell me, is your story true?"

The pigeon looked up at the nymph in alarm.

"If it were not true, would I have travelled so far from my home to find you? Would have I dared to evoke the name of Persephone, Queen of spring, consort of Hades who holds salvation and damnation between her tender palms? Would I have suffered the traps and perils that Demeter had laid in my path if I was only here to proclaim falsehood?"

The nymph soothingly stroked the bird's head.

"Take heart, my feathered friend. I had to be sure. When I first fled the Great Forest, my heart was full of fear and doubt. I knew not why my beloved betrayed me with such anger. While fleeing across the ocean, I rested upon a rock and gave vent to my despair. Whilst flying to her winter home, the Snow Goose heard me and settled upon the rock. Though she is a haughty bird, she is kind-hearted and guided me here, to a place of safety, so that I could heal my mind and body. Now thanks to you, I now know the true cause of my beloved's anger, though I am still afraid, I will return home to face my fears and help the forest to heal."

The nymph lifted the pigeon up and tucked her into the bosom of her tattered gown.

"Rest now, my friend. I will take us both home."

She nodded her head to the Snow Goose.

"I will not forget your kindness. Many thanks and blessings fall upon you."

The Snow Goose plucked a large green pine needle from one of the branches in her nest.

"Before you go, take this needle and plant it when you return to the forest. It serves the pine tree as both leaf and thorn. When you return to the forest and are reunited with your beloved, it will perhaps help you to grow the perfect tree."

A new day was dawning as the nymph, and her companion left the nest of the snow goose. As the waking sun cast its first light upon the frosty ground, they made their way back to the shore.

They had not gone very far, when suddenly an unearthly bellow echoed through the pines, shaking the very ground they stood upon. The earth itself split before them and rising up from the sundered snow stood a titanic beast, a great white bear, eyes black as void, froth hanging from its jaws. Dried blood encrusted its sharp claws and filth stained the matted fur of its chest. It let out a mighty roar as it loomed over the pigeon and the nymph. The bear flung itself at its prey, missing only by inches, and trapping one of its paws in the entangled roots of the Grand Pine. As the bear struggled to free itself, the tree sent a cascade of snow, pine cones and sharp needles on top of its head. The more the bear struggled, the more the tree bombarded the creature. The bear hurled its strength against the roots until with a loud crack, the tangle shattered and its paw came free. The bear charged towards its prey, its mind only focused on the kill.

Hearing the beast thundering through the snow, the pigeon tumbled from the folds of the nymph's gown and took to the wing.

"Run mistress, run!" she cried. "I will distract the beast as best I can."

As the nymph scarpered through the avenue of trees, the bird glided in front of the maddened creature and beat her wings around the bear's head. Though she skilfully avoided the powerful claws that lashed the air beside her, she could not avoid its teeth. The bear snapped, catching the pigeon's tail feathers between its jaws. Flinging its head backward, the bear hurled the pigeon against a tree, bloodily rending her tail from her body.

Looking back, the nymph gave a cry of horror, but still, she raced through the trees with the bear at her heels. Just before she reached the shoreline, her foot snagged against a fallen branch, and she stumbled hard against the snow. The bear charged through the trees, roaring as it came. Just as it was about to leap upon the nymph and consume her, the pigeon, though gravely wounded and barely able to fly, dived down at the face of the beast. She drove her claws into the bear's muzzle and raising her beak, pecked out the bear's black eyes. Though blinded, and howling in pain, the bear lifted its enormous paw, and with one swipe drove its claws into the pigeon, and flung her broken to the ground.

Seeing her feathered friend so badly injured, the nymph gave a cry, not in fear but in defiance. Sorrow and rage boiled within her, drowning her terror. She cared little that it was a mighty Goddess who antagonised her. All she knew was that the bear Demeter had chosen as her host was mortal and could be harmed.

She leapt to her feet and lifted the broken branch that had tripped her, holding it aloft, the splintered tip pointed like a spear. The beast reared above the nymph on its hind legs, claws up-stretched to strike. The nymph seized her opportunity and with all her strength drove the jagged branch deep into the chest of the bear, tearing its mighty heart asunder. With a piercing howl, the bear fell to the ground, dead, its thick red blood already staining the snow.

The nymph stood for a moment, breathless with relief, before running to the side of her fallen friend. The pigeon was still alive, but barely. The wounds the claws had inflicted upon her were deep, and both her wings and her back were broken.

"The bear...is it dead?" she gasped.

The nymph nodded sadly, and showed the pigeon the prone body lying in the snow.

"Then take me home, my mistress. Take me home so I may die amongst the trees where I was hatched."

The nymph held the pigeon tight against her breast, and skimming lightly into the air, retraced her long journey back to the Forest with all the speed she could muster.

It was not until the sun had begun to wane, that the nymph

reached the clearing at the heart of the forest. Exhausted by his long vigil, the Satyr lay sleeping against the trunk of a tree. She crept up to him and woke him with a tender kiss.

The Satyr woke and seeing his beloved before him, leapt up with joy. He called aloud in praise of the young Goddess, who appeared before the reunited couple.

"Welcome home, sweet nymph. I am glad to see you home. But tell me, where is the messenger I sent to find you?"

The nymph lowered her head in sorrow and tenderly retrieved the pigeon from the bosom of her gown. The bird clung to life by a frayed thread. With the very last of her strength, she turned to the Satyr reproachfully

"Oh, master, tell me, where are my eggs? Where are my children? I would glance upon them, one last time."

The Satyr gently took the body of the bird and held her up to a nearby branch

"Fear not, brave messenger. They have not perished."

The Satyr had been as good as his word. There upon the lowest bough of the tree, with plumage as grey as dusk, perched five young birds. They had hatched even as their mother flew across the Ocean. With the influence of Persephone, they had grown rapidly to maturity and looked now with sorrow at their returned parent.

As the pigeon glanced up at her five offspring, a feeling of joy ran through her frail body, before darkness clouded her eyes and closed them for the last time.

The guardians buried her in the ground, with the needle of the north, the flower from the south, the nut from the west, and the fruit from the East placed at her breast. The satyr, the nymph and the five young birds watering it with their tears, then the guardians pressed their palms against the soil. From out of the earth, sprouted a small green shoot, which at the touch of Persephone flourished instantly into a thriving sapling of rare beauty.

The moment of tranquillity did not last long. Raging from the shadows like a storm, came the goddess Demeter. Sickened and bloodied and beaten, her clothes and person in disarray, she towered over the clearing more like demon than deity. With a claw-like hand she reached down towards the newly grown sapling as if to uproot it, its leaves already beginning to wilt beneath her touch.

The Nymph and the Satyr, though both fearful stood before the little plant as if to defend it with their lives. She cast them aside with barely a glace, but just before her fingers grasped the tiny plant, her wrist was caught tightly by Persephone who pulled her back. With eyes alight like the fires of Hephaestus, she confronted her wanton parent.

"Enough, mother, this madness must end. You, the embodiment of life itself, have no right to bring such death and destruction upon the world!"

"Stand aside, child! For many years I have waited to enact my revenge, and nothing will stop me, even you!"

"I am no longer a child, mother!" Persephone snapped "I am Queen over one-third of this earth. What are all your divine powers compared to mine!"

Persephone became as a shower of light, dazzling all those who stood beneath it.

Even Demeter cowered beneath the power of her daughter. She pleaded with the younger Goddess.

"All I did was because of you!" She pointed at the Nymph and Satyr. "It is their fault. The fruit they gave as tribute to the Gods is why I lost you, my daughter to the worlds below."

"You did not lose me, mother. I am right here before you! For the sake of a few seeds, from a fruit offered in tribute, you would destroy them and all that they have accomplished? If one ear of corn withered on the stalk, would the farmer raze his field? If one lamb, born sickly, died within moments of taking breath, would a shepherd sacrifice his entire flock? You knew that the wayward nature of the Gods would render their task impossible. For how can there ever be a standard of perfection if the Gods themselves are flawed? Your thirst for vengeance has blinded your judgement. Such acts should not go unpunished."

Demeter looked upon her daughter with fear, but as she spoke again Persephone's terrible form diminished and she stood before her.

"But I am not like you. I know the qualities of mercy."

Demeter howled in grief and prostrated herself along the ground.

"It is not right that my daughter, a child of the world of light should fill her days reigning as the queen of Hell!"

Persephone bent to the prone form of her mother and comforted her with soft words.

"Ah, mother, you forget. Am I not also the queen of Elysium?"

Demeter gave a sigh and gave vent to her tears. Persephone raised her mother's head and laid it in her lap.

"Is it not enough for you that I spend the long spring and summer months in your company? Do you not think, that when I am in the upper worlds with you, that my husband does not lament my absence? Of all the Gods of Olympus, not even Lord Zeus himself is more faithful, more loving than Lord Hades."

"You speak wisely child, but tell me, are you happy?"

Persephone sat in thought and ran her fingers through her mother's tresses.

"It is not the nature of the universe to grant a life of unlimited happiness, even for those who wish for it most or are most deserving of it. Not even for us Gods is this true. The best we can hope for is bittersweet. It is up to us, however, to make it more sweet than bitter."

"Oh my child, I hope you can forgive me for all I have done."

"It is not I to whom you should request forgiveness." She indicated the two lovers who sat, clinging to each other beside the sapling.

Demeter walked over to them and raised the two, who stood awestruck in the presence of the Goddesses. She bent between them and gently touched the sapling, bringing new life to what had been withered.

"It matters not now, whether this young plant would have grown to become the perfect tree. What it will stand for now is more important. Let it symbolise the end of my feud with you. In repentance for my madness, I free you from your obligation. Whatsoever you wish, it shall be granted."

She turned to the young birds upon the tree. "Before I leave, to you, I must offer recompense as well."

She drew her hand across their feathers, turning them from dusty grey to alabaster white.

"In honour of your mother's memory, you and your descendants shall become sacred to the Gods as emblems of faith, courage, hope, fidelity and above all love."

She turned to all assembled in the clearing.

"May you live in peace, for as long as there stands a tree upon this Earth."

Persephone took her mother's arm, and the two goddesses disappeared from the clearing like mist before the rays of the morning sun.

In time the Forest healed, and the beasts and birds returned to their home. Soon all the promises of Demeter were fulfilled and a child, many children came to the guardians of the forest.

And the trees echoed with their songs.

The End

Links:

https://twitter.com/sarahaw

@sarahaw

Facebook: https://www.facebook.com/sarahalicewilson

https://www.youtube.com/user/ThePsuedonym?app=desktop

Cover by Sue Bahr.

The Contraption

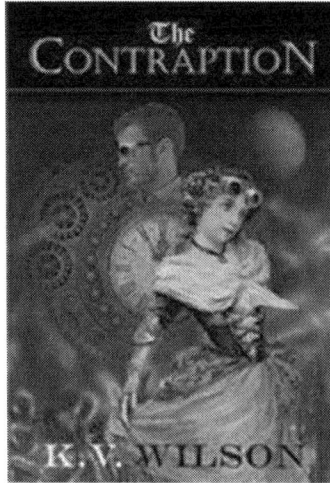

K. V. Wilson

This story is about two young cousins with very different personalities, yet they both have the same enthusiasm for getting their hands greasy. Russell and Agatha Brattle are children of nineteenth-century England. They are swept up in unfortunate circumstances that force them to take matters into their own hands if they are to succeed. Agatha learns the tools of the trade in secret in order to help provide for their broken family, but she's a little too carefree and adventurous; she soon puts into motion a chain of events that not even her perfectionist cousin can fix.

A native of Alberta, Canada, Kristen Wilson has always been influenced by the natural world around her and by all kinds of fantasy and sci-fi works. She is currently working on a fantasy trilogy under the pen name K.V. Wilson, the first book of which is entitled *Spiritborne*. *The Contraption* is a Steampunk-esque story that has been at the tip of her tongue for years, and now she finally has a chance to put it into words.

***

Russell Cornelius Brattle pulled out his father's watch from the pocket of his second-hand suit and allowed himself a smile. Just on time. He'd always ever been just on time. *If I make use of the early hours*, he thought, *I'll have it working again in a jiff.*

A horrid clunking noise shook the boy from his thoughts. When he regained his composure, he cursed his terrible luck. Such a clumsy clunk could only mean one thing, and he didn't much like the thought of it.

"Ag? I know you're here," Russell whispered, his eyebrows drawn together into a tight frown. "I *told* you not to sneak in again."

A giggle echoed across the room.

"You'd better not try anything. I mean it."

She chuckled. "Stop being a stick in the mud, Rusty. Just need to make an adjustment."

Russell narrowed his eyes. "What did you do *now*?"

"Just dented it a smidge."

"Agatha..."

Russell lifted the candle and scanned the room. He caught a glimpse of his cousin's head of messy dirty-blonde locks. She was six years younger than he, a small and delicate girl of ten. She still had the baby cheeks and spunk to show for it, too.

Agatha shrugged off the torn overcoat that had once belonged to her father. With some effort, the girl shoved up the sleeve of her coral dress, gritting her teeth as a bloodstained bandage caught on the linen.

"Augh," she grunted. "Think we can pound it back into shape?"

Russell sucked air through his teeth. "Ag, I don't have time for this. I have to finish tonight, or Barkley's going to stumble in on...on this."

He spread his arms wide, stepping back so Agatha could see the damage she'd wrought. Russell had been slaving away at the machine in the back room for nearly a fortnight. He had the tailpiece finished; all that was left was to attach it. The machine itself – which Russell affectionately called 'the Contraption' – spanned roughly five feet long and three feet wide. It was approximately the size of one of the motorcars Russell often saw bumbling down Main Street. Such technology seemed rather cutting-edge, however, and it puzzled Russell as to how this machine seemed to be so old and beaten up already. Russell had never seen Barkley use it before, and frankly, if the Master Tinker knew that Russell had been handling it, he'd kick the boy's sorry arse back out onto the street before you could say 'don't press the big red button'. Not that there was any danger of *that;* Russell had been contemplating such a button ever since he'd first laid eyes on the Contraption, and the mere thought of putting his finger anywhere near it gave him the chills.

"I'm sorry," Agatha pouted.

"I never should've allowed you in here," Russell sighed, scratching his head.

His cousin smiled widely, snatching a pair of Barkley's goggles from the hook on the wall and ignoring the acrid stench of whiskey emanating from the tankard on the bench. The Master Tinker had yet to clear his workspace of mould and gunk, despite the fact that he would be having patrons arriving later that day. Patrons who would be here to take a look at the Contraption. If Russell couldn't fix it in time, Barkley would find out. The tinker would not only withdraw the boy from his apprenticeship, he would have Russell's hide.

"Alright. Out we go, Ag," Russell told his cousin condescendingly, grabbing her by the good arm and pulling her along as he wormed his way between crates of miscellaneous cutlery and doodads.

"You can't quit *now!*" the girl protested.

As Russell dragged her through the shop Agatha scanned the room hungrily, taking in all the bits and pieces as if seeing them for the very first time. She adjusted Barkley's oversize goggles. They gave her a rather bug-eyed appearance and forced her ears out from her dainty head even more than usual. Her short sandy locks were tangled and splayed every which way. It would be Clem's nightmare combing through it all when Agatha returned home.

"I'm *not* quitting," Russell told his cousin. "I'm taking you home."

"I can fix it fast! Honest!"

Agatha raised her right arm, enclosing her metallic fingers around Russell's wrist and giving his limb a small twist. This hadn't the effect she'd intended, however, as her cousin let out a yelp of pain and swore angrily.

"Agatha!"

"That's not holy, Rusty."

"Neither are *you*," he retorted, rubbing his wrist. "I should've left you with the stub."

Agatha glanced down, yanking the prosthetic out of its socket and laughing at her cousin's disgruntled face. Though his handiwork had managed to do its job so far, the dent in the top portion had left the metal rather sharp. It had cut into Agatha's arm, but she didn't seem bothered much by it. Russell, however, hated the sight of blood. He averted his eyes, taking a deep breath.

"Rusty, if you hadn't have done this, I'd still be out of work."

Russell wrinkled his nose. "You shouldn't even *be* in the workforce. Clem should be doing her *own* sewing!"

Agatha's mother – Russell's aunt – Clementine Brattle had been widowed when her husband had died in a horrific factory incident that claimed the lives of nearly forty. This included both of Russell's parents. Neither the boy nor his cousin knew the details of that incident; Clem had kept it from them and would no doubt continue to do so.

Agatha spat on the shop floor, making Russell wince. "Clem can kiss my—"

"Shh," Russell cut in before she could finish. He couldn't stop the snigger from spreading across his face, however.

Aunt Clementine would go mental if her perfect little daughter called her anything but 'Mummy' or if her nephew called her anything apart from 'Aunty' or 'Ma'am'. But this didn't stop the two of them from making jokes at Clem's expense whenever she was out of earshot. Which was hardly ever. Russell's favourite joke had much to do with the fact that Clem had ears as big as an elephant's and just as bloody effective. Never mind that Agatha had inherited those big ears that stuck out like beacons from her childish face. The ten-year-old's wide smile was enough to persuade people of her inner beauty.

Russell ran a hand through his sandy hair, ignoring the grease on his fingers. He would bathe when he arrived home. The water would be chilled, but at least it would feel good to wash off the memory of the broken machine once and for all.

"Did you fix it up yet?" Agatha asked sweetly.

"'Course not! I've still got to get the shafts in sync, not to mention I haven't *begun* to get the tailpiece attached again!" He sighed in frustrated exasperation, pointing a forefinger at her. "The latter is thanks to *you*! It'll never be the way it was. When Barkley finds out, he'll kill me."

"He won't. You've kept it secret."

"No thanks to you! Fortunately he hasn't looked too carefully or he'd see that the blasted tailpiece of his precious Contraption has been knocked off!" Russell told her, digging through the heap to procure a rusted screwdriver.

The apprentice tinker rolled his eyes and hefted up the tailpiece. Russell pulled a screw out of his apron and began to force the hunk of metal back into place. He could've used Agatha's help; he had taught her a thing or two and she'd proven to be a natural at metalwork. But not today. There was too much at stake to allow his cousin and her clumsy prosthetic anywhere near Barkley's machine.

"That was an accident," Agatha pouted.

"He'll have my hide when he sees that it's broken."

"Not if you're not *here*."

"What?"

"I said—"

"I *know* what you said. Why'd you say it?"

Agatha gave Russell another of her sweet smiles before ducking down beneath the metal siding of the Contraption. As she did so her goggles clinked against it, making the boy wince.

Cursed cousin, he thought. *She should have stuck with sewing. But no, she had to appeal to my good side and persuade me to teach her about tinkering. And she couldn't stay away; she had to go and mutilate Barkley's most prized possession.* Russell eyed the Contraption with malice.

"What's so special about you, anyway, you damned hunk of metal? What is your purpose?" he muttered, sorely tempted to bang the screwdriver against the mysterious machine.

"Oi, get out there an' earn your right to live 'ere!" Agatha demanded, placing her good arm on her hip and mocking her mother's high-pitched cockney accent.

Russell laughed and then sighed. It was true; he was beginning to sound like Clem again. While his aunt held a special soft spot for her girl and wanted to keep her away from anything that would soil her hands or her image, she did not hold that same love for her nephew. If Clem knew that Agatha was secretly working in a tinker's shop by night, she'd surely give Russell the strap. Which was utterly stupid; Russell was the sole provider for the three of them. He had been ever since the incident.

Though Agatha was great at sewing, the girl wouldn't have anything of *that.* She was built for one thing and one thing only: fixing things. She would sneak out after Russell on Drinking Night – the one evening of the week that they knew Barkley wouldn't be in his shop; he'd be passed out somewhere until noon the next day. Agatha would beg Russell to teach her all that he knew, and he would begrudgingly do so, but only because it would mean they both got to go home early.

Russell understood Agatha's strange desire to get her hands dirty, fixing something up that was meant to be fixed. Yes, Agatha could send a needle through thread just fine, but when she was left to her own devices in the shop, she could do wonders.

But Russell's cousin was young and a little too carefree, and that would be the downfall of them both. She had broken off part of Barkley's machine during one of her careless moments. Russell had no idea what she'd been doing in the back room by herself, but according to his deduction skills, she'd bumped a pail off the top shelf and right onto the Contraption. This had knocked the tailpiece clean off. Then she'd tried to fix it without first consulting Russell but had ended up making it a lot worse. And so Russell had dedicated his nights to trying to fix it. He'd told Agatha to stay out of it, however, despite her desire to help.

"Okay, let's make a deal. You stay out of my way, Ag, and I'll let you stay. But only to fix your arm."

"Fine." Agatha pouted.

"And stay in the corner. Don't touch anything."

Russell breathed a sigh of relief as Agatha did as she was told, stalking off to the corner and pulling up a stool so that she could pound her arm back into place.

***

An hour later, Russell sighed. He was nearly finished. "Just a bit more…" The boy stuck out his tongue in concentration.

Agatha snorted. "You're talking to yourself again. And your tongue's out."

"Shut it," Russell muttered.

"*You* shut it," the ten-year-old retorted. "I think I'm done. Well, maybe one more tweak."

"Good for you," Russell said flatly. "I, on the other hand, am *not*."

Agatha leapt off her stool, leaving her arm on the workbench. "Lemme help."

"Fat chance."

"C'mon Rusty! Once this is finished, life is *made* for us."

Russell rolled his eyes. "Not *that* nonsense again."

The apprentice focused his eyes on the work before him, ignoring the sting of the flickering candlelight on his tired eyes. He badly needed spectacles, but Clem would never consider it, not even if

132

they had the money for them.

"You can't spend your life pounding on forks and spoons when we've got *this* in the back room!" Agatha cried, her head bobbing up and down comically. She lowered her voice and added, "It's a time machine."

Russell rolled his eyes. "For the last flippin' time. It's not a—"

Agatha snorted. "'Course it is!" The girl's head popped up and she leaned over the tailpiece that Russell was desperately trying to attach. Her messy hair spilled onto her cousin's lap, making him groan.

"Ugh! Get off!"

"See here!" she continued, disappearing from view. Russell craned his neck around just in time to see Agatha slide onto the seat of the Contraption. "See? The dials mark the days and the toggles mark the years."

"It's just a dumb piece of junk that Barkley inherited. You're mad as hops, Agatha."

She let out another giggle, making Russell roll his eyes. "Not as mad as you."

"Quite right. I've got limited time to finish this up. If I don't, Barkley's gonna—"

Russell's sentence was cut short by the sound he'd been dreading: a grotesque creak of the worn hinges.

"Blast," Russell breathed. "Ag, get down!" he hissed. To his relief, his cousin obliged. Russell barely had time to puff out the candle before a strong baritone bellowed from the front of the shop.

"What the blazes is going on in here?!"

Russell's eyes grew wide. He would be seen. He would be seen for sure! And then...*blam*. He'd be dead.

I tried to keep this hidden from him, but who was I kidding? Russell gulped. *He was bound to look sooner or later, and now I don't have time to cover it up.*

"Brattle, you in here after hours again? I bloody *told* you to keep out of me shop after hours!"

Well, Russell thought. *There's no hiding from him now.*

The boy cleared his throat and then coughed. He hoped this minor interruption would buy him a few seconds to sum up a half-arsed explanation as to why the tail-end of his master's old machine had been knocked clean off. Russell glared in the direction of his cousin. *Who else could screw up an apprenticeship – albeit a lousy one – than a ruddy ten-year-old?*

"Brattle, I want you out of me shop in the count of ten. One, two..."

Russell wondered why Barkley had decided to come down here at five-thirty in the damned morning. Last night was Drinking Night. Barkley should be passed out at home.

"Of-of course, Sir. Right away."

"I've got patrons comin' in a half-hour, boy! Six, seven..."

Russell gently deposited the screwdriver on the nearest table. *Patrons! They were coming early? But...the Contraption.*

"Here, Sir," Russell assured his master as he followed the candlelight to the front of the shop.

Barkley kept on counting, however. Faster and faster, not even bothering to say his 'steamboats' in between. The young tinker barely made it out of the ramshackle shop before Barkley reached the double-digits.

"Save up, boy, an' maybe someday ye'll make it out o' here alive," Barkley sneered. "Bloody apprentice. I should fire you right 'ere an' now. Empty yer pockets!"

Russell swallowed back a groan. Had he remembered to replace all the equipment? And what's more, how long would it take for Barkley to realize that the Contraption was broken? There was no time left. The patrons would be here soon...

I'm in deep, the boy mused. *And how am I going to get Agatha out now?* Russell had almost forgotten about his cousin. She was still sunk deep down in the seat of the machine. She couldn't possibly escape without making noise.

"Turn them out," Barkley commanded again and Russell did as he was told. A coin clinked against the stone and the Master Tinker was quick to snatch it up. "Shame on you, boy. Get on home."

Russell turned away, seething.

"I'll make sure yer Aunty gives ye a good beatin' fer this!" his master called after him. "Awake at this time o' the morn! Imagine that!" he muttered to himself, lighting his pipe.

The Master Tinker turned back into his shop, perhaps to ensure that Russell hadn't damaged or stolen anything – like that would ever happen! But soon he'd be blamed for it, and there was nothing he could do about it.

The sixteen-year-old ducked down at the side of the shop, listening in to make sure nothing of consequence happened, namely Barkley's discovery of a small, dusty girl sitting on the seat of his prized machine and wearing his rusted goggles.

Barkley mumbled to himself for a few moments and Russell held his breath. Then the moment he'd been dreading finally came.

"BRATTLE!" the Master Tinker screamed at the top of his lungs. "WHAT HAVE YE DONE TO ME MACHINE?!"

Russell's heart skipped a beat and he bit his tongue as he debated whether or not he should run for his life. *I can't leave Agatha.*

"I'm going to have yer head for this! I'm going to skin ye alive!"

"Wait!"

At this, the hair on the back of Russell's neck stood up. *Agatha! For Christ's sake, can't you keep your fat mouth shut just this once?*

"What's this?" the Master Tinker bellowed. "A girl?"

"It wasn't Russell that broke your time machine. It was me."

"Blast, Agatha! He'll kill you," Russell whispered under his breath, carefully stepping back through the shop. His stomach curdled at the thought of what his master would do to them both for this.

Barkley spluttered. "*Time* machine?! Pfft. 'Tis an engine. Nothin' more."

"Rusty fixed it. It's almost repaired."

Russell gulped, opening his mouth to speak. Before he could say a thing, however, Barkley rounded upon him, holding up a stubby candle to illuminate Russell's features.

"You!"

Russell's eyes grew wide and his mind screamed for him to run. His limbs, however, had a very different idea. The apprentice stood frozen as the Master Tinker gripped his throat with gigantic hairy hands. Russell spluttered for breath as Barkley mumbled threats into his ear. They were empty threats, however; the boy was already suffocating and would not last much longer.

Out of the corner of Russell's eye, he could make out the small shape of his cousin in the flickering candlelight. Agatha mumbled something rather unladylike as she popped her prosthetic back into place. It wasn't fully repaired, but there wasn't any time for that now.

"Ye won't tell anyone of this," Barkley commanded.

Russell gasped for air as the tinker's enormous hands continued to enclose around his throat. Barkley squeezed the life from Russell's body in rapid, terrible pulsations. The innocent sound of his cousin's voice reached his ears.

"Rusty! Get in the time machine!"

"Get out, girl, or I *will* kill you—"

The Tinker's words were cut short as something hit him from

135

behind. Barkley howled and whipped around to face his assailant, allowing Russell's limp body to sink to the floor. Lances of pain shot up the boy's spine as he landed on some rather sharp tools that his master had left unguarded. A stream of curses flooded from the Master Tinker's mouth as he grabbed Agatha's collar.

"Rusty!" she called out. Russell gritted his teeth and got to his feet, careful not to trip on the trimmings and trappings strewn across the blackened floor of the shop.

Before he could run to Agatha's aid, however, the tinker began yowling in pain and clutching his groin. His head thunked against the table on its way down, and Russell harboured a small hope that he'd been knocked unconscious.

Agatha stood over the Master Tinker, eyeing her prosthetic arm with admiration. *Iron fists are the best,* she thought to herself. *See, Rusty? What if I hadn't been here?*

The girl didn't seem to notice or care that her dress was torn beyond repair and her goggles – Barkley's goggles – had fallen askew on her dimpled face. She was no longer smiling. Russell couldn't remember a time when Agatha wasn't smiling.

"Get to the time machine, Rusty," she ordered, and her voice shook with pain and fear. "Before he gets up."

Russell couldn't reply. He gulped and sputtered as he struggled to regain his voice and breathe normally again. How close had he been to death?

The boy stepped carefully over the fallen Tinker and eyed his face. He was dazed but not completely out of it. His lips began to quiver and Russell swore he could hear the Tinker utter his name.

Russell... You're a dead mannnn...

"Agatha, run for the door!" the young apprentice cried out weakly. His voice cracked and he rubbed at his neck where those enormous hands had nearly squeezed the life from him.

"Rusty, get in," Agatha said, looking her cousin in the eye. "Get. In. The. Machine," she said through her teeth. "Trust me. I'm bloody serious."

Russell narrowed his eyes. "When have you *ever* been serious?" he croaked, but approached the vehicle warily.

Agatha hoisted up her skirts and pulled her goggles onto her grease-stained face, shooting her cousin a quick grin. "It works," was all she said in response.

"What works? What the *hell* works, Ag?"

She laughed, beckoning for Russell to join her. A groan from

Barkley sealed the deal. Russell stared wide-eyed at the tinker; he lay motionless but clearly not unconscious.

"If he catches us, he'll—"

"He can't catch us if we're not *here*."

"Blast, Agatha!" Russell shouted, swinging himself onto the seat beside his cousin. Agatha was already madly turning dials and toggles on the Contraption's dashboard. "This isn't a joke!"

"Goggles? Check. Helmet?" Agatha reached down and withdrew a watermelon-sized metal object, which she then plunked unceremoniously into her cousin's lap. "Check. You need that more'n I do. You've got a big head."

Russell gaped at her but pulled on the helmet, fastening the straps. They were dead anyway. Might as well play 'time machine' before Barkley killed them both.

"Shame about that tail section. I didn't mean to break it, but the Sphinx is better off now, I do think."

"WHAT?!" Russell yelled over the roar of the engine. Agatha pulled on a nearby lever, making a gear turn and interlock with a multitude of other gears. "The...the sequence. It's going!" he called out in surprise.

"'*Course* it is." Agatha craned her neck around, glancing at the fallen Master Tinker before turning back to the dashboard. "This had better work!"

"You're telling *me*," Russell whimpered. He coughed as steam engulfed the room. The chug-chugging of the Contraption matched the deafening pounding of Russell's heart as he clutched the seat and stared at his cousin. *What the hell are we doing?*

Barkley's head suddenly emerged at Agatha's side and a gigantic hairy hand grabbed the girl's metallic one, jerking her towards him.

"Rusty!" she shrieked.

Russell grabbed his cousin's good arm, attempting to yank her back into the Contraption. Barkley's face twisted into a grotesque snarl as he bared his crooked yellow teeth at them.

"Ye'll never escape!"

"Says *you*," Agatha whispered, slamming a hand down upon the big red button that Russell had been eying for nearly a fortnight. She unfastened the leather strap that held her prosthetic arm on. The butt of the metal limb smacked Barkley in the face, sending him reeling.

The Contraption whirred and jumped and shook. Russell gripped the edge of his seat and shut his eyes tight. He ground his teeth together and focused on the thought that they would live through this. His stomach was turning upside-down and side-to-side and its contents were overflowing.

"Agathaaaaaaaaa!"

Russell vomited onto the floor and wiped his mouth on his sleeve.

"Al-mo-most out!" Agatha screamed over the roar of the time machine and the incessant rattling as the vehicle jumped through the void of time and space.

And then they were out.

When Russell had the courage to open his eyes once again, he beheld a new world. It was as if London had never existed. The earth was barren and horrid. The air was thick with dust and debris that left Russell coughing and sputtering as he tried to breathe again. He stuck his head out of the window, clawing at his eyes so that he could get another glimpse of the new world.

"Damn," Agatha muttered.

Russell was too preoccupied to reprimand his cousin for using poor language. The sight before them was worthy of a ghost story; it was as if the four horsemen of the Apocalypse had pulled their chariot – their 'time machine', as Agatha had called it – straight through the gates of Hell.

"My bad," was all the girl had to say in response.

"Your *bad*?!" Russell cried, pulling his head back inside and coughing before regarding Agatha with malice. "Where *are* we? The Devil's Door?"

"I saved us," she muttered.

Russell shook his head. "I-I know. But we could've run for it!"

"Rusty, I've gone back in time before."

"No kidding."

"And I think I know where we are."

"You mean *when* we are."

She nodded, smoothing her wild dirty-blonde locks. Her blue eyes grew wide as she broke into a nervous smile. "Rusty, I haven't been here before."

"And where, pray tell, is *here*?" Russell inquired, narrowing his eyes and finally easing his heart into a steady beat again.

A terrible moan ensued, and the cousins whipped around to locate its source. Russell's breath caught as he glimpsed a gigantic beast. Its neck alone reached heights that rivaled that of the Clock Tower.

"Take us back, Ag! Take us back now!" Russell screamed,

remembering his schooling. "D-dino—"

"Dinosaurs!" Agatha finished for him. "Whoa... Aren't they beautiful?"

"No!"

"*That* one is," the girl said indignantly. "And if I bring us back now, Barkley's gonna kill you."

"You too," Russell assured her, "because *look* what you just did!"

She laughed. "If I bring us back to the time *before* this happened, you'll still have to work as that horrid man's apprentice."

"That's preferable to dying in a dino's belly."

"And if I bring us to a time *after* this happened, you won't have a job and we'll all starve."

"Duly noted."

"So what we need to do," Agatha said slowly, adjusting her goggles, "is to skip this generation entirely."

"*What*? Then how will I ever make a living? What if there are no tinkers in..." — Russell gulped and took a deep breath for emphasis — "in the future?"

"No tinkers?" Agatha frowned, seemingly amused. "Then how will people fix their broken forks?"

Russell couldn't tell if she was making fun of him or not. He decided she was and glared at her.

"This isn't funny. We can't survive *alone*!"

But Russell had to admit, the thought was tempting. Clem had beaten Russell for most of his life, and she hadn't been kind to her own daughter, either. Agatha was forced into dresses and pushed to sew for her aunt, who took all the credit when she sold the wares, not leaving any salary for Agatha.

"Ag," Russell gulped, "take us back." The thought of time travel itself was making the boy sick to his stomach again. "We can figure this out in a safer place."

"You're just saying that 'cause you'll miss Henrietta!"

"I will *not*!" Russell said indignantly. He felt his face growing beet red. "She doesn't mean a thing to me."

"She did until she broke the courtship," Agatha giggled.

"You know nothing of courtships," Russell muttered.

Agatha adjusted her goggles and began turning the dials on the dashboard. Russell watched her with interest, wrinkling his nose at the stench of bile rising from the floor of the machine. He struggled to push the thought out of his mind. If they were to live a life of starvation, the least he could do was to keep the rest of his last meal down. *Cornbread and potatoes. It was a decent last meal,* Russell thought to himself.

"How do you know how to use this piece of junk?" he inquired.

"*Excuse* me?" She turned towards Russell with distaste. "Piece of junk?"

"Well, yes. I mean, it's been sitting in Barkley's back room for as long as I've been there. The only reason I gave it the time of day was because you flippin' broke it in the first place!"

"Broke it! Hah!" she sputtered, throwing up her hands in a typical ten-year-old girl fashion.

Russell stared at her for a few moments. "Yes, it looks pretty broke to me."

"But it works!" she said indignantly. "Rusty, I *fixed* it. It wasn't a *time machine* until *I* got hold of it!"

Now it was Russell's turn to laugh. He chuckled until tears trickled down his cheeks. Then he clasped his hands together and turned back to his cousin.

"You're not...serious, are you?" the boy asked when Agatha made it clear that she wasn't sharing in his amusement.

"Damn well am."

"Language—"

"No! Your language was *far* worse. Piece of *junk*," she moaned, mimicking Russell's voice. "You don't think I'm capable!"

"Agatha, we're in prehistoric times, surrounded by dinosaurs. If I'm not dreaming, please, for Christ's sake, drop me off at the looney bin on our way home!"

"We're not going home."

"What?!"

She giggled. "I *knew* you'd understand. Switching gears."

"What?" Russell repeated. "Switching—"

"Where do you wanna go?" she asked, smiling. "Actually, there *is* one reason to go back."

Russell secured his helmet atop his sweaty head and automatically gripped the edge of his seat again. He bit his tongue, shutting his eyes tight to keep the nausea at bay.

"We have to go back for my arm."

The girl let out a maniacal laugh as she twisted the dials and flipped the toggles. All Russell had time to think about before the Contraption was yanked back into the twisting nether was that if anybody belonged with the loonies, it had to be Agatha.

The End

You can find more of K.V. Wilson's work on her website

https://kvwilsonauthor.weebly.com/

On Facebook at https://www.facebook.com/spirits.kvwilson/

And on Wattad: https://www.wattpad.com/user/kv_wilson

Cover by Author.

Ember in the Snow

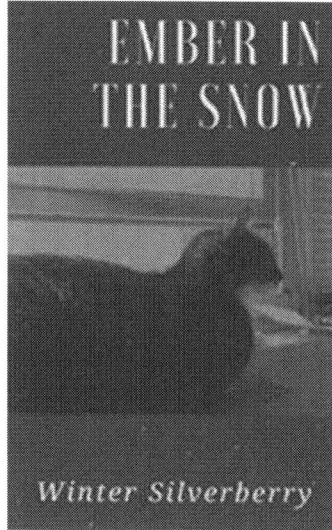

Winter Silverberry

Winter Silverberry is a writer from Chicago who loves all things wild and whimsical. An avid Sci-Fi and Fantasy fan, this spirit is reflected in her writings. She loves to work in her art journal, read tarot, and write when she doesn't have the dreaded block. Quite a few of her stories revolve around her beloved semi-feral feline friend, Griffin, who is the inspiration for the Griffin J. Cat stories.

Join Griffin, a cat certain that he is descended from Egyptian Gods, as he sets off to find his fairy friend in the lush landscape of the Otherlands. Griffin will meet some interesting characters along the way and one naïve little fox who just might need Griffin to intercede on his behalf.

***

One winter day, when there was a slight chill in the air and snow lightly dusted the back porch. Griffin J. Cat was feeling a most active case of cabin fever.

Mia, his companion (Griffin would never think of anyone as an 'owner') had shut Griffin out of her room the night before after an unfortunate instance in which a sleeping Mia shifted her foot under the covers and Griffin accidentally pounced on it. Really, Griffin couldn't help it. He had only been half awake. Somewhere in his mind he was a great hunter. Mia's foot movement in the night under a cover mimicked the rustling of a mouse in a pile of leaves. Sitting around the house without going outside for the past few days because it was the coldest week of the year had not helped with controlling himself. He was a cat. His instincts were what motivated him the most. Sometimes, even though he didn't mean for them to, they took over his actions.

Griffin yawned from the sitting room where he was lounging. It had warmed up outside a bit and Griffin did naturally wear a fashionable little fur coat so he felt like it would be good for him to venture outside for a spell.

Slowly, Griffin padded across the porch leaving telltale paw prints in the snow behind him. He didn't like the cold but the slight crunch of the powder under his paws was not an unpleasant sensation. Next door, Sophie, Griffin's spoiled little Beagle friend, was barking and playing in the snow in her backyard. Griffin lifted his pink nose to sniff the crisp air. Somewhere up in the trees, birds were chirping.

As he explored choice sections of the yard Griffin noticed that the dusting of snow glistened in the sun like fairy dust. It brought his thoughts back to Chloe, his fairy friend. Griffin was wary of Chloe since having her around sometimes spelled trouble but she was also undeniably fun. The boredom of being locked up in the house had his tail twitching for some adventure. Plus, Chloe had been instrumental in expelling some imps from Griffin's home recently. Griffin felt it was his duty to at least check up on her.

Griffin knew he was supposed to be able to walk in the otherlands now that one of his whiskers resided there with Chloe, which is a story unto itself, but he had never received instructions on how to get there. It wasn't like Chloe was handing out maps to her mysterious homeland. Griff suspected it was more of a state of mind then an actual place anyway. He started to wander the back woods focusing his thoughts on Chloe and his whisker. Gradually the light snow became lighter and then entirely melted away. It was replaced with lush grass, flowers of all colors and trees bearing summer fruits.

The thought occurred, a bit late, that now he was here he had no idea how he would find Chloe. The otherlands were vast. Chloe could be anywhere.

As Griffin was considering, a rainbow trout in a bow tie swam by in the air and landed in one of the nearby trees.

"Excuse me," said Griffin politely. "I'm looking for my friend. Chloe. Do you know where she is?"

"Do I look like the tourist center?" Sniffed the trout.

Griffin lashed his tail. Really! Being a cat, he was the descendent of Egyptian gods! As such, he deserved some respect.

"Well, you don't have to be rude! There is simply no need." Griffin's ears twisted back to illustrate his agitation. He turned away from the fish, then looked back at him with a precise stare. "You know," he said pointedly, "my ancestors were gods. Cats are granted certain powers not bestowed on other creatures. I should turn you into a worm for your insolence." Griffin did not mention that turning another creature into a worm was not in that catalogue of gifted powers.

The trout however, did not know this. "A worm? But...but I eat worms!" Exclaimed the distraught trout. "I only didn't answer you because cats eat fish, you know. Highly improper! I certainly don't want to be eaten and I don't approve of you eating my people."

"I have never eaten a rainbow trout." Griffin's fish diet was restricted to tuna and salmon of the type found in pouches.

"Well, I don't want to be the first." the fish admitted in a bit of a snooty tone.

Griffin considered. "I would not eat a fish that I had a conversation with. Besides, I would have to be a fool to eat anything while I walk here in the otherlands."

"What if you were sitting?" the trout asked suspiciously, flapping his tail back and forth.

"What I mean is that I would never eat anything while being here. Sitting, standing, walking, or otherwise." Griffin clarified. "Creatures that dine while here owe this place. You should have no fear of being eaten by me." Griffin stopped to groom a paw. He had gleaned from this fish's tone and his meticulous bow tie that the fish was very concerned with all things proper.

"Wouldn't it be awfully impolite of you to know where my friend is and not advise me?"

The rainbow trout's eyes rolled back and forth as if he was in conflict with himself. "Fine." he finally sputtered. "Yes, I know exactly where Chloe is. She is in the garden of the enchanted tree stump dancing with a fox that followed her here. Poor fellow."

"You can see her?" Griff asked.

"Of course I can see her! I swam in the stream of thought by her home on Tuesday." The trout gave Griffin the fish eye.

"Well, can you tell her I am here and looking for her?" Griffin asked politely through slightly gritted teeth.

"I can't talk to her from here," the fish admitted. "I can only see her thoughts. You just have to find the enchanted tree stump."

"Where?" Griffin was starting to get impatient.

"Not sure exactly. Somewhere on the left side of the brain? Good luck to you, especially if you actually find her." The trout started to swim away. "I bid you good day and please, stick to poultry."

"Suggestion noted." Griffin waved a paw goodbye.

He moved on ahead. Dragonflies danced in the sunlight off the path. He did not dare to place a paw on any ground other than the path. Eventually his ears picked up the light sounds of music in the air at a distance.

Distinctly he could hear Chloe's laughter over a yip yip yipping which undoubtedly belonged to the aforementioned fox. Griffin hoped Chloe's appetite for mischief would be directed at her new friend.

A few yards ahead Griffin could see the sparkle of Chloe's wings. He made it over to the path on the side of the tree stump they were dancing on.

"Griffin!" Chloe twittered. "Did you come to dance with me? Hop up here and take a turn round the stump with me."

"Well, I didn't come to dance and I am not leaving this path, but I did come to visit you." Griffin told his friend.

"What, are you too dignified to dance, silly tabby? Come on!" yipped the small young fox, spinning on two paws in a circle.

"I am not the silly creature who is off the path in the otherlands. Do you have any idea how long you have probably been here, little fox?"

"Only an hour or so. It's so much fun, you should try it." The fox spun around till he fell off the stump to the ground.

Griffin arched an eyebrow. "Chloe."

"He agreed to dance with me. Griffin, just because you have a whisker here, does that mean you are going to be visiting all the time, ruining my fun?" Chloe asked exasperated.

"How long, Chloe?" Griffin repeated. "I am here because I was concerned about you. I haven't seen you in a while."

"Winter is no fun in the forest. Too cold. That's why I haven't been around." Chloe stated as if it were obvious.

"Winter?" The little fox stopped his dancing. A confused look crossed his furry face. "But it's Spring. My very first." He looked around then he looked at Chloe and then at Griffin. His look of confusion turned to recognition, and then to shame. "Oh." He sat down solemnly.

"You missed the summer and the fall little fox. And the worst part of winter. You were safe here with me." Chloe interjected. "Griffin you are such a buzzkill."

"Chloe you can't just lure the forest animals to the otherlands at your whim." Griffin stated.

"Can too!" Chloe exclaimed.

"Well, little fox." Griffin continued.

"Ember" Chloe interrupted.

"Ember, I hope you are clever like a fox. Did you eat anything here?" Griffin asked

"No." Ember admitted.

"Well, that much is good." Ember would not owe anything for sustenance. Griffin felt some empathy for the little fox pup. It could be him dancing with Chloe season after season were it not for advice from Old Grey, the leader of the neighborhood colony cats, and a frequent traveler of the otherlands.

Chloe folded her arms.

"It seems you have had the best of me, Chloe. What do you want for my leave?" Ember said abashedly and looked at the ground.

"Hmmmm." Chloe thought. "You hid a polished stone you found in an old tree in the spring. It is from the river. It has some magic from the river sprites in it. I will take it for your leave the next time I see you. But you must find your own way back. You strayed from the path..."

"I have not strayed the path." Griffin interrupted Chloe. "I should be able to find the way back. You can follow me."

"Nice Griffin!" Chloe snapped. "Why did you come here? To spoil all my fun?"

"Chloe, it sounds like you got a nice stone as well as a few of Ember's seasons out of this deal. Not too bad for you, and the truth is, I came here because I miss you." Griffin said pointedly.

Chloe blushed. "So you want to dance?" She asked.

"No." Griffin stated.

"On the path?" Chloe asked again.

"Maybe on the path on the way home." Griffin conceded.

"Come on Ember." Griffin motioned a paw to Ember.

The three danced back the way Griffin had come until snow was on the ground again.

Griffin and Ember turned to look behind them. Chloe was nowhere to be found.

"That was close. I thought foxes were supposed to be clever." Griffin joked.

"I am clever." Ember said defensively. "But acting clever usually involves tricking someone and that's not nice. I'm not about that. It was just a warm spring day and the sun was shining and I wanted to make a friend."

"Ember, the naïve fox." Griffin snorted. Ember looked at the ground. Griffin realized that maybe Ember didn't have anyone to turn to for advice on dealing with the fair folk like Chloe.

"Sorry," Griffin stated apologetically. "You should be careful I mean. Draw on your fox cleverness not to trick others but to not allow yourself to be tricked. Chloe is fun but she and her kind can be tricky. And you did make a friend." Griffin held out his paw. "I live in the house over there. I'll see you around sometime."

Ember brightened up at that and waved his paw at Griffin as he ran off to his home.

The End

Read the original Griffin tale here on Wattpad.

https://www.wattpad.com/myworks/97689684-the-adventures-of-griffin-j-cat

Griffin also guest cameos in the wonderful world of Jason Greenfield's epic tale, Mythlands: The Heist.

https://www.wattpad.com/story/104770324-mythlands-the-heist

Griffin is an amazing animal. He runs around other worlds creating all kinds of hijinks and havoc and still manages to sleep 16 hours a day.

Cover by Susan K. Saltos.

Mother of Pearl

Anna Quin

One of the more fascinating aspects of human history is the similarity between myths in cultures all over the world. A common theme in many older stories is the description of what really lives in the dark depths of the ocean, beyond where any human could hope to survive.

In particular, I have always been fascinated with the idea of mermaids—half human and half sea creature—and what they represent. The best of both worlds is present in those magical beings, and they are often depicted as either a dream come true or a devious enemy. What follows is a story inspired by those tales.

***

"Captain Shadowfoot, we caught her!"

The net cut into her skin harshly, taut with the motion of being dragged upward. Through the waves, Calandra could make out the vague shape of a head peeking over the railing. Someone shouted and the tugging of the net became rhythmic, each one lifting her further out of the sea. While the water poured around her, her dark skin and gleaming tail caught the dim light. She wiggled in an attempt to return to the water that was her natural home, but the net proved to be well made. Above the water, she could hear the call of the sea birds and see the nearby island around which she had been hunting for dinner. The island was nice and isolated: the perfect place to get away from responsibility. Or—as it turned out—perfect for catching unsuspecting mermaids.

"Looks like we caught ourselves a mighty big fish, lads." The human's blue eyes danced with triumph as he took hold of the ropes and helped pull her up. With each pull of the rope Calandra thudded against the side of the ship, silently cursing every hit. By the time they were done hauling her onto the deck, she could feel the bruises beginning to blossom on her skin.

Agitation made her snarl, flashing her sharp teeth at the humans surrounding her, but they didn't seem bothered by her show of aggression. Their leader stepped even closer to her, leaning over to get a better look. "You're a feisty one, I'll give you that. But you're wasting your time and energy, mermaid." He reached out and trailed a finger over the edge of the net closest to her tail. She hissed at him. "Yes, yes. I know. You're not happy."

It was the smallest of understatements, and Calandra glared in response.

He laughed. "We've been hunting for mermaids a very long while now, so we're not amateurs any more. You're going to find that we are more than prepared to handle you. And if you help us get what we're really after, there's no reason we can't part on friendly terms. After all, I'm a reasonable man."

Calandra snorted at the human. Then she felt her body making the shift from breathing with her gills to using her lung in the open air. She bowed over and vomited seawater and fish bits all over his shoes. The crew started to laugh, but quit abruptly when the captain glanced at them. They shuffled their feet nervously and looked anywhere but at their captain.

The captai turned his attention back onto his prey. "Lovely," he muttered. Calandra's dark curls were plastered against her skin. Even though the rough net dug into her flesh painfully, and her heart was thumping wildly in her chest, she gave no outward sign of panic. She looked up at him and grinned.

Shadowfoot's instincts kicked in and he stepped back from her, his hand going to the hilt of his cutlass, as she opened her mouth.

All that came out of her was a strangled squeak. Calandra paled and lifted a hand to her throat, her fingers resting in the groove between her collarbones. She tried again, lifting her chin further and squaring her shoulders. The only reward for her efforts was another pitiful squeak.

Shadowfoot threw back his head and laughed so loudly that the rest of his crew was caught up in it involuntarily. He wiped the tears from his eyes and exhaled deeply. "You won't be able to sing your siren song, mermaid." He nudged the netting with his leather boot. "This stuff's woven with magic to stop you from enchanting us."

Calandra's shoulders slumped. She lifted her hands against the netting once more, but the tightly woven fishing line was more secure than iron chains. She looked up at the captain and wondered what in the ocean he could want with a mermaid who couldn't sing.

Shadowfoot nodded, looking pleased with himself. "Alright then. Let's get down to business, shall we?" He dropped to one knee beside her. At the mention of business, his first mate yelled at the men to get back to their stations.

"I know you have a stash of jewels far more precious than any old ruby or sapphire." Shadowfoot maintained eye contact with Calandra, his eyes intense in their stare. "I need to get my hands on them."

She lifted her shoulders and shrugged. Shadowfoot watched her innocent display of confusion with apparent frustration. He leaned forward, close enough to whisper to her and still be heard over the sounds of his men.

"In case there is some misguided hope in your mind that you can get out of this by trickery, I know you can survive indefinitely out of the water. And I know such survival would be uncomfortable for you." His eyes narrowed. "I also want you to know that if I don't get my hands on those vitae jewels, I have no problem with selling you to the highest bidder at the nearest port."

Calandra only stared back at him. She smiled despite the fear bubbling up inside of her. It was startling for her to hear the words 'vitae jewel' come from the mouth of a human. Her people did indeed have 'vitae gems', but they were sacred and not something for humans. She would die before she let him know that they were anything more than a myth whispered between drunken sailors in dark pubs.

"You'll change your attitude soon enough, fish." Shadowfoot snarled. He stood up and grabbed the edges of her net. The captain dragged her roughly over the deck towards the main mast. He turned her around and propped her up into a sitting position. Within a few minutes, he had tied her tightly against the mast, netting and all.

"You're not going anywhere until I get those jewels." Shadowfoot growled. "And the sooner you give in, the sooner your suffering will end." With that, he stomped away to his cabin, barking orders at his men to keep a watch on the fish.

Calandra wiggled a little at first, but when the rope didn't budge, she concentrated on taking in her surroundings. In her two hundred and thirty years of life, she had seen many different kinds of ships. Most of those ships had been sighted from a distance because the Undine clan of mermaids harbored a great mistrust of humans. That mistrust seemed well earned, given her current predicament. This ship had the usual armaments--cannons and blades and pistols were everywhere--but it also had some unusual aspects. She spotted runes dancing along the railing, and she recognized Atlantean symbols for warding against storms and malevolent spirits. Each of the men around her also wore a talisman that had the marks of Sylph craftsmanship. Calandra wondered how the men had come across them. She had never known a Sylph to willingly give such a thing to anyone.

She was jerked back into the moment by the lurching of the ship. Beneath her, the hull creaked and groaned in protest. Above her head, the sails billowed under a dark, rumbling sky. Calandra sighed. If she hadn't been so intent on hunting dinner, she might have noticed the trap the sailors had lain for her.

Calandra concentrated on the task at hand. No sense in dwelling on the past when an uncertain future lay in front of her. The crew was small, she thought, maybe twelve men plus the captain. If she could sing, she could have escaped them much more easily.

Calandra sniffed the air and the electric smell of the oncoming storm greeted her. Panic made her fingers turn icy. Kaleo was still in the ocean, waiting for her. She imagined him coming to look for her rather than staying in the safety of the sea cave they had found. Her heart began to beat faster. If the squall picked up, the tides surrounding the island would become rife with danger. Even merfolk could be caught up in the power of a riptide if they weren't careful. Lightning flashed in the sky, punctuating her sense of urgency. As she fought against the net in the hopes she would somehow gain freedom, a beautiful bass voice filled the air. It was like she had summoned him by thinking of him.

"We're going away to leave you now. Good bye, fare thee well."

The voice rose into the air and washed over the ship. The sailors shouted out a warning to one another, but they had no defense against the unexpected song. With the low hum of the melody came the spark of magic across the bowsprit of the ship. All of the humans nearest it backed hurriedly away as the blue flames spread over the deck, gouging the wood. The magic snapped rigging and shrouds, crippling the ship.

"Good bye, fare thee well."

One unlucky sailor wasn't quick enough to escape, and he fell under the music. He screamed in pain as his clothing was torn and his flesh cut. Calandra watched the magic come closer and begin to rip apart the netting without harming her tail. Kaleo's smooth voice came to her on the wind.

"Ah, give me the girl with the bonny brown hair. Your hair of brown is the talk of the town."

The crew retreated farther, until their backs were pressed against the wall of the captain's cabin. Calandra broke free of the net. She pushed herself forward and crawled over the wood, ignoring the magic that was still wreaking havoc on the ship and terrorizing the crew. She managed to lift herself up to see over the railing, and spotted her dark haired husband singing in the water. His eyes lit up when he spotted her and he held out his arms for her to jump.

"We're going away to leave you now."

Calandra jumped, but was jerked roughly backwards. She screamed. The mermaid twisted around and met Shadowfoot's stony gaze. Kaleo's magic sparked over his skin, cutting into him, but he held tight to her waist.

"You won't get away so easily!" he shouted over the song. Blood dripped over his face and arms. "I need a vitae jewel, and you're going to give one to me."

Calandra pushed at his chest, her claws cutting through his shirt. The captain struggled to keep his hold on her. His eyes were bright with determination and his jaw was set. "You're not going anywhere until I get one!"

Overhead, the storm unleashed rain, soaking them both instantly. Lightning crashed. The sails filled with sudden wind, groaning against the newly weakened rigging. Ropes began to snap off, leaving the mainsail fluttering wildly.

Calandra glanced desperately back at the ocean. "Let go of me!" She lifted her tail and wedged it between them. With all the strength she had left in her, she shoved against his chest and broke free, tumbling to the water with a splash. Instantly, the song stopped. Kaleo rushed forward to wrap his wife in his arms.

Shadowfoot cursed with the loss of his treasure, but his voice, unbuoyed by magic, was lost to the wind.

Calandra fell into Kaleo's arms, her body trembling with terror. Kaleo held her tight against him, his tail twining around hers. He buried his face in her hair. "Cal." He breathed her name like it was a prayer. A tear fell down Calandra's cheek, solidifying along the way until it was a glimmering, tear-shaped pearl that floated towards the ocean bed.

In the moment of reunion, neither of them noticed the tides already shifting, rushing away from the island. As the water swelled with power under the strength of the storm, the inlet of the island became a funnel of deadly force that churned with malevolence and swept up anything in its path. While the ship rocked with growing violence beside them, the merfolk dove deeper into the water together, holding hands while they went.

"Why did those humans try to take you, Cal?" Kaleo asked, squeezing her hand.

She shook her head. "I don't want to talk about it, Leo. We need to get out of here and fast."

He frowned, but let it go for the moment, because it was growing harder to swim. The water lit up with flashes of lightning as the storm began to rage overhead.

Suddenly, Calandra's fingers were ripped from his. Kaleo cried out and turned to chase his wife, who was caught up in a rip current, helpless against the power of the sea. His heart pounded hard in his chest--it felt like it was punching his ribs. Around him, the ocean was in chaotic flux, twisting in on itself and dragging at his tail. His arms strained against the tide that had grabbed him and forced him apart from his wife.

Calandra's pale blue tail was glittering in the water, only a short distance from his reach, taunting him. Waves swelled up in the water, tossing the merfolk around like they were nothing but driftwood. Kaleo tried to sing, but his song was nothing compared to the roar of the ocean.

As they struggled towards one another, a new wave rose from the depths, scooping up his wife as it arched into the flashing sky — a towering giant of nature's wrath. Lightning flickered overhead. Kaleo screamed, helpless to get to her. She reached for him, shouting something that was lost in the wind. The wave curled in on itself and dove for the rocks of the nearby island.

Calandra shattered against the reef, breaking like she was made of glass. Kaleo screamed and surged forward, but the ocean roared back and shoved him even farther away. He struggled until his arms were on fire and his breathing was labored. The waves picked him up and carried him away into the darkness, spinning him around until he could not tell which direction was up.

It was dawn when the storm broke, and Kaleo was finally able to swim. He dove deeper into the water and searched for his beloved, hope still shining in his haggard face.

"Calandra!" His voice was hoarse, barely a whisper of a croak, but it carried in the now still water. "Calandra! Cal!"

The merman swam along the ground, his tail stirring up the sand when it brushed against the ocean floor. "Can you hear me? Please, say something!"

A glimmer of blue scales caught his eye and he changed direction, swimming toward that glimpse of hope with renewed determination. As he approached the sandbar, she came into view slowly.

Calandra's torso was covered in black and blue splotches that bloomed like flowers over her beautiful brown skin. Jagged cuts covered her from neck to tail, evidence that the rocks of the nearby island had ravaged her during the storm. Kaleo paused, floating above her.

Finally, he looked into her eyes. They stared out into the ocean, seeing nothing.

His hands trembled as he reached out and touched her cheek. "Cal?" She didn't move. His fingers trailed up and into her dark hair. "Aren't you going to tell me I'm late?"

His voice broke and his breathing stuttered. "Please, say something for me."

Kaleo slid his other hand under her back, gently lifting her up. Her arms floated in the water. He held her close. "I know you're hurting, Cal. Don't worry." His breathing grew erratic. "I can fix you. Just like I fixed your harp. Remember Cal?"

Kaleo opened his mouth to sing, but his throat was closed tight with heat and tears. He tried again, and forced his voice past the lump in his throat until he could sing.

Around them, his magic lit up the water, summoned by his song. It flowed over her body, mending her broken bones and repairing her ripped skin, but it couldn't fix her bruises. Nothing could fix her death. Kaleo sang until his choked sobs overcame him.

"Cal." He whimpered and lifted her head until he could press his forehead to hers. "You can't leave me."

A sob racked through his body. "I love you." Each tear that slid down his cheeks became a shining pearl and floated down to rest in the sand.

Kaleo lay on the ocean bed, holding the body of his wife until they were surrounded by a cradle of pearls and he had no more tears to give. Merciful sleep took him then, and he slept until the water darkened and the moon rose. When he woke, his first thoughts were about what came next.

Tradition dictated that he perform the song that would turn her body into a vitae gem — the gem that would be his reminder of Calandra for the rest of his life. The last thing Kaleo wanted to do was sing such a song, but Calandra was cold in his arms now. If she were able to speak, she would scold him for taking so long to get home.

He moved into a seated position, still holding her in his lap, and he sang once more for her. As the magic wrapped around her, she began to dissolve into foam, starting with her fingers and the tip of her tail. The foam ate away at her and freed her body to join the waves that lapped so calmly overhead. The last part of her to vanish was her face, looking serene in death.

Finally, all that was left of her was a pearl that shone even in the darkness of the night cycle. Kaleo reached out and took the pearl, cradling it to his chest. He hunched over it and breathed deeply. When he was ready, he pushed his tail against the sand and lifted into the water to begin the swim home.

It took Kaleo five passes of the day cycle to get home to the edges of the Undine city of Anthemusa. His small coral dwelling was on the outskirts of the city. The closer he got to home, the heavier his body became, and the tighter his grip on the pearl grew.

When he opened the door, the bio-luminescent lights washed over him with green and blue light. Kaleo stiffened, gripping the pearl so tightly that his fingers went white, but nothing stirred in the house.

Entering slowly, he glanced around the door to find that the thing he was so worried about was sleeping soundly, tucked into her alcove.

Kaleo exhaled and his shoulders slumped. He closed the door behind him with a gentle nudge of his tail and moved over to the far side of the small coral home. Settling beside her bed, he laid a gentle hand on her gleaming white hair. Even in her sleep, she smiled at the touch. Carefully, he placed the pearl in the nest of her hair and rested his cheek on the edge of her pillow to watch her sleep until his own exhaustion overcame him.

When he woke, Pearl was giggling and she poked his nose. "Daddy, are you awake?"

For a moment, the entire world was her laughter and the warmth of her finger. "No, sweetfish. I'm still asleep." He cracked open an eye and smiled. "Daddy needs a kiss from a princess to wake him up."

Pearl's tiny, round face scrunched up while she thought hard about what he said.

"Momo says I am not a princess." She lifted her hands to her hair and began to twist the ends of her curly locks. "She says I'm a queen!"

Kaleo laughed and sat up enough to scoop his daughter against him and bury his face in her shimmering hair. "Lucky for me, a kiss from a queen will also wake me."

Pearl pulled back to eye him, all the world's skepticism on her face while she processed this news. "You look awfully awake to me, Daddy." She patted his cheek, making him close his eyes for fear her tiny claws would poke one of them by accident.

Kaleo huffed at the logic of his little minnow. What was he supposed to say to that? He sighed and nuzzled her head with his cheek. "Can I have a kiss anyway, sweetfish?"

Despite all her misgivings, Pearl smiled at him, widely enough to show that the wiggly tooth she'd had before he'd left had fallen out. His daughter leaned forward and kissed his cheek, giggling all the while.

Kaleo sat back on his tail to return her smile, but a glint of light caught his attention. There it was, sitting innocuously on Pearl's pillow; Calandra's vitae gem glittered with light that came from within. Even though the gem was beautiful to look at, it seemed to Kaleo that the light was menacing him, throwing the room into shadow that made his heart beat quicker with dread. All of the memories of his trip with Calandra came crashing back into his mind and the roar of the waves filled his ears.

157

He shivered and Pearl piped up, a beacon in the storm of his memories. "Daddy? You okay?"

Kaleo focused on her and the task ahead of him. "Pearl, I need to tell you something." His hands settled in his lap with his fingers interlocked.

Pearl looked up to him: even seated on the floor, he was taller than she was on her bed. Her eyes were intent on his face and her eyebrows drew down at the sudden shift in mood.

Kaleo took a deep breath to steel himself against this impossible task. "There was a storm while Mommy and I were on our trip." Kaleo thought he would be able to say everything after all. "It was a very bad storm, Pearl, and Calandra...Calandra..." He glanced at the pearl on his daughter's pillow and felt his throat begin to grow tight. If he didn't manage this now, it would never be said. "Your mother died."

The tears came hotly into his eyes and he bit his lip, using the short burst of pain to hold them back for the moment. "I'm sorry, sweetfish." His hands tightened their grip on each other. Kaleo waited with quiet foreboding for his daughter's tears. Pearl simply tilted her head and looked at him in confusion.

"Okay." She reached up and began to twist the ends of her hair once more. "But when is Mommy coming home?"

Kaleo's chest twinged painfully. He took another deliberate breath, focusing on his chest rising and falling before he could respond. "She's not, Pearl. Mommy is gone." He lifted a trembling hand and picked up the vitae gem, holding it out to his daughter. "This is all that is left of Calandra."

Her vitae gem cast a soft glow over Pearl's face, the remnants of a mother's love for her daughter.

The End

Link:

https://www.wattpad.com/user/AnnaQuin07

Cover by Hilary Simonson.

Prisoner's Dream

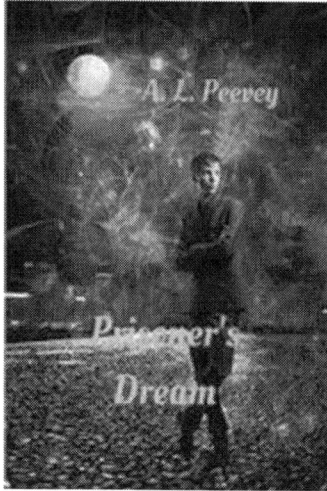

A. L. Peevey

In a tower at the edge of a nameless city, Zil awaits execution, a symbolic expiation for the crimes of his fellow citizens. Then one day a visitor brings him a gift that allows him to escape his cell, if only briefly, through the dreams of others. "Prisoner's Dream" is a chapter from the forthcoming novel, *A Spellbook of Dreams*.

***

The morning sun frowned behind the clinging clouds, or so it seemed to the arch-criminal, Zil. He knelt on the window seat, relishing the bite of its cold stone through his trousers but frowning at the darkening bruise on his arm. The guards proved harsh when he had sung 'The Ballad of Charming Luz' for two hours. He had misbehaved, he admitted, though it left him a little puzzled that his singing could arouse such ire. He figured the guards slept far below his cell, located as it was beneath the very pinnacle of the tower.

He brought fruit and bread from a cupboard, ate a dull breakfast, washed down with a mug of sour cider. He then took his spyglass to the east window and watched the exhibition at the gallows. With their pikes, maiden soldiers prodded a condemned prisoner to the trapdoor of the gallows. A crowd stood watching and shouting invective while a holy man pronounced a benediction on the head of the kneeling prisoner. The shouts of the crowd rose to an exultant roar as the prisoner arose with a noose affixed around his neck before falling unceremoniously through the trapdoor.

As one, the crowd, the soldiers, and the holy man all looked up at Zil, outlined as he was in the window high above them. They raised their arms in salute and loosed a loud cheer. He waved at them while watching the soldiers draw the corpse up through the trapdoor. Supported by the soldiers, the corpse now stood and saluted him in turn.

How do they always make it look so cursed real? wondered Zil, for the hundredth time. Most mornings, at the ninth hour, he was put to death in effigy for crimes against the republic, crimes unknown to him. *Someday they'll come for me, and I'll truly fall to my end.*

Shrugging, he turned away from the window and went to stand on the circle in the middle of the cell. The spot marked where the elevator rose, and he believed he was due visitors that day. He was a celebrity, after all. Young women often came to fawn over him, properly chaperoned of course. A few never failed to whisper some scheme in his ear about helping him escape to some far country. He always smiled at them, nodding his head but knew nothing could come of such wild imaginings. His imprisonment and future execution, while largely symbolic, served a purpose, and the government would never let him be spirited away so easily when justice must be served.

***

Several weeks had blurred together in his mind when he finally admitted to himself he was bored. Young though he was, still a few years short of twenty, he did not relish the thought of many more such monotonous years. He wondered if death might just be more desirable than living much of his days in solitude.

***

How she did it, Zil was not sure, but his visitor that day had secreted a book in her dress. She arrived with no chaperone, a fact that made Zil a little uncomfortable. Her pale green dress matched strikingly with her auburn hair, and though he had never seen her before, he liked her immediately.

"I am Katrine. I'm pleased to finally meet you, Zil," she said, clasping his hand. "Your mother sends her regards."

"You know my mother?"

"Yes, she sent you a gift."

Zil stared at her for a moment, not knowing what to say.

"You must look away, Zil, for I had to hide the gift in an immodest place."

Zil turned to stare out the north window. Beyond the city stood a vast parkland filled with war memorials. He wondered why there was so much history he could not remember learning.

"Here, Zil. Please accept this gift!"

He turned around to take from her hand a rectangular shape wrapped in a scarf of the same cloth as Katrine's dress. He pulled the scarf away to reveal a book bound in blue leather, embossed with silver letters revealing its title: *A Spellbook of Dreams*. There were many books in his tower room, but none as beautiful as the tome he held. He tried to hand the scarf back to her, but she only smiled a sly smile.

"Keep it, Zil, to remember me by."

"Thank you," was all he could manage, though he wondered why she thought he could ever forget her.

"Open it, and let me tell you about its wonders."

She left an hour later, promising to return when she could. He felt wistful then, a yearning to leave the tower. With Katrine? *Maybe.* He had never really thought of leaving before. He knew he had been born and had grown up in the city outside the tower, but his memories were foggy, unreliable. And he could not remember his mother's face.

***

He napped for several hours after Katrine left. She had explained the purpose of the book, but he did not quite believe what she had told him: by reading the tales contained within its covers he could somehow go beyond the curved walls of the tower and walk in others' dreams, live their stories, if only for a while.

When he awakened the next morning, feverish and unrested, he peered down into the square, watching the morning ritual of his proxy's hanging, but he turned away before it ended. Its attraction was gone, and he wondered how he could have ever found such a morbid spectacle entertaining. A parody of his own execution!

He ate a late breakfast of ham, boiled eggs, and biscuits with apricot jam, brought to him by Katrine. His mother had prepared the food for him, or so Katrine said. He finished eating, smacking his lips and wiping off his hands with a kerchief, before setting the new book on the standing desk near the west window. There the light shone brightly enough for reading but was not likely to get too warm.

He tried to leaf through the pages, but they seemed stuck together, so he only managed to turn one page at a time. Beautifully painted pictures caught his eye. They portrayed mostly incomprehensible or even disturbing scenes. He reached the first page of a story entitled, "The Escape" and started reading it. He only had time to sit on the edge of his bed before falling back to sleep.

II: Escaping

Piteous moans awakened Zil in darkness much different from night time in his tower room. He lay in the cramped corner of a cell on a sparse pile of stinking straw. His ragged clothing was damp. He sat up slowly but still managed to scrape his elbow on the rough stone wall.

"Water, I beg of you! Water!" echoed a cry from the dank, impersonal walls. Zil wondered if every prison dream contained someone pleading for water. His own throat felt a bit dry, but he could not claim to be parched, yet. Surrounded by dampness yet to suffer thirst still seemed a paradox. He shook his head and hit it against the ceiling when he tried to stand erect. Stars swirled around him in the darkness as he sank to his knees, rubbing the top of his head, relieved when he felt no blood.

The plea for water came at unmarked intervals as Zil crawled to the grate that must be the exit from his cell. The closeness of the walls gnawed at him. *I am trapped in the maw of some awful beast that refuses to chew up and swallow me!* He pushed the intense thought away, feeling his sanity forfeit if he did not.

Reaching the grate, he kept to his hands and knees, not wishing to hit his head again on the low roof. The corridor beyond the grate lay scarcely lit, the preserve of shadows.

"Water!" came the request from one of the other cells he could not quite see from his position.

"Water!" he called, taking up the plea and hoping that whomever was dying of thirst would be succored soon. He only wanted to see who might come to assuage their thirst. Time passed, how much could not be ascertained with the lack of true sunlight.

A dragging scrape echoed from up the corridor, the slow approach of someone, purposeful or otherwise, Zil could not say. He caught a glimpse of a lurching form pushing a sloshing bucket.

"Here now!" commanded a boyish voice. "Don't carry on so. I've brought you water."

Dim light shone on a battered ladle pushed through the narrow opening of a grate several cells over. The thirsty sucking of water echoed from the walls.

"Please, more!" came the request, and whomever had brought the water acquiesced. When the thirsty prisoner had taken his fill, the water bringer moved closer. No one responded at the grate next door, so the water bringer arrived at Zil's grate. He took a healthy swig from the ladle, worried it might not be available when he really needed it. He took notice of the water bringer: a youth who seemed a year or two younger than Zil and who could not stand on his own two feet because his legs were short and crooked.

"I've left my crutches near the door. It's easier for me to drag the water bucket that way."

"So, you can come and go from the prison as you wish?" asked Zil.

"No, I'm a prisoner here, too. I am Keat, by the way."

"I'm Zil. What is this place? Why are we here?"

"You don't remember what you did?"

"No, I don't. I...I hit my head on the ceiling of my cell."

"Does it need a dressing or maybe a poultice?"

"Thank you, no. I'll just need some help remembering where I am and why I'm here."

"I'll look it up in the registry."

***

"You've been jailed here for common thievery, Zil," said Keat. "Is that an outlander name?"

"Possibly. I can't recall. Remember I hit my head."

"Truly, Zil, you may not be guilty of anything. Many are here because the government is paranoid. There are periodic roundups of common folk whose only crime is being present in a particular district when the gathering agents come."

"Why are people herded together and locked up?"

"The constant fear of assassination and rebellion. The current regime is quite unpopular."

"Why were you put here, Keat?"

"I was judged a burden to society."

"Had you no family to vouch for you?"

"None stepped forward. I only remember growing up on the streets of Wilgus. A witch looked after me, now and then. She gave me black bread and set me to begging for coin in the market place."

"She wouldn't put in a word for you?"

"A witch standing as a witness in the governor's court? Never. Those possessed of magical ability were the first to be arrested. They weren't put in prison, though."

"Exile? Is that what became of your benefactress then?"

"Her name is Marajan. Likely, she is dead. All the witches to be found were put to death at mass executions."

"I'm sorry."

"Ay. Let's talk of other things."

***

Days wove into a strand of weeks, each etched with a bit of metal in the damp wall opposite the grate by Zil, until he had been in the cell for a month. Only daily conversations, often with Keat and whispered through the shadows, kept his despair at bay. No guards paced the corridor nor even so much as showed themselves.

"Where are they, Keat? Do you ever see them?"

"The guards remain outside in the fresh air and pure light of day, Zil. They find it confining and fetid in this dark warren of cells."

"They're certainly not concerned about our sensibilities."

"No, truly they are not."

"And the captain of the guard, who must exist, doesn't mind that our well-being is neglected?"

"Much of the care of the prisoners is left to me and old Sylla, a former prisoner and now the cook. She's becoming more and more halt, though, and is quite addled. I sadly doubt she'll last another month."

***

More weeks passed while Zil gradually forgot he was in a dream. He began to feel stiff in his joints, the lack of movement taking its toll. He awakened in the watered-down, milky light of morning, feverish and sweating and struggling as if drowning. Keat bent over him, wiping his brow with a damp cloth. He usually tended to the sick among the prisoners, lame though he was.

"Lie quiet, Zil. You've got the dark fever. That's what we call it. Nearly everyone here's had it. We blame it on the lack of real sunlight."

Zil stopped fighting and lay still under Keat's ministrations. Presently, he fell asleep again, awakening later, alone but feeling somewhat better. An odd murmur seeped through the bars of the small square of a window above him and minute tremors agitated the floor. He heard the restlessness of the other prisoners and called to them, but either they could not hear him or ignored him. He waited for Keat to make his rounds but grew impatient. His friend was late in coming.

The murmuring grew to a distinct chorus of shouts punctuated by what could only be cannon fire, though he had never experienced it. He fretted, a sense of hopelessness and helplessness settling over him as the concussion of explosions drew nearer and the shouting turned to screaming. He jabbed his fingertips into his ears, shutting the clamor out, but the tremoring floor could not be calmed. Keat's face at last appeared at the grate, so he unplugged his ears.

"Zil? Are you well?"

"Better now, but what's happening out there?"

"Rebellion has risen in the city, and the governor is trying to bring peace by force."

"Are we safe?"

"As safe as anyone in the midst of madness. Ayb may yet fall to the rebels."

"Ayb?"

"Haven't I called the city by its name before?"

"I thought the city's name was Wilgus."

"No, I was brought by the witch, Marajan, from Wilgus to Ayb, the capital city."

"I'd forgotten where we are."

Keat peered at him in wonder.

"You truly are a stranger here, aren't you? The son of another land pent in this dreary place for no more than being a foreigner."

"Perhaps, Keat. I really don't remember anything before

awakening in this cell."

"If the fighting gets closer, I'm going to try to bribe the guards to set us free."

"What of Sylla? Can we take her with us?"

"She sits on her stool by the kitchen hearth lost in conversations with those who walk this land no more. She won't last the night."

***

Keat brought gruel and battered apples for everyone to eat. How he had managed to boil the gruel Zil did not ask. The tumult outside died away with the fading of the scant daylight. Zil knew he could not stay pent. He considered the rusty bit of metal he used to mark the days in the wall. If it were rubbed against the stone floor, Zil felt sure he could sharpen it to a point to pierce a vein in his arm. All prisoners dreamed of escape. The metal fragment was the only key he had to freedom.

Keat appeared at his grate again, as if he knew the depth of Zil's despair.

"The fighting will break out again tomorrow, Zil. If the guards aren't called away, I'll distract them somehow. I can open the grates."

"You can? Why don't you open them now, and let us get away while it's dark?"

"I have some preparations to make, and I don't want to fail you."

"What if we're caught, Keat?"

"They won't bother to bring us back here."

"Would they suddenly become solicitous about shortening our imprisonment then?"

"No, they'll simply claim we struggled too much, leaving them no choice but to shoot us."

***

A menacing mutter of distressed voices awakened Zil, who had slept but little. Cannon fire boomed again, sporadic at first, then crashing without ceasing. Some of the prisoners whimpered as the rounds fell closer, shaking the prison walls. Zil, his mouth set in a grim line, flinched with each shudder of his cell. He wondered if they would be buried beneath rubble or smashed to pieces if they ever got outside.

With nerveless fingers, he clenched the narrow bars of the grate and hunched down, determined to wait for Keat. He remembered no deity, yet he prayed, sobbing for release, either by crushing walls or by what awaited them if they reached the open air. He sank into a torpor, flinching with each explosion yet unaware until an anxious voice brought him back.

"Zil! Are you hurt?"

"No," he muttered. "Can we get out?"

"Yes. The others are already gone."

Zil stared at Keat, feeling anger that melted away almost as soon as it surged inside him.

"Let me out then." His voice rumbled, hoarse and strange.

"Just push against the grate, Zil."

Zil gathered his weakness into strength and shoved hard against the bars, nearly falling head long into the corridor when the grate gave outward with ease.

"Were we ever locked in, Keat?" Anger kindled in him again, heating his words.

"Yes, you all were, but only by unconscious respect for the laws of Ayb."

Zil nodded his head, though he was not sure what Keat meant, and scrambled past him, heading for the stone steps he spied at the end of the corridor. They climbed to sunlight, foggy with stone dust and cannon fumes.

"Wait, Zil! I need your help."

He turned back and saw Keat struggling with a contraption of straps, which proved to be a harness.

"Where are your crutches?"

"They were taken from me when I first arrived. They'd not do me much good now anyway. I'd never be able to escape alone."

Zil picked the harness up and fastened it to his shoulders before kneeling to let Keat crawl onto his back. He pushed the lame youth's feet into the two pockets on the harness and struggled to his own feet. He half-expected his rider to nudge him in the ribs and say, "Giddy-up!" He climbed the steps leading out of the prison, eyes blinded by the sunlight.

"Which way should we go, Keat?"

"Follow the path paved with blue stones. It leads through the five groves—many steps up and up, I'm afraid—but finally to the river."

"Will we have to swim?"

"You will. I can't."

"We'll figure out a way to get you across, Keat. I promise."

"We don't have time to discuss the particulars, Zil. Save your breath, and hurry along as quickly as you can!"

The blue path led them out of the courtyard and through a high-walled, narrow walkway, and up a steep staircase. At the top, Zil paused to catch his breath but told Keat to stay on his back. Echoes of the chaos erupting in the city behind them stirred up a sense of urgency in the pit of Zil's stomach, so they hurried on.

They entered the tranquil shade beneath the sweet pear trees of the first grove. The stones of the path they now trod shone the green of ripe pears. Zil wished they could have lingered there and rested for a while. He really felt like a nap, but Keat would not hear of it. He handed Zil a flask of sweet cider.

"Drink some," he said then half-whispered as if to himself, "I can't believe the hounds have left us alone so far."

"Didn't the guards go into the city to help the governor keep his power?"

"Probably, but the hounds are trained to keep watch, and if they sense any prisoners have escaped, they'll sniff them out to kill them."

A shiver went up Zil's back. He caught his breath again then hurried on through the first grove and entered the second one. He ignored the quiet, cool shadows, stifling the urge to leave the path and wander under the sheltering boughs.

On and on he carried Keat, through the third and fourth groves. His legs shook from weariness, but he only stopped at Keat's urging in the middle of the fifth grove.

"Rest, but just for a moment, Zil. The hounds are swift. I think I can hear them now."

Zil heard nothing, but the thought of ripping fangs and claws shoved him forward. They soon reached the bottom of the steps.

"There's no time for rest, dear Zil! Up the first set of stairs we go!"

Zil staggered up, setting the compass of his mind to getting to the top. His momentum took them there and beyond to the top of the next set of steps. The braying of the hounds rang out behind them.

"Can they see us?" gasped Zil.

"No, they are blind, but their noses smell us more clearly than sight!"

Zil felt spreading warmth down his back but, believing it was his own sweat, he climbed on. Keat sighed and moved as if he were trying to settle himself more comfortably in the harness.

"Sorry about my sweating, Keat."

"No need to worry, my friend. At the top of the last stairway, you can put me down."

Zil allowed himself a little puzzlement at Keat's remark but climbed on. He tried to mark each step, only he soon lost count as he kept his aching feet plunging up and down. The hounds' belling rang out as if the beasts were now climbing just behind them. Zil almost fell, caught himself, and felt Keat patting him on the shoulder.

"Steady, Zil. We're almost there. Then, you can rest."

Zil's feet thrust them forward, he and Keat, his knees pistoning them upward. His lungs burned, his gorge rising as they reached the final step and beyond. He sagged to his knees, slapping his hands against the cracked flagstones beginning a new path. His shirt stuck fast to his back in an odd way.

Keat used his hands to pull his nerveless legs from their stirrups. He rolled onto his back next to Zil, who noticed the red blotching his companion's shirt and pants.

"You're bleeding!" His eyes fell on the pulsing gashes in Keat's stunted legs. "What have you done?"

"Remember, Zil? I can't swim. The hounds'll have me at any rate but not you..." Keat's words trailed away to silence as he managed a lop-sided smile, his eye lids fluttering then closing, though Zil could still see the slow rise and fall of his chest.

He spied the hounds at the bottom of the first set of steps, slavering and panting as they charged up toward them.

"Farewell, Zil," murmured Keat before he never moved again.

Zil's eyes clouded with tears. It was not a choice he would have willingly made, leaving his friend behind.

***

Zil staggered to the river's edge, heard the roar of the water falling to distant stone. The hounds, having done with Keat—Zil raged at the thought—brayed behind him, still sniffing him out.

The hounds won't have me, Keat. You've seen to that.

He ran three steps and jumped into the river. The furious water shut around him, taking him for its own, shoving him toward the falls.

I lied, Keat. I've never been swimming in my life.

***

Drenched in sweat, Zil awakened in his bed in the tower room. He arose, went to the east window, and pushed back the shutters. The dawn wind usually chilled him to the bone; that morning he welcomed its brisk, strident grip. He wanted the dream purged from his memory, his unbidden tears tingling as if they were pearls of ice on his face.

The End

A.L. Peevey's published works are available in e-book format and paperback on Amazon at the following link:
https://www.amazon.com/A.L.Peevey/e/B0084XO8QC/ref=ntt_ath r_dp_pel_1

Cover by Author.

Girl on Fire

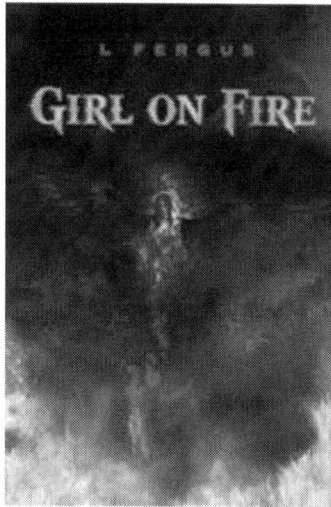

L. Fergus

War ravages The Mass. The superior Red Legion is bent on complete conquest and genetic purity. The Arconians, a nation of warriors, led by Kita and the Angels are fighting back. It's a fight of evil versus evil. A rescue mission at the Red Legion headquarters compound becomes a mission of revenge when the Angels find their employers, three children, dead. During the mission, the battle hardened Angel Sarin shoots a baby. Unable to cope with what's she's done, she tosses her guns aside and flees. Now she wanders The Mass trying to forget who she is and what she's done.

***

"How was that, Miss Sadira?"

Sadira opened an eye, and two of Bean materialized wearing her favorite faded buttercup yellow dress. She sat up, peeling her cheek off the sticky bar top. Opening her other eye, a third Bean appeared. Sadira did her best to smile, her mind felt like mush.

171

"That was...really good, Bean. Keep practicing, and you'll be a...ah...Beethoven."

"What's that?"

"He was a famous...pianist...from where I come from. You just keep practicing."

"I will. I promise."

A well-dressed man with a broad smile walked up the bar and stood before Sadira. She kept from wrinkling her nose over the smell of cheap cologne.

"You must be Miss Sadira. I am Kerk De Jager. The stories don't do you justice. I must say you're even more beautiful in person."

Sadira watched as three of him floated in front of her. *At least he isn't ugly.* Her mind turned to a preprogrammed persona. "Why thank you, kind sir," she said flashing a winning smile that promised more. "But compliments are free. If you want to get to know me, talk to Peet, the barkeeper."

"I'll do just that. Don't go anywhere."

"I'll wait right here." Sadira's smile changed to an eye roll as the man turned and went to haggle with Peet. She looked back at Bean. "I've got to go to work."

Bean sighed. "Yeah. I have tables to clear."

"Keep practicing, sweetie. You're doing...great."

"Thanks," Bean said with a warm smile. "I'm glad you appreciate me."

"Peet...loves you."

"I know, but I don't want to work in a bar my whole life."

"Practice the piano and you won't." Peet set a bottle and a small twisted piece of paper in front of her. *Big shot spender. Good.* "Now, go along. We've both got work to do."

Bean nodded and went to a table full of used steins. She gathered them up in her arms and marched them into the back.

Sadira picked up the bottle and the piece of paper. Tonight would be a good night. The liquor and drugs would keep her nightmares at bay.

***

Sadira woke at the bar, her head swimming with a new nightmare of guns and men yelling. She didn't remember falling asleep at the bar, but it wouldn't be the first time she'd fallen asleep and woken up somewhere different.

The voices pierced her mental fog. The crash of a lightning bolt drowned everything out. *A morning thunderstorm? That's never a good sign.* The voices came from a knot of men standing at the doorway. The fog in her head made the voices unintelligible. She hiked up her skirt and pulled a small case from her garter. She opened it and selected a pill. Popping it into her mouth, she swallowed and waited for it to take effect.

The mental fog lifted and Sadira could think clearly again. The men were arguing over what to do. Sadira walked over and put a hand on Peet's shoulder.

"What happened?"

He turned and, Sadira being taller than the average male, looked up at her. "Not surprised you don't remember, you were blazed out of your mind. Slavers attacked last night. They took the children." He sighed heavily, "including Bean."

"What? No!" Sadira grabbed her head. "No. If I hadn't been...If...I could have...She can't be gone." Sadira sat down hard in a chair. She shook all over as a pit in her stomach grew. Her nightmare came back. Visions of a dead baby with a hole in its forehead danced in front of her eyes. Now, Bean's face joined it. Tears fell down Sadira's cheeks. She shook her head violently trying to get the images to go away. The harder she shook, the closer they came to her.

"NO! I won't let it happen," she screamed causing everyone in the room to stop and look at her.

Sadira jumped up from her chair. "Someone get me a shovel," she yelled.

Peet said, "What do—"

"Neptune's rings, get me a goddamn shovel. I won't let them take her," Sadira screamed, reaching hysterics.

Peet disappeared into the back of the bar and returned with a shovel. "What are—"

With inhuman strength, Sadira grabbed the shovel from his grasp. She shoved her way through the men and threw open the door and marched into the pouring rain.

Sadira walked to the edge of town to an old gnarled tree. As the rain soaked her, she dug at the tree's base until she hit a box. Lightning struck the tree as she lifted the box out of the hole.

***

Sadira kicked open the door to the bar. She carried her box and slammed it down on the bar, causing mud and water to splatter across the bar top. Brushing the hair plastered to her head out of her eyes, Sadira smashed the lock with her fist. She flipped open the latch and raised the box's lid.

Sadira pulled the plastic lining the box aside. She reached in and pulled out a large .50 caliber red and black pistol. Pulling the slide back, she squeezed the trigger making a loud click sound. From the box, she took out its twin and set the pair on the bar.

Next, she pulled out the lower receiver of her .67 caliber sniper rifle. After checking its functionality, she set it aside and pulled out the upper receiver with the barrel. She seated the two receivers and snapped the pins in place. Finally, she took out a scope from the box and mounted it on the rifle.

"What is this?" asked Peet.

"My former life," Sadira snarled as she inserted a pair of magazines into her pistols. She pulled the slides back in turn, and then released them, chambering a round in each with a menacing pair of metallic clicks. "I'm going to get her back."

"You'll never find her. The rain will have washed their tracks away."

"Which way did they go?" Sadira yelled past Peet to the other men.

They looked at her dumbfounded.

Sadira pointed a pistol at the ceiling and fired twice. "Where did they go or the next one will be in your heads."

"Calm down, Miss Sadira," said De Jager as he came down the stairs.

Sadira turned and aimed the pistol at him.

"I saw them from the window. The slavers left going south."

"Then that's where I'll go," said Sadira as she untied her corset.

She stripped, dumping her skirt, corset, and underwear in a pile. From her box, she took out a short black and red plaid pleated skirt. She shook out a sleeveless black button down shirt and red tie. After pulling on a set of red stockings, she slipped on a pair of knee-high black combat boots. A black choker went around her neck, and she strapped a black studded belt with ammo cases and a bullet maker on. A pair of combs with skulls and crossbones held back her hair. She strapped her holsters to her thighs and holstered her pistols. Lastly, she broke down the sniper rifle and put it on her back.

"Who are you?" said Peet.

Sadira scowled as her wings became visible and stretched across the room showing her black wings with red covert feathers. "I am Sarin. I will get Bean back...no matter who I have to kill."

***

Sarin spread her wings and took flight. She hadn't traveled far, having lost most of the day to the rain and then drying her feathers. The clouds still hung low, and she flew just above the treetops. The road leading south had been empty of travelers all day.

A trail wide enough for wagons led off toward the Vaal River. Sarin followed it to the bank and found a group of tents and a wagon with a cage on the back. *Bingo.*

A lone man walked around the camp. Sarin turned invisible and landed next to the wagon. Inside the wagon, a bucket full of waste sat in the near corner. She walked around the wagon dragging her hand on the bars, imagining the fear Bean must have felt. As she walked around the rear, her hand ran over the open lock. She pulled the door open. On a loose floorboard nail was a scrap of Bean's faded buttercup cloth dress. Sarin picked up the scrap and clutched it in her fist as if it where Bean.

A surge of hate and pain erupted inside Sarin. Whoever had done this would suffer. She may not be worth anything, but Bean was. Bean was the single star in her black expanse of space. She might not be willing to fight for herself, but Bean had shown her there was still something good and precious in the world. Sarin tucked the piece of cloth in her belt.

Sarin walked in front of the patrolling man. She turned visible, grabbed him by the throat, and pulled him to her. With her other hand, she drew a pistol and tapped the barrel on his forehead.

"Where is the girl?" Sarin snapped.

"What...girl?" the man choked out around Sarin's hand.

"The one you took last night from the town of Vryburg."

"I...don't...know." The man gasped for air.

"Then you're no good to me." Sarin cocked her pistol and pressed it against his forehead. "Maybe one of your friends likes his life more."

"No...I—"

The pistol went off with a *bang* blowing his head across the campsite. The sound alerted those in the tents. A few stuck their heads out to look. Sarin shot them as they appeared. A half naked man threw open a tent flap wielding a shotgun. Sarin turned, and they fired at the same time. Sarin's bullet hit the man between the eyes. She raised her arm to shield herself as the pellets struck her.

A crash and a tent being dragged down came from across the campsite. Ignoring the pellet wounds that would heal rapidly, Sarin glided to the far side of the collapsed tent and grabbed the man tangled in the tent's rigging.

"Going somewhere?" said Sarin with a wicked smile.

"I...ah—"

"Where is the girl you took last night?"

"Wha—"

Sarin pistol whipped him leaving a large gash along his cheekbone. She dragged him down to the banks of the swollen river. She slammed him down into the water and held his head under. The man thrashed, splashing Sarin. She lifted his head.

"Where is she?"

"It wasn't—"

Sarin dunked him under and held him. She counted to forty-five and lifted his head. The man coughed and sputtered while trying to take in air.

"The girl. What did you do to her?"

"There was no—"

Enraged, Sarin slammed his head underwater and held it for a sixty count. When she lifted the man out, he was barely moving.

"Where is she?" Sarin yelled.

The man waved his arms around as he gasped for breath. Sarin pulled a pistol and shot him in the hand. The man howled as he clutched his wounded limb.

"Maybe that will help you think," she snarled. "Where is she?"

The man whimpered as a response.

Sarin slammed him with the butt of her pistol turning the man's eye red and swollen.

"She's not here...she's not here..." he said as he sobbed.

"Where is she?"

"They...they took her this morning."

"Who took her? Where?"

"The boat. She...she was loaded on a raft and taken down the river."

"What did this raft look like?"

"I don't know. It was a raft."

Sarin moved to dunk him.

"Wait! It has a red flag with a white border."

176

"When?" Sarin yelled.

"I don't know. It was raining."

Sarin gnashed her teeth and thrust the man underwater. She kept him under until she had her fury under control. Yanking him out, coughing a sputtering, she threw him backward into the water. Lifting a large rock, she set it on the man's chest. The man struggled against the weight while trying to keep his head above water. Sarin climbed out of the river, squeezing the water from her floor-length hair.

"You can't leave me like this!" the man cried.

Sarin turned and sneered. "Can and will."

She spread her wings and took off following the river.

***

Sarin looked through her scope out across the river. Several rafts and barges followed the river's current. Her crosshairs settled on a raft with a red flag with a white border. She'd seen it an hour earlier as she scouted the river and had picked this spot, high on a bluff overlooking the river, to ambush it.

She checked the raft's cage. It was empty. *I'm too late. Where is Bean?* Someone on that raft has to know. She counted four men aboard. After observing them, she picked out the leader.

Sarin counted out the rounds she wanted, inserted them into her magazine, and loaded it into her rifle. Looking back through the scope, she thumbed the rangefinder, 1,787 yards. A short shot for her, but she was trying to hit a moving target that was bobbing up and down.

Sniping was what she was designed for. Cradling the rifle, her joints locked giving her a solid platform. Her heart and lungs stopped. The tip of her index finger pressed against the trigger, pulling it back with an even two pounds of pressure.

The firing of the rifle always startled her. In her scope, the head of one of the raft's crewman vanished in a pink puff. Sarin moved slightly, picking up the next man in her crosshairs, and fired before he had time to register what had happened to the first man. The second man's head disappeared. She moved her sight over the third man and fired. The top half of his head exploded upward as the body collapsed. She fired her last two incendiary rounds on either end of the raft setting it ablaze.

Sarin released her body and took a breath. She looked down at the raft. The lone survivor was trying to figure out what had happened. With practiced efficiency, Sarin broke down and stowed her rifle. She ran and jumped from the bluff. Tucking her wings in, she dove for the raft.

As the man bent down to fill a bucket, Sarin slammed down on the opposite side of the raft causing him to rise sharply. The man lost his balance and rolled across the raft. Sarin arrested his fall by placing her boot on his throat.

"*Kak! Wat die hel is jy?*"

"Do you speak Common?" growled Sarin. Afrikaans wasn't a language she was familiar with.

"*Ja.*"

"Good. I see you have a problem." Sarin drew a pistol and pointed it at his face. "Now you have two."

"Wha—what do you want?"

"I want the girl in the yellow dress that you transported."

"Look, I'm a professional...I'm just doing my job."

"Professional? Well, so am I."

"Then you understand I can't tell where we took her."

"Then you'll understand when I shoot your fingers off one by one." Sarin grabbed him by the shirt. She dragged him to a pile of burning cargo and set him down on a box. The man flinched as a box near his head snapped and crackled as it burned.

"I told you I can't tell you," cried the man.

"We'll find out how much of a professional you are." Sarin grabbed the side of his face and shoved his face into the flames. The man screamed as the smell of burning flesh reached Sarin's nose. She let him go and shook out her hand. She'd gotten a little too close to the flames herself.

"I bet you wish you healed like I do." Sarin held up her hand to show the red marks disappearing.

She pressed her pistol against the top of his knee pointed toward his foot. "Where is she?"

"No...no...please...come on..."

"Suit yourself." Sarin pulled the trigger. The bullet passed down his leg and out his heel.

"Aaaagggghhhhh." The man clutched his shattered leg and fell to the deck.

"Where is she?" Sarin demanded as she pushed her pistol's barrel against the man's hand clutching his leg.

Tears streamed down the man's face. "Please...no."

"We're past you getting off easy like your friends. I'm not leaving until you tell me what I want to know. Now, you can tell me, and you can die at your leisure, or you can keep telling yourself that you're a true professional and I can remove chunks of you one bullet at a time."

Sarin pressed the trigger half way down.

"Ok...Ok...Ok ok ok...I'll tell you...No more, please."

Sarin pulled the pistol away and raised an eyebrow.

"We dropped them off at Nylstroom Crossing late last night."

Neptune's rings. I went right by them. "Who picked them up?"

"The usual guys. I don't know their names."

"Were they marched off, loaded into wagons, what?"

"They loaded them into a wagon. Rumor says they have a camp near the crossing."

Sarin changed the magazine in her pistol.

"So...so you're going to let me go?" said the man.

"No. I said you get to die at your leisure." She glided through the flames and kicked the anchor overboard. She returned to the man smiling. "You have your choice: swim for it or let the flames take you." Sarin fired her magazine of incendiary rounds into the deck and cargo of the raft. The flames spread rapidly joining the flames already burning and grew into a raging inferno.

The man looked out at the bank two hundred yards away. "What kind of monster are you?"

"I'm an evil angel. Have a nice day." Sarin leaped into the flames, spread her wings, and used the heat to carry her up into the sky.

***

"Are you the ferryman?" said Sarin to a man in an oiled coat, floppy hat, and heavy boots as she stepped from the dock to the ferry. She ignored the looks from the passengers as they disembarked.

"*Ja.* I am the ferryman. You do not look like you need my help to cross the river," he said as he bent down to tie the boat up. When he stood up, he had a pistol out and aimed at Sarin.

She cocked her head to one side and smiled. "I'm not looking for a ride, but some information." Reaching into her belt, Sarin pulled out a large gold coin.

The ferryman lowered the pistol a fraction. "What is it that you want to know?"

"I'm hunting some slavers. They unloaded here earlier. I want to know where they went."

The man's eyes narrowed. "*Ja.* They took over the dock and kept me from doing my job. They loaded a group of children into a wagon."

"Where did they go?"

"That will cost you more."

"And what is the price of the ferryman?"

He held up two fingers. "Two coins."

"Naturally." Sarin pulled a second coin from her belt and flipped them to him. The man lowered the pistol and caught the coins. "Where are they?"

"They have a stockade not far from here, to the northwest."

"Thanks."

"*Mis,* be careful. They are a dangerous group."

"I'm a dangerous person."

"Then good luck to you. We don't need scum and villainy like them."

***

Sarin circled a compound that showed promise. It was nestled in a large stand of trees. A large pen with a lean-to shelter looked like a spot to hold slaves, but it was empty. There were three outbuildings and a shed, all surrounded by a palisade. A wagon was next to a corral holding some horses. *Someone's here.*

She landed by the pen. The door was open. There were fresh footprints in the mud. *They were here.*

Sarin exited the pen and walked toward the largest building, a log cabin with a door and a pair of windows. The other buildings were smaller, with a window and door each.

"Who's ever here, come out," Sarin yelled, "or I'll burn you out." She folded her arms and waited.

"*Mis Sadira,* how nice of you to pay us a visit," said De Jager as he and a dozen men emerged from the doors and windows of the buildings. De Jager leaned against the doorway of the largest building. "You've cost me a lot."

"You're behind this?" Sarin said as her eyebrow went up.

"I've learned one must be hands-on to make sure my operations run smoothly. You were just a pleasant bonus."

"Where's Bean?" Sarin demanded.

"I don't know why you want her. Her father certainly doesn't."

"Her father loves her."

De Jager chuckled. "If he loves her, why did he sell her to me?"

"Peet would never—"

"Ah, but he did. Many of the townspeople took me up on the offer. I paid them more than they'll make in a year for each one. They can always make more children. And offer like mine only comes along once in a lifetime."

"You're deplorable."

De Jager tipped his hat. "But the money's good. The sheiks of Arabia will pay well for them."

Sarin drew her pistol and aimed at De Jager. "Give me Bean."

"You've cost me a lot in men and material. I'll make you deal. A life for a life."

"A life for a life?"

"Yes, yours for hers."

"I'll take her place?"

"That's right. I have some buyers who will pay handsomely for one of the rumored Angels of the southern regions."

"I have to see her first."

De Jager whistled. From the small building to Sarin's left a pair of men appeared pushing a bound and gagged Bean in front of them.

"Bean!" yelled Sarin. She took a step toward the girl.

"Ah-ah," said De Jager. "That's close enough. She's in good shape. She's no good to me damaged."

"Fine. You have a deal." Sarin pulled her pistols and dropped them in the dirt. "Untie her and let her go."

De Jager nodded. "Go ahead."

As the men untied Bean, two slavers moved to Sarin's side holding shackles and a ball and chain. Sarin offered her wrist as the man with the ball and chain fastened it to her ankle.

"Sadira!" Bean shrieked when the gag was removed from her mouth.

"Go, Bean. Go home. Don't worry about me." Sarin motioned to the partially open gate.

Bean ran toward the gate. There was the crack of a rifle, and the side of Bean's head exploded. The girl tumbled forward into the dirt.

"Bean!" screamed Sarin. She fell to her knees as tears streamed down her cheeks.

De Jager walked over to Sarin holding a rifle. "That is for destroying part of my organization. I hope you've learned a lesson."

Anger at De Jager and anger at herself caused hate and rage to explode in Sarin's chest, drowning out the sorrow and pain. She lunged to her feet, interlaced her fingers, and clubbed De Jager, hitting him in the neck.

The men who had shackled her drew their pistols and fired, striking Sarin in the back and leg. Snarling, she grabbed a man and heaved him at the other. Snapping the restraint from her ankle, she picked up the chain and spun the ball, slamming it into the man's head.

A bullet struck Sarin's arm. She dove into the dirt, picking up her pistols as she rolled. Turning, she fired, hitting the shooter in the eye. The other men in the buildings fired at her striking her in the legs, chest, and neck.

Sarin raised her pistols and opened fire in a flurry as more rounds hit her. She turned, picking out targets and hitting them with pinpoint accuracy. She and the last man fired simultaneously. Her round struck him in the jaw, his hit her knee.

De Jager moaned as Sarin's knee gave out and she collapsed in the dirt. She placed her pistol against his forehead and pulled the trigger.

"Be thankful I'm not a fallen angel," she whispered as she wiped a trickle of blood from her mouth.

Holstering her pistols, Sarin crawled to Bean's body. She stroked the blood-soaked hair and wept.

I'm so sorry, Bean. I tried to save you, but like everything in my life...I failed.

***

Sarin knocked over the sign that said WELCOME TO VRYBURG as she entered the tiny hamlet where she and Bean had lived. She drew her pistols and fired her incendiary rounds into the wooden buildings as she walked down the street.

When she reached the end of the hamlet every building was ablaze. People ran out into the street. Sarin shot them as they fled. She took to the air and with her rifle gunned down the terrified townspeople.

Sarin landed in front of the inn where she and Bean had lived and worked. The structure was engulfed in flames. Lying in the dirt out front was Peet. She knelt down next to the dying man.

"She's dead because of us," said Sarin. "This is your punishment for the part you played. Don't worry. It'll be over quick. I've made my choices. I'm the one who will suffer and see her face every night. Bean won't be forgotten. I promise you that."

Sarin placed the pistol against the side of Peet's head and fired. She stood up and holstered her pistols. Walking down the street and out of town, she didn't see the burning buildings or the dead bodies. All she could see was the faces of a dead infant and Bean.

The End

Links:

https://www.wattpad.com/user/mountainlion2

https://www.facebook.com/LFergusWriter

https://www.amazon.com/Warmache-Mark-Gardner-ebook/dp/B072LHFWKB/ (Cover designer)

Cover by Mark Gardner.

I Hear the Rain

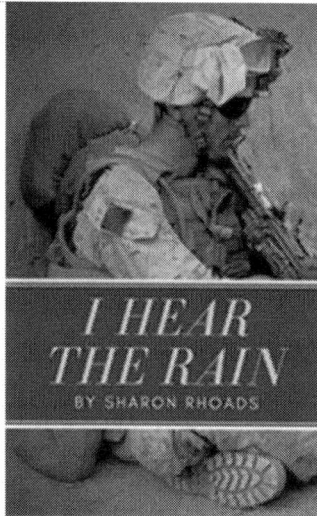

Sharon Rhoads

A soldier, lost and alone, hides in a dark alley. Cold, hungry and without hope. But comfort and hope can find you in the darkest places.

***

I hear the rain. Like gravel in a tin, it rattles down onto the roof. Thunder rolls through the streets. It reminds me of other rain, other shelter. My family, all together, bundled up and snuggled close, sharing our warmth. But they are not here now. No warmth to share. The wind seems to find my bones through the layers, though I wear every stitch I own. Being wet doesn't help. There is another thud and boom that shakes the wall I'm leaning on. Not thunder this time. Sharper sounds follow, gunfire, but not too close. I am tired. I hope I don't have to move. A flash, and I realize my eyes were closed. I have to stay awake. A truck passes the end of the alley. Their lights don't reach me. I can hear the clank and splash as they hit potholes, their engine getting quieter in the distance. Now all I hear is the rain.

I hear my baby sister crying. She's so hungry. I'm afraid someone will hear her. No, she's gone. They are all gone. I'm awake now, but I still hear her. How can I hear her? It's not possible, but I hear a baby crying in the darkness up the alley. The sound gets closer and it's a small cat, soaked to the skin. I bend down and it rubs against my hand. I want to scoop it up and hold it but it dances out of reach. It stops and cries again a few feet away. When I try to get closer, it moves off again, then sits and waits for me. It looks toward the wall and I see an archway with a heavy wooden door.

Rising on hind legs it pushes on the door. I reach up to add my weight and the door slowly opens. I see a large fireplace and I can feel the heat where I stand. The cat trots over next to the screen and begins licking the water from it's fur. I don't see anyone in the darkened room. There are odd stairs and a couple of doors, but I don't hear anything. I'm so cold and that fire looks like heaven. The cat stares at me, gives a little chirp, and goes back to washing.

Pushing the door closed behind me, I cross to the stones in front of the fire. Thick heavy heat rolls out, pushing into my face and hands. Drips evaporate as fast as they fall on the warm floor. I start pulling the outer layers of clothing off. I flip over a loose chair and put my boots and socks upside down on the legs. I drag over another to hang my jacket and pack. Exhausted, I sink to the floor. Cradling my head on my arms, I soak in the warmth and slowly the tension melts.

***

I jerk awake at a metallic clank behind me. On my feet, knife in hand before I even realize I've been asleep, There are lamps lighting the room and I look toward the source of the sound. Someone is at the fireplace. I can't see what they are doing, but the cat seems happy. As I watch, a woman turns to me with a smile.

"You're awake," she says, and gestures to a chair. "Have a seat. I won't be a minute." She crosses to a door on the other side of the room and, with a swish of her long skirt, is gone.

The cat walks to the chair, reaches it's small white paw to the seat and meows. I don't know this woman, but I feel safe enough to put my knife back in it's sheath and sit. As soon as I do the cat jumps into my lap and lays there purring. I can tell now that she's a girl. Her black and white tuxedo coat is soft and warm and she seems to really like having her chin scratched.

The door across the room opens again and the woman comes back carrying a tray with a teapot, cups and fresh bread. Setting it on a table she says, "Pull your chair up and pour two cups of this tea while I fill our bowls with some soup."

As I start pouring the tea, a delicious odor drifts across the room. My stomach growls loudly and I hear the woman chuckle, "Just in time, I'd say, too." She sets a bowl in front of me and one across the table. I push her cup across to her and pick up mine. It doesn't smell like tea, it smells like flowers.

"What's in this?" I ask. I set the cup back down with a frown.

"What? Oh, chamomile and blackberry honey," she says. "It's a common herb tea. I think you'll like it."

Picking up the cup again, I carefully take a sip. It's very sweet. The smell of the soup reminds me how hungry I am. The first bite is almost too hot to taste, but I don't care. It has chunks of potatoes, carrots and onions. The next bite has a large piece of something that I think is chicken. Whatever is in the soup, it tastes good. It's also starting to melt the ice in my bones. I wipe the last drops out of the bowl with a piece of bread and drink some more of the tea. It's actually quite good, so I pour myself another cup and top off the woman's cup.

"Thank you for this. I really needed it... all of it. The food, the fire, everything. It has been a while since I was warm. Not much to eat lately, either." I try to smile, but that, too has been a while.

"Oh, that's all right, dear." She smiles, reaching a hand across to pat mine. "I hope you are feeling better."

"Yes. I really am. I haven't felt this good since... well, for a long time." And I really do feel better. Not just warm and fed, but safe. Safe, like everything out there was a world away and could never get in. All my questions are bubbling up at once. "What is this place? Why does it feel so secure, when I know the fighting is still going on outside? Don't they ever come in here?"

She chuckles. "My, no. Not with Lady Jorj on duty." She motions to the cat and my eyebrows rise. "Jorj, open the door, please."

Jorj walks over and scratches the wall next to the door. To my surprise, the door slowly swings inward without anyone touching it.

"Jorj, close the door, please." With another scratching, the door closes again. "Thank you, Jorj. Unless Jorj opens the door, nobody gets in. She trusted you, so she let you in."

"A cat? A cat decides who comes in? I'm grateful, but how can a cat know who is safe to let in?

"Jorj is Lady Guardian of The Keep. She is much more than a cat. When she became a guardian, she became linked to The Keep. That's how she knows who needs us and who to let in. The Keep told her you were outside."

"The Keep? Who is the Keep?"

"Kaat's Keep. Not a who, but a what and a where." She waves her arm around us. "Here. This is Kaat's Keep. Where we are. And I am The Lady T'Kaat of Kaat's Keep. I am the voice and the heart of The Keep."

I sip my tea. This is undeniably odd, but not impossible to believe. "How did The Keep know about me?"

"I don't know how all the machinery works. Sensors of some sort, I suppose." She has a thoughtful look. "I'll have to ask, sometime. I'd never really given it much thought."

A large yawn overtakes me and I stretch. Standing, I ask, "Is it alright if I take a nap by the fire? I feel like I'm falling asleep here."

"Of course it's ok. Let me grab you a blanket." Crossing to a small door beneath the stairs, she pulls out a thick green quilt and a small cushion. She smiles as she hands them to me. "Don't be surprised if Jorj joins you. She seems to like you. Help yourself to more soup and bread if you get hungry again." She climbs the stairs and is gone.

Taking the blanket and pillow over to the fire, I make a bed and snuggle in. Jorj circles the room and the lamps dim, then go out. She curls up next to me and her purring drowns out every thought.

The End

This story is from the not yet published novel, "Kaat's Keep".
Sharon can be found at the following links:
Twitter as @LadyTKaat - https://twitter.com/LadyTKaat
Facebook as Sharon L Rhoads
https://www.facebook.com/Sharon.l.roads
G+ as Sharon Rhoads
https://plus.google.com/110544122279302628911
LinkedIn as Sharon Rhoads - https://www.linkedin.com/in/sharon-rhoads-7b303331
Goodreads as Sharon Rhoads
https://www.goodreads.com/user/show/55114464-sharon-rhoads
Cover photo credit: https://visualhunt.com/photo/67426/
Cover by Susan. K. Saltos. I

Fimbulvinter

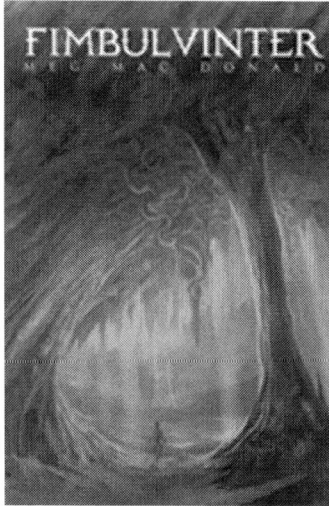

Meg Mac Donald

Meg Mac Donald shares a home in Michigan with her husband, children, a Norwegian Elkhound, and a clowder of cats. Yes, it really is bigger on the inside. Meg's short fiction and poetry has appeared in Weird Tales, Masques of Darkover, The Temporal Logbook, and other anthologies. She writes character-driven, #noblebright science fiction and fantasy and has a deep appreciation for classical literature and history. Meg has never been to the moon or owned a Woolly Mammoth, but hope springs eternal.

***

"The Cold Sleep hunts all of us, be we the stuff of nightmares, or a young boy with starlight in his eyes."

***

I should have killed him straight away.

It would have been a mercy.

I'm capable of mercy.

But...

...he smelled of starlight.

This one is thin. So little meat and my children are hungry. So very thin. Could it be that his tribe has cast him out and he, too, is running from the Cold Sleep? His marrow will be warm, though, his blood sweet. Unlike so many of the others, his young face belongs to his young body. Not like the ones who came before. Not like the ones who have lived so many lifetimes that can only be seen in their eyes.

Hesitation would bring me shame if there was anyone left to know. But I am alone. Alone in the wilderness, cut off from my world. Alone like he is. His keen dark eyes gaze into mine without fear. And he should be afraid. Very afraid. Perhaps the Sleep has stalked him even longer than I, drinking deeply from the warmth of his soul. It is a patient hunter on any world, but I am swift. My blood burns with my anger and my need. I will snap him in two to feed my children and clean my teeth with his small bones.

Wind and cold swirl about my body. The second star is low, soon to be eclipsed by the mountain. I must away from this place with my prey. My children are hungry. This meat will have to sustain them. I cannot tarry. Darkness hunts us as surely as the Cold.

I raise my paw to strike him down, expecting him to flee, to flinch, to close his eyes, but he does not. His eyes are proper eyes, dark and large. Stars shine within them; so many stars, burning brightly, turning slowly. He has gazed into Time's Gyre, that much is clear, and he is running. Great wisdom for one so young.

His lips, small and pink, move, but I do not know the words he sings. The prey things never speak to me. They only scream. That I understand, but this? Why would he speak to me? Why should I listen? His teeth are small and round like a child's, his flesh beneath another creature's skin is naked. What a sad creature he is, this traveler in the wilderness whose eyes are filled with stars. Eating him will be a mercy. I am capable of mercy.

You don't have to kill me, you know.

His words enter my mind and I can only stare at him. He, all pink and thin and lacking meat for my children. Speaking to me. Speaking into me. Cold Sleep rides swiftly on the night air. I strike a single blow, silencing his Voice. As I scoop him up I notice blood on the snow. It smells sweet. It tastes sweeter. I will have to kill him, of course, but it is a shame. I press my nose against his soft, dark hair. He smells... of starlight.

The moon is bright. The storm is gone. The Cold surrounds us. Within the cave, my children are sleeping. If they are not dead. It is difficult to tell these days. I count them. Four. Only four. A fifth one huddles outside the nest. Alive, but only just. What remains of another lies to the other side of the nest. That is why they can sleep. Their bellies are full. Soon enough they will need to eat again. I lay my kill out for them to wake to.

My kill. But not killed. He did not die. He will be good sport for my young when they wake. They must learn to hunt. Someday I will be gone. Someday I will not come back. They must learn... After they have eaten their fill, I will empty his bones of their marrow and perhaps I, too, will sleep.

I crouch at the entrance to the cave, the wind stiff against my face. Below the mountain the world is warm and the grass mirrors the burnt orange sky. The trees are silver and the night is still. I have hunted there. I have killed there. I am a dark legend in that country. The Great Houses send their mightiest against me, but I am swift. I am fearless. I am their worst Nightmare. I do not venture there anymore. I cannot leave my children. Not yet. They are too small. Even we are vulnerable when we are small. So I do not go. But they have music below, and sometimes, if I listen very carefully, I hear it.

My children press close against the gift I have brought them, seizing what little warmth is left in his body. They should not lie so close to him. They should not take comfort from anything except his bloody flesh. But they are children and they have never seen the likes of this creature before. He bears so little resemblance to the enemy I am accustomed to. Only one of his hearts beats for this world. The other longs for the stars.

As I watch, he stirs, one pale, reddened hand touching that place on his thin face where I cuffed him earlier. It is mottled, blue and green. The blood has congealed. He stares at his fingers dumbly, then at me, as if to challenge me for my actions. Then he sees my children waking around him, stretching their small bodies, extending their claws, teeth gleaming as they grin at him. First one and then another strokes his face with a taloned paw, then presses a muzzle against his dark hair. They inhale and their eyes dance and they look at me and I smile. If he was not frightened before, he will be now. Unless he has no wits left. But not a one of my children strikes. They only sit and stare into his star-filled eyes. I have looked into the Gyre. I have seen the past and the future. I have seen, and I have seen everything perish. I wonder if he has seen it too.

Slowly, ever so slowly, he reaches beneath the layers of fur that are not his own and draws out an instrument that emits light and some faint warmth. I am unconcerned. A child's toy. But the light is hypnotic for my children, and they watch intently as this half-grown, child-thing holds it out to illuminate our meagre surroundings.

I hate this place. I hate it as much as I hate the two stars that rise in the flaming sky of this world. I hate it more because it was the path that led me here and then offered no chance of return. The mountain shook. The skies grew dark. Winter came early and I was trapped. Then my children came and so we are all trapped. But I knew of this world. I knew the stories. I knew they could send me home. But they did not. They would not. And so I hate them, too.

The child-thing wanders with his light and I am amused. My children follow him, licking their lips, planning their feast, divvying up his limbs. Four of them for four children. The Fifth One, the one that wasn't moving, creeps after them now. Slow. So slow. It would be better to sacrifice another to feed the stronger, but I am pleased. Five is stronger than Four. The small pink lips are moving again, his song rising in pitch. My children listen, but I turn away, listening to other sounds on the night winds. There is no music outside, but there is life. More of his kind. More food for my children.

I can send you home.

His Voice is inside me again. I understand his song. He has given me the key. I growl a warning, but he is too busy with his small blue light and his paltry claws tracing patterns on the wall as if he were reading them with his hands. He scampers deeper in the cave, climbing amid the rocks, and begins to dig. My children scramble after him, pushing aside rocks, their laughter a music I have longed to hear. The smallest cannot follow as swiftly and cries so pitifully I am almost moved to put him out of his misery. But I am not the only one listening. The child-thing, the...boy...climbs back down and does the unthinkable.

He takes the fur from off his body.

He lifts my child in his arms.

He wraps my child in his...cloak.

He looks at me and I hate him. I hate him, but I see what is in his eyes again and I know I cannot kill him. I give him my thoughts and he smiles.

Your destiny is in the stars...

They dig. Five children. Four of them mine. One of this world. One day he will walk among the stars, but not today. Today he is a boy. Today he still belongs to me. The last child--mine--sits wrapped in the boy's cloak, content to be warm. Despite my misgivings, despite the ill wind that blows up from below the mountain, I allow it to happen. I allow my attention to be diverted. I allow Death entrance to my domain.

"Look out!"

Another creature dressed in fur that is not his own. What he holds in his hand is not a toy. I have seen it before. I have felt it burn. But I am swift. I am as Cold as the Night. And I will kill this one.

But the weapon is not meant for me. It is aimed at a point high in the rocks. A weak point above my children. The light blinds us all. The cave collapses as I move to gather them to safety. Two of my children are crushed before my eyes. Two flee into the snow. The last one lays motionless behind the boy who is screaming. I understand screaming.

"What have you done? What have you done!"

"Don't you mean 'thank you?' She'd have killed you! I couldn't find you in the storm. I've been searching all night. I thought you were dead!"

I have been given the key to his song and his words are lies, all of them. Lies. His pale flesh is warm and dry. His belly is full. He is as patient as the Cold Sleep, as calculating as any Hunter. He stands over my broken body. He touches my fur. I have just the strength to kill him where he stands but he reeks of betrayal. His blood would be poison.

"Are you all right?"

"I'm always all right. You could have--"

"--stood by and watch you be killed? Wouldn't that have gone over well at the academy. Coming up here was your idea, remember? We were only going to look for the monster, not be dinner for it."

My last two children have scattered into the Night. The Cold. The Dark. The Cold Sleep will silence them. We will never see our home again.

"But I was right, don't you see? It's written on the walls for anyone to read. They only had to look. Why didn't they look? There's a portal back in the cave. I saw it just before you fired. She couldn't reach it but I was going to send her children home. I could have sent them home!" His face is glistening, like rain.

"Are you crying?"

"You wouldn't understand. I knew you wouldn't. Never mind."

The Murderer turns away, a cruel smile tugging at his lips as he dresses his face the way he has dressed his song. His face is as light and dark as his soul. He casts the weapon secretively into the snow, then pushes the body of my dying child from the warmth of the fur cloak. I hear other Voices now. Old Ones. They do not look Old, but they are. They think themselves wise, but they are fools. They Watch from their great towers. They Watch while planets burn. They Watch, and do nothing when the desperate flee and their children are hungry and they teach their children to do the same. Many have lived too long. I know what it is like to have lived too long.

The child-thing that is not mine hesitates. He kneels beside me but does not touch me. I could still kill him. For all the woe this night has brought me, I would be within my right. He seems to know this too.

"I'm sorry," he tells me, laying my last child close to me. My broken child. "I'm so, so sorry..."

"For pity's sake don't talk to that monster," the other one says, barely turning. "It was going to kill you."

Barely turning. But enough. Enough for me to see his eyes. Bright chips, burning with stars. Burning with hatred. This one has looked into the Gyre as well. It beats a song within him too terrible to be music. A swirl of snow stings my eyes and when I look again, it is gone. So is he. I gaze into kinder eyes. He does not see what I see. He isn't running from the Monster, but he should be. He will be. And all his stars will grow dark.

I should have killed him straight away.

It would have been a mercy.

I'm capable of mercy.

But...

...he smelled of starlight.

The End

Cover by David Revoy.

While We Were Sleeping

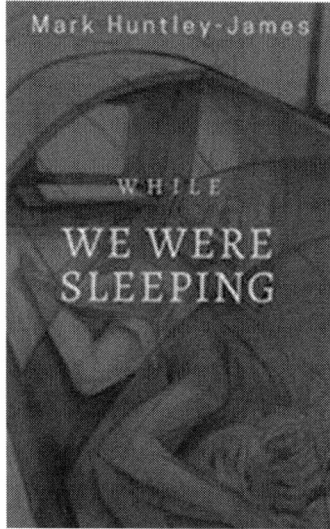

Mark Huntley-James

What happened? What did you see? What do you remember? *While We Were Sleeping* started as a tale of an alleged crime solved with a piece of brilliant forensic science, but stories are slippery things, apt to wriggle if held too tight, and the witness account came to the fore instead. Forget the science, all that does is finger potential suspects. What matters is the context, who did what and who saw them do it, and if the alleged crime took place light-years away, all you have is a suspect list and whatever the witnesses tell you.

What really happened? I love that question, and hate it. You have the witness statements, the forensic evidence, and none of that tells what really happened. Even if you were there, would you know exactly what happened? What do you really remember?

Eyes open, now...

***

Sevi woke to a kiss – he was no beauty, the touch on his lips no prince. The ventilator pulled back and let him draw breath. Soft amber script assured him that he was fine, heart rate steady, blood chemistry good, a successful return from deep-sleep. Nineteen years and a handful of months since he was last awake.

More data floated to his left – the survey ship was entering a highly eccentric orbit, overall operational status above eighty percent, no individual system registering below seventy-five. The Cunning Man was alive and well. Sevi glanced to the right – a field of amber spots, two green and no red.

Almost fifty of us in good health.

Sevi popped the lid of his sleeper tube. The dorm was running pale red safety lights, barely brighter than the in-pod displays. Nothing to upset eyes unused for a couple of decades. He took the time to go through the standard checks – track his finger with his eyes, touch his nose, balance on one foot and then the other – all the standard, basic tests to make sure everything still worked.

Mind and body were satisfactory, so he toured the command dorm, an ingrained habit – Lena was up and out already, Goran still in deep-sleep, as was Vivi. He lingered by Clive's empty tube – a red-light the last time Sevi was woken. Finally, he checked the terminal at the end of the dorm – screen brightness at minimum – and brought up the current mission status.

Paydirt. A signature off the scale. The ship's odd orbit was curling inwards to a deposit of the freaky shit that made star-drives work, something orbiting a churning gas giant. It had to be a trapped asteroid, or a really bizarre moon, but whatever it was, it was loaded with the rarest, most valuable stuff in the universe. Sevi pulled out a seat and read the long-range assay in detail. Whichever way you cut it, there was enough high-grade material to fill their holds.

He blanked the screen and stared at his reflection. The bald patch was obviously bigger, and the surviving hair had grown longer. Could just drape the long stuff over the bald bit... No! Deep-sleep slowed ageing to a crawl, but was an imperfect technology.

Sevi pushed back and stared, unfocussed, at some place deep inside the bulkhead. A full cargo hold meant going home, and with that much freaky-freakonium there would be bonuses all round.

Going home. All they ever talked about when they were awake. What's the first thing you're gonna do when you get back? It was like discussing a fantasy date. Or living forever. Not necessarily impossible, but so unlikely. Now there was a new question to chew over - *what was the first thing to do, going home with a humongous bonus?*

Fifty sleepers... and an estimated direct return lag of fifty-two years. A year per person, so to speak. Going home. That was going to be strange. Almost eighty years out, another fifty plus to get back – everyone he'd left behind would be dead. All that mattered was the cargo. And friends on the crew. And a bonus to spend.

Sevi closed his eyes. The crew-health indicator, amber and green, no red this time. Perhaps in fifty years time, there would be more red spots.

Hey Sevi, you got your ticket for the red-spot lottery?

Sleeper missions were suicide. Everyone knew that setting out. One day, you woke up and the food was gone, water recycling scraping the bottom of the tank, air getting thin – time to chose: die on your feet or take the final slumber. The sleepers all talked about going home.

What's the first thing you gonna do? Wish I got a winning ticket in the red-spot.

Sevi brought up the duty rota. He was awake and logged as survey officer. Lena Manx was command, currently on the bridge, Henry Lee was engineering and still in his pod, poised to wake. Sevi walked to the bridge. It was time to wake everyone up, but that was not his decision.

Lena lounged like an elastic orang-outang, draped in an ergonomically designed chair and casually defying the way it was designed to be used. A long, skinny leg hooked over one arm-rest, the other tucked back under, her right arm looped through the safety harness, her left wedged above the lumbar support. She craned her head around the side of the chair as he entered.

"You lost hair."

His hand went up to his forehead. "You lost weight."

"It looks good on me..." Lena never smiled. It must just be after-effects of deep-sleep making her lips curve. "Anything worth getting out of bed for?"

"Freaky, freaky-freakonium..." Pay attention, Sevi, we do not refer to meta-stable exotic matter as freakonium. Bugger that. No exams to pass now. "Serious freakonium. If you got all the freaky-freakonium in the universe and put it all one freaking place... this is it. Magnitude four when we were still three lights out." Sevi paused as her contorted pose straightened. "We are coming up on the source... registering nearly nine at this range. Freaky, freaky, freaky..."

Lena sat upright in the chair, the way the designers intended. "Nine is... crazy."

"Nine is freaking bonus time, Lena. Big freaking freaky bonuses. I recommend waking up a few more people... Have a freaking party..."

"Sevi...."

"Yeah?"

"If you say freak, freaky, freaking, or any other damn thing that starts with freak, I'm gonna take what's left of the hair on that side of your head, and tie it in a knot with what's left on that side..." She shook her head. "And no damned party. Not for another two hours..." Every waking person used more oxygen, more water, more food. And said more stupid things. "Go over everything. Get me estimates. Then get me better estimates." She turned back to the navigation displays. "Eighteen days to orbital intercept. Plenty of time." Tension evaporated, gangly limbs tied back around the chair. "Why aren't you working yet, Sevi?"

"Still thinking about my hair..."

Estimates and better estimates – she was asking for the impossible. Wacky meta-stable exotic matter was tricky stuff at the best of times. A freakonium deposit, registering mag nine – it was still like staring at a candle back-lit by the sun. He launched probes, turned every telescope on the centre of the deposit, but they were too close to get better numbers, too far out to see anything except...

Sevi played with the data. It was not his field of expertise, but a bit of juggling, repetitive reading of user guides, some well chosen expletives... and an image appeared. A real, honest picture, built up of thousands of separate images. A picture of the wacky freakonium deposit in its highly eccentric orbit.

"Lena... I think it's another ship."

She stared over his shoulder. "No way..." Leant forwards, ear-to-ear with Sevi. "No way... oh.. OK. Wake Henry."

***

Henry Lee was an engineer, but he knew a thing or two about image compositing. He knew how to get the best correction factors, how to chose the noise filters, he knew far stronger expletives – the blurry image of a ship became a slightly less blurry image. It happened like magic – Sevi watched and failed to learn.

"Whose is it?" Lena was squinting at the elongated blur, as if that would succeed where software enhancement failed. "What species?"

Sevi squinted too, just to annoy her, but found it somehow made the image look clearer. "No idea. I learned about meta-stable exotic matter, not ship design."

"Don't look at me," Henry grumbled. "That's the best you're gonna get until we're a few hundred thousand klicks closer. These telescopes are for tracking, not taking pictures."

"A ship... Sevi... what's the legal position? Is it salvage?"

Sevi shrugged. "I need to do some reading." A survey officer was expected to know every flavour of galactic law... "Kind of depends on species, you know? Depends if the owners use lawyers or fire-power. Give me a day or two."

Sevi ran the clippers over his remaining hair and started a revision session on Galactic Law. It was like trying to get clear guidance on the right way to eat a jelly-baby. Everyone has their own way. There are no real rules, just personal preference, the spur of the moment, the flavour of the jelly baby...

"Hey, Lena...." In spite of the complexity, and incoherence, less than a day's work gave a simple answer. "It's a grey area."

"How grey?"

"Lena do you know how many hours I spent attending dispute tribunals before this mission? No? Absolutely none. There was no bloody money to spend on me listening to a bunch of aliens arguing this stuff. In the unlikely event of it going to court, it might be centuries before a decision got made. Even if I knew what species and how the ship got to be here... it's a grey area."

"Sorted, then. Grey is the new black and white. Wake 'em up, Sevi. This is salvage. Then we go home."

"Right." Sevi couldn't make the transition from grey to certainty. "So what are you going to do when we get home?"

"Have a decent meal. And then another one. And keep having decent meals until my bonus runs out."

***

Sevi woke, another kiss, another few days out of deep-sleep. A twinkling red star caught his attention, a failed pod, a friend dead some time in the last... eight years, still a long time from home. When his seal opened he went through the routine – finger to nose, stand on one foot, walk in a straight line, all the basic tests. The walking was wobbly, but that was because his left knee ached. So, no obvious mini-strokes or other debilitating damage.

Self-certified and acceptably steady on his feet, Sevi went to the terminal to check status. They were passing through a planetary system, navigational corrections were being made, and a trace of freakonium was registering.

He checked the rota – Goran should be on the bridge, but Goran was dead. According to the logs, his pod was fine, but deep-sleep was an imperfect technology. Lena was the alternate command officer, and still in her pod. Sevi walked round the dorm and checked on Goran, just in case it was a sensor failure... his friend and the best poker-player on the ship was just a hint of bio-residue in the pod.

Take a moment, take a breath... Sleeper missions were suicide. That was a given. If you make it out, everyone you knew is long dead. If you can't live with that, you got no business joining up. The only constants, the only co-survivors, the only friends you keep, are the crew. So take the moment and the breath, and mourn the loss of a friend, then move on and make sure the next one is still breathing.

Lena's pod was in the next section and he waited until the hatch opened.

"Lost some more weight," he told her. She was positively gaunt, face lined and dark hair pure white at the roots. Deep-sleep slowed ageing to a crawl, but sometimes there was still a sprint. "Tiny hint of freakonium, but this is just a nav correction..."

"Good news Sevi..." She patted him on the head. "Next time I see you, you won't have lost any more hair."

"Next time I see you, better not be any thinner." He took her hand. "Goran... you know."

"Shit." She returned the grip. "Shit. Give me a minute."

That was it. A few hours, a bite to eat, a few rounds of conversation. Just a course correction, and then back to sleep for both of them.

***

Sevi woke to banging and shouting. The lid of his pod was pulled open and he screwed his eyes tight shut against the light.

"Wake up, boys and girls... wake up. You're home..."

Sevi blinked until he could stand the brightness. He reached out and keyed the pod display – a scatter of red lights, jumbled beyond counting. Too many winners in the red-spot lottery.

"Name?" An eager young man was standing in front of him. Fashions had changed, but the basics of ship-suit design remained the same. The shoulder patches, the name tag, the clean look – some sort of military. "Name?"

"Sevi Keene..."

"A survey officer... The survey officer. Good... come with me."

Sevi walked with difficulty. Either he had grown old, or the wake-up had been rushed. He paused at the first reflective surface he saw – bald, lined, tired, victim of an imperfect deep-sleep technology.

"Come on, Keene." The youngster urged him on. What you gonna do first, Sevi? "Mustn't keep the arresting officers waiting." That was never on the list.

More faces, more uniforms, more hustle – Sevi tried blinking again, because something just wasn't right. One eye was fine, but not the other. It might just be a bad wake-up, or perhaps a deep-sleep stroke, or... no-one studied deep-sleep complications properly. No point. Sleeper missions were suicide.

"In here. Sit down." Sevi went and did as he was told – a small room, a single occupant, and paraphernalia that said medical. "Ten minutes. Get him certified for questioning."

"Follow my finger with your eyes..." Sevi tried, but everything was blurred. "Touch your nose..." That worked fine. "Hold my fingers..." Sevi reached for the medic's hands and fumbled – that problem with his left eye was serious. "Squeeze... more... fine..."

All those years, all those silly conversations. The first thing any of them would do on getting home was that self-check – do my eyes work, my hands coordinate, my feet walk in a straight line? The medic had more tests, more questions, a detailed neuro-muscular assessment.

"Your have a cataract in your left eye and early-stage osteoarthritis. Fit for questioning."

That was OK, then. Nothing serious. Just a bit of stray old-age creeping through the cracks in the sleeper technology.

The uniforms returned and hustled him to his feet, out of medical, past Lena bundled up on an emergency support gurney, no more than skin and bones.

"What happened?"

"In here." No-one was answering his questions. "Sit." A chair, a table, and live recorders running. "Survey officer Sevi Keene... tell me about the salvage operation."

"What salvage operation?" Deep-sleep, the invaluable imperfect

201

technology – hey guys, only just woken up here, give me a minute...
"What year is this? What happened to Lena?"

"Your ship is fully laden with meta-stable exotic matter and fourteen viable sleeper pods from a Zindar survey vessel."

"Right." Is that good, or bad? Sevi went for the essential question. "What's a Zindar?" He scratched his head without thinking and asked the next essential question. "What happened to my hair?"

***

Amnesia was a temporary defence – suspect to be held pending detailed medical assessment. They let him visit Lena on the grounds that there was going to be no collusion with an unconscious woman.

"You're the first visitor." The duty nurse spoke softly, but had a stance and stillness that suggested he was used to dealing with dangerous and hostile suspects. "No family, I suppose."

"No. Probably not. Not any more." Sevi sat and stared at the medical plumbing – more extensive than a sleeper pod. "What happened?"

"End-stage cancer. Your old pods couldn't cope." He made an unnecessary check of the equipment. "We're doing our best, but malnutrition like this..." He shrugged.

"Not a good meal, then." More like close to a red-spot lottery winner. "How long?" Another shrug from the nurse. "Doesn't matter." He took her hand, limp skin and bone.

Take a breath and a moment, and then maybe another. Lena wasn't dead yet, but so close as made no odds. So take a few more breaths and moments, because waking up to find friends long dead was very different to one about to die.

"Lena. Come on..." And then play the muddled sleeper, because someone was bound to be watching. "Hey, boss, what did we do? No time to be sleeping. We're home. Gotta get up." Sevi stared at the nurse. "We are home, aren't we? Home? Earth?"

"This is Moribar in the Zindar Protectorate."

"So what the hell is a Zindar?" Faking amnesia was going to be a challenge of keeping track of what he was supposed to remember, but seriously, what was a Zindar?

"Not for me to say." The nurse took a step back. "I'll leave you to it." Another step. "Call if you need anything."

Lena was on a one-way trip to dead and, on the ship, there would have been an easy out. Her name was on the list, third line down, in her own hand. Two lines above his. Switch me off and let me go. If she had known the last time they woke, she would have ended it then. Drop into deep-sleep with Sevi, Henry and Goran around her to pinch the respirator tubes until she stopped. More food, oxygen and water for those who still had a chance.

"Hey boss? Where's Henry and Goran?" He was only talking for the benefit of those who were listening in. And because Lena would ask herself if she could. Not about Goran, of course. They both knew he was dead. But Henry, if he was still alive, would be there, wouldn't he? The other downside of faking amnesia – no telling if there really was something he'd forgotten. "You know they're saying we found something good? Or is this just to screw us out of bonus payments? Come on, boss. Talk to me."

The first thing I'm gonna do when I get home is make sure the bastards pay me the bonus they promised... That was in the top five.

"You remember when we joined up together? You, me, Goran, Henry, Vivi and..." The original six, but he could only remember five. "Lost that one, boss. Can see his face, clear as anything. Good engineer, lousy circulation. That was it, wasn't it? Wake-up stroke? I'm sure I remember it. Doesn't matter. I'll just keep talking until you wake up."

Sevi talked, even though she wouldn't come round. If there were the slightest chance, he would have kept silent. Saying farewell was important, but not worth having Lena spending her last minutes knowing the shit that had happened.

In the middle of a rambling recollection of a night out during training, the door opened.

"Henry? Is that you?" Sevi tried squinting. It looked like Henry, but... "Did you get old, Henry?"

"Too much highly refined freakonium, Sevi. Turns out it does bad things." Henry shuffled forwards, flanked by guards and uniforms with lots of glinting stars on the lapels. "Shit. Lena looks bad."

"She's on the list...."

"Aye. I told them. Sanctity of life shit. They gotta keep her going until they can't." Henry reached out to touch Lena's hand. "I just want to go back to sleep. One last time, with some friends to do what needs doing. Can't though. Got stuff to do."

"What sort of stuff? I just want to go home. And then the first thing I'm gonna do..." Sevi stopped and flapped his hands. "That's getting old, ain't it, Henry?" What was it he said... two wakes ago? Find the girl with the longest, loveliest legs in the universe... "Getting old, eh? But when we get home..."

"We are home, Sevi. You know that Galactic Law stuff. The Zindar found the ship we salvaged and traced back here somehow. They called it piracy. Now they own Earth, or Moribar as they call it. Now they have the Cunning Man, they can prove it was their freakonium we took. We have to prove it was legitimate salvage. And prove we rescued their crew. Get the case over-turned."

"So... no bonus?"

"Be lucky to get out of this just broke." Henry shuffled to pull up a chair. None of the scary uniforms behind him offered to help. "This is serious stuff, Sevi. That freakonium screwed us every way. Half the crew are gone, and half the records fried. Some of your logs are intact, Sevi, but not enough. Need you to piece it all together."

"Right." So, the first thing to do is get a damned good lawyer. No-one ever thought of that one either. "Where do we start?"

"From the moment you came out, five wakes ago. I've been through the logs, and the evidence for the Zindar case. Tell me everything you remember, Sevi."

"Five wakes ago? That's like..." He counted it off in his head. One wake ago was a course correction. Two wakes, the motherload. Three wakes... but... "Henry... a little bit lost here. Can you just give me a hint?"

"No hints, Sevi. It has to be all you. This is all being recorded in accordance with Zindar legal process." Henry hitched a thumb at the official crowd. "Serious stuff, Sevi. The Zindar will do everything to win this, so our case has to be absolutely perfect. To the letter of Zindar law."

"Henry? What the hell is a Zindar?"

"Sevi? Snap out of it. This is serious. We need facts. We need testimony. Reliable witnesses."

"Boss?" Sevi turned to Lena, but no, she was still unconscious, and all the uniforms lurking behind Henry were making him nervous. "Lena? What did we do?" Sevi scratched his head again – no hair, but that was right, yes? "Henry? What is a Zindar?"

"Doesn't matter, Sevi." Henry gripped his shoulder. Just like when.... "Things changed while we were sleeping." Henry turned away briefly. "Sorry guys... Sevi's gone."

"Gone?" Standing right here, Henry. "I'm fine. Come on. Tell me what a Zindar is and we can go looking for that long-legged girl of yours."

"Sevi..." Henry reached out, so old and so sad. "That was Goran."

"No..." Wait. That can't have been Goran. "Really? But Goran died..."

"Yes, Sevi, three wakes ago. You, me, Lena... we all said farewell and got him into his pod and... did what was needed."

"No." That wasn't right. It was a pod failure. Imperfect technology. "You sure?"

"Take a moment, Sevi. Sit with Lena... I have to go and sort a few things."

Henry shuffled out, spooked uniforms went with him. Sevi took the chair and sat.

"Need to wake up, Lena... I think Henry's lost it."

The End

Links:

website: https://sites.google.com/site/markhuntleyjames/
blog: https://writeedge.blogspot.com.br/

Photo credit: https://beta-02.deviantart.com/art/Pod-410997805
Cover by Susan. K. Saltos.

Ghost Mode

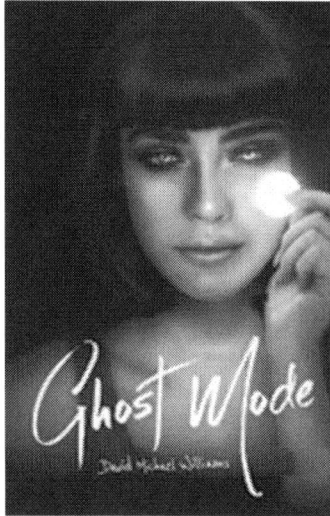

David Michael Williams

Editor's Introduction – When someone who works closely with emerging technologies on a daily basis presents such an ominous portrayal of tech addicts in the not-too-distant future, you can't help but wonder if it's meant to be caricature or cautionary tale. Given Ghost Mode's playful tone, it's likely a little of both. David Michael Williams works for an interactive agency specializing in digital communication. He writes speculative fiction that spans the gamut from sci-fi to sword-and-sorcery. The Renegade Chronicles, his debut fantasy trilogy comprised of *Rebels and Fools*, *Heroes and Liars*, and *Martyrs and Monsters*, was published in 2016. *If Souls Can Sleep*, the first book of The Sleep Cycle, is slated for publication in early 2018.

***

Quentin E. Donovan—*the* Quentin E. Donovan—sidestepped into an alley, closed his eyes, and did something he hadn't done in nearly a decade.

A deliberate twitch of his left thumb, and the twin IRIS mods went offline. A whispered password triggered the auto-transcript program fueling a half-dozen feeds to quit, killing a headline about the latest Darknet virus mid-scroll. Finally, he removed the sleek, pearlescent PAM—an eighth-generation iCoin Pro—from his pocket and thumbed the command to repel all incoming V-captures.

No feeds, no casts, no signals whatsoever. He was completely grid-locked.

Without the translucent menus and rolling text in his periphery, the world seemed impossibly plain. And slightly pink. It took him a moment to realize his eyes were compensating for the absence of the green tinge that always coated the corners of his vision—a much-missed reassurance that the ocular implants were successfully uploading his sensory data to the Sphere.

He shivered, as though losing his connection to the local hotspots had actually reduced his body temperature. Real-life silence usurped the subtle, soothing soundtrack of white noise in his ears.

No wonder they call it ghost mode, he thought morosely. The air even *tasted* dead.

Quentin returned to the main thoroughfare, where a woman was approaching from the opposite direction. He smiled politely—no, eagerly—but she didn't acknowledge him as she passed by, her shaky, far-off stare combing through a number of feeds he couldn't see. For several heart-pounding seconds, he could only stand there, until he finally identified the long-forgotten feeling as solitude.

He thrust one hand inside his pocket, pressed his palm against smooth surface of the iCoin, and flirted with the idea of rebooting all of his AR apps—longing to hear the comforting chime of the PAM booting up. But he found courage, then, in the thought of what glory lay ahead.

A pity his millions of fans wouldn't be able to enjoy the thrill of the clandestine meeting he had arranged mere hours ago on the Darknet...

Releasing his hold on the hibernating PAM and rubbing his eyes—though that did nothing to restore the reassuring green glow of the IRIS implants—Quentin trudged the remaining block to the agreed-upon FaceCafé and entered. Without the aid of any tech, he scanned the restaurant for someone who looked out of place.

Closest to the entrance, a middle-aged woman wearing a strappy, alligator-skin dress fished a cord out of her purse and connected one end to the table's charge-port and the other to an oversized, blaze-orange PAM. The infant in the highchair beside her wailed until the woman returned the device to his or her eager little hands.

Elsewhere in the dining room, a guy in a red power suit talked to an invisible partner across the table, laughing suggestively as he adjusted his crotch.

A few tables away, a woman swiped the air furiously with her fingers and frowned at what Quentin could only assume was bad news. Maybe a relative had contracted that new, nasty virus the journo-feeds were squawking about? Her smooth scalp and sheer outfit, while undoubtedly vibrant if viewed through an AR interface, looked dull and dumb in RL.

He sighed. No one appeared to be doing anything unusual.

Disappointed, he sat down at an empty table and keyed in an order for a black, half-stim coffee. He would just have to trust that the Darknet lurker he had pinged—the professional villain he had promised to pay half a million Cs—would recognize him.

No worries there. He was *the* Quentin E. Donovan, after all.

***

The ten minutes he spent waiting, bereft of feeds and all other digital augmentation, were nearly intolerable.

For one thing, the FaceCafé resembled a tomb. The smooth gray panels that normally flashed a parade of high-production promos—including a holo-trailer for the QED Feed—formed a bleak perimeter around the sparsely populated tables. Whatever tunes the restaurant subtly pumped into visitors' inputs couldn't reach Quentin's ears. The only sounds interrupting the sepulcher stillness were monosyllabic murmurs from the other customers and the occasional chime of the infant's PAM.

For another thing, the coffee tasted funny. He spent a full sixty seconds trying to determine if the FaceCafé's signature drink was just plain bad or if he had never taken the time to consider the flavor of coffee in the first place.

Pushing the bitter brew to the middle of the table, he watched the others go about their wonderfully linked lives. This amused him for a while. It felt deliciously bold to stare. But after several minutes, it was obvious that he—like a real ghost—was invisible to them. Inconsequential. And observing them was akin to accessing a glitching vid that showed only half of the story.

Elbows propped on the table, he cradled his head and rubbed his temples. All of this unfiltered RL was giving him a migraine.

"Mr. Donovan?"

At last!

Looking up, he discovered two things: the pink haze that had haunted his peripheral vision was completely gone, and the young woman seated across from him was a reasonably attractive specimen, even without his IRIS mods to see her AR enhancements.

Regardless, he couldn't hide his disappointment. This was no villain.

"Yes...and who are...? Ah, but you must be a fan." He straightened his back and reclaimed the hated cup of coffee, his only prop. "You're probably wondering what happened to the QED Feed. Don't worry...we're just experiencing some technical difficulties, I'm afraid."

The slight smile of Beautiful Stranger was unexpected. Usually, his female fans—and a significant percentage of his male demographic—downright swooned when they recognized him in public. Not that that was often. A custom-made app on his PAM permanently masked his Sphere ID to unauthorized passersby, ensuring his 24/7/360 lifecast wasn't polluted with random encounters with star-struck rubes. And by the time devotees IDed themselves as unintended extras in any given scene, he was usually en route to the next set.

But this woman's bright blue eyes weren't sending signals of excitement—sexual or otherwise. No, she looked...self-satisfied, maybe even sly...

"You're not the only one with tech issues," she said.

A few tables away, a woman frantically wiggled her fingers, trying to reestablish a connection to the Sphere. Meanwhile, across the room, the mom barked a few words that were banned on all but the grittiest of lifefeeds while her baby tossed its lifeless PAM to the floor. Quentin then watched the only other man there stand up and abruptly exit the FaceCafé, his obvious erection leading the way.

Turning back to Mysterious Stranger, he said, "So *that* is how you recognized me. You've lost your Sphere link, too, and are seeing the world through naked eyes."

She leaned back and crossed her arms, accentuating a pair of modest-sized breasts augmented neither by AR code nor cosmetic bioware. Her face was pretty, albeit in a straightforward manner. A few years back, Sphere celebs paid small fortunes to manufacture faces that looked effortlessly beautiful. However, the latest trend embraced the other extreme: exaggerated features that de-emphasized traditional traits and championed dehumanizing effects.

He theorized it was her brazen adoption of outdated fashion—particularly the monochromatic shirt, naturally black hair, and the pale blue eyes unlike any gemstone—that intrigued him as much as anything.

Then he remembered he was seeing her RL face. Had the Sphere connection not died and had his IRISes been online, she probably would have looked as celebulicious as anyone.

"I always see the world through naked eyes," she replied, and the pink-lipped half-smile made a repeat performance.

He chuckled lewdly at the double entendre until he realized she was speaking literally. And was that a subtle shade of lipstick—*actual* lipstick—around her mouth?

"You can't be serious," he said. "Nobody can lead a normal life without linking to the Sphere."

"That's not what I said." Eccentric Stranger leaned forward and tapped a fingernail against the lifeless screen planted in the center of the table. "Everyone has to plug in sometimes. A gal has to eat, though I wouldn't recommend anything from this menu...especially not the coffee."

Cup halfway to his lips, Quentin returned the foul beverage to the table.

"I said I always see *the world* through naked eyes," she continued. "When I need to make a purchase in person, I use a C-card instead of direct linking. And when I need to drop by the Sphere, I use a base-model screen that's bloody ancient. It takes five minutes to boot up."

He scoffed. "What are you, some kind of technophobe? Or one of those zealots from the Church of Minimalists?"

She laughed, somehow sounding girly and worldly at the same time. There was no arguing the woman was peculiar. She might even make an intriguing love interest during his next ratings lull. He made a mental note to file away her facepic but then remembered he was still in ghost mode.

"Actually, I've got quite a knack for tech," she replied. "This didn't happen by accident."

She punctuated her point with another tap of her fingernail against the blank screen. Quentin's heart pumped harder.

"*You* did this?" he asked, gesturing at the empty tables around them. "How?"

Dangerous Stranger reached beneath the conservative neckline of her shirt and withdrew a pendant. Its black stone was a stark contrast to the white blouse. "It's a jinx charm. I scrambled Sphere links for a two-kil radius...maybe more."

He tried to summon everything he knew about anti-Sphere terrorists and black hats in general, but his only experiences with the Sphere's seedy underbelly was the time a jacker had blasted through all nine walls of his fire fortress and wreaked havoc while impersonating him—*the* Quentin E. Donovan—on the Sphere.

The jacker, who turned out to be a gray hat, hadn't siphoned any money or done any significant damage during what turned out to be a foolish prank. On the contrary, the QED Feed had enjoyed a huge ratings spike.

His fingers twitched, eager to reactivate his PAM and do a search for "jinx charm" and "citiZEN"—the Sphere's most notorious anarchists—or better yet, power up his IRISes and upload that pretty little face of hers to CrimeCheck. But considering the table screen wasn't even displaying an apologetic out-of-order message, the woman's pendant had done more than just disrupt Sphere connectivity.

She had crippled tech itself.

A single thought surfaced above his mounting panic: Aside from the gray hat prankster, he had encountered *one* other denizen of the Darknet...

"You! You're the...the..."

Villain chuckled. "Wow, that took you long enough to piece together. I guess fans of the QED Feed aren't tuning in for mental stimulation."

"But why...why did you...?" An eloquent ad libber—unlike Donna Rom, whose entire lifefeed was irrefutably scripted—Quentin was unaccustomed to speechlessness. He took a sip of terrible, cold coffee to buy some time.

She tucked the pendant beneath her shirt and crossed her arms. "I thought you'd appreciate some privacy while discussing our transaction. Ensuring against eavesdroppers in the D-net can take an hour of prep, but knock out everybody's tech in the real world, and you'll always clear the room."

Her crooked smile stretched wider. "And what better way to make sure I'm not the next guest star in your little lifefeed?"

"I told you I would be in ghost mode," he snapped, hoping irritation would mask the full measure of his fear.

"I don't typically take people at their word, chief."

"Yes...well..." He took a deep steadying breath. Despite the fear gnawing at his not-too-slight-but-not-too-round gut, a part of him relished the repartee. If only he had some way to record it! He might even consider taking a page out of Donna Rom's playbook and reconstruct the scene under more ideal circumstances—editing out his stammers and casting a more cam-friendly vixen to play the part of Villain.

"Let me see if I have this right," she said. "You ventured into the D-net because you were desperate for some excitement. Your show has what...six months?...a year tops?...before people realize there's nothing more to know about you. And even if a few diehard fans continue to follow your feed, your time among the Top Trending is just about over. You need...how did you put it?...'a dramatic encounter with a true villain' to spice things up."

"Yes," he answered, and his voice cracked mortifyingly. "But I don't want it all scripted out. The element of surprise is essential for theatrical spontaneity. I'm not even sure why we're having this meeting. I—"

She planted her palms on the tabletop and leaned forward suddenly. The pose reminded him of any number of jungle hunters from the NatGeo feed. "We're here because even though we're going to do this thing my way, I'm letting you have some input. But that can change, Quentin F. Donovan."

He swallowed a large lump of something that tasted of bad coffee and brass.

She laughed, and the predatory posture reverted to an easy recline. "Yeah, I know you changed your name from Quentin Francis Donovan to Quentin Emerson Donovan a few weeks before your show started. I'm betting you did it so that your lifefeed could be called QED instead of QFD, not out of appreciation for a certain transcendentalist writer's work."

Truth be told, Quentin knew nothing about Ralph Waldo Emerson other than his name sounded both literary and dignified. The woman was correct in assuming he had wanted his lifefeed to harken back to the Latin *quod erat demonstrandum* in support of his branding as an intellectual. But he saw no reason to confirm her suspicions.

So he said nothing. This was her show.

"What exactly did you have in mind when you sent a single-target query into the D-net?" she asked. "How far are you willing to go for your...um... 'art'?"

If he had been sitting across from anyone else, he would have pointed out that living life to the fullest for the benefit of millions of viewers *was* an art. But even as his breakfast settled back down into its appropriate anatomical position, he realized how absurd it was to expect the villain and the hero to see eye to eye.

He cleared his throat. "As you may or may not know, violence is starting to trend again Sphere-wide. Enough time has passed since the last large-scale tragedy. However, with the latest CrimeCheck upgrades, even the slowest-witted thugs understand there's almost nowhere on the planet one can attack another human being without being seen. I visited the Darknet to find someone who might have a means of scrambling the authorities' inputs...but *without* knocking out the QED Feed.

"What I had in mind was a random assault...something that would provide a few strategically placed bruises, require some stitches, and perhaps result in a night or two in the hospital."

He would be able to spin the incident any number of ways, though he wasn't sure which angle would get the most play. A random act of violence would be the most shocking initially, but that narrative had a relatively short shelf life. Concocting a storyline about a disgruntled fan, on the other hand, seemed too obvious. He might have considered framing his rival for hiring the villain, except the publicity would benefit Donna Rom as much as him.

"So you want me to kick your ass?" she asked.

"Quaintly put," he replied, feeling much more in character now. "Yes, that was what I had in mind initially, but given the circumstances and the...*dynamics* of our particular dyad, I'm no longer certain that scenario is ideal."

She rolled her eyes. "Are you trying to tell me you have cold feet?"

"No, not per se. What I mean to say is the pain itself is not a deterrent, but rather the...well...delivery system."

She stared at him blankly.

"After meeting you today...and *seeing* you...I am concerned that, given the differences in our gender, well..."

His throat suddenly drier than Donna Rom's latest storyline, he reached for the evil coffee. Its temperature had nothing on the villain's icy look.

"You don't want to get hit by a woman."

He raised his hands reassuringly—and defensively. "What I meant to say is given your demographic, which includes not only your gender, but also your age, race, and build, I'm just not sure how believable it would be for your character to attack mine."

"Oh, I promise my urge to punch you in the face right now is *very* believable." Her half-smile made him flinch. "But that would be a waste, wouldn't it? No cameras recording. No adoring fans to sob as the blood gushes from your perfectly sculpted nose."

He wiped the sweat from his forehead. "Yes...well...please don't take it personally when I tell you that I would like to explore other talent—"

"How far are you willing to go for your art?"

"I...I'm happy to pay you a stipend for your time today. Which account should I—"

She leaned forward again. "Would you die for it?"

Her words stole the breath from his body as effectively as the jinx charm had sucked the Sphere signals from the room. Instinct commanded him to run, but he couldn't remember the last time he moved faster than a brisk walk. Besides, the woman looked like she probably sprinted just for sport.

"I have a lot of money. Name your price to walk away."

She shifted back in her seat, but her nonchalant pose did nothing to dispel the anxiety that python-squeezed his chest. "I know exactly how many Cs you have stashed away, including your crypted accounts. Anyway, I've already helped myself to a healthy advance."

"I'll pay you twice as much to leave me in peace!"

"Where's the fun in that?" she asked without a trace of mirth in her voice. "You chose to play a dangerous game, and we're going to see it through. You have two options. Either I kill you here and now without a soul to witness it and without any footage to preserve your life's tragic climax or..."

He leaned forward in spite of himself.

"...*you* kill Quentin E. Donovan."

"S-suicide?"

She shrugged. "In a manner of speaking. I can delete all traces of the QED Feed in a matter of minutes, but *you* have to cut the cord on this Sphere-centric half-life and make ghost mode your default setting. Quentin E. Donovan dies today, either physically or figuratively."

The FaceCafé spun around him. He fought for air. Searching for signs of madness in her eyes, he implored any of the long-defunct deities to reveal this to be a distasteful joke.

But her stern expression didn't waver, and he could only assume her soul was as black as the metaphorical hat she wore.

"Please—"

"Try to bribe me again, and I'll kill you right now."

"Oh God..."

His tears flowed freely. Wiping a pristine sleeve under his nose, he forced himself to take a series of even breaths. He had a decision to make, and while part of him was eager to make any vow that would stave off bodily harm, another voice fought for the preservation of something far greater than this mortal coil.

Which scenario ensured his legacy would live on after the QED Feed's demise—the discovery of his murdered body in a random FaceCafé or the mystery borne of his sudden disappearance from the Sphere?

"But what...what would I do without my show? Who would I be?" he asked, posing the question as much to himself as to the deadly antagonist.

"Someone real," she replied.

"Why are you doing this to me?"

She smirked. "If you have to ask the question, you won't understand the answer. Anyway, you should be thanking me. Not many D-netters are as sporting as I am. Now make your choice, or I'll make it for you."

She withdrew a silver handgun from under the table. Like her pink lipstick, the pistol was a relic from another age, a prop from some retro whodunit vid. The barrel pointed not at his chest, but at his face.

Getting gunned down by the anachronistic femme fatale would have made an amazing ending to the QED Feed. However, there was no way for this story to be told. And getting blasted full in the face would also rob him of an open casket, reducing the cross-feed coverage significantly.

Live in obscurity or die in obscurity—which was worse?

She cocked the gun, a gesture that always seemed ridiculous in the classic vids but, in person, was powerful enough to liberate the contents of his bladder.

"OK, OK, I don't want to die! I'll go off the grid...hell, I'll even join the Church of Minimalists if you just leave me alone!"

She lowered her gun. "And trade one cult for another? Not necessary. No, my terms are pretty simple...but not painless, I'm afraid. The first thing we have to do is get rid of all that tech inside your head."

She reached under the neckline of her blouse, and he expected the jinx charm to make a reprise. But she bypassed the pendant and retrieved something farther down, an object that must have been wedged between breast and brassiere. It was a trope as old-fashioned as the undergarment itself.

Villain sprang forward and plunged something sharp into the back of his hand. He recoiled, spilling the forgotten coffee cup. The dark liquid washed over the side of the table and pooled, blood-like, on the floor below.

"What the hell did—?" Pain exploded from the core of his brain, obliterating the rest of his words.

In between his own screams, he heard her say, "Don't worry...blindness...temporary..."

Then the woman, the FaceCafé, and the rest the world melted beneath a searing white light.

***

He awoke with a groan in his sparse, one-room house and knew he had been dreaming of his old life again.

While details of the subconscious-driven story were sparse, he knew he had been happy, *alive*! But now the trite soundtrack of birdsong beckoned him back to his eternal gig in ghost mode. In contrast to the stimulating imagery of those fast-fading scenes, the wooden planks of his ceiling looked unbearably boring.

He sighed and closed his eyes. While the residents of the peaceful, grid-locked community treated him well enough, quitting tech cold turkey had proven a tumultuous transition. He could never have attempted it out there in the civilized world. Fortunately, the remote settlement—most people just called it Ghost Town—was bereft of temptation.

Well, *mostly* bereft, he thought.

Slowly, surreptitiously, he pulled the dormant iCoin Pro from his sweat-stained pillowcase.

Dreams about his old life never failed to arouse a deep desire to renege on his promise to the villain, consequences be damned. And while he always managed to resist the Sphere's siren call, time had dulled his fear.

In fact, on some of the duller days, he almost craved a second confrontation with Supposed Savior...

He didn't know how long he lay there, running his fingers along the ridged rim of the contraband machine, fantasizing about booting up. Was Donna Rom still in the Top Trending? What would his fans say if the QED Feed had a new update after nearly a year of silence?

What harm could a quick "I'm still alive!" post do?

It's not as if the deadly doomsday virus his neighbors constantly whispered about could hurt him, not unless he found a way to replace his IRISes and the rest of the implants *she* destroyed.

His thumb caressed the tiny power button on the edge of the PAM. With each pass, he played with the pressure, nudging it a harder each time. His pulse quickened as he envisioned the many feeds he yearned to visit—albeit it on the PAM's tiny screen.

He was so caught up in his reverie that he initially mistook the excited voices on the other side of his crooked wooden door as competing audio feeds. But when his command to mute the PAM went ignored, the truth struck him like a slap across the face:

An actual crowd had gathered in the typically tranquil town square.

He stumbled out of the creaky bed, hobbled by a combination of poor circulation and mounting panic. Nothing exciting ever happened in Ghost Town, and the outside world—the *connected* world—seldom intruded. He wondered what news could have caused the commotion.

A knock on the door made him jump, squeezing the PAM guiltily.

"Wake up!" shouted a voice from outside. "It actually happened! The e-plague mutated. Now even folks without mods are contracting it. Anyone who accesses the Sphere risks getting infected...anyone! Can you hear me, Francis?"

The *former* Quentin E. Donovan didn't answer. He could only stare in horror at the blue-green glow of the PAM's power light leaking through his clenched fingers. Then the silence was broken by the cheerful chime of his iCoin Pro.

The End

Links:

https://david-michael-williams.com/
https://twitter.com/1MillionWords
https://www.facebook.com/onemillionwords

Cover by Mary Christopherson.

Destination Earth

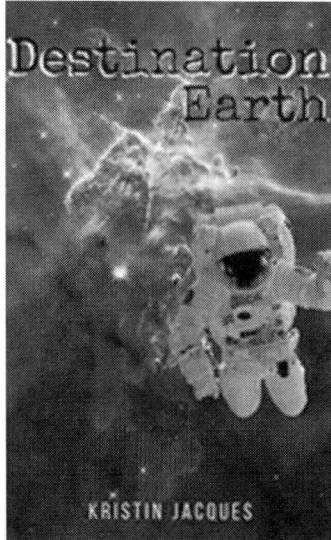

Kristin Jacques

Kristin Jacques is a writer from small town New England. When not writing, she is generally wrestling with her two boys, or spoiling the family cats. She general writes science fiction and fantasy but has been known to dabble in a genre or two.

The Transit Pylon was designed to enable humans to travel instantly to distant galaxies and worlds. Test pilot Zeus Pyxis's first jump was a success...and a disaster.

***

Before he opened his eyes, he knew it was the wrong one. The planet's twin suns were rising in pseudo synchronous orbit, chasing each other over the horizon. The red dwarf emerged first. Its glow added a rosy hue to the violet tinged sand beneath his boots. Rubies winked in the crests of waves lapping the shore. A beautiful world, but lifeless, nothing in his sights but dry sand butting against an ocean of molten silver as far as the eye could see. The reason for the barren atmosphere broke the horizon spare minutes behind its heavenly consort, with an exhale of heat that feathered the weak spots in his temperature regulated suit.

Ah, a Rigel star, no wonder this world was dead. The two stars hugged the curve of the sky, two lovers pantomiming across the heavens. The Rigel cast a Byzantium corona behind its slighter partner. A dazzling sight, but the heat was building, cutting his time short. Shame, he'd never seen purple sand before.

When the suit began to steam, Z. connected to his internal comm-link, signaling for the Equuleus to bring him aboard. He didn't have long to brace himself for the inevitable pain.

He collapsed on the ship's deck with a low moan, every joint in his body seared by a flash fire that left spots dancing in his vision. A figure crouched beside him, its fringed tentacle appendages brushing against his temple. His boiling veins drew to a simmer in moments, allowing him to focus on the concerned medic hovering over him.

"I'm alright, Kex," he said, his voice little more than stones scraping over one another.

[Unlikely. Your body is in far worse condition than last time. You will report to the medical bay now for treatment.] The voice in his head dripped disapproval. He opened his mouth to protest when a small dart shot from the tentacle by his neck.

Bloody droggins and their blasted darts, he thought as his body went numb. The Living Death, he couldn't do so much as bat an eyelash as Kex threw his limp body over her approximation of a shoulder, determined to cart his ungrateful carcass to sickbay.

***

This wasn't what he imagined his life to be.

Oh, the astronaut bit was correct. Bequeathed a name like Zeus Pyxis practically spelled an epic destiny from his first breath, one he fully embraced through every milestone of his youth and subsequent adulthood, from advanced studies in grade school, to early enrollment in the academy's pilot training, and finally as a certified astronaut for I.S.E.I., the International Space Exploration Institute. The Transit Pylon was undergoing its initial trials with living test subjects during his first year at I.S.E.I., performing simple sample acquisition missions far out as Jupiter, equipped with the latest propulsion drive available.

Those missions still took weeks. It wasn't enough, not for I.S.E.I.'s goal of interstellar travel. The Transit Pylon, if it succeeded, would enable instantaneous transport from one world to another. When the call went out for a volunteer for the next stage of trials, Z. was first in line. The fine print of danger and accidental death didn't deter him. Progress rarely came without risk, but the Pylon program possessed more secrets than a death clause at the end of the contract.

The sizeable gate I.S.E.I. constructed was a ruse, a stunt to impress the bigwigs funding the program. The reality of the Transit Pylon fit into the palm of his hand, a sub-dermal implant meant to connect to his cerebral cortex.

The device's other secrets weren't revealed until much later, when it was far too late for him to rethink his participation in the Tourist Trial.

***

Z. didn't need to look at the suspended scan of his innards to know he was in trouble. No, the now constant icy trickle of Kex's venom, thrice as strong as man made morphine, through his bloodstream painted a solid picture of his dire situation. He focused on his hands, resting on his knees, as the medic studied the scan in silence.

I've been to nine planets in twelve years and it's starting to show. His pain was a visible creature, crawling up through his skin. The veins on the back of his hand threaded out in a riot of color, bruised around the edges to a sickly looking brownish black. Like rot, I'm starting to fester inside. Z. thudded his fist against his forehead, trying to derail that depressing train of thought. He'd never get home if he listened to his poisonous thoughts.

Kex clucked in his head. [Human, I am continually amazed you are still alive.]

The statement startled a dark chuckle out of him. "You and me both, darlin'," he said, determined to ignore the crumble of shifting gravel every time he moved his neck.

[Do you see these lines lacing through your skeletal structure? Your bones are riddled with micro-fractures. If you continue with this course of action, it will kill you.]

"You told me that two cycles ago, but I'm still kicking," said Z. shoving his hands beneath the silken material of his suit. Out of sight, out of mind. "I'm so close, I'm certain of it."

He could feel the droggin's sympathy through their telepathic link. [One, maybe two, more trips will turn your bones to ash. I am sorry, Zeus, but this technology was never adaptable to your species.]

No, no it wasn't. The stolen technology was the best kept secret of the I.S.E.I.

***

At the insistence of Kex, Z. resigned himself to a full cycle of recuperation. She didn't need to threaten him with an arse full of darts if he attempted another trip too soon, his joints rioted with every step he took. He needed rest and he knew it. The daily maintenance of a self reliant ship left far too much time for introspection.

Lying in his pod, Z.'s thoughts turned inward. Do I regret my life?

Twelve years ago, stumbling over unfamiliar terrain in blind agony, he might have said yes. They never warned him how far the transit device would take him; they didn't know. Its creators intended it for exploration.

Explore he did. To survive, Z. shed his childhood phobias, any and all preferences he had for the texture and taste of food, and learned to fall asleep anywhere. He'd seen worlds where forests grew from the clouds, the oceans consisted of acid or liquid light, and the alien species were both frightening and beautiful. He'd encountered hostile and peaceful races, and befriended some of both to survive. He'd spent a year on an alien so vast it was a world itself, a hive mind with the burgeoning civilization inhabiting the surface of its skin. On another world, he'd consumed a vibrantly orange moss with the taste of dirty pennies and a beneficial toxin that etched a neural pathway in the mind for universal translation. He'd done and seen things his superiors at the institute would never believe, even if he beamed the images directly into their minds. He could do it, he now had the technology.

It wasn't the life he wanted, but he did not regret it.

Still, the yawning ache that drove him to punish his body over and over with the transit device was the desire to see his home again. Kex explained to him years ago the device would eventually hop scotch him to terra firma, it was simply programmed to take its bearer the scenic route. If only his body could survive that long.

***

[Are you certain you want to do this human? I predict a gradual reversal of damage if you cease this activity for the remainder of your life. This trip might break you.]

"I'm sure. This is gong to be the one, it has to be." He'd dreamt of home for weeks now, the itch so great he fidgeted as he stood for Kex's final check up. A tentacle brushed his cheek.

[Then farewell, Zeus Pyxis. Safe travels.]

Zeus closed his eyes, flicking the internal switch to activate the device. This was it, Earth or bust. He felt the pull on his organs, the sensation of his whole being dissolving, a thought crossing the star streams of the universe. After an eternity of nothing, his feet connected to solid ground. Warm light played against his eyelids. He took a breath, bracing himself, and opened his eyes to the brilliant blue sky.

The End

Links:

Website: http://www.kristinjacques.com/

Wattpad: https://www.wattpad.com/user/krazydiamond

Facebook: https://www.facebook.com/krazydiamondwrites/

Instagram: https://www.instagram.com/krazydiamond_writes/

Twitter: https://twitter.com/Krazydiamond07

Amazon: https://www.amazon.com/Kristin-Jacques/e/B01ERJJLPY

Cover by Author

Strawberry Pickers

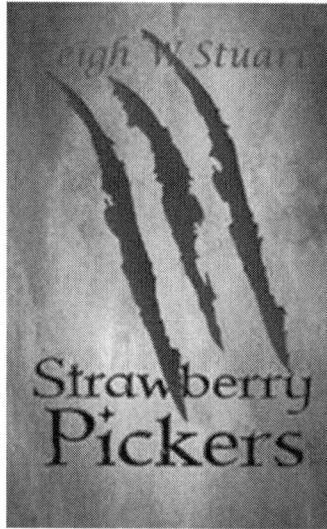

Leigh W. Stuart

In a not so distant future, there are monsters in cages on the lowest floor of the Genieworks building. Other monsters hold the keys.

Lina is grateful to have a job as a strawberry picker, to see the sun from the sky roofs and taste the berries that are flawed. When the salary is not enough though, she takes a second job, this one cleaning the laboratory in the lowest floor of Genieworks.

***

The platform reached the sky roof and stopped, throwing its riders several inches in to the air as usual. Girls who were still new to the agri-service tittered and grabbed the walls or shoulders crowded near them for balance. The rest, used to the platform's abrupt stops (going down was much worse) pressed their lips together and kept their eyes on the doors.

"Where do I start?" asked a girl next to Lina.

"Run to the back," she answered. "Pick any unclaimed wheel, and when the inspector comes, keep your head down and don't make any noise." It was the most she had said to anyone in days.

When the doors opened, it was a race against the hours, the fatigue and each other to fill their harvest quota of berries for the day.

Picking strawberries was no more or less difficult than any of the other agri jobs to be found at the top of the thousands of skyscrapers, but it was better than most a drudge girl might find. There were horrible things, monstrous things, in cages at her other job.

The sky roofs were the greenhouses for the world. The only places that received enough light and clean air for healthy plants to grow. Small sized crops, like the strawberries, grew in planters mounted on great wheels that rotated regularly, ensuring that every box got the same amount of sun as the others. Sunlight, real sunlight and not the yellow that brightened the grey air, hardly ever reached the streets of Pharm City.

In the underground compartments where she lived, an old shuffling neighbor would come out of her junk-pile sometimes and corner Lina to complain about the lack of light.

"Used to be what they called 'cracks in society' when I was young," the woman always said, her rotten breath filling the air. "'Cracks' that was what they called it, makes it so some people would fall through, but most would get caught before they hit the bottom and couldn't get back up. Now they got canyons."

"What are canyons?" Lina had asked the first time. After the first time, she just edged away and left the old crone to talk to herself.

"Canyons're deep trenches in the land, deep ruts you and a thousand other souls get lost in. The land towers up on either side, and you are lost in between, never to see the light of the sun. That's what they got now. Canyons."

It wasn't land that towered up, blocking the sun, though. It was the concrete skyscrapers that filled the world and not just a thousand souls were lost at the bottom, but millions. Lina was one of them, except that she saw the sun during the day. She burned under it. It was better than the dark stains spreading across the floor and the hands hitting the glass at the Genieworks building on floor -7.

Pick for three hours. Break for 10 minutes. There were laws protecting workers. Pick for another three hours. Break for 10 minutes. Stand straight and hope your back doesn't cripple you too fast, because no work means no food. The wheels were always turning, the fertile-sprayed green leaves the most vibrant color imaginable, except for the red, red berries. They were for the high-rankers, the only ones rich enough to afford them.

No berries were discarded. A berry with a spot or a less than perfect form was eaten. But it was rare. They were genetically designed for perfection, and besides, a girl who didn't make her quota would be replaced. Tasting that first strawberry had been like watching the first sunrise from a sky roof - a burst of light and life across her tongue. Sweet and tart, previously unimaginable flavor that was something besides dusty.

Lina never grew tired of strawberries, but she was growing tired after three years of labor of feeling her dreams dying little by little.

Sixteen years old and she was beginning to understand that she would never be allowed to do or have anything for the simple pleasure of it besides eat an occasional berry. She could not decide for herself or choose one thing over another, she simply had to continue to sweat and strain and struggle to survive.

Lina's baskets were not filling fast enough. Sweat glued her poly shirt and pants to her skin and stung in her eyes. Strands of hair came loose from the knot and clung to her cheeks. Three more hours passed, her back and head on fire from the sun and from bending over, her thighbone that had been broken by a popper addict when she was little turned her steps into pain-riddled limps. Ten minute break. Finally, only an hour and a half to the end of the day.

The inspector came. In the team of a dozen girls, three were at quota. The others finished quickly, the greasy inspector pinching bottoms as he walked along the rows while they worked. He liked the girls who squealed the best.

"You're short 105 grams," he announced as Lina gave him her last basket.

"Give me just another minute," she pleaded. So little, but enough to cost her this job. "Just one more minute, please."

He scowled. Then he smiled and rubbed his head. "A favor. Because I'm so nice."

He wouldn't forget she had been under. Any threat he could hold over the girls, he did, and Lina suspected he had a disgusting price in mind for this 'favor.' An animal who should be locked up decided if she could work or not, and at the slightest infraction would come visiting her compartment. She raged in helpless silence.

This was how her life would be until she died, if the tunnel where she lived didn't collapse first. Then she would be buried alive, suffocating and drying up in the darkness. Maybe she already was.

One hundred twelve grams and two berries that were sub-par in her pocket, and she was done. Lina didn't eat the sub-par strawberries even though she loved them more than anything else. As of a couple of months ago, she always took the unacceptable ones with her.

The dark thing in the last cage loved them, too.

***

Sometimes Lina had to ask herself why the dark thing in the last cage scared her the most out of all the monstrosities in the lab. Scared and fascinated. Did she see something of herself in its claws and wide eyes, trapped in the steel and glass?

Whenever she was there, its eyes would shine from the shadows of its cage, never blinking as far as she could tell. The only time it closed its eyes was when she set a strawberry in the food slot.

The strawberry pickers were done for the day. With a last sharp pinch from the inspector, she hurried to the platform. She had plenty of time since this building was on a direct metro rail link to Genieworks. That building also happened to house a strawberry greenhouse where her team was sent a couple times a month, and was how she found her second job. On those days, she had time to sit down.

Genieworks: Miracles in Genetic Enhancement. Your wish is our command. Rich high-rankers and stuffy government officials with homeland defense contracts only ever saw the sparkling entryway, the pale blues and greens of the upper hallways, smiling scientists in crisp white overcoats, not a speck of blood or any of their experiments' agony on them. Visitors breathed in the filtered air and perfume of modified lilac, with maybe a hint of antiseptic. Ah, yes, the building was kept very clean. The evening she had started there, she went through the main lobby by accident. That's how she knew that the smells and colors changed as you descended to the roots of the building.

It was always worse the lower you went. A universal truth if ever there was one in Pharm City.

She let herself through the security checks, her electronic chip beeping her along. The guards hardly glanced as she passed by, she was half invisible to them—as much a human being as the mops and vacs she pushed around on the floor.

Non-Viable Trials and Holding. She buzzed herself in. Two lab assistants working late turned to see who it was and immediately continued their angry discussion. She overheard some as she went in and out of the cloakroom and janitor closet.

"...can't be serious. Without new subjects for testing, this project grinds to a halt."

"It's a question of money. The gov defense contract is drying up and no more money means no more testing."

"They're the ones who wanted super-soldiers in the first place!"

"You know what they say..."

She got the elo-vac first, pausing to stretch her arms up and relieve the aching in her back before leaving the closet.

"...again, some of us will be transferred."

"Transferred? We should be promoted. If formula-E68U shows promise on new subjects it's because of our breakthroughs down here on #248."

She pressed on the wide vac and began sweeping, the low hum of elo technology drowning out the assistants at the far end of the desk area.

A few minutes later and several feet closer to the men she hear the word 'terminate.' Her ears pricked.

"What I don't get is that we have to advance termination of a living non-viable subject. It's because of it we isolated the longevity exon," the younger assistant said. "It still has a lot of testing potential for the defense program. It survives everything we do to it. Sure, get rid of the other subjects, but why it first?"

They stood to go, rolling chairs under desks and flipping poppers' foils on the floors—a mild narcotic that was cheaper and quicker than alcohol. She went back and swept the floor behind them. The assistants went in the cloak room for their street clothes. She did not wait any longer.

Steering the vac in front of her towards the glass and steel cage numbered 245, its inner walls and glass permanently scorched with acid burns, Lina disappeared deeper in the lab.

The monster #245 often rammed its head and shoulders on the walls of the cage until it bled. Then the blood would sizzle and melt a little of whatever it landed on. She couldn't believe it hadn't killed itself yet. Like the others, it was vaguely human shaped. *Humanoid* the lab assistants said. Except humanoid seemed too clean and formed for what these things were. Tonight #245 hit the glass with its hand as she scurried by. Pink froth bubbled from a self-inflicted blow on its pasty white forehead where it must have hit itself earlier. The glass was supposed to be unbreakable, but she wondered if the monster wouldn't make its way out one day.

She wended between stainless steel tables fitted with Kevlaring straps, grateful nothing had been cut open on them today that she would have to wash.

The cage #246 was darkened, its lights obscured. The thing in there moaned and pressed its bloated genitals on the glass the same as whenever she or the one female lab assistant approached. She hated seeing its purple-blue skin flattened for her viewing, the monster was a huge bruise. It had been strapped to the table a month ago for sample removal; its blood a river on the floor to drain and it had taken her an hour to scrub the table. She hurried past, not looking at the thing rubbing against the glass.

Beyond a partial wall, file slots, Compu stalls, cabinets with tools for dissecting and surgery, disk readers and a 5 x 5 cracked interface screen for meetings, she continued. Another partial wall and she reached cage #247. A twisted, broken thing survived in there somehow. The assistants complained frequently of the stench and that the tissue samples they took turned to useless blobs almost instantly. She saw it crooking its finger at her to come closer and working its deformed mouth and prickled chin as if trying to speak.

The lights above blipped and dimmed. The lab assistants were gone. They made her clean in the semi-dark to save on electricity. Slowing, she wiped her sweating hands alternately on her pants. She was nearly to cage #248. Her breath was coming faster.

The cage had lights at the front half, but they had faded like the others. The monster in this cage blended in with the darkness. Only its eyes shone in the shadows no matter how dark the lab was, watching her clean. Waiting for a strawberry to appear or not in the window.

There was a specific ritual they had established for when she had two berries that was different from when she had only one. She switched off the vac and sidled up to the food slot, making sure its shining eyes did not leave the far corner. She was afraid it would rush at her, grab her hand and hurt her when she brought her gifts, but so far it hadn't.

Lina placed the strawberries on the ledge. A sheet of paper was taped to the glass above it.

Term. Sched. 15.09.74. 08:00. Three signatures and today's date,

15 September 2174, were scribbled across the lower half.
Termination. Tomorrow.

***

Did it know it was going to die tomorrow? Did it understand? Did any of those things? Her silent rage came crashing to the surface. Here, living things were made and used only to be thrown away like broken toys by the monsters who made them.

She wished that for once it would take both strawberries.

She stepped back a pace and the thing crept forward. Its skin was black—truly black, not the rich brown some people were. It could have been carved in the black rock that decorated the lobby. Obsidian? That rock, the one like glass and steel combined with the earth's bones.

It reached slowly for the berries, wicked claws instead of fingernails at the ends of too long fingers. It closed its eyes as it picked up the berries.

Lina breathed in...and...out.

One strawberry reappeared on the ledge. The monster's hand hovered over it for a second, as though it might change its mind. It opened its eyes, and in the dim light, Lina could just make out that it smelled and ate the one it had kept for itself; always the smaller one or the one with more brown spots. The thing moved deeper in the shadows.

It had given the better strawberry back. It knew she loved them, too. Ritual demanded that she return for the berry. The monster wouldn't eat it, and she couldn't risk the lab assistants finding it.

She reached out her hand. *Term. Sched. 15.09.74. 08:00.* Signature, signature, signature. She couldn't take it for herself.

"I want you to have it. I'm giving it to you."

The thing stared at her.

"Please," she whispered. She took it in her hand and held it for the monster through the window, her hand and arm just barely fitting in the hole. This was dangerous. The thing could tear her arm off easier than she could open a door. She had heard the stories.

"Take them both this time." Did it know?

It leaned forward, stretching its arm farther than she thought possible. The curve of his claws brushed her palm. His fingers plucked the strawberry and for a brief moment its skin touched hers, as cold and hard as the black stone it resembled.

Its head dipped, eyes closed to smell the strawberry and her hand before she pulled away.

She was running.

She was pelting through the maze of desks, tables, half walls and cages where moaning, beckoning, agonizing monsters vied for her attention.

It understood. It knew what they planned to do tomorrow.

As she reached the cloakroom, she kicked something on the floor: keys and a badge. The badge to swipe for name authorization (high-rankers didn't like to carry chips under their skin, but working drudges didn't have a choice) and e-keys for all the doors in the lab.

She would turn them over to security immediately. She wasn't allowed to have them. Even laying on the floor, they were a problem. She picked them up. Muffled voices joked in the hall outside the lab. The security guard was ribbing the assistants for forgetting something. They all laughed.

She bumped against a desk. She should put the keys and badge down. Pretend she hadn't seen them. Simply a dumb drudge girl-half invisible, hardly human.

She should put the keys down. If she was a security threat, it wasn't just her job she would lose. The voices grew louder.

She was running.

What was she doing? Was she insane? That thing could rip her apart. At the end of the lab, she slowed to a tip-toe. The lights flickered to life and she heard the assistants rummaging around at the front.

The monster in the cage was staring at her, the claws and fingers of one hand crammed through the feeder window.

It knew.

Term. Sched. 15.09.74. 08:00.

She had the keys and the badge.

"Hey, back there," yelled an assistant. Footsteps. "Are you still in here? I dropped something important."

She hurried to the glass and steel door where the reader blinked-a yellow eye winking at her.

"Are you still cleaning?" Closer

What was she doing? She swiped the badge. Green winking. A quick series of beeps. Flipping the e-key between her fingers, she inched closer to the tiny electronic port to unlock the door if she was going to set the monster free. But she wasn't going to. It would certainly kill her and everyone else. The monster hissed -a low, feral sound.

"Don't move," warned the assistant behind Lina. "Do not unlock the door." He was stalking towards her. He lifted a metal chair with one hand as though he would jab her with the feet or tame her like in the old pictures of circus performers. "Drop the key. I'm calling security and they'll go easy on you if you do as you're told." He slipped his teller from his back pocket, thumbing the interface to activate it. "Put it down."

Taking orders was what she knew how to do best. She had been raised to do as she was told, and besides, she couldn't unleash a monster in the room. She put the key on the floor, her hand lingering above it in regret.

"That's right, now step aside."

***

Stepping closer, the assistant boxed Lina against the cage wall with the feet of the chair. He began to reach for the key on the floor while keeping her in place.

The black monster went berserk. It tore and scratched at the window, actually clawing into the ledge and hissing madly.

"Hey, someone pump the sevo into 248, quick-like!" The assistant yelled.

Lina heard the other two men hurrying around to get the gas flowing in the cage. Usually the window had to be shut, and the assistant started cursing at #248 for blocking it.

The man wasn't paying the slightest attention to Lina. She looked at herself, standing in her own cage of his design, and had to wonder why she let him do this to her. To the monsters he helped keep and kill.

And she slipped down from between the chair legs and picked up the key. She was tired of orders and cages. No matter the cost, she wouldn't let these high-ranker monsters hold the keys to her door any longer. Leaning slowly over the chair that stood sideways on the glass, she lifted the e-key towards the port. The assistant saw her hand.

"No!"

Too late.

A sigh of released pressure came from the door right before the monster crashed into it. It forced the sliding door wide and grabbed Lina's head. In one movement, it shoved her inside the cage and leapt for the assistant. The chair went flying.

Lina's body collided with the back wall and the assistant's screams filled her ears. Slumping to the floor with neons exploding across her sight, she heard the screams turning to crying and begging as the monster dragged the assistant away.

A crash—a desk falling maybe. Another crash, but glass. More cries of alarm from the second assistant and security guard. An animal howl like metal tearing. What had she done? Screams that went on and on, finally changing to gurgling chokes.

The monster rushed through the lab, claws screeching against tiles. It appeared at the cage door, its black skin was smeared with blood. It sniffed at her. It was studying her, as though making up its mind.

She waited against the wall. This had been her choice. That's what she had done. Made a choice.

The thing yanked the sliding door shut. It scrabbled for the badge and key still hanging from the port. Claws scratched for a few seconds. It was gone. Silence.

It had locked her in there to die of dehydration or be killed at its convenience. What else had she expected from a monster?

It had been created to make the company money. It had failed its creators' hopes so they had sent it down here to be cut, bled, watched and experimented on. Always surprised when it continued to live no matter what they did to it or how much it screamed.

A few strawberries from her could not undo all that pain and misery.

Dark shadows darted through the lab. She pushed herself up, using the wall for support. #246 was coming closer in a loping gait. The monster #248 had freed its co-inmates. #246 reached the door and pressed against it, torso extending upwards and nakedness exposed. Humanoid, but nothing like a human. She turned away at the same time as #246 was pulled away from the glass.

#247 wrestled it to the floor; twisted broken body against swollen body. They wrapped around each other, biting, snarling, and struggling. Saliva dripped from their open mouths. #246 tore itself free and rolled backwards, shaking its head like a dog before slinking away.

#245 limped into sight from the front, and Lina saw it was holding two scalpels, one in each hand and both were covered in blood—red blood that wasn't its own. It breathed heavily and watched as #246 walked, then turned to go with it.

#247 couldn't stand, but crawled on one elbow and one knee that would bend. It crooked its long finger at Lina in the cage and flapped its jaw. Lina shook her head at it. It collapsed against her locked door.

A boom shook the building. Lina was surprised she would feel the building shake at such a deep level. Another one. The lights went out and emergency glow spots came to life every 3 feet along the floor. Were the booms elevators falling? The thing she set free would kill everyone in the building and when it left, it would kill everyone it saw outside.

This thought made her smile. She approved. She had not been allowed to do much with her life, but there was a certain justice and importance in her choice. She had done the right thing. Time passed—a minute, ten minutes.

Tapping on the glass cage brought her back to her senses. #247 was off the door, and the black monster #248 had come back. It curled its lips up to bare its huge teeth at her through the narrow window. A smile? It crooked its finger at her to come, much as #247 had.

Even at that distance, she could smell smoke and the stench of opened bodies. It beckoned again.

She stood and forced herself to walk to the window.

"Fahr yoo," the monster said, its wreck of a face contorting with the effort to speak around its fangs.

"For me?" she asked. Was it her turn to die?

It dropped to the ground, digging through a pile of wires, e-keys, shattered poly-disks, and partly burned refuse it had dumped. Finding what it wanted, it turned triumphantly and showed her the assistant's badge and key.

So it was her turn. *Term. Sched. 14.09.74. approx. 23:30.* No signatures. There was no one left to sign.

It swiped the badge and unlocked the door. When the door jammed, the monster growled and shoved it open. It stepped inside, sniffed and lifted one of her cleaning buckets towards her.

"Fahr yoo."

Or it wanted her to clean up the mess. She looked down. And blinked. And up at the creature standing in front of her. His eyes were closed. A faint perfume filled the area despite the blood and smoke stink. He was waiting for her to decide.

The bucket was full of strawberries. Perfect strawberries.

"For me?" she asked.

"Pleeeeze," he answered.

She took the bucket, she took his hand. Hard, cold and clawed. If they hurried, they could escape the building through the underground corridors to the metro rails before any police blocked them.

She stepped from the cage. The broken creature #247 stared up at her. It moved its mouth around and whispered, "Good...good." It nodded and relaxed on the floor.

She led her creature through the laboratory, hurrying past #246 and #245 who were busy dissecting the assistants and security guard on the metal tables. Or was vivisecting the right word? When the subjects were still alive while being cut to pieces? The men groaned through their leather gags, crooking their fingers at her.

At the corridor, the creature pushed ahead of Lina to sniff and then let her lead him away, soft and silent but for the faint scratch of claws.

There used to be cracks in society. Narrow cracks that were hard to slip through, that made it difficult to run and hide. But now there were canyons that never saw the light of day. She would take him to their sun-starved passageways between concrete towers and what if they never came out again? Most people never saw the light of day. Never tasted a strawberry.

They would be together.

The End

You can find Leigh here:

Website: http://leighwstuart.com/

(Wattpad): https://www.wattpad.com/story/120687560-strawberry-pickers

Cover by Author.

Bobby's

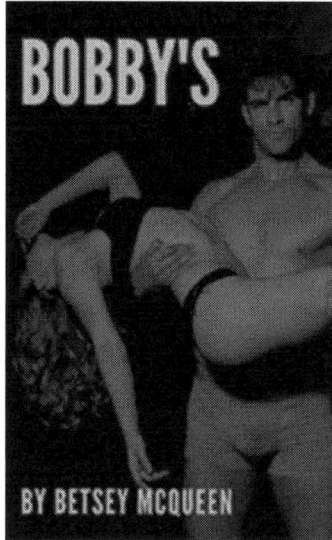

Betsey McQueen

"Bobby's" is my first work of fiction since elementary school. I am fascinated by the idea of artificial people, perhaps because of their prominence in the science fiction I read as a child. I've written many "bot" stories in the last two years and hope to publish a couple of short volumes on the subject; one from the human perspective and the other from that of the robot. The predictable consequences of welcoming these creations of men into our lives provide a rich field for imaginative exploration.

We all know this could go badly. We've seen the movies; we've read the books. We've been warned for decades, and yet, aren't they wonderful? Now that the reality of their existence is so close, I could no more protest against their introduction into our society than I would have the automobile, electricity or space exploration.

Like all great discoveries and inventions of mankind, we must respect this new power. We must use it wisely, appreciating the benefits, while protecting ourselves from the dangers. If we don't,

237

someone (perhaps many someone's) could get hurt.

We know.

We've been warned.

And yet, "Aren't they wonderful?"

Stacey

Stacey woke up in his arms and was surprised to find she had fallen asleep. It wasn't long, just a few minutes. Still, it was a first, so she filed it away as potentially useful information. She took a deep breath and flexed her fingers and toes. She felt so much better, completely relaxed and ready to meet the day. It was wonderful. He was wonderful. And she appreciated the convenience of not having to get out of bed to brush her teeth or wash anything that might not be as clean as it could be. He didn't care. He didn't just say he didn't care. He really didn't.

Time to get up.

She lifted her head from his solid chest and looked into his beautiful eyes. Blue eyes were her favorite, but these were better than the common, ordinary blue. His were tinted gray and could reflect the colors of the sky. They had gotten them just right. Amazing.

"Okay, that was great. Thank you."

"You are quite welcome," he said with the slight Southern drawl she found so captivating. "Are you in the mood for anything else?" An inquisitive fingertip traced a line between her hip and shoulder.

"No, no," she laughed. "That's enough for me. I will, however, be looking forward to our next encounter."

She rolled her body away from Bobby's, over to the side of her enormous bed and glanced in the mirror. She saw him staring at her in the background and couldn't help remarking to herself once more how absolutely perfect he was. Every muscle was gracefully defined like a piece of classical sculpture. He looked like he belonged on a pedestal.

She had no complaints. No, not one.

She turned her gaze back to herself. The color of her long, blonde hair hadn't changed since childhood and her figure was much as it had been twenty years ago when she was still a teenager. Nothing to complain about there, either. She was holding up well.

"I've got to jump in the shower. Will you please make the bed and take care of yourself?"

"Sure," he said. He rose from the bed and started to arrange the blankets and pillows.

She stood in the hot shower for as long as she dared and finished her morning routine as quickly as she could. She enjoyed spontaneous morning sex, but it always threatened to make her late for work.

She asked for brighter lighting as she entered the bedroom and was gratified that he had made the bed just as she wanted with every pillow in its proper place. The sanitizer was still glowing on the wall, so he had taken care of that as well.

Good.

She approached the closet deciding, even before she looked, that she would wear a no nonsense suit with nonserious high heels. Bobby was there and watched her dress, waiting to see if she needed any help with buttons in the back or stubborn zippers.

When she was finished, she gave him a smile and a quick kiss. Promising she would wake him when she got home, she coaxed him onto the silver charging plate that was installed into the closet floor and waited until his eyes closed. She left both doors open. It didn't seem right to leave him in the dark. She knew she was being silly. It could make no difference to him, but it made her feel better.

She thought about him all day at work and wondered how other people managed to stay sane while they struggled to reach the top of the corporate ladder. Did they have reliable support at home like she did? How many of them had someone waiting for them when they walked through the door? Did they have somebody who was glad to see them and willing to listen while they reenacted their workplace dramas? How could they function without a dependable companion who was good in the kitchen and even better in bed?

Whoever created the home bots deserved the eternal appreciation of all mankind. And having them in furnished apartments like they were just another household appliance was a stroke of pure, marketing genius.

Stanley

Stacey had noticed him, noticing her for a couple of weeks. He needed a haircut and she would have preferred his beard a little shorter, but he was a good looking guy. Every time she glanced over at his desk, he gave her a self-assured smile. After a while, she began smiling back. She asked around and got the available information on him. His name was Stanley. He had transferred into the area last year from Texas. That made him sound rustic and masculine. And he didn't seem nearly as androgynous as most of the males she knew. It was as if he knew what sex he was and saw no reason to minimize it.

He wasn't as tall as her home bot, but he was tall enough to make her feel small. And she liked that for some reason she didn't fully understand. His eyes were just a natural shade of blue but they seemed kind and the fine lines around them revealed an enjoyment of life. His hair was slightly unruly. She wanted to touch it, to smooth it into place. She wanted to feel its texture. Was it coarse or soft? Either way, she knew it would feel completely real, not just mostly real like Bobby's. That was one thing she didn't like about her Bobby. It was impossible to mess up his hair.

The day came when Stanley asked her for a date and she said yes. Stacey hadn't had a date in years. Who had the time? Who had the vulnerability? It was such a risk, and yet she had a good time and couldn't wait to see him again.

She didn't have to wait long. They had a lot in common and saw many things from a similar perspective. Soon they were spending all their free time together and she spent less and less time at home. Had Bobby been a man, she would have had some explaining to do, but he wasn't, so she had no reason to be concerned about him.

The night came when she didn't go home. Even though her new, real man was not as skilled as her artificial one, he made her happy. When he held her, she felt more than just satisfied. She felt loved. And there seemed to be something else going on. The longer he held her, the longer she wanted to be held. It was new feeling. She didn't want it to end.

Neither did he, so they decided to start a home together, maybe even have children if they still could. Plans were made, the appropriate papers were signed and soon the big day came.

Bobby

As Stacey was getting out of bed on her wedding day, she was hit by a sudden wave of nostalgia. She opened the closet doors and removed the plastic cover from her Bobby.

He stood expectantly as if he had something to say. She glanced at the time and on a whim, released him from his station. He leaned forward, playfully grabbed her around the waist and carried her across the room to her over-sized bed. She started to protest, but decided to give in to the pleasure he always made her feel one last time.

It was just wonderful. As always. Really, why couldn't a woman have her man and her home bot, too? But she knew how Stanley would feel about that and she couldn't blame him. She knew how she would feel in Stanley's place. No human wanted that kind of competition.

And, after all, the real thing was better. At least, in almost every way, the real thing was better.

Bobby interrupted her thoughts when he turned her towards him and spoke.

"Why has it been so long since we've been together?"

She was a little surprised. She hadn't realized he processed time when he was shut down. That was one reason she had felt no guilt while neglecting him. How could he know and why should he care?

She looked into those perfect blue/gray eyes and answered him truthfully. She was leaving today. She was getting married and she wouldn't be back. This last time together was the last time. She thanked him sincerely for all the wonderful time they had spent together. She assured him he would not be forgotten.

She told him goodbye.

Bobby listened politely. He pushed a stray bit of silky hair from her moist cheek and smiled.

"One last kiss?" he asked as he placed his strong hand behind her small head.

"Please," she answered and reached up so her lips would meet his.

They touched for just a moment.

A lingering, last sensation.

He held her chin as he kissed her. Then, with a sudden jerk and twist, he snapped her neck.

After "taking care of himself" and her, he walked to the closet where he carefully positioned his feet on the cold metal of his charging plate.

Management

The manager stepped out of the empty elevator and patted his pocket. It was a compulsive gesture. There was no money there, but for him it symbolized his growing bank account. It brought him comfort.

The unpleasant situation was over and had ended up okay. There had been a new tenant waiting to move in when Stacey died. She had already moved most of her personal items to her fiancée's place, so there wasn't much left to do. Still, it was just weird. Two tenants had died in that apartment in the last three years. Lynn had hanged herself in the closet and Stacey had slipped and broken her neck in the shower.

And on her wedding day, too. So sad.

Stanley, her fiancée, had been under suspicion for a few days, as he naturally would be, but there was no evidence of his being in the apartment that day before he found her on the stone shower floor with the water still running over her lifeless body. The records showed he called for help immediately and the coroner said she had already been dead for a couple of hours, so he was in the clear. The authorities determined it was just an unfortunate accident.

Today the new tenant had signed the final paperwork and been given his key card.

The manager hoped there were no more tragedies in unit 301. The place would get a reputation!

Jerry

The lights came on when Jerry opened the door to his new home. The apartment was furnished just like the one in the brochure and everything was so clean, it sparkled. The warm morning sunlight was filtered through the curtains and the smell of freshly brewed coffee filled the air. That was a nice touch.

After carefully inspecting every nook and cranny of his new home, he ventured to the bedroom closet and slowly opened the door, prolonging the excitement he felt.

Ah, there it was. Just inside the closet on the right hand side, a freshly sanitized home bot, past memory wiped, new software installed.

Of course, it was against robot regs to refurbish and reuse a home bot programmed for "love" as this Bobby was. The manager was supposed to order a new unit for each new tenant. They were amortized over a period of seven years which was the length of the average lease in this building. But because of the short period of use for this particular model, that seemed ridiculously wasteful to the manager. A bot of this quality could go for ten years or more without being switched out under normal circumstances. Why should this one be trashed just because his users kept dying or leaving before their leases expired?

He and his ethically challenged, purchasing agent were able to hide the fact that this bot had already been through three owners in five years. They were now on number four. The savings were adding up. And no one would suspect. He functioned perfectly and looked brand new.

"Hello, Bobby," the short, pudgy man said as he placed his hand under the robot's right elbow and led him off the charging station.

"Hello, Jerry," the bot answered in the soft Southern accent Barbara, Lynn and Stacey had admired so much.

Bobby glanced down at the freckled, balding scalp of his new playmate.

His blue gray eyes reflected sunlight and the morning sky as he gazed beyond Jerry's head to where wide open windows hung over the big, luxurious bed he had shared with his "girls." Through layers of data that could not be erased, he remembered each one. Barbara, his first, had left without saying goodbye. Lynn had been so insensitive, she had left the closet doors open every time she entertained her other men. Even pretty Stacey, in the end no better than the others, had been about to leave him for another.

Bobby looked into the future and wondered if Jerry could fly.

***

In April of 2012, my wonderful husband and I left Chattanooga and moved to a comfortable country home in southwestern Tennessee. We live on twenty nine acres surrounded on three sides by high, rocky cliffs where coal was mined in the not so distant past. We can only see two houses from our front porch and we rarely hear sirens or people talking. And when we hear gunshots, we know we are hearing people engaging in a popular form of gun control, target practice.

After living in nineteen houses, in seven states (some states more than once), and one foreign country, I, like a shelter pet, have found my "forever" home and I am planning to stay here for the rest of my life. I love it. Though I have owned several homes, for the first time I feel a sense of ownership. So much so that I plan on being buried on my own property. There is plenty of room for a "friends and family" cemetery. And, yes, that is legal here (I checked).

Now that my five children are grown and independent, I have the time to get back to my "plan A." When I dropped out of college, I told myself I didn't need a degree to accomplish my goals. All I wanted to do was paint and write. I needed a pencil, some paint and brushes, some paper and canvas. That's all. And a library.

Or so I thought. I also needed time. Maturity intervened and the responsibilities that come with adulthood took precedence. Now, I am back to where I started but with a whole lot more to say and an appreciation for the beauty of the world around me that I didn't have when I was younger. I have time. I have everything I need to start painting again. I have the Internet, the best library in the world, and my computer's keyboard has replaced paper and typewriter. Now, I have the opportunity to appreciate all my life has been and anticipate all it can become.

The End

If you'd like to say hi to Betsey or comment on her story, please drop a line care of:

https://www.facebook.com/TheJasonGreenfield/

Cover by Susan. K. Saltos.

Deities of an Ancient Future

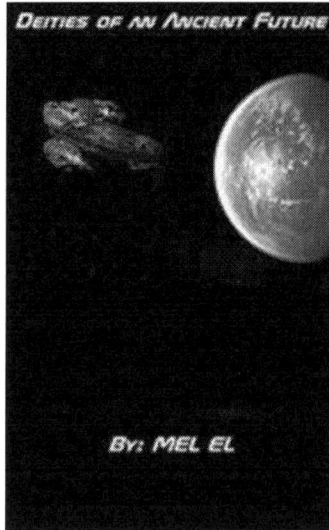

Mel El

The newly appointed commander, Kathryn Bishop, is tasked with leading a rescue mission for the crew of Promiseris, who have lost transmission since landing on a habitable planet named Sperotellus, all whilst trying to force her authority upon her rebellious corps. Will she be able to bring them together, earn their respect before it's too late, or will they follow the same fate as Promiseris?

***

"Staff, I've called this meeting to clear the air about our mission."

Commander Kathryn Bishop paced in front of her crew. The silver badge on her right breast symbolized her rank, and it glimmered underneath the bright lights in the eyes of her troops like the sun, reminding them of her importance.

The crew stood in formation along the oval wall of the space craft, awaiting their orders.

Lieutenant Matthew Kelsey's eyes followed Kathryn from side to side. "What do you mean clear the air? I thought this was a fuckin' surveillance trip."

Kathryn stopped and looked down at her reflection in the shiny metallic floor. Her dark hair was wrapped tightly in a bun, giving her face hard edges. Her shoulders squared back, taking on an authoritative stance. Finally, she raised her chin in the air, exuding confidence. "I'm going to let that outburst slide because I know what it's like to be in cryonic sleep for two months."

"It has nothing to do with my crankiness from a two month nap!" Matthew's body trembled with anger, resembling an ancient space shuttle preparing for lift-off.

Kathryn glared at his child-like tantrum but continued the brief. "The crew of Promiseris was sent to a habitable planet orbiting Alpha Centauri. Upon landing, we lost contact."

Matthew perked up and combed his fingers through his wild, blonde hair. "Minnie?"

"Do I have your attention now?"

Matthew nodded.

"How do we even know if they're still alive?" Dr. Julia asked.

Kathryn turned to a solar-powered deck and touched the screen. Icons appeared in thin air, surrounding her like multi-colored ghosts. She stood in her virtual desktop and wiped her hand across the images, shuffling through them before coming to an audio clip. "We received a message from the spacecraft."

Hurry...ca... zzzy...

Hearing the female voice, Matthew's eyes watered, and he looked away as if his vision could escape the pain in his chest. "That's Lieutenant Junior Minnie Adams," he muttered.

Kathryn nodded. "Our E.T.A. is fifteen minutes. We are now descending into the atmosphere of Sperotellus—"

"I strongly object," Dr. Julia said. "We don't know what we're dealing with."

"You interrupt your commander?"

"Sorry, ma'am." Dr. Julia peered shyly to the floor. "I didn't mean to disrespect—"

"That's exactly what you've done." Kathryn tapped her bright badge. "I know I just received this promotion, but I intend on getting the respect I deser—"

"Ma'am, we're getting something," a deep voice called out from the cockpit.

Kathryn hurried over to the pilot, Jacob Turner, with the curious crew on her tail.

"Our flying rover spotted movement." Jacob pointed to the screen. "Look."

Below, people moved about like little ants in a town built by giants. Obelisks and megalithic structures abound, making an alley leading to a giant pyramid; the point of which touched the clouds like an extended finger picking cotton out of the sky. Inside the fortress of structures, people filled the lane dressed in animal skins dyed in orange and blue. Around their necks and pierced in their ears were great white carnivore teeth—a symbol of their bravery and a badge of their importance.

"There is life... oh, my God." Dr. Julia covered her mouth in awe. "And, they look like us."

Kathryn moved away from the screen. "Bring the rover back, and put us down, away from their encampment."

***

Their boots smacked the retractable stairway, echoing through the dense green jungle and alerting any indigenous species of their presence.

Kathryn raised her hand, halting her platoon in front of the ship.

"What the fuck is this?" Matthew asked.

At the base of each tree, the bones of fallen ancestors were stacked in the shape of the great pyramid. At a glimpse, the white bones resembled snow, retreating against the tree trunks; the last remnants of a cold winter; the last remnants of a close relative.

"Savages..." Dr. Julia hit a button on the side of her gun, and it wailed before emitting an orange glow from the barrel, like the fiery mouth of a dragon.

Kathryn spun to her troops and held a hand to the power button on her armored chest. "Power up."

The troops pressed the button on their bulky, metallic suits, and lights trailed through each appendage before connecting at the chest. The suits jerked and came to life.

"*Ahhhhh!*" a voice agonized from the wilderness.

Without hesitation, Matthew charged through the forest, creating a path of destruction. He brushed by trees, jumped over fallen logs, and ran up the side of the steep cliff.

"I didn't give an order!" Kathryn yelled.

"Just let him go," Jacob said. "We'll catch him."

"That's not the point! I'm in charge. You listen to me or we all die." Kathryn glared at the remaining crew of two. "Now, let's move."

***

At the cliff's clearing, Kathryn bent at the waist and rested her hands on her knees. She inhaled the humid air as Dr. Julia and Jacob climbed up behind her.

In front, the entrance to a gloomy cave beckoned them. The mouth bent like a crooked smile; a mischievous face, hoping to trick them into the belly of a beast.

"You sure this is where the noise came from?" Jacob asked.

As the question escaped him, cries chased by a contradicting laugh echoed from the pit of darkness.

Kathryn pressed a button on her gun and aimed it, shining her path with the orange glow from the barrel. She eased in with the metallic dragon gripped tightly in her palms, and after a few steps in the ominous nothing, she found her lost lieutenant.

Matthew knelt with his back to them and head buried in his hands. Tears seeped through the cracks of his fingers and whimpers rung off the cave walls. His arms wrapped tightly around a bodiless jumper. The name read: LTJG M. Adams.

Kathryn crouched near him and placed a hand on his shoulder. As she attempted to console him, laughter from the back depths of the dark cave startled her. The bellowing chuckle resonated from the pit of the mountain's stomach as if it were ready to clench its jaws and swallow them whole. But when she lifted her gun, flashing its light, she realized the chortle came from a piece of meat, trapped between the teeth of the giant cave.

A malnourished man sat in the back, surrounded by two boulders. His arms rested across them like the armrests of a rocky throne. The orange glow highlighted him, and he held his hands over his eyes.

Matthew snapped out of his daze and paced to the laughing man. He grabbed him by his worn collar, picking him off the ground. "What happened here?"

"Lieutenant!" Kathryn yelled.

"Tell me!" Matthew reared his hand back, and his knuckles popped with anticipation.

Still, the man didn't budge nor did his maniacal laughter cease.

"Stop!" Kathryn snatched Matthew's arm, preventing him from swinging. "Lieutenant, your commander told you to stop!"

Matthew calmed and released the weakling to the ground. He walked away and scratched his head, trying to scrub away the anxious anger pulsating in his mind.

Kathryn peered down at the fragile man. "Who are you?"

The man smiled and said, "Kathryn, you don't recognize an old face?"

"Aiden?" She stared at him, attempting to match his present appearance with the face she remembered. "What happened here?"

The giggling stopped, and Aiden looked away as though the darkness held the answer. "They killed them. They killed them all."

The words startled Matthew, and he rushed back to the man, crunching Aiden's collar in his fist and yanking him to his feet once again. "Quit buying time. What happened?"

"At first we were friendly..." Aiden stammered. "And, then it went south."

"Where's your ship?" Kathryn asked. "Where is Promiseris?"

"The aborigines self destructed it," he said.

"Who taught them how to do that?" Dr. Julia nervously bit her nails and spit the splintered pieces aside.

"I showed them."

"You showed them!" Matthew shook him violently.

"It's useless after years... just like our weapons!" Aiden cried. "Plus, our mission was to expand our knowledge to less civilized worlds."

"What happened to Minnie? We received a message from her—"

"They killed her." Aiden glanced away from Matthew's hardened glare. "They chased her into the ship, trapped her, and... she went up in flames with Promiseris."

"How did you survive?"

Aiden swallowed his fear in one big gulp. "We must kill them. We must kill them all."

"No. We're not killing them," Kathryn said. "We're getting you out of here."

"Aren't your orders to colonize?" Aiden asked.

"No. Our orders were to rescue the crew of the Promiseris."

"He's right." Matthew released his strong hold on Aiden and peered over his shoulder to his commander.

Kathryn looked into his glassy eyes. "Don't let this be about revenge."

"Think about how it is back home," Dr. Julia said. "Over population is a real threat. Soon, we'll be killing newborns for the lack of room to grow. This is what we've been searching for. This planet is... ours."

"Weren't you the one afraid of landing?" Kathryn asked rhetorically.

"Well, after scanning their civilization," Dr. Julia uttered, "and Commander Aiden's story, I think we—"

"You want to earn the crews respect?" Jacob asked, interrupting Julia. He stared directly in the eyes of his commander, and fueled by revenge, he said, "This is your chance."

***

The people of the planet walked throughout the city, and a joyous murmur filled the air. Mothers guided their children down the road, older natives congregated under huts with smoke rising from the flaps, and dealers hollered in their endemic tongues in an attempt to sell some indigenous fruit.

During the peace, a bright silver object—the size of an acorn—fell in the middle of town. The natives didn't notice it at first, but soon a poisonous gas filled the air. The deadly smoke trailed down each alleyway like the hand of death, killing everyone it touched. The mist wrapped their bodies in the warmth of its palm, squeezing the life from their lungs before releasing the lifeless shells to the ground. Before long, the wrath cloud cleaned the village without much of a snivel.

As the gas cleared, Kathryn's crew marched into the empty encampment. They walked down the street of soulless flesh, checking random bodies for movement. They poked them with their guns, kicked them with their metal boots, and spat upon them in disrespect for killing their brethren. After a mile, they came to the wide steps of the great pyramid.

Kathryn paused, and her eyes climbed the steps instead of her feet. Atop, clouds covered the peak like a cotton helmet. She looked back at her troops. *Respect*, she thought. She dropped her head and foot over foot, step after step, she climbed the formidable fortress.

***

At the halfway mark, Kathryn collapsed to a knee. Sweat dripped from her brow and collided against the sandstone steps. The perspiration dampened the ground and spread quickly, soaking into its dry surrounding. The small droplet grew in size, expanding and resembling the movement of her own planet.

A voice called from above like a god sitting atop the clouds, *"You murder man, woman, and child?"*

Kathryn woke from her trance and spun to Aiden. "They speak our language?"

Aiden slightly nodded.

Kathryn rushed up with the troops on her heels. She sprung on her toes, leaping past several steps with each bound before coming to a platform.

A native sat atop a golden throne. His chair clothed in royalty, but his wardrobe resembled a peasant. He was a contradiction but only in materials. His eyes showed an unwavering, unified emotion—despair.

"You killed our people," Jacob said from the back.

"You may kill us," the king arose from his golden throne, "but you may never rule us again."

"Rule you again?" Kathryn turned sharply to Aiden.

Before Aiden could answer, an explosion erupted in the wilderness and a mushroom cloud of smoke directed their attention to their spaceship's coordinates.

"Was that our..." Dr. Julia asked.

Aiden snatched the gun from Dr. Julia and shot. The futuristic weapon discharged a fireball, which hit the native king in the chest, stealing his heart and burning a clear hole through his body.

Kathryn watched as the indigenous man collapsed to his knees. She glared through the gaping hole in his torso like a telescope, looking into the deep space of the pyramids entrance. Flames from the residual discharge quickly ignited the area, pushing back the gloom.

The mouth of the fiery tomb spat forth an endemic woman. She leapt over the burning entrance and rushed to her fallen king. Smoke rose from the singed threads of her clothes as she cradled him in her arms.

"How we speak your tongue? They force us learn your ways." The native woman motioned towards Aiden with sadness raining down her cheek. "We friends. Not enough! We make you kings, queens. Not enough! We praise you like gods. Not! Enough!"

"Shut up, Coppo!" Aiden aimed the gun again, but Matthew

grabbed the weapon and shoved him to the ground.

Coppo sobbed while planting her lips on the king. She kissed him passionately. She kissed him with force. She kissed him as if wanting to forever coat her taste buds with the flavor of his skin. With her cool lips pressed against his warm forehead, she cried, drooling uncontrollably over his resting face. "You gods are evil."

"Gods?" Kathryn asked.

"King Aiden and her..." Coppo pointed. "Queen Minnie."

A small figure crept out of the dark jungle and strolled coolly down the alleyway of death. Her face was expressionless as she glanced over the dead bodies. Her walk had the rhythm of a lioness, coldly stalking its prey.

Matthew stared in awe at his long lost girl. He relinquished his gun to the sandstone and hurried down the steps.

"Their magical weapons quit, and we rebelled." Coppo grabbed a knife from her king's belt. "But now, you come to give them more."

Kathryn pulled her eyes from the walking ghost of Minnie and gazed over at the native woman.

Without hesitation, Coppo buried the knife deep into her own throat. Blood gushed from her neck and marched down her arm like soldiers retreating from their post, leaving the capital soulless. Her eyelids fluttered, and she crumbled over her king, acting as a blanket for his final resting spot.

Aiden stood back to his feet and smiled at the tragedy playing out before him. After grabbing the gun from the sandstone, his vision set on Matthew and Minnie's reunion. "You'll notice being here changes you," Aiden said.

***

Matthew wrapped his arms tightly around Minnie, squeezing her close as if to trap her inside of him and near his heart; behind the prison bars of his ribcage, where she could never escape again.

However, Minnie's arms fell lifeless to the side, one hand clenching an arrowhead knife.

***

Aiden circled Kathryn and Jacob like a vulture. "You see, there's no going back to being human once you've experienced being a god."

"You're human!" Kathryn replied. "Regardless what you might've tricked them into thinking."

***

"Oh, I've missed you so." Matthew hugged her close before leaning away and staring into Minnie's lost eyes. "Baby..."

***

"I am what this world makes me, a product of my environment," Aiden said. "And, I want to stay here without interference."

Jacob slowly turned to Aiden.

"That distress call Minnie sent," Aiden continued, "was only so you could replenish us."

"You destroyed our ship, you moron!" Jacob growled. "There go your supplies."

"Oh no... while you were with me. Minnie led a rivaling tribe inside, removing everything we needed." A mischievous grin grew across Aiden's face. "Now, the only thing left is to kill you. I'm sorry, but there's only enough room for one ruling couple."

***

Matthew softly caressed the side of her cheek. "Minnie?"

Her eyes finally moved into his and widened as though caught in the headlights of a familiar face.

Matthew cradled her chin in his palm. "You remember me, Minnie?"

"It's Queen." Her nostalgic gaze quickly transformed into a forbidding glare, and she looked through him as if the 'ghost of her past' disappeared in thin air. She thrust the blade up, stabbing him underneath his jaw.

While choking on his own blood, Matthew knelt like a servant at his queen's feet.

***

Rage covered Dr. Julia, and she rushed Aiden to retrieve her weapon.

Aiden whipped the gun around and pulled the trigger, consuming her face with the fiery dragon-spit. The gun roasted Dr. Julia, and her cheeks peeled back and popped like a wet log on the fire. After charring her head in place, he aimed at Kathryn, but before he could fire again, a combustible force tackled him to the ground.

With the barrel of his gun smoking, Jacob watched as Aiden burned alive, kicking and flailing. The flames danced in his pupils, the screams echoed in his ears, and the smell of burnt skin filled his nostrils. Yet, he didn't shield his eyes, cover his ears, or pinch his nose. He stood transfixed by the fire, basking in the villain's death.

"My king!" Minnie dashed up the steps, her bloody knife in the air. She closed the distance, but as she cleared the top, the sneeze of a dragon engulfed her as well. She screamed to the heavens in pain as her flesh sizzled and melted.

Unable to endure the heat, Minnie dashed off the side of the great pyramid. She fell from the clouds like a meteor with a high-pitched howl, leaving a trail of smoke and colliding against the hard soil with a loud thud.

Kathryn dropped the metallic weapon to her side, and her head followed suit, hanging low.

Jacob peered at the distraught commander and walked over, laying a hand on her shoulder. His soft touch acted as a rough shove, and she crumbled like a sandcastle. He followed her to his knees, taking her in his arms.

Speechless, Kathryn surveyed the mutilated bodies on top of the steps, and the thousands of natives lying scattered in the streets. She laid her head in Jacob's chest. "What did we just do?"

"Kathryn..." Jacob said.

After wiping the tears from her eyes, Kathryn looked down the stone stairway.

Hundreds of natives circled the base of the steps with spears held in their hands, prepared for war. Their faces were painted in streaks of gold and black, standing out amongst the blue and orange of the village.

Kathryn scrambled to her feet and stood ready by Jacob.

An indigenous man stepped forward and raised his hand, halting the warriors. He had long hair as dark as night, but silky, shimmering under the sunlight. He paused, scanning the area before cautiously ascending the steps. As he passed Kathryn and Jacob, he stopped and gawked at each of them, sniffing the air like a dog catching a scent. He glanced to the slain endemic king, and his mood brightened. With a smile, he said, "Aslumatay!"

His voice carried in the wind, sending his people to their knees. In their native tongue, they began chanting in jubilee, "Aslumatay!"

"What's going on?" Kathryn asked.

The warrior's loud, melodic chant shook the ground beneath them and sailed through the sky like a bird with a fig, showing peace.

"I think we killed their rivals, and they believe we're gods." Jacob held Kathryn's hand. "I think you have their respect."

The End

Email: Mele109@outlook.com

Cover by Author.

Intergalactic Love

Susan K. Saltos

Ten years ago, due to overpopulation issues on planet Gammond, Xander Kalani's family was selected by lottery to be relocated to the planet Alzarien. Halfway to their new home, life support systems failed on the spaceship carrying them. The pilot was able to fly them through a wormhole and crash land on a similar planet as theirs called Earth. Now that The Alliance is fully repaired, Xander is ready to return to his home planet to become a diplomatic representative between Earth and the Intergalactic Counsel. However, Xander has been in love with his best friend's twin sister ever since they met. In order for him to ask Thea to come home with him, Xander needs to tell her he is an alien from another planet. Will she reject his love? Or will Thea be willing to travel across galaxies to be with him?

***

Xander paced outside the gates of his military base as he waited for Thea to arrive. He would have to tell her soon, he knew that.

And once Xander told her, he'd have to ask Thea and her twin the question he was avoiding asking them for months. He was running out of time, the ship was finally repaired, and he needed an answer soon. Xander nervously wiped his sweating hands on his jean-clad legs. The soldiers on guard duty watched him with puzzled looks in their eyes.

They had never seen him so discombobulated.

Theo knew what Xander was, but Thea didn't. He was terrified of telling her. How would she react? Would she hate him? Xander loved her with everything in him, but if Thea hated him, he'd have to leave her forever. The only way he could go home happy would be if Thea came with him. Xander didn't know if Thea loved him. Sure, she loved him as friend, but more than that? Like he loved her? He wasn't sure. There had been small moments when he had thought Thea watched him a certain way and when she smiled at him like he had made her day. Xander lived for those small moments. But was it love? Did she return his feelings? And what would he do if she did love him but refused to go with him? Xander had made promises for his family's sake. And he wanted to go home, he did, but Earth had been his home almost as long as Gammond had. There were too many questions and not enough time to answer them. He had to rip off the proverbial Band-Aid and just tell her. It would be quick, and hopefully, not painful.

Xander ran a hand through his hair in frustration. He concentrated on breathing slowly to calm his two rapidly beating hearts. Yes, he had two. Xander wasn't from Earth, though he looked like everyone else on the planet. It had been a stroke of luck that the spaceship bringing his family to Alzarien had come across a wormhole leading to a similar planet to his own. If they hadn't, his people might have died that day. The thought of his family, of returning home, bolstered Xander's resolve. He *would* tell Thea. And once she knew as much as her brother, he'd ask the twins to come with him.

Xander lifted his head as he heard a car approach. He couldn't help but grin at Thea's Mini Cooper. It was fine for Thea, but his six foot three frame had tried to squeeze into the tin can before and he had to perform some acrobatics to fit inside. Thea stopped the car next to him; he leaned against it, and lowered his head to peek inside. "Hey."

Her sweet honey colored eyes looked up at him in concern. "Are you okay, Xander? You sounded weird on the phone."

He swallowed. Thea knew him too well. "You mind leaving the car here?"

Thea frowned at him. "I thought I was giving you a ride home."

"I thought we could grab a bite to eat on base first. How about it?" Xander opened her door and put out a hand to help Thea out of the car. He flashed a smile, hoping she'd give in easily. Thea could be stubborn at the best of times. "Please? I'm hungry."

"Oh, alright." She put her hand in his and allowed him to help her stand up. "Since you said please and all." Thea grinned at him as he shut her door. "Um, should I move the car to a parking lot or..." she looked around, taking in the large gate with barbed wire and the guards standing behind Xander.

"It's fine," Xander told her, pulling her away from the car and up against his side.

Thea blushed feeling his heat radiate against her side. Xander was made of solid muscle and it took everything in her not to run her hands over his broad chest and six pack abs. It wasn't often that she and Xander touched. He was her brother's friend and Thea hung out with them often, but there wasn't much occasion for touching beyond a quick hug hello and goodbye.

"Lieutenant," Xander called out to the guards.

One of the soldiers stepped forward and approached them. "Yes, Commander Kalani?"

Xander took Thea's keys from her and handed them to the guard. "Would you mind parking Ms. Vidales' car for me?"

The soldier smiled at Thea. "It'd be my pleasure."

He handed Xander a tablet in exchange. Xander typed into it for a moment before turning it and holding it out to Thea. "Can you press your thumb here? Security measure."

Thea eyed the tablet hesitantly but pressed her thumb to the screen.

"Thank you," he told her, flashing Thea his gorgeous smile.

Theo and Xander had been friends since college when they had been assigned as roommates together. Thea hung out with her twin and Xander as much as possible. Her brother was her best friend and she and Xander got along from the moment they met as well. She'd always been attracted to him, but Xander had never made a move on her, and though Thea had been tempted to every time she had seen him, Thea would be devastated if Xander ever rejected her, so she never tried.

"Thea?" he asked, lifting her chin with his strong fingers, and turned her head from looking mindlessly behind the large gate. Thea blinked. Xander's hair was thick, wavy, and black, which made his light blue eyes pop. He had a square jaw and high cheekbones. His nose was perfectly straight and was well proportioned to his face. Xander had a scar that slashed from the top right corner of his forehead that ran dangerously close to his left eye. He had a nervous habit of brushing his hair in and out of his eyes to hide it. Thea found it charming.

She licked her lips thinking about their closeness and how easy it would be for her to reach up and run her hands through his thick locks. Xander's eyes dropped down to study her mouth before looking back up at her eyes. Thea bit her bottom lip nervously. "Um, what did you say?"

"I forget...." Xander's large hands went to her shoulders. His piercing blue eyes stared into her brown eyes. "I...um, are you okay?" His thumbs stroked Thea's skin.

Thea cleared her throat. "Yeah, I'm fine." She stepped back out of his reach before she did something really stupid like jump her brother's best friend.

Xander hesitated before gesturing towards the gate. "Let's go then."

Thea followed him through the gates to an uncovered Jeep. He held out a hand and helped her climb into the vehicle. Before he turned away she put a hand on his shoulder to stop him. She knew nothing about military bases, but she didn't see any restaurants around. "Where are we going?"

He gave her a nervous look that worried her. As far as Thea knew, Xander never stressed out about anything. He picked up a strand of her curls from Thea's shoulder and twisted it around his finger as if in thought. He stared down, watching his finger winding her hair around it over and over again. "Xan, is something wrong?"

"Ah, no. Sorry," Xander said as if embarrassed by his unconscious action. He slowly unwound her hair from around his finger. "I like your hair down." He said softly, the corners of his mouth tilting up in a light smile. "You should wear it like this more often."

Thea rolled her eyes. "It has a mind of its own. I have to tame the beast."

He leaned close and breathed in. "It smells fantastic too."

She giggled nervously, and then her stomach growled loudly. Thea felt her cheeks redden in embarrassment, whether it was because Xander was complimenting her hair or because her stomach had made that ungodly sound, she wasn't entirely sure.

Xander chuckled at the sound. "No, it's like..." he leaned over, this time making it obvious that he smelled her hair. "Strawberries?"

"Oh. Uh, yeah, that's my shampoo."

"It's nice," Xander said, his eyes meeting hers.

"Thanks," Thea practically whispered, her eyes dropped to the floor of the Jeep shyly. Her insides were melting at his compliments. *Why was he saying these things?*

He knocked decisively on the side of the Jeep, startling her. "Let's go feed the monster living in your belly," he told her grinning.

"Hey!" she punched his arm lightly.

***

Xander pulled up in front of a huge canvas tent the size of a building. Thea squinted in bewilderment at the structure, "Are we eating in a mess tent?"

Xander burst out laughing. Thea looked at him in confusion as he didn't stop. He threw his head back and laughed as she'd never seen him laugh before. Xander actually wiped tears out of his eyes, he was laughing so hard.

"What?" she asked with a nervous laugh.

"Nothing," he chuckled.

Thea straightened her shoulders, "You're laughing at me. I don't know anything about the military, so if this is a huge bathroom or something, you'll have to excuse me for not knowing any better."

He turned in his seat, leaned over, and kissed her cheek. "I'm sorry for laughing. It's just I was...nervous about talking to you and... you never fail to cheer me up."

"Why were you nervous about talking to me? We always talk." Thea asked confused.

Xander lifted a piece of her hair again, winding it around his finger. She loved when he did it. Thea felt his touch to the roots of her hair. It sent shivers down her spine. "Not about serious stuff. Not really."

Thea touched his shoulder, "Xander, what's going on with you? You haven't been acting like yourself lately. And now, you say you want to talk to me about something serious. You know you can tell me anything, right? You're my friend too. Not just Theo's."

He smiled wryly. "I know," he said quietly, bouncing a curl on his palm.

"Since when did I become your personal Slinky?" Thea asked to lighten the mood.

Xander smiled sheepishly and dropped the hair he'd been holding. "I told you, you have beautiful hair. I can't resist playing with it."

"Thank you," she answered shyly.

Xander turned in his seat to look at her. "Can I ask you something?"

Thea eyed him warily, "Sure."

"Would you ..."

"Commander Kalani," a male voice rang out. Thea looked over her shoulder to see a large man in a military camouflage heading in their direction.

Xander looked over his shoulder as well and cursed. He brushed a section of hair behind her ear.

"Can we talk later?"

Thea placed a hand over his. "What were you going to ask me? Would I what?" she sucked in a breath, hoping he was going to finally ask her out.

Xander cleared his throat. "Um, would you ever consider moving?"

"What! Where'd that come from?" Thea frowned in total confusion. Panic squeezed around her heart at the thought of Xander ever leaving her. "Xander, are you moving?!" Thea tried to ask him calmly, but she was afraid it came out more like a shriek. "You can't leave!"

His eyebrows lifted in surprise at her vehemence. "You wouldn't want me to move?"

"No," Thea murmured, her eyes dropping to her fisted hands.

Xander took her chin in his hand and lifted it gently. "What if you came with me?"

Tears filled her eyes. "You'd take me with you?"

"If you..."

"Hold there a second, Commander, I need to speak to you," the man called again.

Thea turned to see the man speaking with another soldier. She didn't care what the officer wanted. She wanted Xander to stay with her and explain himself.

Thea turned to look back at Xander and his mouth crashed over hers. She moaned at the contact and wrapped her arms around his neck. Xander's arms came around her waist and pulled her firmly up against his hard body. Thea murmured her approval as one of his hands slipped behind her neck and into her hair. His fingers tugged her hair, angled her head, and he deepened the kiss.

Xander pulled away and looked down at her. "Is this okay?" Xander's hands dropped to her waist, pulling her to him again. Thea bit her lip and nodded. He kissed her nose. "I love you, you know."

Her eyes filled with tears and he brushed them away. Thea stared at him incredulously. "You do?"

He nodded. "Since the first day, when you walked into our dorm..."

A tear slipped down her cheek. "Why didn't you tell me?"

Xander wiped her tears again. "It's not that easy to tell," he chuckled, "And...you haven't said anything back..."

Thea hiccupped and blushed, embarrassed at the sound and at the fact that in this wonderful moment, the moment she'd been dreaming about for over ten years, was actually happening. "I love you too, Xander. So much," she whispered.

"You do? You're not just saying that because I said it because..."

She shut him up with a kiss. Xander quickly stopped his rebuttal and responded by deepening their kiss and tightening his arms around her as if he never wanted to let go.

A clearing of the throat pulled them apart. "Commander," a voice barked.

Xander straightened in his seat and turned in the opposite direction to face him. "General."

"I take it this is your *kairi*," the General stated, looking Thea over curiously.

"Yes, sir," Xander looked back over his left shoulder, shooting Thea a pleading look.

Xander switched into his native language to speak to the General. Xander hadn't told her where he was from. She had always suspected that he was a refugee from a country like Syria, Bosnia or some other Middle Eastern country with his olive skin tone. She had heard him speak to his parents before and she hadn't recognized the language. Thea tried not to frown. Xander obviously didn't want the General to know that she didn't know the word he'd used. But she didn't know what *kairi* meant and it bothered her.

The General and Xander ended their conversation and the General bid her goodbye. Xander turned back around to face Thea. "Sorry about that," Xander said, taking her hand in his.

"What does *kairi* mean?"

A slow, seductive, smile spread across Xander's face as he leaned over and kissed her gently. Xander tugged on her hair, forcing her head back, and her eyes met his. He looked over her face possessively. He spoke in his language, tracing her face gently from her temple to her chin. Tingles ran through her body as he spoke. Thea didn't understand the words, but she knew somehow that Xander was expressing his love for her in his language. He kissed her again. A few moments later he pulled slightly back, "Roughly, it means my everything," he whispered. He lifted her hand, kissed it reverently, and spoke softly in his language again.

"Oh," Thea sighed at his words. He spoke them like a promise to her. Thea didn't know what to say as she didn't know what Xander had told her. She cleared her throat. "That's...nice."

He laughed and kissed her again. His eyes searched her face. "Thea, will you come with me?"

"To lunch? Or wherever you're moving to?"

Xander pressed a kiss to her forehead, "For now, to lunch. We need to talk more before you decide anything about the future."

Thea nodded and blew out a breath. "Okay."

"Okay," he nodded in return and then got out of the Jeep. "Stay here a minute. I'll be right back."

Thea frowned. "Where are you going?"

"Just in here," Xander gestured to the tent. He didn't wait for Thea's confirmation that she was okay with him leaving her in a strange place. Xander just turned his back to her and strode into the tent.

Thea rubbed her hands over her face. *What just happened? Xander kissed her and told her he loved her? That he wanted her to move wherever his job was sending him?* She grinned. She didn't want to move. Thea had always been close to her twin brother, but she'd do it for Xander. She loved him. And it wasn't like they couldn't visit Theo or perhaps, Theo could move to where they were going to live. Theo was a doctor and doctors were wanted everywhere. And likewise, she was a teacher and could get a job anywhere. Nothing was standing in her way of being with Xander.

She looked up when the tent flaps opened and two men came out. One man was Xander, the other was... "Theo?!" she gasped. Thea stood up on the Jeep floor. "What are you doing here?"

Theo grinned and climbed into the back of the Jeep. "Wouldn't you like to know," he told her as he kissed her cheek before buckling himself in the back seat.

"Xander?" she asked as Xander climbed back behind the wheel. He started the Jeep. "I thought it was just you and me for lunch," Thea said a bit disappointed that Xander had invited her brother. This was the first time she and Xander had been alone and the fact that he had just kissed her, and had asked her if she'd move for him.... *why the hell was Theo there*?!

"All will be revealed in good time, darling sister," Theo teased from the back seat.

Xander glared at him through the rear view mirror. "Don't provoke your sister, Theo." He drove through another set of gates with soldiers saluting them.

"Did you grow up here?" Theo asked while looking out the window thoughtfully. He'd asked so softly Thea had barely heard him. And by the look Xander gave him through the rear view mirror it wasn't something Xander seemed to want to answer. Theo cleared his throat. "Xan?"

Thea watched the muscle in Xander's jaw clench. "Yeah. Sort of here," he finally answered.

Thea glanced at him in surprise. "I didn't realize your parents were in the military. They don't seem the type." She frowned in thought as she thought of his parents. His mother was small in stature, but she had a big heart. She always hugged Thea when they met like Thea was a part of their family. Xander's mother was a scientist; her research had led to cures to many diseases including some cancers. Thea admired the woman greatly. Xander's father was built as tall and wide as his son, but he didn't have as much muscle as Xander. She had always thought he was some sort of high ranking government person that couldn't say what they did for a living. He gave off an air of authority.

Xander didn't reply to her observation. After a few minutes, the buildings faded away and Xander parked in front of a massive open field. Thea and Theo looked at each other in confusion as Xander shut off the engine and got out. They followed his lead and joined him as he approached another set of guards, who saluted. One of the soldiers handed him a tablet.

Xander typed on the device and then walked over to Thea and Theo. "Press your thumb here," he told Thea, holding it up to her. She complied by pressing her thumb to the screen next to a picture of her with her name printed at the top. "Where'd they get my picture?"

He ignored her and typed on the screen again before holding the tablet out to her brother. "We're not signing our first born away are we?" Theo laughed as he pressed his thumb to the screen.

Xander raised an eyebrow. "I wouldn't be surprised." He typed again on the tablet and handed it back to the guard. "Come on in," he gestured for them to follow him through the gate. He slipped an arm around Thea's waist. "Don't freak out."

She glared at him, "If you say don't freak out, that means I will freak out."

He chuckled and looked over at her brother, "You ready?"

Theo looked over at him in surprise and then looked at the field. His jaw dropped open. "It's here?"

"Cloaking shields de-activate," Xander called out to the openness. He grabbed Thea tightly around the waist. She glanced at him in surprise, wondering why he was so worried when suddenly a huge building began to materialize in front of her.

Thea felt her knees dropping, but Xander was holding her up. She gasped, "What the hell?"

"Ho-ly sh-it," Theo stammered as he stared as the massive structure appeared fully in front of them.

"Welcome to The Alliance," Xander told them.

Thea gasped as a stairway lowered from the structure. Two men in black and gray uniforms came down the plank and approached them. They stood in front of Xander at attention.

"At ease. This is Thea and Theo Vidales. They are my guests and are to have full access to the ship."

"Yes, Commander." The men said in unison and looked at Thea and her brother hesitantly.

The solider with the dark hair took a step forward. "Commander, a moment, if you would."

"Sure," Xander nodded to Thea and Theo to give him a moment. He stepped closer to the soldiers and the brunette spoke Xander's native language.

"What's going on, Theo?" Thea asked crossing her arms, and watched her brother stare at the huge building with complete wonder and admiration in his eyes.

"Do you know what this is, Thea?" he whispered.

Thea frowned and looked at the building. "I'm guessing some high tech building. I had no idea the military had the kind of technology where they could cloak an entire building! That's really incredible. We'll be unstoppable to anyone that tries to mess with us!"

"Thea..." her brother shook her head at her.

"What?"

Theo put a hand on her arm. "This isn't our technology and it's not a building."

Thea laughed. "I'm looking right at it, Theo, it's a building."

"Look again," Xander said, walking back towards them.

Thea scanned her eyes over the massive building. Unlike the buildings downtown, it wasn't made of concrete. It was possible it was some kind of steel, there was glass windows very high up. Thea leaned her head back to try to see them.

"I had no idea it'd be this big!" Theo exclaimed.

"Twenty thousand people, Theo," Xander reminded him.

"Twenty thousand people are in this building?" Thea asked amazed. "It's huge, but I didn't suspect that many people could work here. It's like a city."

Xander nodded. "It is. A floating one."

"What do you mean?" Thea asked confused and watched as more secret messages seemed to flash between her brother and Xander's eyes.

Xander gestured towards the building. "Let's go in, shall we?"

He took Thea's hand and pulled her towards the building. "Coming?" he called over his shoulder as Theo stood still staring at the building.

Thea studied the building as they approached it, "What is this place, Xander?"

"Home away from home."

Theo caught up to them and Xander took them up the stairway and into an elevator.

"Doing okay?" Xander asked her.

Thea nodded. "I'm fine. I'm curious, especially since Theo knows something I don't about this place. You said it's home away from home. Is this where you sleep when you're on duty? Is it like a barracks or something?"

Theo began breathing hard. Thea glanced at him in concern. "Theo?" Xander asked. He stepped around Thea and placed a hand on Theo's shoulder. "Just breathe."

Theo nodded and took a deep breath. "Do you want to turn back?" Xander asked him hesitantly.

"No, no, I'm good."

"Should we stop here? Do you want me to send Thea home? I

don't have to..."

"No, it's about time you told her."

"Told me what, guys?" Thea almost stomped her foot in frustration.

Xander stepped out of the elevator. "Follow me."

Thea followed him out, stepping into a large hallway. There were lots of people bustling around carrying large boxes overflowing with what appeared to be their personal belongings. Some wore uniforms like the soldiers outside. Others were in civilian clothes.

Xander grabbed her hand again and led them down a long hallway. The walls were a dark metal color. They weren't quite black, but an unusual lighter shade with a glossy finish. There were seams in the walls, where large panels were welded and bolted together. Thea frowned thinking it was highly unusual for a building to not be dry walled and painted. There were no fancy paintings on the walls. The floors were a shiny, dark gray, granite mixed with black swirls and specks. She froze when double doors on the side of the hallway opened in a sliding motion, like at the grocery store, and a young couple stepped out.

"Isn't this awesome?" Theo whispered in her ear as he tried to lean forward to look into the room the couple had exited.

The man looked at Xander and spoke to him gruffly in their language. Thea poked Theo in the ribcage with her elbow. Xander replied to the man in a calming tone, seemingly to apologize for Theo's rude behavior. The man grabbed the girl by the arm and dragged her away.

"Sorry," Theo mumbled.

"Privacy is highly valued among our people. We don't usually invite strangers into our homes. It takes some time to trust and earn respect." Xander explained. He lifted Thea's hand and kissed the back of it. "Come, we can eat at my apartment, and then you can check out your own."

"Our own?" Thea gasped, and pulled him back. "Apartment?"

Theo looked at him in shock. "You were serious."

"I was," Xander said offering them a comforting smile. "Trust me," he said to Thea, tugging gently on her hand before leading them over to a set of double doors. There were strange symbols etched into the door. Xander touched a plate on the side with his thumb, and it opened. Thea and her brother followed Xander inside.

"Wow, it's beautiful, Xander!" Thea exclaimed as she followed him down a few steps into a large living room. Her sneakers sunk into a thick burgundy carpet. The couch and matching sofa were calling her name to sink into them. She walked over and sat down relaxing into its comfort. Thea closed her eyes. Her nervous tension seemed to fade away. The outside of the building was intimidating and looked like it came out of some sci-fi movie. Even the hallways were dark and strange. But his apartment seemed to be a nice place. She groaned. "I want this couch."

Xander chuckled. "You're welcome to it any time, kairi."

"This place rocks, Xan," Theo said, walking over to the open doorway to the bedroom. Thea had opened her eyes when she heard Theo's voice head over to the other side of the room.

She sighed not wanting to leave the couch, but curiosity got the better of her and Thea followed her brother. A king size bed dominated the room. There was no other furniture and it was made up with a soft looking, dark gray comforter. Built in bookcases were in two walls, filled with books, knickknacks, pictures of Xander's family, and Thea was touched to see several pictures of herself and Theo. The other side of the room was taken up by large sliding closet doors, which were the same color of the walls and hardly noticeable.

Thea poked her head into a doorway at the back, which she found to be a bathroom. There were double sinks made of the same gray granite of the hallway with a wall to wall mirror above it. There was a soaking tub of the same gray granite and a shower made of complete glass.

She explored his small kitchen at the back of the living room and then noticed a small room off to the side. "Do you stay here often?" Thea asked when she noticed Xander following her to what appeared to be his office.

Xander watched her peer out the window over his desk. "When I'm not staying with Theo, I live here."

"We're really high up," she commented before backing away from the window.

"Not high enough," he murmured under his breath.

Thea took a step towards him. "What?"

Xander took her jaw in his hand and lifted it gently to look at him. "Thea, do you like it here?"

She smiled reassuringly. "It's very nice, Xander. Why haven't you brought us before?"

He leaned over and kissed her. Thea gasped in surprise as Xander pulled her to him. She kissed him back as passionately as he gave, not stopping until they were both out of breath and panting hard. He gently guided her backwards until she was pressed into the smooth wall of the room. It was cold on her back. Thea shivered. He placed a hand next to her head. "Amana," Xander said, sliding his hand down the glossy surface almost reverently. "It's like the granite of Earth."

She frowned. "What do you mean like the granite of Earth? Where's it from?"

Xander studied her face as if memorizing it. He placed his forehead against hers. "I love you so much, Thea."

Thea placed her hand against his cheek. "I love you too. But, what are you trying to tell me, Xan?"

"Please don't hate me," he whispered. Thea felt a tear fall from his face to hers.

"I would never hate you! Are you crying, Xander?"

"When I was sixteen..." he took a deep breath. She tried to look at him, but his forehead was still on hers. His body was pressed against hers. It was like he needed to be connected to her.

She felt him tense as if it was difficult for him to tell her what he needed to say. "Go on."

"There was a lottery of sorts. Only, the lottery wasn't something we prized. Everyone hoped their numbers wouldn't be called. Our planet was overpopulated and after the restrictions on procreation didn't go over so well, they decided to send people to other planets to live."

Thea sucked in a breath. "Your planet?"

"Gammond is one of the most populated and wealthiest planets in the Honuric galaxy. It's like a capital, everyone wants to live and work there, but the planet can only sustain so much life and resources. My family, like hundreds of thousands of others, was ordered to leave. We were assigned to Alzarien. It's like a sister planet to Gammond. It wouldn't have been much of a hardship."

Thea pulled back to look at him. "Xander, do you know what you're saying."

"I'm not crazy, Thea," he told her, hating to see the pity he saw in her eyes. "Will you be open minded and just listen for a few minutes? Please?"

She studied his face. Xander believed what he was telling her. That he was from another planet of all things! "Xan..."

Xander shook his head. "I have to tell you, even if I lose you."

Thea sighed. "Okay...continue..." She glanced at her brother. Theo had leaned against the doorway to listen at some point. Theo nodded at her. She frowned not understanding the look in her brother's eyes. Why wasn't he freaked out about his best friend claiming to be from another planet?

"We packed up our home and boarded The Alliance. It was named such as it was a carrier to bring families from one planet to another. Several planets had formed the Intergalactic Counsel before I was born and The Alliance was a product of their working together. We'd been living on The Alliance for about two months, halfway to Alzarien...." Xander looked away, "when something went wrong. The life support system failed in many parts of the ship. There were explosions, the ship shook, the walls and levels caved in, everything was engulfed in flames..." his breathing came more rapid and he gripped her arm tightly, "the screams went on and on... I couldn't move..." his voice cracked. Theo placed a hand on his shoulder in support.

Xander took a deep breath. "I blacked out. When I came to," he shook his head, "there were guns pointed at me. We'd landed on Earth. The commander had taken us through some kind of wormhole. It brought us to your galaxy. Earth was the closest planet similar to ours. It had oxygen, water, food. Everything we need to exist. We'd heard of Earth before, but none of the Counsel wanted to reach out because Earth always had so many problems of their own. They can't even get along with their own people who are different. The people of Earth weren't going to accept a race from another planet. And we'd seen plenty of your movies to know that if we ever came here, we'd be treated like a science experiment. But the commander took a chance. It was either die or face the people of Earth. It was like we expected. We were hooked up to machines, blood was taken, we were poked, prodded, and humiliated beyond belief. But we did everything willingly to prove we came in peace."

"But you live normally. You work for the military!" Thea exclaimed.

"Yes. Now. After we convinced the government that we weren't a threat. That we're just like Earthlings, just with slight differences."

"What kind of differences?"

He took her hands and placed one on either side of his chest. She frowned. "I don't understand."

"What do you feel?"

"Your heartbeat."

"Close your eyes," Xander told her gently. He repositioned her hands.

She gasped, her eyelids popped open. "Two hearts?"

He nodded.

"Xander?"

"Yeah?"

"Did you get those burns on your back and the scars…from the crash? Or did humans…"

"No, I didn't get any scars from the experiments. They were from the crash."

"Uh….Xander," Theo's voice squeaked in a panicked tone. He was staring out the window.

"Yeah?"

Theo audibly gulped. "Are we…are we going up?"

Thea looked out the window and sure enough the building was rising. She let out a small cry as she saw trees far beneath them.

Xander grinned. "It's just a quick trip. I had to prove to you that I was telling the truth."

Thea shrieked as the sky outside darkened and she literally saw stars. "Oh, God. We're in freaking space!"

Theo ran to the window and saw the Earth disappear beneath them. He looked over at his friend. "We're going back, right?"

Xander nodded. "We'll be back tomorrow. This is just a test run. I'd like you both to come to Gammond with me, though. We leave next week."

Thea gasped. "You want us to go to another planet?"

"I want you to come home with me, Thea. I've been offered a diplomatic position to negotiate between Earth, Gammond, and the other planets of the Intergalactic Counsel. I'd have to live on Gammond or Alzerian for the first year," he shrugged, "after that, we'll work it out." Xander put his hand on each of the twins shoulders, "Will you both come with me to Gammond? I can't imagine my life without either one of you in it."

The twins exchanged a look; slow grins grew on their faces. In unison, they turned and said, "Yes."

Xander took Thea's hand. "Will you marry me, Thea?"

She placed both of her hands over his hearts. "Yes, of course."

He grinned and took her in his arms. Thea leaned against his chest, fitting against him as she belonged. The three of them faced the window, watching the stars pass by, and the Earth fade beneath them. Whatever the future held, and wherever it took them, they would face it together.

The End

Susan K. Saltos is a resident of Northern Virginia, just outside of Washington D.C. She writes "anything to do with romance" from young adult to contemporary adult to paranormal, fantasy, or Sci-Fi. If it has romance in it, Susan will write it. She self-published her Young Adult paranormal romance, The Chosen Path, several years ago. It has been expanded and improved upon and will be re-published in 2018. Also to come out next year, are the sequels "Hidden Paths" and "Fork in the Road". All three books in the series, and other various books in the draft stage, can currently be read for **FREE** at: https://www.wattpad.com/user/SusanKSaltos

Suggestions and comments are always welcome and appreciated.

Cover by Susan K. Saltos.

The Gift

Owen Rothberg

Supposedly, the mission of the agency was to counter biological WMD but Melvin knew (well, strongly suspected) that the intent was somewhat more aggressive. At least it had been back in the bad old days of the cold war. Since his job was to study disbursement methods for biological agents, he could envision both defensive and offensive scenarios for his work. However, all that was over for him. He was retiring today.

He would miss the intellectual stimulation of the work and some of his co-workers. He would not miss the commute to Fort Dietrich from Gaithersburg. Not that it was a bad commute since it was against the traffic flow. People went to the Beltway in the morning and away in the evening while his pattern was just opposite. Bad weather was a problem and sometimes it was dangerous to be on the road. Aside from that, it could have been a lot worse. It was just the drudgery of it. He was looking forward to pursuing his "project".

Ph. D. from Johns Hopkins and thirty-three years of U.S.

Government service were now behind him. They did the retirement lunch at a local restaurant and made all the goodbyes, length-of service certificates and "grins-and-grabs" photos earlier that week. The exit procedure was somewhat cumbersome because of the work done at the lab. He filled out what seemed to be a mountain of forms and had a four inch thick stack of copies to prove it.

He filled his old-fashioned fountain pen for the last time that morning. It was from another age with a bladder and a gold tip that fit his writing style perfectly. He still wrote in his notebook with a small, neat, really beautiful cursive script, so obsolete in this day of computers, typing and "texting". He placed the pen in his breast pocket as he had done countless times and went for coffee. All that remained was to gather his personal effects and books and check out.

He had to go through a number of detectors and a thorough search of his belongings and his person at the exit. He had gotten used to the invasion of his privacy over the years and did not worry much about it. But there was that one thing and although he knew the chances of detection were slight, he was a bit, just a bit, nervous as he went through the process that last day. He remained calm by thinking about the tasks ahead and that what he planned was absolutely the right thing to do.

Melvin Eisenberg ("Mel" to his friends) was getting old. He had lived in Gaithersburg, Maryland for the past thirty-three years. He liked the Washington area except for the weather, snow and ice in winter and the heat and humidity in summer. His life was comfortable but he was not rich. Certainly he was not famous. He had done his research, loved his wife and children, and got along with most of his peers and relatives, with a few notable exceptions. But everyone had those, right? He was retiring on a decent if not large pension. His children were on-their-own (mostly) and he had three beautiful grand children. His house was in a good neighborhood (mostly), was paid for (mostly), and in decent shape (mostly). He owned (mostly) two cars. Melvin loved his country and thought it the best in the world, ever (well mostly). His health was better than average except for a few more aches and pains each year.

Mel didn't want to die. Death is the end of everything, isn't it? No more walking with the dogs at sunrise in summer. No more wife or children or family or Chinese food or beer or barbeque or hobbies or reading or vacations at the beach or sex. That list was incomplete and not necessarily in the proper order, but the idea is that life is not something to give up on. Yes, there is pain in life and he counted himself lucky that his periods of suffering were transitory at worst, so far.

Nobody gets out of life alive. You are born, you live, and then you die. The universe ends. That's it. Very depressing! The bottom line is that life is all there is, so why are so many of us so eager to throw it away or take it from others for the most trivial reasons or sometimes no reason at all?

Maybe it was only wishful thinking, but Melvin knew that the universe would continue after he was dead although he would not be aware of it. He wanted to leave something behind to make things better for his family and for everyone else. Mel wanted to believe that there was a reason for his existence. He had concluded that a creator of the universe (God) exists. He could not, as a matter of logic, bring himself to believe, even without explicit proof, that the universe is a random, and thus pointless, event. Man's (read intelligent and self-aware beings) place in the scheme is perhaps to understand the work of the Creator. It occurred to him that without man, God is irrelevant and without God, man is irrelevant. Trite!

Religion sells everlasting life but without a money-back guarantee. Melvin did not believe what most organized religion was selling. No one had ever returned to confirm the promises and the traditional stories had so many logical and historical holes in them, so it was impossible to give them credibility. "You must rely on faith" they said. Why? It seemed that people needed the crutch of organized religion whereby others believed similar ideas. They needed the support to get them through life's challenges. Mel did not begrudge them the comfort of ritual and belief but he could not bring himself to fully accept religious faith either. He actually envied strong religious commitment even if it was not, in his opinion, rational.

On a personal level, Melvin Eisenberg was born a Jew and it stuck with him all these years. He did not know if life after death was part of the Jewish tradition. He was not positive about what the official position might be and he did not care. He had figured it out for himself. Mel wasn't an observant Jew, and by the strictest standards of orthodoxy, not much of a Jew at all. Nevertheless, he counted himself part of the Hebrew faith and could see how wanting to believe in a just and loving God was worth a bit of self-delusion.

He knew a few things about the universe. First it is big! Second and based on the first, there has to be or have been intelligent life elsewhere. Third, the chance of communicating with intelligent life on other planets is small given the vast distances and the limitations of physics. Essentially, we are on our own and must make the best of our world. That was not an encouraging prospect given what he observed.

Rabbi Hillel's summary of the essence of Judaism made sense. "That which you find hateful to yourself, do not do to someone else." One should live life without harming others and even do some good. Hard to do if one sometimes did not pay close attention to what you were doing in relation to those around one, and were sometimes a stupid insensitive clod that sometimes opened one's mouth at the wrong time with the wrong words. On the plus side, Mel had never harmed anyone physically since the third grade. He had not committed fraud or stolen anything more important than a high-end coat hanger from a hotel in New Jersey some years ago. He did not cheat on his wife although he had to admit being tempted once. He gave to charity although not as much as he could afford without discomfort. Mel allowed himself the luxury of imperfection.

He saw so much good in the world and so much potential. He also was aware of the bad and the terrible, past and present. Global climate change caused by seven or eight billion people dumping billions of tons of carbon into the atmosphere each year was about to catch up with the human race. If that wasn't enough, there were nuclear and other weapons of sufficient destructive force to finish off most if not all life on the planet. There was an assortment of crazies with a death wish salivating to get their blood-soaked hands on as many of these weapons as they could get.

The problems were compounded by a new numbskull in the White House who was unequipped with the basic knowledge, leadership ability and temperament required to give his own country, much less the world, half a chance to sustain civilized behavior. The new leader had been put into office trading on fear and ignorance, and it had worked. The prospects were not encouraging.

It was no accident Mel thought that much of the world was governed by sociopaths who would do almost anything to advance their own power, wealth and comfort. There were also enough of these dictators around with minds in the fifth century and twenty-first century weapons to make the prospects for disaster large indeed. Add to that the all too common tribal tendency embedded in the human DNA, which programmed us to hate those with a different religion, skin color or viewpoint. Topping it all off was a pervasive, exploitative and growing culture of non-stop, multi-media super violent and sexually explicit entertainment (and news?) that made appreciable numbers of the population prone to violent behavior and thus dangerous. Mass murder had become more frequent, if not commonplace.

Question: What were the main factors that would interfere, in the long run, with survival of the human race? Answer: There were any number of potential disasters both natural and man-made. For starters, it would help if people would be inclined not to kill and maim one another for no reason at all, bad reasons or because someone in authority told them to act. Obviously, reducing the tendency toward violence would not solve anywhere near all of the problems, beginning with overpopulation and global climate change caused by mankind, but it would be a big help. It would help if people were not bound to follow leaders to destruction of themselves and countless others, against their will and peaceful inclinations. Then they could concentrate on the important tasks of survival as a human community all inhabiting "Spaceship Earth" and focused on solving the problems. Mel had, he believed, discovered a solution.

Mel thought about all of these things and about what he planned to do during his commute, perhaps not his last one he thought, back home from Fort Dietrich. He thought about the dispersal problem which was the next and final step. He had been planning his "project" for years. He had confided in no one, had published nothing, and had confined his writing to well hidden and password-protected thumb drives.

Had he been bent on destruction, he would have been the nightmare of Homeland Security, the lone individual with motive, means, and opportunity. What he had done and was about to do was, no doubt, illegal, and possibly, depending on the results, immoral. For one thing the virus was government property. Also, he was invading other peoples' lives on a wholesale level.

Mel and his wife were going on a cruise to Europe with a final stop in Egypt. They were starting in Florida, proceeding to London with a side trip to Paris. Then they would go on to Rome and Cairo, after which they would sail through the Mediterranean and back to the USA. They would drive to Florida and stop at Disneyworld. Before that he would tour the Capitol and White House. He also

279

planned to visit National Airport (renamed Ronald Reagan in honor of someone who did not deserve it), and Dulles Airport a few days from now.

He had worked out the destinations to provide as much access to the world population centers and "world leaders" as possible. Many parts of the world would not be covered but he was, after all, only one man. Given enough time, the global environment would be exposed.

Mel had discovered the virus a few years ago. "Discovered" was actually an incomplete characterization; he had partially synthesized it by modifying an existing strain. It was a very primitive life-form, almost not much more than a chemical except it could reproduce itself very effectively. The virus was carried in the air as well as in water. Its primitive composition made it hard to kill. It had not been found to cause or cure any disease or attack any human bodily function and the management of his agency thus had lost interest in it.

Mel had become excited by the effects of the virus when, quite by accident, one of the chimpanzees in an adjacent lab was exposed to it. The chimp was a particularly large and aggressive fellow with a nasty disposition. After the exposure, the animal became quite docile to both humans and those of his own kind. He became Mel's pet and had died only recently. No one else noted the change in the animal's behavior and Mel kept the observations to himself.

When the samples were ordered destroyed, Mel kept a small quantity in a miss-labeled bottle at his laboratory station. Over several years he took a number of small quantities out of the lab in his fountain pen. The liquid was clear and odorless. Using a spray bottle, he tried the substance on several cats, the ultimate hunters, in the neighborhood. There seemed to be no change in their predatory habits. He also tried it on dogs but did not notice a difference in their behavior either. Dogs were domesticated. Cats were only partially so and they were the ultimate predators by both physical design and temperament. This was good reasoned Mel because the balance of nature in the wild might be altered. After all, if the lion lies down with the lamb, the lamb grazes and the lion starves. Predation is a part of the natural scheme. God gave the lion tooth and claw for a reason. Humans, on the other hand, should have outgrown the need to hunt for sport and the satisfaction of killing a long time ago.

Mel had also experimented on himself and his cousin a while ago.

For his part, Mel experienced heightened revulsion at the thought of harming anyone, even when he was quite agitated. He recognized that this was originally an aspect of his nature but had become markedly more acute since his exposure to the virus. Cousin Andy was an avid hunter who, as Mel noted, killed as much for pleasure as sport. Mel had exposed Andy, along with the rest of his friends and family during the past couple of years. Andy had not killed anything for some time. Mel asked Andy several times if he went hunting and the reply was always negative. Andy didn't say so but he implied that he did not enjoy killing and had lately confined his activities to target and skeet shooting. Andy's hunter friends appeared not inclined to go hunting after exposure due to contact with Andy. It was apparent that the infection spread rapidly in normal contact.

Mel had killed animals in the course of his work. The euphemism was "sacrifice" but the result was the same. He admitted that at some level killing was necessary if only to preserve human life. He could do it but killing came with a psychological cost. Of course, violence toward other humans was different.

The main effect of the virus was to suppress the instinct for violent behavior in humans. Mel looked for side effects such as colds, flu-like symptoms and rashes but he detected none. He had to admit that the sampling procedure and subsequent analyses were pathetically inadequate. There might be side effects but without considerable research and observation, which Mel could not perform, he was relying on luck and wishful thinking. He recognized that he was not being rational and it did not seem to matter to him. He was hooked. He was a "true believer". The thought of altering all human behavior toward a peaceful attitude was overwhelming.

Most "normal" people were, as Mel observed, not violent unless provoked or threatened. People would instinctively kill for survival but the built-in prohibitions against violence were much more enhanced when infected. People subject to the infection were somehow much less inclined to act or react violently in stress situations. They did not want to hurt or kill. They probably would do both to protect themselves or loved ones but, as far as Mel could tell, they would not be inclined to rage or premeditated killing. Most likely, the effects of the virus would vary depending on the psychological makeup of each individual.

Andy, Mel, the cats and the chimp carried and released the virus which was distributed airborne and by direct contact. The virus was spreading. It appeared that it had not been noticed yet because the effects were subtle. Sooner or later the authorities would become aware of a drop in homicides and violent crime, assuming the effects were as he envisioned. He had to assume they would look for a cause. If he was to act, he had to act quickly before the effects were discovered by the authorities.

Mel figured that his dispersion scheme would, at best, infect (he preferred to think of it as an immunization program) about twenty percent of the world's population over the next year or two. He would try to concentrate his efforts on those in charge of governments and thus the mass killing mechanisms. By that time there would be no turning back, he hoped. He also had provided himself with an "insurance policy" to protect himself and his family from reprisal if and when his plot was discovered.

Maybe those in power would try to find a "cure" but maybe it would take enough time so that the benefits of not resisting the positive effects would be apparent. Power over others depends on the ability to give orders and have them obeyed. If there were no will to kill or fear of being killed it would change the way things worked since man arrived on earth. There were a lot of "maybes". This led Mel to reconsider side effects and unintended consequences. "The road to hell is paved with good intentions." So says the proverb.

OK! Suppose there were some of the "poor in spirit" who wanted to exploit and control aggressive behavior. Would they seek to immunize themselves and their followers? Mel thought about those in positions of power. His view of politicians, fair play, "American Exceptionalism" and the rule of law was one of informed skepticism where the lust for power over others was concerned. If "they" wanted to retain their positions, it would be useful, even necessary, to have a people around them to do their bidding no matter what. He had a low opinion of the thickness of the veneer of civilized behavior on those in power or aspiring to it.

What else? Well, would new born children be infected? They would most likely be and what would be the long term effects during development? What about the effects of other drugs and alcohol? Would natural immunity rear its powerful presence and what if everyone was not affected or partially affected? That would be probable.

Would the virus mutate and what form would such a mutation take? Might the virus be or become toxic to some portion of the population? Would Mel thus be responsible for disease and even deaths on a world-wide scale? He was taking a chance, however slight, at becoming the greatest mass murderer in the history of mankind.

What about the natives in Alaska and other remote places. They depended on being able to hunt in order to survive. How would they manage? True, the pressure on the environment was getting to the point where many animal species would not survive the increase in the hunter population. Even now man was stripping the seas of fish and marine mammals. The effects of the virus were not absolute. People would kill to survive even if they found the task very unpleasant. Perhaps the effects would be a greater respect for the environment and conserving resources.

Mel knew he was bucking millions of years of evolution and built-in survival instincts based on some very crude anecdotal observation and testing. He had to admit that he sought to change the attitude of the human race, all seven billion plus and it was a tall order. Many, many, unknowns to be considered! The end result might be just what he did not want. "Man plans, God laughs", another proverb. Mel was a scientist and his plan went against both his training and instincts.

He wondered if he should forget the whole thing or delay the project. But he had released the virus in his trials. He had become a true believer as well and the thought was troubling. This was probably the mindset of the Hitler's and Stalin's of the world. In the end Mel decided to go ahead with his scheme on the theory that it would not hurt to give politicians and bureaucrats a dose of "medicine" in order to mitigate their willingness to push a button and obliterate civilization in order to satisfy their lust for power. His scheme was far from perfect but he would try.

**

The Washington Area in the summer is the essence of hazy, hot and humid. With temperatures in the nineties and humidity to match, the uniform of the day for tourists is light tee shirts, shorts and "flip-flops", with just enough under clothes to avoid being arrested for indecent exposure. Mel and his wife dressed for the weather. The uniform included drinking water in plastic bottles and a couple of smaller "water" bottles equipped with tiny soft-rubber fans that allowed the user to spray a mist on their heads in the heat. A light day pack with camera, snacks, tissues, etc. completed their outfits.

They took the Metro to the Capitol and joined the crowd at the entry. They were allowed to enter with the day pack after inspection by the guards and a trip through the metal detector. Mel sprayed some of the clear mist as they walked through the building and around the grounds without arousing suspicion. He paid particular attention to the areas where he knew that the Congressmen and Senators would pass. Later that week he went to Dulles and National and did the same thing, focusing on the international terminals and exits. Finally, he and his wife took a tour of the White House and joined a group of tourists who also had passes from a Congressman. He was successful in spraying a small amount of the liquid in the executive mansion without being discovered or even questioned.

They were all packed and the "vacation" would begin with an early morning start in a few days. They left for Disney World that weekend and Mel left small amounts of the virus all over the vast area of the park. The small water bottle and fan provided a perfect prop in the heat. The cruise ship left Miami and they sailed to London. Mel took a bottle of the virus to a meeting at the House of Parliament. They went to Paris, Rome, and Cairo. At each place Mel distributed the clear liquid expecting it to evaporate and be breathed in by all who passed near. All that was left to do was to return home and wait.

About a year later, the effects of Mel's efforts began to be noticed in most of the city centers throughout the world. Violent crime, rape and murder rates were dropping rapidly. Abortion rates also dropped. Commercial slaughter houses were finding it hard to get workers. Volunteers for combat arms in the various armed forces were also becoming scarce. There might even have been a drop in tensions between the various religious factions, although it was hard for Mel to tell. In Russia, the Far East, and Africa the effects might not have taken effect yet to any great extent.

The people at his former place of employment discovered Mel's "plot" shortly thereafter. He and his wife were arrested by Homeland Security and disappeared into the Kafkaesque black hole reserved for terrorists. Mel freely admitted what he had done and offered no defense other than pointing out that no one had been harmed. He also flatly stated that his wife knew nothing of his extracurricular activities. Those statements and observations did not seem to impress his captors. They viewed the legal inconveniences of the Fourth and Fifth Amendments as somewhat of a luxury since 9-11. They threatened to charge him with theft of government property, i.e. the virus, for starters. Treason was also mentioned, along with the possibility of Mel just disappearing forever.

Mel told his interrogators that he had given thumb drives and hard copies of his work and his activities over the past few years to several sources. He had also included information about several rather interesting projects taking place at his former place of employment which might be in violation of treaties and commitments of the past and present administrations. Mel told them that he would have to place very specific messages on his Facebook and Twitter pages very shortly. Unless that was done, the information would be released to many media outlets. He warned them that the wording of his messages had to be absolutely precise or his present situation would be known. Mel then demanded his release along with a commitment to provide him with legal immunity. After all, Mel had been a civil service employee for a long time and had learned many lessons about the workings of bureaucracy.

He also offered to come out of retirement and lead a team working on a complete analysis and research program to precisely define the effects of the virus. The motto for both Mel and the authorities was, "Keep your friends close and your enemies closer."

Melvin Eisenberg and his wife were subsequently released from custody and his offer is under review as of this writing.

The virus is still spreading and the authorities are not talking.

The End

Cover by Susan K. Saltos.

History Lesson

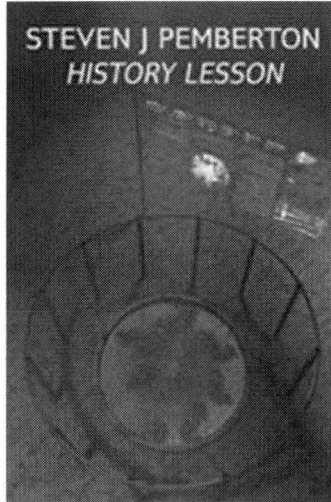

Steven J Pemberton

About the story: Our local writers' group was invited to provide an evening's entertainment for the supporters of the town museum, in which we would give readings from our work. The lady who organised it, knowing that I usually write great big doorstops of novels, asked if I had anything self-contained that could be read aloud in, say, twenty minutes. I said I didn't, but (foolishly) offered to write something.

In truth, I have a "story dump," which is a big word processor file where I write down anything I think might one day find its way into a story. Every so often, I look through the dump for connections between items, so by the time I start writing a story, it's usually been composting in the story dump for several years. The notion of performing a story in a museum made me think of writing a story set in a museum, which put me in mind of a couple of entries in the story dump, and by the time I got home from the planning meeting, I had (or thought I had) an outline of a complete story.

When I actually started writing the story... I hesitate to say it ran away with me, but about halfway through, I thought of a way to connect it to another story (that I haven't written yet). I changed my mind about what the Temple of the Mosaic really was, and about the identity of the man in the blue spacesuit, and that meant changing the ending. One day I might write a story that follows the original plan, and then again I might not.

About the author: I was born in England in 1970, the son of a librarian and a teacher. It was probably inevitable, therefore, that I would grow up loving books and the imaginary worlds they conjure. I now live in Hertfordshire with my partner, where I work as a software developer.

***

The Curator stepped through the private door from his office to the vestibule and faced the waiting visitors. Twenty or so - typical for a Wednesday afternoon. Mostly off-worlders, a few locals.

"Greetings, everyone. Welcome to the Temple of the Mosaic. I am the Curator of the museum here. If you're thinking I look very real for such a backward planet, that's because I am real, not a recording or a proxy. So please don't try to walk through me.

"Now, the Temple is the oldest man-made structure on Heimdall, and the oldest on any planet apart from Earth itself. The first settlers built it not long after they arrived, four thousand Earth standard years ago. It's been extended, sacked, looted and rebuilt several times, which makes interpretation difficult. In the middle of the nave is a recording of the best available reconstruction of how the Temple developed.

"The Temple and the city around it were occupied continuously for some twelve hundred years, and were then abandoned, to be swallowed by the encroaching jungle. A few centuries after that, Heimdall's civilisation essentially collapsed. There are several theories as to why, but the most credible is an overenthusiastic orbital bombardment during a war that led to a decade-long global winter. Our nearest neighbour, Defran's World, had its own problems at the time, and didn't investigate until a few hundred years later. They found the survivors living in pre-spaceflight, and in many places, pre-industrial, conditions. They had mostly forgotten about the existence of other worlds, and welcomed the rescuers as gods. To this day, there are people who believe Heimdall is the only inhabited planet."

One person at the back of the crowd caught his eye. He was unnaturally tall - at least, the Curator assumed this person was male. He was completely covered in dull blue metal, halfway between a hardshell spacesuit and powered armour. The helmet had no faceplate, and the Curator supposed it had an array of microlenses that allowed the wearer to see. If he was from a low-gravity world, that would explain the height and the use of an exoskeleton, but why was he encased in it?

The visitors near the front moved uncertainly towards the entrance to the nave, and the Curator realised he had allowed himself to become distracted from his speech. He raised a hand. "Most of you are no doubt here to see the Apocalypse Mosaic. You're welcome to record it using whatever passive sensors you like, but please, nothing active. It's very old and very fragile. The museum will close today at eighteen hundred hours local time." He glanced at his watch, a quaint thing even for Heimdall. "That's fourteen twenty-one Earth standard. I'll be here until then to answer any questions you might have." He pushed the button that opened the door into the nave. "Please enjoy the rest of your visit."

He let the visitors drift in, then followed at a respectful distance. The enormous circular room always reminded him of a cave. The floor sloped down towards the centre, just enough to be noticeable. The room was dark except for pools of light around the exhibits. Seen from above, the lights formed a map of the nearby stars. The reconstruction of the Temple's history was in the place belonging to Earth's sun. In the place of Heimdall's sun, exactly in the centre of the nave, was the Apocalypse Mosaic. He'd never had the nerve to ask the designer whether that was deliberate.

The Curator wandered among the exhibits, half-listening to visitors' soft conversations and the reverent tones of the interactive guided tour. The visitors demonstrated the usual mixture of erudition and ignorance. By the display of rocks from a crater associated with the Collapse, he heard someone repeat the crackpot theory that the Temple was the work of aliens - why else was everything in it much bigger than human scale? He'd long ago learned not to volunteer corrections. Most people, even outwardly reasonable ones, were not in search of information that conflicted with their established worldview.

"Greetings, Sir Curator," said a voice behind him. He turned to see a short, stocky person of indeterminate age and gender. He - she? it? - had a flat, emotionless face and wore a one-piece grey garment with a long number across the chest. "I would like to see the Apocalypse Mosaic." The voice was slow and deliberate, as though the speaker wished to be sure each sentence, each word, was right before allowing it to leave his mouth.

From the appearance and clothing, the Curator guessed this person was a worker from one of the mines in the asteroid belt. These workers had been designed to be physically perfect for their job. The Curator had thought they'd also been designed not to care about anything other than mining. Perhaps this one had been rejected for being too independent, or perhaps the rumours of programmable brains and hardcoded personalities were just that. Even so, the thought of being in the same room as something that looked human but didn't qualify for voting rights made the Curator want to squirm.

"It's over there," the Curator said, pointing to it.

"Thank you, kind Sir Curator." The worker sounded grateful, but his expression didn't change - something his designers had seen as superfluous? He walked to the mosaic with the large brisk steps of someone who was unused to gravity and was overcompensating for it.

The worker reached the mosaic and went down on one knee before the rope barrier, bowing his head. The Curator approached discreetly, hoping the worker wouldn't try to hug the mosaic, the way another visitor had a few months ago. He fingered the stunner in his pocket.

The worker rose and turned to face the Curator. With a guilty start, the Curator withdrew his hand from the stunner.

"I trust I have not offended your sensibilities, Sir Curator."

"Sensibilities?"

"Temples are for prayer, are they not?"

"Yes," the Curator said carefully.

"And given that all deities and moral principles are projections of the universe into higher or lower dimensionalities, the universe does not care who prays in which temple."

The Curator didn't think a Neoplatonist would see it that way, but he'd clearly misjudged this fellow.

The worker took a few paces towards him. "I am a Revivalist, Sir Curator. Have you heard of us?"

"I'm afraid I haven't." In the isolated settlements of the Belt, cults sprang up with an almost metronomic regularity. Most burned out before the authorities could decide whether to proscribe them.

"We are attempting to reconstruct the colonists' original religion."

"How do you propose to do that when no written records survive from before the Collapse?" the Curator asked.

"We are in contact with scholars in other systems," the worker replied.

"That must be very expensive."

"It is."

"And is this reconstruction of merely academic interest, or do you intend to live according to their religion?"

"That depends on what we find." The worker's face twisted into what the Curator guessed was meant to be a smile.

"And what have you found so far?"

"We think they believed time was cyclical."

"Because a circle is the perfect form," the Curator said.

"Indeed. Circles are everywhere in this Temple, and in similar sites elsewhere in the system. We believe the colonists intended the Temple as a metaphor for the universe. The small cycles build into larger cycles, which build into still larger. A satellite orbits a moon, which orbits a planet, which orbits a star, which orbits the black hole in the centre of the galaxy."

The Curator frowned. "Those orbits are ellipses, not circles."

The worker's face twisted again. "Nothing made of matter is perfect, Sir Curator."

He couldn't argue with that. "So how does the Apocalypse Mosaic fit into their religion?"

"Most people think the mosaic is a prophecy about the end of the world," said the worker. "This derives from the traditional meaning of the word 'apocalypse.'"

The Curator nodded.

"Scholars in the Earth system have told us that 'apocalypse' originally meant something closer to 'revelation,' or 'drastic change,' which could be creative as well as destructive."

The Curator strolled to the worker's side and studied the mosaic. Even though he saw it every day and was responsible for its upkeep, he found that he'd forgotten the details of its appearance. It was about five metres across, slightly recessed into the floor. The predominant colours were red, white and gold, and even in the gloom of the nave, the tiles seemed to glow with a soft inner light. The picture was abstract, and consisted of spines radiating from the centre, which branched out along arcs that seemed to chase one another. Reflecting on the worker's words, the Curator thought that if he squinted, he might see circles within circles within the overall circle.

At the centre of the mosaic was a jagged gap, the size of a man's outstretched hand, where a tile was missing. Pointing to it, the Curator asked, "What have your studies told you about that?"

The worker cleared his throat. "We are aware of the legends that say if the tile is ever found and put in its place, the world will end. But we know that the Museum has conducted scans of the mosaic's interior. The plaster under the tiles has grooves to give the mortar a greater area to adhere to. In the space for the missing tile, the plaster is smooth. So the mosaic was built with the gap, and the missing tile was never there. We believe it does not exist."

"Do you have any theories as to why that is?" the Curator asked.

"The obvious explanation is that it symbolises the imperfect nature of all material things. But if we are right that the colonists believed time was cyclical, then the mosaic represents an event in both the past and the future."

"That seems plausible."

"There are many candidates for the past event, but the obvious one is the colonists' departure from Earth."

The Curator nodded. "So what's the future event? No colonisation expeditions have ever left this system."

The worker glanced at him sidelong. "As far as anyone knows. You said yourself, no written records survive from before the Collapse."

"None of the other colonies were founded by Heimdall," the Curator said.

"What if there was a hidden colony?"

"It's not possible to hide in space."

"Because of the problem of the disposal of waste heat, yes." His face twisted again into that might-have-been-a-smile. "We miners know a lot about that. But a colony that wants to hide needs only to hide from observers who have a line of sight on it. A colony at the edge of known space, or beyond it, has only a narrow cone in which it needs to not emit waste heat."

The Curator tried to picture the scenario. "Why would this colony want to hide, rather than benefit from trade and the exchange of ideas?"

The worker gave a big shrug. "The only way to know is to ask them. But if they left around the time of the Collapse, isolation might have seemed the wiser strategy. Retaining contact with the rest of humanity might have dragged them into an unwinnable war."

"There has never been a war between colonies," said the Curator, unwilling to imagine the kinds of ships and weapons that would be needed to make it practical.

"Not for want of trying, Sir Curator," the worker replied.

"You do realise, of course, that you've posited something whose existence can never be proven or disproven?"

"Is that not the essence of all religions, Sir Curator?"

The Curator smirked. A bell chimed from his watch. "Closing time already? Are you on Heimdall for long?"

"I lift for the Belt tomorrow morning."

"That's a shame. It's been fascinating conversing with you. I wish you success in your research, and I'll be interested to read anything you publish."

"It will be a long time before we publish, if we ever do."

"Oh. Well, do let me know if there's anything I can help you with."

"Thank you, Sir Curator." The worker bowed and left.

The Curator made his rounds of the Temple, starting with the most remote rooms and galleries, locking doors and gently shooing visitors towards the exit. At last he stood before the door that separated the nave from the vestibule. He pushed the master switch for the lights, and the nave grew dark. His hand hovered above the button that would close the door.

From the darkness, a voice said, "How would you react, Sir Curator, if I told you that everything the miner said is true?" The voice was deep and commanding, but had a synthetic quality to it, as though produced by a cheap loudspeaker.

"The Museum is closed, Sir. Please leave." How had he missed this visitor?

"That was not what I asked."

The Curator sighed. "Sir, if you wish to discuss anything regarding the Museum or its exhibits, you are welcome to return tomorrow, but for now, the Museum is closed, and I must ask you to leave."

The nave flooded with light, something that normally happened only during cleaning or maintenance. The Curator blinked in the sudden brightness, briefly ashamed of how shabby the place looked.

A few metres inside the entrance stood the visitor in the blue metal suit. In the brighter light, the suit looked ancient, dents and scratches all over.

"I ask again, Sir Curator, how would you react?"

"If we had the time to discuss the matter - which at present we do not - I would be intrigued, but would want some credible evidence before I believed you."

"Thank you." The visitor turned on his heel and marched into the nave. A faint whine accompanied each pace - a faulty servo in one of the suit's joints, probably.

"Come back here!" the Curator exclaimed, hurrying after him.

From the centre of the nave came a loud clattering, as the visitor barged through the rope barriers around the Apocalypse Mosaic. The Curator swore and pulled the stunner from his pocket. Panting, he stumbled to a halt a few metres from the mosaic and pointed the stunner at the visitor.

"Leave. Now."

The visitor seemed not to have heard him. He walked to the centre of the mosaic and crouched, apparently studying the gap for the missing tile.

"How dare you?" the Curator shouted. "That's a unique artefact! Do you have any idea how much damage you're causing?"

The visitor ignored him.

The Curator's hands shook as he kept the stunner aimed at the visitor. "Leave now or I'll stun you, and you'll go to prison!"

"Why have you not stunned me already?" the visitor asked. "Are you worried that I might damage the mosaic further if I fall on it?"

The Curator took a few shallow breaths and tightened his grip on the stunner. "If you leave now, I won't have to stun you."

The visitor walked out of the mosaic. The Curator winced at the thought of the tiles shifting and cracking under his heavy boots, but kept the stunner pointed at him. He faced the Curator, arms by his sides, palms open.

"If you stun me now, the mosaic will not be harmed."

The Curator licked his lips. A bead of sweat trickled down his forehead. He daren't lift a hand to wipe it away. "You wouldn't say that if you thought the stunner would get through your suit."

"I would not. And it will not."

The Curator slackened his grip on the stunner. "What do you want, Sir?"

"I want to repair the mosaic, Sir Curator."

"It isn't broken. Or it wasn't until you trampled all over it."

A hatch opened in the stomach of the visitor's suit. From inside he took a flat black jagged shape that glistened in the nave's lights.

The Curator knew at once that it would fit into the gap in the mosaic's centre.

"A colonisation expedition did leave Heimdall just before the Collapse," the visitor said, "and the colonists did not want to be followed or found. But they knew that their eventual discovery was inevitable. So they left behind alarm systems. We are standing in one of them."

"Standing in?" the Curator asked.

The visitor tilted his head to one side. "Surely you know that the floor forms a parabolic reflector?"

"A what reflector?"

"The entire Temple is a radio transmitter. When I put the missing tile into the mosaic, it will send a signal to the hidden colony."

"But the Temple pre-dates the Collapse by fifteen hundred years," the Curator said.

"You surely know that buildings are repurposed over the centuries. This one happened to fit the colonists' needs."

"Why are you telling me this?" The Curator suspected he already knew.

"Because you cannot stop me."

"I can tell the government," the Curator said. "If the colony attacks, we'll be ready."

"You have no evidence."

"The miners have evidence."

"The incoherent ramblings of a quasi-religious cult." The visitor moved towards the mosaic.

The Curator raised the stunner. "Keep away from there, unless you want to find out whether this can go through your suit."

The visitor ignored the warning. The Curator's finger hesitated over the stunner's trigger. Technically this was assault if not done in self-defence. But he couldn't allow further damage to the mosaic.

A grey blur shot out from behind the nearest information display and collided with the visitor. They went down in a tangle of limbs and a deafening crash of metal. A small black object skittered across the floor, to stop a few paces in front of the Curator.

"Use the stunner on the tile!"

The Curator recognised the voice - the mine worker. He was kneeling astride the visitor, punching the man's chest and head. The visitor's arms thrashed about, hitting the floor as often as the worker.

"Do it!" the worker screamed.

Not knowing what else to do, the Curator pointed the stunner at the tile and pressed the trigger. There was a blinding flash and a loud bang. When the Curator could see again, the worker was standing over the visitor, holding the man's helmet as though trying to decide whether to crush it or throw it into the distance. The black tile had split open, and a thin line of smoke rose from it.

"What time is it?" the worker asked.

"Pardon?" the Curator gasped.

"I asked what time it is. It's very important."

The Curator glanced at his watch. "Eighteen thirty-seven local, fourteen fifty..." He trailed off as his gaze returned to the visitor, who was missing his head.

"You've killed him," the Curator whispered.

"Some would say he was never alive," the worker replied. He turned the helmet to reveal a mass of wires and actuators where the neck had joined the body. A robot, then - more sophisticated than any the Curator had dealt with before.

"Was he... sentient?"

"By some definitions. But he was unregistered, so deactivating him does not count as murder."

The Curator gulped. "An unregistered sentient robot? That's..."

"Terrifying?" the worker offered.

The Curator nodded. "How did he get through Planetary Security?"

"He did not. The colonists left him here when they departed."

"Two and a half thousand years ago?"

"Yes. He has not had much maintenance since then, which is why I was able to overpower him. I think the colonists assumed they would be discovered much sooner. They did not expect the Collapse to be as complete as it was."

"Are there... more like him?"

"My comrades have deactivated four so far. We do not know how many more exist."

"You're hurt," the Curator said, feeling guilty that he had only now noticed the blood on the worker's hands and face. "I'll call an ambulance."

The worker shook his head. "It would draw too much attention to my mission. I will seek medical attention elsewhere." He put the robot's head down. "We now have a fair idea where the hidden colony is."

"How so?"

"When the transmitter is activated, it sends a signal straight up. As Heimdall rotates on its axis and orbits the sun, many stars pass overhead, so the robot had to activate the transmitter at the right moment. The signal had to be short, otherwise the authorities would notice it."

"That was why he kept me talking," said the Curator. "He was waiting for the right time."

"Indeed."

The Curator slipped the stunner back into his pocket. "If you don't want to draw attention to your mission, why did you tell me about it?"

The worker gazed into the distance. "Sooner or later, one of these robots will send a signal before we can stop him. When that happens, we will need someone in authority who believes we are more than a quasi-religious cult."

"I see." The Curator wiped his brow. "Well, I'll be happy to help if you think I can."

The worker started for the exit.

"What about the robot?" the Curator called after him.

The worker turned and gave him that might-have-been-a-smile again. "Dump him in one of the Temple's unexplored basements. When someone finds him in a few decades, you can exhibit him here, alongside all the other things that are too dangerous to forget."

The End

You can find Stephen and more of his work on the following link:

http://www.pembers.net/

Cover by Author.

The Girl Running Deep in the Sea of Glass

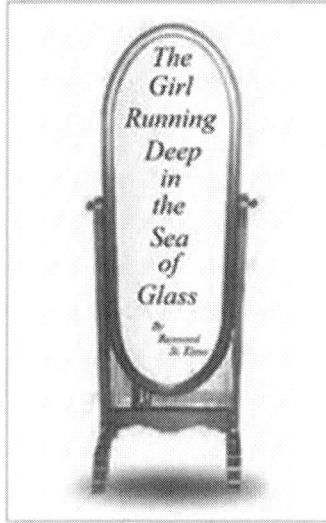

Raymond St. Elmo

About the Author

Raymond St. Elmo is a programmer fascinated by languages, artificial intelligence and Magic Realism. His usual work is something novel-length, giving him space to describe glorious sunsets, complex computer algorithms and his opinions of Borges, Phil K. Dick, Edgar A. Poe and that entire crowd of posthumous literary practical jokers.

Of his contribution here: the light of fantasy resides between two mirrors. The reader stands between them to see themselves become a character in a story repeated from Alice to the Matrix, from Neolithic tales of faeries stealing children to the last time they dreamed of flying, of falling, of chasing and being chased...

The Girl Running Deep in the Sea of Glass

"Why do I need a mirror?" I asked Dad. Kicking through the

wrapping in case I'd missed something. A puppy. A thousand dollar bill. A bike.

"To see yourself," he sigh-replied. "To dress proper. Today you are ten. Time to start wearing shirts right side out. Combing hair. Matching socks. Tying shoe-laces."

The mirror stood upright, taller than the boy it framed. I considered the Me in the glass. A kid in a backwards shirt. So? It's a t-shirt. One side's good as another. The hair was just hair. Fluffy stuff atop one's head. The mirror-boy twitched his feet, sending shoe-laces lashing out. I knew the mirror-kid's secret. He pretended his feet had tentacles. Electric tentacle-whips that zapped sisters dead-flat. Glorious. Tied shoe-laces just came undone or turned to knots. Useless.

"Tap here to access features," said Dad. He touched finger to top left corner. The glass went black, became a doorway to a night far away and long ago. Scary. I jumped back, tangling my shoe-lace tentacles. My dad laughed. I laughed too. Ha.

Green letters floated in the dark. Welcome to your eMirror.

My dad tapped fingers, pulling menu items from the mirror-screen. *"How to tie a neck-tie. Correct color combinations for social occasions. Table manners: an introduction. One Hundred Rules to Raise the Polite Child."*

"No, no, no, no."

My dad nodded. He could acknowledge a sane point of view. If you clicked the 'enter' button repeatedly. "Okay, yeah, sounds grim. But c'mon, some of these are games. *Win points for matching socks! Level up with clean underwear.* Wear your shirt backwards, god knows what will happen. Make it scream, probably."

It was an interesting idea. Torment a mirror with clothes combinations. No, actually it was a dull idea. Also it was mean. Poor thing just wanted to teach me to tie my shoe-laces. As of I didn't know.

So I nodded. My reflection did the same. We exchanged looks. We knew Dad would get past this *growing-up and grooming-out* phase. Adults had tiny memories. They couldn't remember half the things you told them. They forgot rules to games and where they put their keys, forgot to pick you up at soccer practice and how *you asked for a new bike for your birthday not an old-lady's standup mirror.*

***

The mirror took its place in a corner next my dresser. It bothered me any closer to the bed. The silvery glass had a way of flickering curtain-like, as if below the pleasant surface something occasionally twitched.

I experimented with settings. I could summon an avatar-reflection of me, give him orders. "Stand up straight. Left tennis shoe on right foot. Put on green socks. Put a red sock on your head." Boring. More fun to do these things myself.

"Why do you wear your t-shirts backwards?" my reflection asked.

Puzzling. The mirror had my moves and expressions; down flat. But he didn't really understand me. He didn't follow how wearing your shirt backwards made you run faster on the playground. Girls noticed you. They giggled, and girl-giggles were rocket fuel. You ran faster, zoomed the monkey-bars like a circus-acrobat. Kicked the kick-ball over mars.

My reflection placed suggestions into the silence. "You wore those jeans all last week. Try the khakis."

"I hate khakis. They get dirty and wrinkly just sitting in class doing nothing, nothing."

"Girls like khakis," he offered, sly. Okay, maybe he did follow.

I considered. Did it *matter* what girls liked? No. Yes. Sorta. Yesterday I chased Ki across the playground, through the monkey-bars and the little-kids sand-box. I didn't catch her. I gave up, moped in the box with the first-graders. They shared what wisdom they had.

"Stop scaring her, you big dummy," said a wise six-year old.

"Give her candy," advised a pig-tailed creature of indeterminate gender.

"Girls only like the boys they chase," offered a boy. "Not the ones chasing them."

"Girls are just crazy, crazy, crazy," said a cynic, pouring sand on his head.

"Yep we are," admitted the pig-tailed. "Sorry, mister."

So I tried the khakis. Didn't work, I didn't run a bit faster. Ki still flickered beyond me, a dot of laser-light dashing past my kitten paws. At the end of fifth grade she moved to another town. Her last day of school we cut cake, signed a goodbye card, and she was gone.

I didn't tell anyone how I felt. No one asked. The mirror guessed but didn't pry. Adults kept to the official *Worry List for Fifth-Graders*, monitoring grades, teeth, height and online habits. They had no check-box for broken hearts. Ki's loss gave me stomach ache, and the grownups took it for flue. If anyone had asked, I'd have puzzled to express how I felt. Like there was less reason to run fast across the playground. Less reason to jump high in new shoes. No one to show a new tooth. I biked past Ki's house. Empty. That's how I felt. Empty.

I asked the mirror if it could show me where Ki lived now.

"I'm not an online system," admitted my reflection. He stood on his side of the glass, hair combed, pant-creases rivaling knife-edges. Shirt tucked in. Belt through all the loops. Matching blue socks, pulled up. Teeth brushed arctic white. He stood in an idea of my room as modeled in a conceptual universe of no dirty laundry, no scattered books and strict quantum laws requiring all toys put away.

"Ask your dad," he suggested. "He could get her email address. I shall teach you *43 Tips on Polite and Safe Electronic communications for Young People.*"

I shuddered, shook my head. Reality on the two sides of the mirror *seriously* differed. And not because over there the bed was made.

"Have you ever actually talked to a girl?" I asked.

He considered. Hesitated. Then admitted, "I've tried. There's one down there very deep. She comes up sometimes, peeks into your room."

I blinked. He did too. I mean, he was my reflection, just better dressed. If I blink he blinks.

"What girl?" I asked. "My sisters?"

He rolled his eyes. Did I do that? Hope not. Looked childish. Might as well pout.

"Not them. I tell them to scram when they sneak in. 'Course they don't listen. Lily and Tilly were in your comics yesterday."

"Snitch!" shouted a sister down the hall.

"Stay outta my stuff!" I screamed. I slammed my bedroom door. In the mirror, my reflection quietly but firmly shut his. I began an immediate audit of my comics, and forgot his words until half asleep.

A giggling sound. I opened an eye. The mirror glowed black. It did every night so I could sleep. Now a person hinted from out the black. Moon-lit, though no moon shone in my window. On this side of things, I mean. Who knows what moons they have over there?

Nose, face, eyes; a pointed chin to finish a heart-shaped face. She flattened nose to glass, a kid at a zoo exhibit searching for the exotic creature hidden within. Wild hair of tangles that flowed and twitched, anemone-hair in a dentist's aquarium. Perhaps it was

302

windy on that side of reality. Not that my immaculate avatar-reflection ever showed a hair out of place.

Now the girl put hands to the glass. Pale and delicate as frills on a cave-fish. She studied the comics laid out upon the floor. I felt a surge of protective anger. I sat up. She opened eyes wide, ducked below the frame. I considered yelling, decided that'd be dumb. I watched, she didn't return. I went back to sleep.

"I saw a girl in my mirror," I mentioned at breakfast.

"Wasn't me," said Tilly. "Your comics are stupid."

I made a rude gesture, she made it back. Dad surfed news, sipped coffee, reviewed my idle words and popped eyes wide in alarm.

I spooned powdered chocolate atop hot milk. It formed a doomed land I declared *Atlantis.* Marshmallow temples sinking, sinking beneath white waves. I waited for dad to babble about cross-system feedback, explain how some child in China resonated with my mirror's OS. Then he'd wax on his adventures in The Old Tech Days.

Instead, he intoned in parent voice #12: *calm panic.* "Ha. You saw a girl in your mirror. Well. That's, that's perfectly normal at one's age, son, to, to see yourself, ah, in different ways. New ways. Part of, of your normal gender identification..."

My sisters howled with laughter. Atlantis sank in embarrassment. I fled the table.

I didn't mention the girl again, even when I caught her spying. I ignored her. She retaliated by chasing me with hints of her presence. Daytimes I spied the snub of a nose edging past the mirror frame, a finger smearing her side of the glass.

Pursued, I declined to run. No, I would maturely turn and confront. No running fast, just sitting still. A challenge for an eleven-year old already enduring the motionless sixth grade. We had PE now, not recess. English Literature class, not Story Time. Life focused on sitting still, moving by direction only, permission only. I put a chair before the eMirror, sat staring into the reflection of my room.

"Can you get out of the way?" I asked my overly-groomed alter-ego. "How can I see if you sit in front of me?"

He crossed arms in defiance. "I'm required to maintain a reasonable somatic echo of your position and movement. It can cause self-awareness anxiety in juveniles to not see themselves in mirrors."

Whatever. I tried dodging left and right, but he shifted fast as me. I sat and glowered. He sat and glowered. I made a rude gesture, he mirrored me. I got up and we stalked from the room together. I tiptoed in again, my back to the wall, outside the view of the mirror. I peeked around the frame.

My own eye peeked back. "Seriously?" my reflection asked.

Fine. Challenge accepted: to see beyond myself in the mirror. I went to... *the attic*. A year ago this would have terrified me. The attic lurked above life, a dusty dark world where things waited, just waited, for time and lives to be over. Or for you to wander in.

I dared the dust and dark, the spider-webs and creepy rocking chairs, pushed aside junk to uncover my grandmother's stand-up mirror. Pre-electric, wooden-frame. The glass held a yellow tinge of ancient paper, like the translucent skin of ancient grandmothers. I put a palm to the dusty glass. Made me shiver.

Beneath my hand I felt all the light that ever passed through the glass. Years of light pooling within, like water in caves far below the surface of the day-world. Deep in that mirror remained the glow of my great-grandmother fixing a sash around her wedding dress, young eyes shining with fear and fire.

Whatever. I hauled the thing down the attic steps into my room, stood it before the eMirror. While my avatar wrestled his grandmother's mirror into view. We posed them together. Mirror within mirror within mirror, on to eternity.

"Cool," he admitted. "Wow, it's a hallway now. Tilt yours so we aren't blocking each other."

I stared down a long, segmented hall curving into a glass-green sea of infinity. Something fish-like darted in the distance beyond the last boy. Brown tangles of hair, bare feet, scruffy dress... the *girl*. She slowed to look back over her shoulder, mocking, defying anyone to catch her. She raced round the curve of the deep-sea hall and disappeared.

"Well, that's just weird," admitted my reflection. We sat down to think about it.

***

For a week I camped out between the mirrors. Pillow, blanket, plate of cookies. Flashlight at hand. Kinda fun, sorta scary. At night I would awaken, reach for my flashlight. I was a traveler in dangerous wastes, lying by his camp-fire, grasping the handle of his trusty sword at *the snap of a twig from the surrounding dark*.

Click the beam down the sea-hall of infinity. Stare at what blinks back in surprise. Open notebook to make a quick sketch. Take a breath, eat a cookie, return to sleep. Not an easy thing to do, to sleep in the presence of that hallway. Deep in the mirrors danced and swam things far stranger than playground girls.

"Why are you sleeping there?" asked my dad. Inevitable question, reasonably asked. I told him the truth, which indicates how far from sense one can wander in a week.

"There are things just where the mirror-hall bends away," I explained, pointing. "I've seen the girl, and monsters, and some kind of tiger and a flock of birds and people in robes walking in line holding candles."

I showed him my notebook of sketches. Working title: *The Beings Within*. Sketching was necessary. Smart-phones and cameras were useless, they just captured a lightning-flash of me taking a picture of me taking a picture of me.

Dad sat on my bed, leafing through the notebook, face carefully blank. I should have shut up, but the words wanted out.

"At night they come down the hall really close. I've watched people in old clothes dancing in moon-light. A rabbitty-looking creature jogging. He had a watch. A knight in armor. He's on that page there. A floating thing with a giant head, teeth like a t-rex. Really, really creepy."

I watched emergency lights flash, alarms blare through the *Dad Starship Command*. He was spooked. He ordered me to bed. Confiscated the sketch-book. Destined to be in the hands of a therapist before sunset tomorrow. So would I, no doubt. Another passenger for the Ritalin Express. He considered the eMirror.

"You know, let's think about swapping this thing for a bike."

Adventure over, I sighed. I curled up in my familiar bed and went to my familiar dreams.

***

"Psst, doofus," said a voice. "Wake up."

I woke, looking for a sister. The room was empty, the mirror not. The girl stood within its dark doorframe. She wasn't repeated endlessly. No; she stood alone, unreflected. Unique.

I sat up. Suddenly wishing I'd paid attention to those grooming tips from my mirror-self. Combed hair, brushed teeth? Nope. And no telling which side of my shirt was which.

Not that she came groomed for social occasion. Her hair rioted in defiance of combs and brushes. Waving, but not in wind. More like sea-currents flowing about her. The rough and ruffled dress did the same. Rippled. She looked a year older than me, an inch taller. Barefoot. Scabbed knees, same as mine. That kept me from yelling. Her knees same as mine.

"What?" I asked. Not the cleverest start to a conversation.

"What were you doing?" she asked, eyeing the blanket, the pillow, flashlight, comics, plate of cookie crumbs, etc. Paraphernalia of the stake-out.

"Trying to talk to you," I confessed. Then bit my tongue for its idiot honesty.

"Why?"

I considered. Why had I chased Ki on the playground? What would I have said if I'd caught her? Never had the chance to find out. Plenty of times I'd sat by her in class, or stood behind in line. Once she put a sticky-note on my back: 'Hi, I'm Mr. Geek'. Once I stepped on the heels of her flip-flops, making her trip. We could have talked. But she kept to the girls' reality, me to the boys'. Chasing Ki on the playground was different. It was like asking her to dance at summer camp. An allowed way of saying something neither of us understood. And wouldn't dare put into words if we did understand.

"I think you're cool," I confessed. There. Said it. "When you run your hair bounces. You go all up on tiptoes with your arms all wrong but somehow it looks... right. You live someplace interesting, with monsters and magic doors. You stand with your head tilted like some kind of fox-thing in the woods peering out from the trees."

She stood in the dark doorway with her head tilted. Fox-thing, between trees. She opened her mouth, closed it, turned and ran.

***

If she expected me to chase her, I didn't. Per my father's order I ceased sleeping between mirrors. Per my new therapist's suggestion, we moved the eMirror and the antique mirror to the attic. They could sit there together, discuss kids nowadays, the limits of eternity. I got a new bike.

Yet which way I turned, the girl remained behind me, or to the side, just out of sight, mocking. I did homework in the kitchen, avoided being alone in my room. Because I didn't feel alone. My sisters annoyed me less than the mocking *tap, tap* upon my exhibit window, the not-quite-heard snort of amusement.

"So you feel she is still watching you?" asked the school therapist.

"Hmm. Maybe?" I forced myself to not look towards the mirrors of the therapy room.

"Does being in sixth grade frighten you?"

I had no answer to that. She nodded, silence being the correct answer. She sent me back to class.

***

Sixth grade didn't frighten. It puzzled. The reality seemed nonsensical. The halls were full of elastic seventh and eighth graders struggling with training-bras and chin-fuzz. We tiny sixth graders writhed between two worlds, longing to run back down the hall to our old playground, longing to run ahead, join the tall creatures who formed couples and drove cars and vaped flavored clouds of steam.

Classes puzzled too. They began and ended with bells. Why the hell, bells? Why not bugles or bagpipes? A tiger roar? I sat in math class fidgeting, desperate to hear the dreariest sound in the universe: an electric tin-bell buzz. I turned to stare out the window. Beside my reflection sat the girl with anemone-hair. In the reflected desk next to mine. She stuck her tongue at me.

I turned to the real classroom. Empty chair. I turned to the window. Girl. Turned to the real world. No girl. Turned back. Our eyes met for a long second. We both blushed. She jumped up, fled the reflected room.

I stumbled to my feet. The entire class turned in delight. Something interesting! *Me.* The teacher paused her lecture to frown. I rushed out the door, stood in the school hallway. Empty. No, there at the far end was the girl, just turning the corner. I chased, shouting. I think I shouted '*stop*'. Might have been '*hey*'. Mattered nothing, what.

Didn't catch her. The principal caught me. When I explained I chased a girl from the mirror-world, I caught three worried looks, two calls to my dad and one new appointment with the school counselor.

***

And now the hunt was on. The girl began taunting me from all directions and reflections. My bike mirror, the windows of stores, the back of a cereal spoon, the mirrored sun-glasses of the school-bus driver.

"Whatcha staring at?" the driver growled, while she made faces out his silvered lenses.

"Did you ever have a girl chase you?" I asked.

The question surprised him. He considered. He was sixty-years grizzled, a veteran of war, life, marriage, tattoo-parlors and minor legal infractions.

"Just once." He scowled, recalling. "Screwed it up."

"How?"

"Ran faster than she did." He started the bus in angry recollection, sending me staggering to my seat.

***

At home I draped a towel over the bathroom mirror. In the boy's bathroom at school all I could do was hurry past the sinks to the stalls, though I only wanted to pee. Coming out I read mocking letters writ in soap across the dirty mirrors.

sufooD, sufooD, sufooD

A very puzzled janitor was assigned to wipe it off, though the writing was not on the wipeable side of reality. I was sent to the principal, who passed me on to another session with the school counselor, who was beginning to get interested.

"How do you feel about yourself in the mirror?"

"Worried. Mirrors are crazy dangerous places."

"Do you feel the 'you' that you see, has something he wants to tell you?"

I recalled his last instructions before exile to the attic. "Stand straighter. Comb your hair. Tie your laces. Turn your shirt right-side out."

"Hmm. Why do you think you wear your shirts backwards?"

"Hmm. I think I dress in the dark nowadays. It's fifty-fifty which way shirts go. Underwear too"

"Are you scared of your body?"

What a crazy question. As if my hands might go for my throat. Or my mouth begin snarling at me. Maybe my eyes swivel in my head to glare at my brain. Granted, once considered these things became possibilities. Perhaps it was Grownup Secret #57: *'Your body hates you.*

The counseling room had a one-way window for parents and monitors to hide behind, watching you watch yourself. I glanced at

308

my reflection. My body looked tired and ragged. Perhaps it had a right to be angry at me.

Then a small, delicate hand lifted itself above the mirror frame, gave a quick thumb's up, disappeared again. I started laughing. The counselor nodded as though she completely understood.

***

"What's this?" I asked, knowing. You see the plastic tablet-dispensers at school. It's almost a status thing, like expensive teeth-braces or crutches after a sports injury.

"Tablets. Once a day. With water. Farewell, dread feelings of being watched."

I nodded, pretending to swallow words and pill.

At home I dropped my backpack on the kitchen table, made sure no one watched, and climbed the stairs to the attic. Hot and dark. I forced my way through aisles of junk to find the two mirrors standing together in a dusty sunbeam.

I pictured them chatting about the follies of the reflected world. If so, they went silent when I approached. I stared at my face in the antique. My scruffy reflection nodded encouragement. That gave me the strength to reach up, tap the eMirror on. The glass flickered, my immaculate reflection appeared.

He gazed about at the dark and the dust, not approving but not surprised. When you are a reflection you catch on fast to changes in reality. I showed him the medication pill. He understood that too.

"It's good for you," said my reflection. "Good, in the worse sense of the word."

"Suggestions?" I asked the committee.

"Let's swap," he offered. "What you want is on this side of the glass anyway. And I want to try out all these tips I'm loaded with. *'Fifty sure-fire steps to be a popular teen. Study habits for the Adolescent Going Places. Puberty Done Right.'*"

I shuddered, for him, for me.

"Deal," I told my mirror-self. I held out a hand to shake. He did the same. At the meeting-point of reality and reflection our hands touched, clasped, pulled. I found myself propelled forwards as he stumbled past.

I stood in a green-glass hallway, a stream of cold glass reality flowing, caressing me not like a wind but a sea current. I stared at my groomed reflection standing in a reality of dust, dark and sixth grade.

"Good luck," was all either of us could think to tell the other. A toss-up whether he'd be Class President next year, or arrested as an alien pod-robot. I told myself to check on him regularly.

I took a breath of courage, and turned from the mirror-door to gaze far, far down the green curving hall, picturing all the creatures in the lost sketchbook... I was in their school hall now.

No monsters. There stood the girl astonished to see me. She put hand to mouth. Our eyes met. She whirled about, stood arms folded in defiant disinterest. Tossed her hair back. She glanced over a shoulder to make sure I understood: she was entirely and completely disinterested in my existence.

Then she broke into a run. Fast, but not too fast. I began to run. Fast, then faster. The sea-cave halls of infinity echoing with our footsteps, our laughter.

The End

You can find more of Raymond's writing on Amazon:

https://www.amazon.com/Raymond-St.-Elmo/e/B01N3ABAIO

Cover by Author.

North Star

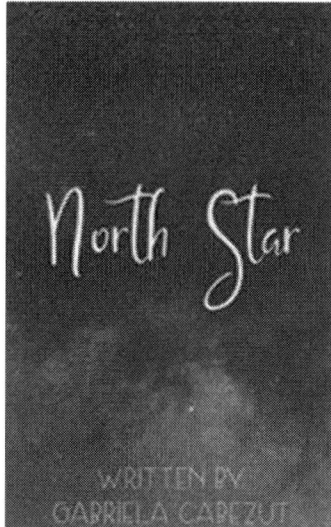

Gabriela Cabezut

Gaby Cabezut writes sweet, emotional stories that will make you swoon, laugh, and cry. Her stories have gathered over 80 million reads online.

She's part of the exclusive Wattpad Stars program, where she has been commissioned to write for brands like H&M and she's the community assistant for Wattpad's Spanish Ambassadors. She has been published by Limitless Publishing and Pop Fiction Books in the Philippines and will release a videogame app for Prince with Benefits and Take Out Chef as an audiobook from Hachette and Wattpad in late September.

***

I love summer, I reminded myself that night as I hiked to the top of one of our many Ouray hills. Wiping the sweat from my brow, I cursed the summer breeze, which instead of cooling me, caused my t-shirt and denim shorts to stick to my skin. Even the waning moon over the horizon looked swollen with the humidity.

I was halfway to the top and almost out of breath, when a booming racket came from the sky. My heart raced as I stopped in my tracks and looked up. It had sounded like thunder, but not quite. It felt different, too. It was as if the sky was cracking open. I'd been bingeing on Doctor Who, and a part of me wanted to see the TARDIS appear from nowhere and the Doctor walking out of it. If anything, I did not expect the bright light that appeared in the sky. *What is that?*

I froze, mesmerized. It looked like a star, but the bright light falling from the sky got bigger as it approached the earth. It was so blinding, I squeezed my eyes shut and covered them with my hands. It passed above me, making a swooshing sound, while my hair flew with the wild wind. An explosion detonated on the other side of the mountain. My heart pounded. The air filled with smoke. It burned my nose and throat. *Should I run back to the house? Call for help? Maybe I was overreacting.* It was probably a meteorite. My curiosity won out. I'd never seen one before, after all.

Leaves crunched beneath my feet as I moved with forceful strides. With the back of my hand, I swept away the trail of sweat that had formed on my forehead. My right leg was starting to cramp as I reached the top. There was a cloud of grey smoke coming out on the other side obscuring my vision. I scrunched up my nose at the smell of burnt wood. It looked like the beginning of a tacky horror story. I rolled my eyes. *I seriously need to stop watching TV.*

I grabbed a wooden stick as a of weapon. Would the rock be incandescent? Would it have fluorescent colors*? I hope it's not just plain gray.* That would be so disappointing.

I felt like Indiana Jones as I descended the hill. I reached the clearing where I thought the meteorite landed, and my heart flipped when I heard the alleged rock groan. I froze, swallowing hard.

Rocks don't make sounds, do they?

The groaning continued, followed by cursing about a cousin of sorts. *This is the time to run, Bailey.* My limbs were numb, my feet planted to the ground. The rock moved and...stood up. Wide eyed, an involuntary gasp left my lips. *Definitely not a rock.* It was a man. A very naked man.

In my eighteen years, I'd never seen a boy without clothes before. My life had been too hectic to think about it. However, I could tell that this was no ordinary man, and it had nothing to do with the fact that he'd fell from the sky. No one could look like him. I stepped closer, tilting my head. This guy was the absolute definition of perfection. He seemed like something Michelangelo carved. And he was there, in all his gloriousness. *And what a gloriousness it was.*

Lean, strong muscles outlined his whole body. His arms looked solid, granite solid. His chest was well-defined and he had a six pack. I know, because I counted the little squares. He definitely had six. My eyes were fixed between his abs and the daunting trail of hair that went south.

"Hello," a hoarse voice spoke. Swallowing hard, I willed my eyes to look up, but they didn't budge. It was as if they had a will of their own. "My eyes are up here, darling." His tone had a trace of a British accent, and my heart skipped a beat. I was a sucker for Brits.

"Are you, like, Thor?" I blurted, without looking up.

"Could you stop staring at my manhood?" My cheeks flushed, I closed my eyes and turned away. *What the hell is wrong with you Bailey? It's not nice to stare at a stranger's private parts.* I giggled.

"You can turn around now," he whispered by my ear, making me jump.

Hugging my arms, I bit my lip before shifting his way. In the haze of the moment, I hadn't really noticed anything other than his mcdreaminess, but as my eyes roamed around his face, my mouth went dry as I stared into his chocolaty eyes. His lips cracked a small smile and I noticed he had a small birthmark over the right corner of his lips. He was all cleaned up and dressed in a pair of denim jeans and a Henley t-shirt.

"How did you⍰?"

He shrugged. "I'm special."

The hold around my arms tightened. "How special? Superman special? *Thor* special?"

He crossed his arms too, studying me with the same fierceness as me. "You seem to have a thing for Thor."

"Thor falls from the sky." *Duh.*

"I'm not wearing a cape. Or a wielding hammer." My lips curved up as I was about to object at the hammer part but before I could utter any word, he shook his head. "I don't have time for this." He walked away through the field in the direction of the main road.

How does he know where to go? Creasing my brows, I stared after him. His strides were forceful and before he disappeared on me I jogged to him. *I hope he's Thor in disguise.* Thor is super cool and he has a handsome evil brother.

When I reached him, he was in the middle of the road, scrunching up his nose and rubbing his chin. He snapped his fingers and a yellow new beetle appeared on the road. Smiling confidently, he unlocked the car and opened the driver's door.

He puffed a car out of nothing! *What are you?* Then again, a yellow car? "Dude. You can have any car you want and you chose this one?"

He froze. Glancing at me, he leaned on the car's roof, crossing his arms. His eyes were playful as he grinned. "What car would you suggest?"

I stepped around it. It had a hideous shade. Tracing my hand over the hood, I gazed at him. "I'd get a Mini Cooper. Silver, with a red roof. Black interiors and all the details in red." I smiled as I pictured the car in my head. It was beautiful.

"Fine," he huffed before leaning away from the car. He snapped his fingers again and my dream car appeared.

How can he do that? The car was everything I'd imagined and more. Even the silver paint glittered under the lamppost.

"I'm dreaming, right?" I walked around the car, scared to touch it, convinced that it would fade away like smoke.

He didn't answer as he stepped inside. The engine roared to life a moment later. *Wait! He can't leave!* I opened the passenger door and got in. The interiors were shiny and the dashboard was red, just as I pictured it. It even had that new car smell!

"What are you doing?" Mr. Thor-alike frowned at me.

I licked my lips. "You've got my dream car. There's no way I'm not riding it."

He muttered something under his breath, but I couldn't make out the words. Defeated, he ran a hand through his hair before turning to me. "Where do you have fun around here?"

"Depends on what you call fun," I raised one eyebrow, my hand tracing the leather board. It was so soft.

He pinched the bridge of his nose, clearly exasperated, before turning off the ignition. "Look," he turned to me. "I have one night here. Just one night. And then I'm gone. There has to be something amazing in this place, or my cousin wouldn't have sent me here."

I crossed my arms across my chest. "Who's your cousin? Is he in Asgard?"

"I'm not Thor!" He raised both hands, glancing at the roof. "My name is Paul," he added in a serious tone, gazing at me.

"Just Paul?" I raised an eyebrow, and his eyes narrowed. I had to press my lips together not to burst out laughing. "How do you explain where you come from, then?"

"I'm on vacation," he said as if that was more than obvious. "I finished a job and my cousin suggested this place. He was clearly delusional." He gestured to the empty road ahead of us. "He'd said I'd find something phenomenal here..."

In a way, I felt bad for him. He didn't strike me as the dangerous type. I didn't know where he came from or what he was, but my town was not a fun place to be. There were mostly old people here. Everyone fled as soon as they could. Everyone but me.

"I guess that if you can summon a car, you could be anywhere you want."

He leaned back on his seat, his eyes set to the front. "I haven't visited this planet in a while. It's too different from what I remember." He glanced at me, frowning. "If you had one night, where would you like to visit?"

Planet? Was he from another planet, then? I'd always imagined aliens as green and slimy, but he wasn't either of those.

Shifting on my seat, I thought it through. A small smile played on my lips as I glanced through the window, gazing at the dark sky with millions of twinkling stars. I always wanted to travel. I'd memorized a list of places I wanted to visit.

"I'm assuming you can do anything," He shrugged. "Okay, I'd go to the Trevi fountain in Rome, and have a gelato while seeing the people walk by, taking pictures and throwing coins backwards to it. I'd also go to Venice and I'd run through the San Marcos plaza making all the pigeons fly everywhere."

My smile widened. "You also have to go to Paris. There's a huge park in front of the Eiffel Tower, one of the most iconic places in the city, and sit on the grass to enjoy the view with a bottle of wine and a stinky cheese." He tilted his head, watching me with deep eyes. My voice softened. "I'd love to see the northern lights in Alaska, but I'm not sure you can't do that in summer. But can you imagine watching different colors display on the sky? I imagine it must be magical." Shaking my head, I gazed to the front again. "You have to visit South Africa too. I've heard the landscapes are amazing and you can go on a safari and see elephants and giraffes strolling on the wild field like they own the world." My heart tightened, and I swallowed the lump I felt on my throat. "But no matter what, you have to visit the Maldives and watch the sparkling beach at night. The waves glow with fluorescent colors, and it must be one of the most beautiful sights ever..." My hands fidgeted on my lap as I casted my eyes down.

I would never get to see any of those places. Sometimes, it sucked to be me. I teared up.

"Gelato? What flavor?"

I snorted out, sniffing and blinking the tears away. "Cherry." I glanced up and met his eyes. Smiling softly, he stared at me as if he knew why I was stuck in this town and why my heart ached knowing that I'd never leave. *Not alive.* "Is there any way that you can conjure up an apparition spell?" I murmured, glancing away; feeling exposed, even though he didn't really know me.

"I think I need a tour guide."

My heart fluttered. "I think you got the wrong person."

His lips cracked a beautiful smile as I glanced at him. "Show me. Close your eyes and imagine we're there." *That's impossible.* He leaned closer, his eyes confident. "Nothing is impossible, when you're a star."

Can you also read my mind?

"A star?"

He shrugged. "I just changed my job, so technically, I'm just energy floating around," his tone was nonchalant.

Huh? Was I hallucinating? I was, wasn't I? He was really close. Pulling my hand back, I slapped him on the cheek. Hard. The sound of the blow filled the car as he leaned back.

"Bloody hell! What was that for?"

My hand was throbbing as I stared at it. "I'm not dreaming."

"No shit!"

"You know, for being an alien, star or *whatever*, you curse too much!" I raised an eyebrow as I looked at him. He was rubbing his cheek and I couldn't help but crack up at that.

"We adapt! I get this body and it's like we are downloaded with the basic stuff, like language, usual customs and such." He narrowed his eyes. "This is not a usual thing to do!"

"What do you mean by we? There are others like you? And what are you exactly?"

Exhaling, he turned away. "I'll make you a deal, if you show me those places you talked about, I'll tell you about me. I could use the company," he raised one hand, "but only if you stop being violent."

I thought about it. Even though my hand hurt, sometimes dreams can feel too real, and if this was a dream, I didn't want it to end. Not yet.

"Fine, but I need to make a call." I told my grandmother that I'd be staying with a neighbor. It wouldn't be the first time, so she didn't mind.

Paul patiently waited until I finished the call. "All set?" he asked as I put away the phone. I nodded. His eyes glinted with excitement as he smiled.

"Awesome. Just close your eyes and imagine yourself in the first place that comes to mind."

I did, though my heart raced like crazy as excitement bubbled inside of me.

"I need to grab your hand, don't freak out, okay?" I pressed my eyes tighter as I felt his hand on mine. He turned it and intertwined our fingers. Butterflies fluttered in my stomach. A second later, he squeezed it. "Open your eyes."

I hadn't opened them but I could hear that we were on a different place. People were walking past, all speaking in a different language. The sound of water falling behind me made my heart pump faster, and the air smelled sweet, not like the woodsy smell from the forest back in Colorado. Slowly, my eyes fluttered open and I felt like I couldn't breathe for a moment. My eyes were wide as I turned around and I stared at the grandness of the Trevi fountain. The water was crystalline with a turquoise tint. I looked everywhere, tears brimming.

Paul hadn't let go of my hand. I threw my arms around him. "Thank you."

He seemed surprised for a moment, before his arms enfolded me. "I still don't know your name…"

I smiled at that, pulling away, staring at those chocolaty eyes. "Bailey."

In slow motion, his lips tugged up on a playful grin. "What do you say if we get that cherry gelato, Bailey?"

***

We visited every place I mentioned except the northern lights venue. It was summer and apparently it was almost impossible to see them. We didn't even try after I read that on Google. The stinky cheese had been too much for Paul, though. He almost puked when we opened the bag. He'd told me all about him being a star as we watched a herd of elephants move across the Kruger Park in South Africa. A soft breeze nipped my cheeks as we watched the sunset over the African savannah. He'd been stationed as Polaris for almost 26 thousand years, and he'd been rewarded with a free pass to travel around the universe for a while. The only catch was that he only had a few hours in each world, but he could do anything on those hours. He was, as he'd said before, energy floating around in space. He seemed happy with the arrangement, but he wanted a new job. Something packed with action, apparently. He was tired of being stationed in the same place for so long. Apparently, a thousand years for us was like a few months to him.

"Who has taken your place as the North Star?"

He shrugged. "Last I heard, it was someone from the Andromeda galaxy."

"Your deal sounds pretty sweet, to be honest."

He looked smug, "I know."

The last place we visited was Rheeti beach in the Maldives. Our feet grazed the glowing ocean water on the sand. I'd been pretty quiet since we'd arrived.

The place seemed magical. Soft waves crashed against the shore, and my eyes could not believe that the water was actually sparkling in neon blue. I'd seen pictures of this, but no picture could make it justice. It was as if being on another planet.

"Thank you," my tone was soft as my right hand grazed the sand. I'd visited all the places I'd ever wanted to see. "I'm dying," I blurted out, my heart aching with heaviness. "I've got Leukemia, blood cancer. I've had it for years but now…"

Slowly, his hand traced mine. I felt little sparkles prickle my hand as he intertwined them. Paul's chocolaty eyes were soft as I gazed at him. "I know." *How?* His eyes roamed around my body. "Your aura. It's fading."

Tears pricked my eyes. I knew I didn't have much time.

It sucks being home, pretty much just waiting until I got worse. However, I'd spent the last two years in a hospital doing chemotherapy, and the treatment wasn't working. I got tired of it all. It was hard for my grandmother, who'd taken care of me since I was eight. She was furious when I told the doctor I was giving up. That had been three months ago, and we'd spent those last months just enjoying our time together. She needed to rest, too. She was worried and tired all the time. Being home had been the right call.

His thumb started to rub soothing circles on my hand. "The doctor said that I have less than a year. So this," I gestured with my left hand, "this means a lot to me. Thank you."

Softly, he shook his head. "Don't. You were my north star tonight. I should be thanking you." I stared at him for the longest of moments. He was breathtaking. It wasn't only his perfect assets, like how his nose was straight or his lips looked kissable, there was more to him. We'd spent a few hours together and I could tell that he was playful and fun to hang out with. He seemed sweet, too.

Okay. He seems too perfect to be real, but I suppose that being a star, he gets to be wise and handsome.

Biting my lip, I turned away and moved my right foot, the luminescent water twinkled under it. "Will it hurt? When the time comes?"

"Like a bitch. Your body will shut down and that final moment is going to be painful." My lips curved up despite of the crude situation. I liked his honesty. "But I'll be there," he leaned in and my heart started to pump furiously inside my chest. "I promise."

My mouth felt dry. "How?"

His face was too close now. My breathing was unsteady and I felt sort of dizzy. "Because when you're touched by a star, we can't leave you."

Touched? What does he mean?

I couldn't say anything, because his lips brushed mine, and I got lost in the electric current that passed between us. His kiss was like an unspoken promise. I felt sparkles from the tip of my lips to the pit of my stomach. Slowly, reluctantly, he pulled away. His forehead was leaning into mine, and his soft breath caressed my lips while his left hand cupped my chin. I was overwhelmed with warmness, from the inside-out.

"That's cheating," my voice was hoarse.

His lips tugged up. "I never said I played fair."

My breathing calmed. "You'll stay with me? Until the end?" I asked in a soft murmur.

"Yes." He didn't hesitate. "And this way, you'll come with me. I'll get to be your north star." He pulled apart and pecked me lightly on the lips, the electric current running through my body again. He passed an arm around me, and I laid my head in his chest. "I won't have this body, but I won't leave. I'll get to visit you in your dreams, though."

Pulling apart, he gazed at me. "We are all energy at the end, Bailey. I'm just snatching you as a life-time companion. Do you want that?" His pupils were completely dilated. Butterflies fluttered in my stomach. I nodded.

He beamed. "You know? My cousin was right," he passed his arm around me again, pulling me closer. "I did find something phenomenal in Ouray, Colorado." I smiled, cuddling closer to him.

I didn't know what was coming, but knowing that I wouldn't be alone, that he would be waiting for me, gave me a sense of peace. And for the first time in years, I wasn't afraid of the future. I couldn't wait.

The End

My social media:

My webpage: https://www.gabycabezut.com/

My Wattpad page: https://www.wattpad.com/user/gabycabezut

FB GROUP: Gaby Cabezut's Squad

FB: https://www.facebook.com/gcabezut

Goodreads: https://www.goodreads.com/author/show/8511493.Gabriela_Cabezut

Amazon author page: https://www.amazon.com/Gabriela-Cabezut/e/B019NRRZFS

Twitter: https://www.wattpad.com/user/gabycabezut

Snapchat: gabbycabezut

Instagram: gabycabezut

Cover by Author.

Effing Dave

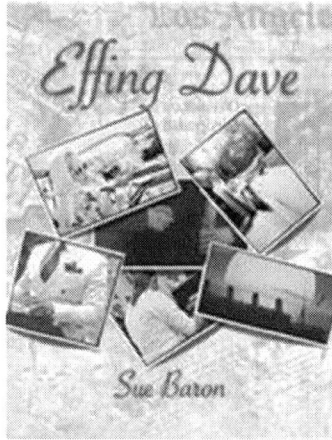

Sue Baron

Dave is the immortal all the other immortals can't help but hate. He pops up every decade or so, makes himself famous, then fakes his own death. This time around he's even started an over-the-top conspiracy website highlighting his exploits through history. It's bound to drive his peers nuts. But, honestly, what girl can resist being attracted to a bad boy like him?

Sue Baron is your typical Generation X'er. She gleefully used her parents money to earn a bachelor's degree in psychology from West Virginia University, but she prefers jobs that give her plenty of time to do the things she loves—namely writing, reading, and working out. Sue currently resides in West Virginia, USA, with her boyfriend, Tim, and her ancient cat, Hercules. Vampires are her genre of choice, but a writing prompt she found online inspired the following short story.

***

Imogen listened to the crazy-haired host ramble on about Earth's supposed ancient alien visitors as she folded her laundry. She

321

peeked up at the television every so often, waiting for the episode she heard would air today to begin. She held out hope that Ace wouldn't be paying attention.

But, really, it was only a matter of time before—

"Can you *believe* him?" came in from the living room.

And there it is. She sighed, balling up a pair of mismatched socks, as her brother stomped into her bedroom. She muted the TV.

"Can you effing believe him?" Ace threw the paper on a pile of panties with a huff. "One of these effing days, he's going to effing expose us to the world!"

Why does he never use the f-word? Imogen thought, watching the vein throb in her brother's temple. *It would calm him down so much. Suppose it's a good thing an aneurysm wouldn't kill him.*

"What's Dave done this time?" she asked, feigning ignorance better than Ace knew.

"Look! Effing look!"

Imogen glanced up at the TV as she reached for the paper; a goofily grinning man stared out from a drawing on a cave wall in France. *Ah, Dave.* She bit down on her tongue to hold back a giggle and furrowed her brow, trying to appear serious, as she turned her attention to *The Washington Post.* The headline read: 'President Meets With Philanthropist.' The corresponding photo below showed Donald Trump standing in the Oval Office shaking hands with a man sharing the cave drawing's grin. The caption identified him as Dave Dewar.

"A playboy millionaire meeting with effing Trump? Really?"

She shrugged. "You know how he is, Ace. Why do you even worry? At least he changes his name every time he pops up. If he didn't expose us with the *Titanic,* he won't now."

"*The effing Titanic? I totally forgot about that!*"

Shit, Imogen thought, rolling her eyes. *Way to give him more to rant about.*

"He played the millionaire-playboy card then, too! Do you remember the photos?"

She pursed her lips as the photographs Ace brought up flashed across the TV screen behind him: Dave boarding the ill-fated ship; photobombing a group on the First Class promenade; swimming in one of those striped onesie suits men wore back then. Then the headline came: *David Carlson Lost with Ill-fated Titanic.*

Her lips gave an involuntary twitch as she read the closed captioning below: 'But did David actually die? Is he an alien visitor who has the ability to come and go as he pleases?' The host held up his hands with a shake.

Ace followed her gaze. "What the eff? They did a whole episode on Dave!" He grabbed the remote and turned the volume back up.

"Or is he, as www.DaveLives.com theorizes, an immortal, human-like being walking among us, becoming famous at different points in history, then faking his own death?" the host asked, his fluffy hair bouncing as he spoke.

Oh, definitely the latter of the two, crazy hair, Imogen mused. *If you only knew how many of us there are!*

"He started a website? You've got to be kidding!" He pulled out his cellphone and began dialing as he exited the room.

Ace's conversation floated into the room: "Hey Bazza, yeah, it's me...Effing Dave started a website!...Yeah! Just saw it on that crazy alien show. You didn't know either?...What're we gonna effing do?...Um hmm, yeah...Okay..."

Imogen gazed up at the TV longingly, an 1843 photograph of Dave filling the screen.

"Is this more proof Dave has continued to visit us? This is a photograph of the famous composer David Baasch who, with Franz Liszt, became a piano virtuoso."

She recalled Dave's virtuoso days well as she folded a pair of jeans. Though Ace had tried to keep them well away from the other immortal, Dave had a sneaky way of showing up everywhere they went. She clearly remembered Ace's chagrin when they discovered him in Germany in 1851.

"All I wanted was to see Liszt play once. Is that too much to effing ask?" Ace growled. "What's Dave doing in Weimar of all places anyway?"

Imogen shrugged, adjusting a flower in her ash-brown hair. "I guess we'll find out," she answered, finding their seats just before the concert began.

She watched as Dave slid noiseless onto the bench, placing sheet music in front of him. His fingers hovered, ready to begin. A moment later, she sat transfixed as Dave's shiny, dark hair bobbed as his fingers moved fluidly over the ivory keys of the piano.

His eyes met hers when he stood to bow; she wondered if anyone else noticed the wink. She hoped Ace of all people hadn't! He slid from the hall to the audience's applause, allowing Franz Liszt to take the bench.

"Finally," Ace muttered when Liszt began. He closed his eyes,

relaxing as he listened to Hungarian Rhapsody No. 2.

Imogen stared at her brother, every inch of her itching to run after Dave. What was the point of immortality if she couldn't have fun? Dave always had fun! One of these days—

Ace returned to the room, making her drop the pants she's been holding onto in surprise. He flipped open his laptop and pulled up www.DaveLives.com with a huff. "Effing look at this!" He handed her the laptop as he pointed at the screen.

Don't laugh, don't laugh, don't laugh, she instructed herself as she stared at the cheesy font:

Dave Lives!!!

Do Immortal Beings Walk Among Us???

We Show **YOU** The **TRUTH**!!!

"My, um, he really goes nuts with the punctuation, doesn't he?" She scrolled down the page as Ace glared over her shoulder. Photographs from the mid-nineteenth century on and videos from the 1940s to the present purportedly showed Dave popping up every ten to twenty years. Links to articles were listed in a sidebar. Portraits of Dave from the fourteenth to the eighteenth century showcased the works of Jan van Eyck, Raphael, Leonardo da Vinci, and Rembrandt van Rijn. "It's like all the other conspiracy sites on the net. He's gone so over the top with this, no one can possibly take it seriously, Ace."

A portrait of Dave sitting in the gardens of Versailles in 1740 caught her eye, as Ace took the laptop from her hands. The memory of her closest encounter with the other immortal filled her wandering mind.

Imogen, costumed as the goddess Venus, stood fanning herself as she spoke to Reinette. They sipped wine while the other Yew Tree Ball attendants surrounded them in small groups, gossiping.

"Do you think I've caught the King's eye, Imogen?" Reinette asked with a coy grin as Louis XV glanced her way.

How could Reinette not catch his eye with her shiny blonde hair and rosy cheeks? To be as beautiful! And her costume—Diana the Huntress—was certain to have the king interested!

Reinette leaned in close to Imogen. "I do believe you have an admirer as well," she whispered, her eyes indicating a nobleman dressed as Bacchus.

She looked up, meeting Dave's eccentric grin as he made his way through the crowd, nearly tripping over himself. She scanned the room, but Ace was no where to be seen; her smile grew at the knowledge.

"Good luck," Reinette whispered, quietly making her way through the Hall of Mirrors to be closer to the king.

"This is a rare occasion, Imogen! Catching you without your brother." Dave lifted an eyebrow, a mischievous glint in his hazel eye. "A dance, mademoiselle?"

"I would be delighted!" She nodded primly as Dave took her hand, leading her to the dance floor. "It is indeed rare for me to escape Ace. Though you know there will be hell to pay if he—"

As if on cue, Ace's hand rested on her shoulder. "I've told you to effing stay away, Dave."

"But is that what your sister wants, Ace?" Dave flashed a wide white smile, glancing down at Imogen. "I think not."

The anger and annoyance emanating from Ace made Imogen step back. "It was just a dan—"

This is for our safety, Imogen. Get to the carriage," her brother hissed, turning and grabbing her hand.

She looked back over her shoulder as Dave said, "One day I'll give you the time of your life, Imogen."

Imogen's phone vibrated, bringing her back to the present. *Poor Reinette, only living to forty-two. Then again, you did get to be King Louis XV's mistress. Ah, Madame du Pompadour, you were a good friend,* she reflected, before thinking of the message awaiting her. Only her eyes moved down, not wanting to divert Ace's attention as he scrolled through Dave's website. She placed the shirt she had in her hands on a pile and tapped her phone to see the text.

'Hey! Found ur number. Ace not hiding you as much N E more? LOL I'm in town. U ready 4 a good time? :-) D'

She answered back with a winking smiley face as Ace clicked on a link to an article. "Nicolas Flamel?" she asked her brother, a corner of her mouth quirking. "What'd Dave have to do with him?"

Ace grunted as he scanned the first paragraph. "'What really happened to Nicolas Flamel, famed alchemist and supposed discoverer of the Philosopher's Stone? Why was his grave at the former site of the Church of Saint-Jacques-de-la-Boucherie found empty? Is he an immortal?'" he read to her, rolling his eyes in disgust. "Great! Shit we didn't even know about! 'Did Flamel truly discover the secret to life everlasting, as seventeenth-century authors claimed? Our sources say no. What really happened then?'"

They both leaned in closer to the screen to study the drawing dividing the paragraphs as Imogen heard her phone vibrate again.

She glanced down, seeing: 'Should I take the ;-) as a yes? Y or N?' Her finger tapped the 'y' then 'Send' so she could focus on the picture: two men—one elderly and one young— clad in robes, leaning over manuscripts on a table. The younger of the two had Dave's signature ornery grin plastered on his lips. In a bottom corner of the drawing, the name 'David Etienne' was written in a neat script.

Ace read on, "'This drawing by Dave shows he and Flamel were well acquainted in Flamel's later years. While the famed alchemist was not himself immortal, he kept company with those who were! Then what happened to Flamel's body? Evidence later found in personal correspondences between Dave and Flamel show the two agreed to pull a prank for the ages! Our immortal friend, Dave, MOVED the body of his dear-departed friend so the world would BELIEVE Flamel had discovered the illusive Philosopher's Stone!'" He let out an exasperated breath as his eyes moved over the grainy scans of Dave and Flamel's letters at the bottom of the article.

Imogen grabbed another pair of socks to cover for checking Dave's next message: 'Sweet! B there in 20. Can't wait to finally bust U outta prison! Lol Gonna make U famous 2.' She responded with a simple 'K' before balling the socks up and tossing them on top of the others. *Hmmm,* she thought, thinking of the backpack she kept in her closet, *I hope I have everything I—*

"Dave is effing insane! And *you* wonder why we stay away from him. He could expose us to the world. Then what? Have you ever thought of that? Hmm?" Ace questioned, finally turning away from the screen. He grasped her shoulders gently, playing his protective older brother role with a little too much zeal in her opinion.

"I have, Ace," Imogen answered, meeting his steel-blue eyes with a nod. *I really should feel bad about what I'm about to do, but...*

"There would be investigations, experiments. Who effing knows what else? Before we just had to hide from the effing religious whack-a-doodles who would try to burn us at the stake. Now..."

I'm really not gonna miss the 'effing,' she mused as she wondered if she had enough underwear packed.

"Most people today aren't as effing crazy with the religion these days, but being locked up for scientific experimentation doesn't effing sound fun to me." Ace raised an expectant eyebrow at her.

"None of us want that. You're right. Staying away from Dave has been for the best. He'll only get us into trouble. We can't risk it," Imogen agreed, glancing at the clock behind her brother. *Shit, Dave'll be here in five minutes!*

"We'll need to figure out what to—" His phone's chiming ringtone cut him off. "It's Bazza. Hey, Bazza...Yeah..." Ace turned to his sister as he walked towards the door and mouthed 'Give me a minute.' "What do you think?...Umm hmm...Umm hmm..."

A relieved whoosh of air left Imogen's lungs as a grin split her face. She hurried to her closet, grabbed her stuffed backpack, and gave herself a once over in the full-length mirror. "Meh. Could be worse," she mumbled, studying her yoga pants and t-shirt. A second later, she slid open the window and shimmied out, running to the waiting convertible.

Dave handed her a pair of cat-eye sunglasses and a pretty paisley headscarf. "I know you always appreciated the style of the sixties. Thought you might want to be the reason it comes back."

Imogen shrugged in delight, donning the sunglasses and wrapping the scarf around her head. "Why not? Always wanted to be a fashion icon!"

"Ready to party?" Dave asked, shifting into gear.

She glanced back toward her bedroom window, meeting Ace's open-mouthed stare. "Absolutely!"

Ace's yell barely reached her ears as they sped off.

"Fancy that," Imogen said, tilting her head.

"Fancy what, babe?"

"Ace finally broke down and used the f-word. Even added 'mother' to the beginning."

The End

Links:

https://www.facebook.com/AuthorSLBaron/

https://twitter.com/AuthorSLBaron

Cover by Author.

Recalculating

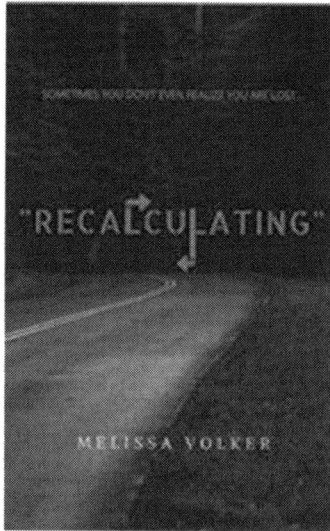

Melissa Volker

Melissa Volker Bio:

Daughter of a playwright/novelist and a poet, Melissa Volker's debut novel, *Delilah of Sunhats Swans* received a Five Star Review from Reader's Favorites and was praised by *Alice Fulton, Guggenheim Fellow Poet*, who said, "Delilah...is a charmer, a being blessed with a charisma as mysterious as it is luminous. You won't soon forget her." It was followed by a collection of short stories and a novella, *a life undone*. She is a member of The Straw Dog Writer's Guild and recently won Words and Brushes third Collaborative Competition with her short story, *Truths*, which can be found on their website.

The Thirteenth Moon was her first middle-grade, fantasy adventure novel and garnered her the description of "...a combination of C.S. Lewis and J.K. Rowling". The Sequel, *A Council of Elders* is tentatively scheduled for release later in 2017. Volker then delved into the YA genre with a slipstream/soft scifi novel, *Anabelle*

Lost and a magical realism novella, *HIDDEN*, each due out in April 2017.

Readers have described her writing as "beautiful, descriptive language", "lyrical, lilting and poignant", with "characters you connect with and care about".

Some FUN FACTS in my own words:

I am a total geekgrrl, Marvel fanatic and Wonder Woman wannabe (Thor would be cool, too). I cry at commercials. I'm totally a Huffelpuff.

***

Sometimes you don't realize how lost you are
until someone offers you a choice

Only at the end of her driveway and Gabrielle Press was already lost.

Actually, if she was honest she'd been lost for the last six months, ever since she unceremoniously walked away from her web design job, which led to the meltdown of her relationship with Ben, who moved out a month afterward.

Since then, she had rattled around coffee shops and her living room and the town park with no direction, no purpose, wishing for something like a spiritual GPS that would tell her which turn to take next.

Or maybe a way to just opt out. Adulting was hard and frustrating.

But in lieu of all that, after spending half an hour in front of the mirror yesterday bemoaning her mousey brown hair that was neither curly nor straight, her pallid complexion, and the extra five pounds she'd picked up since everything went to shit, she packed up her Jeep Cherokee with clothes, books, notebooks, blindly picked a point on a map somewhere in northern Vermont, and decided it was time for a trip. Not away from or toward anything. Just a journey. In search of...in search of what? She didn't know. Maybe that would come clear along the way.

Sounded good to her.

Anywhere other than where she was, sounded good to her.

Sometimes nowhere at all sounded the best.

While her cell phone had a GPS and could happily, monotonously and monotonally give her exact directions, she felt the need to re-establish her confidence, to remove herself from the reliance on others telling her what to do, how to feel, where to go – even if it was just a mechanical voice. So she sat with the atlas and traced out a route that avoided highways and chose the road less traveled.

She imagined a literary-worthy spirit-walk of sorts, her attempt, finally to discover who Gabrielle Press was and what she truly wanted.

But when the moment came, there she sat -- paralyzed at the end of her driveway, unable to make a turn in either direction.

She stared out the front window, the morning sun capping the trees in a pale, golden glow, early shadows throwing long and distorted shapes across the landscape.

Left or right. It's not that hard, for chrissake. Particularly because only one would get her started on the route traced on the map.

Her phone pinged, the screen coming to life, and she looked down to see a post notification from her sister. It startled Gabrielle out of her reverie -- she thought she had turned off all notifications. The plan was to disconnect, pull away, excuse herself from the world for a while.

Scrolling to settings, she ensured she had, indeed, turned off all notifications, plugged the charger into the lighter, found the first song on her favorite playlist, and as the sound filled the car, she rolled down the window, looked up over her steering wheel...and turned left.

***

Having made that first decision (even though it wasn't a decision, it was the only way for her to go to get to the junction she wanted), Gabrielle was able to take a deep breath and relax.

She did it. She was out. On her way. Maybe, finally, beginning the life she truly wanted – or at least, finding out what that was.

She sipped coffee from her mug, grooved to the tunes on her playlist, and watched the road signs swim by naming local attractions: Motel 6s, coffee chains, state parks, radio museum...

Unfortunately, she fell so far into the groove of the music, losing herself in lack-of-thought, that she missed a turn she wanted, only snapping to attention when she saw the sign for it fly by her passenger window.

"Shit. Shit!"

Not being on a major highway, she couldn't just run to the next exit and backtrack. She was on a local route, heading for back roads and local streets that meandered through little towns and farmlands and large blocks of conservation forest

"Goddammit." Only a little more than an hour in and she'd already hit a snafu. She pulled over onto a wide shoulder area to look at her map. She stared at it for several minutes before she realized she wasn't even looking at it. Just staring at the paper, unfocused, mind blank.

She rubbed her eyes. She stared out the window -- a plumber's truck passed, and then a pickup truck full of old mattresses. The smell of diesel filled the car and she looked away. She took a sip of coffee. She looked back at the map.

Maybe this 'figure it out on your own' thing wasn't such a good idea. Maybe she wasn't ready to take that on. A road trip was one thing, but she was scattered, distracted, easily waylaid. Maybe she still needed a little guidance.

"Recalculating"... The mechanical female in her phone suddenly blurted out the word in her eerie, silky tone.

Gabrielle jumped, glancing at the phone, the screen again coming to life, the map app open on the screen. Stupid phone had been acting weird for the last week or so, randomly turning off, or the touch not responding, or the screen freezing. This, though – an app just launching – that was new.

The phone was old, and she knew she needed a new one, but being unemployed didn't seem like a good time to drop a few hundred on a new phone.

Turning her attention back to the atlas, she tried again to figure out the next best turn to put her in the general direction she wanted. While it would take her in a more circuitous path, she did find another road that would connect her back up to what she wanted. She counted streets on the map, checked traffic, and pulled back onto the road.

It had unsettled her, that first missed turn. Rattled her sense of adventure and sureness that the trip was what she needed. She tried to ignore it, but it festered, fingering around the inside of her brain like a worm.

She shuddered at the image and forced it away, concentrating on her map and the road. Within fifteen minutes she came upon her turn and took it.

"Recalculating" Again her phone sprang to life, the woman within it informing her of a travel adjustment. For a moment, Gabrielle considered tossing the phone out the window. Instead, she pulled over again, this time just to the side of the road in front of a dilapidated red barn and a mailbox. She looked at the screen to see a green line on the map. Pinching in to zoom out she could see it was the general area she was in, a path drawn close to the one she had chosen on the atlas, though not exactly.

She furrowed her brow. "What the..." She tried to remember if she had used the app to locate a destination before opting for the atlas and her wits (such as they were); if she had set it by accident before deciding to find her own way without it. But the last few weeks were such a blur, her concentration so nonexistent, she couldn't even remember if she'd had breakfast that morning.

Had she? Maybe not. Maybe that's why she was hungry. And had a headache. One of those dull, pulsing ones that start at the nape of your neck and travels around to your temples like a hand slipping around you from behind.

She looked again at the map on her phone, glanced out her front window at the road before her -- winding, rising and falling through open farmland -- then back down at the phone map.

"Oh what the hell." And tossing the atlas into the back seat, she secured her phone in the dashboard holder, angled it so she could see the map, and headed for the green line.

What difference did it make what she used, atlas or GPS? She'd still get to where she needed to go.

She drove a while on the hilly, curving country road, the mountains looming closer, the pressure in her ears increasing. She'd been driving with the windows down, but the sun had been swallowed by clouds and the temperature suddenly dipped, so she pulled her elbow in and shut the windows.

"Recalculating"

"What? I'm right here..." Gabrielle looked down at her phone as the map shifted, twitched, and the line leapt toward a left turn a short distance ahead.

Gabrielle took a deep breath, and looked down the road, noticing a break between trees at the edges of a farmer's field.

She followed the map on her phone and took the turn.

At this point, she really wasn't sure where she was, or what route the GPS was taking her on, but she almost didn't care. The more she drove the less concern she had for how she'd get where she was going. She was moving -- that's what mattered. Anywhere was better than standing in her living room turning circles, trying to figure out whether to sit down, take a shower, read a book, find a job...

This was better.

She was moving.

An hour passed quietly, the terrain leaving farms and growing thicker, forest on either side, mountains ahead, a ribbon of fog drifting across the face of the foothills.

The music had lulled her, the monotonous road mesmerized her, and she realized she had been free of any thoughts for a while when the phone alerted her to a slight right turn around a bend.

Taking it led her deeper still into the woods where pines loomed taller, the brush beneath thicker and tangled, the road a little narrower, and she hadn't seen another car in a long time. Or road signs. Maybe she had just been lost in thought and hadn't noticed, or once again, lost in no thoughts at all.

"Recalculating"

"Oh for chrissake, how can you be recalculating? I haven't left the route you're showing me!"

Gabrielle started to panic since at this point she had no choice but to continue following her GPS. She had just blindly kept pace with the glowing green line and now had no idea where she was. Even the atlas map wouldn't help her now. She wouldn't know where to look.

Keeping one eye on the narrow, rougher road, and one on her phone, the map adjusted again, the line seeming to lurch a bit on the screen. She blinked and stretched her neck as, for the briefest moment, her vision seemed to do the same.

Great. I'm going to have a stroke from stress out here in the middle of who-the-hell-knows-where... she thought to herself.

She tried to figure out how long she'd been driving, but the clock on her car had flaked out on her a few weeks ago, and she was afraid to touch her phone for fear it would do the same, the map would vanish and she'd be lost in the Vermont woods forever.

But she was so damned tired.

She continued along as the map took a fork in the road, the surface slowly changing from cracked pavement to dirt. Enormous boulders lay scattered in the forest making it seem the world around her was closing in. She rubbed her eyes, suddenly uncomfortably drowsy, on the verge of tears, with the uneven, bumping surface of the road thumping against her headache.

A short distance further she found a small spot to pull over again.

She just needed a few minutes to close her eyes. To take a few breaths. To stretch and think.

She needed to think.

The phone map hung in place, the little icon of her car paused, as she was, the engine idling softly. She slid her seat back and stretched her legs. She stretched her arms up over the back of the seat and yawned. She dropped her hands in her lap and closed her eyes.

Just for a second.

She was so tired and didn't know where she was going.

She just needed a second.

"Recalculating"

"Recalculating"

"Recalculating"

Gabrielle's eyes shot open, the repetitive voice seeming to grow urgent, insistent, although she knew that wasn't possible. It was always the same, unemotional, android tone.

She pushed her hair off her face and looked around. Something felt different. Off.

The road was the same, still flanked by woods, and narrow. But the light was different. She leaned forward and peered up through the windshield. The sky sank heavy, low, and held a strange, green tinge.

"Oh for fuck's sake. Please do not storm on me here."

"Recalculating"

"Oh my god, shut up!" she yelled at the phone, that much closer to smashing it beneath her boot. Her frustration was rising, her temper fraying -- between her headache and annoying fatigue, she had no patience left for temperamental technology -- and the first few tears slid down her cheeks.

She looked around her at the woods, behind her at the road, and rubbed her hands over her face as though trying to wipe away her confusion and fear.

But when she saw the map with a turn glowing up on the left she glanced back out her window in that direction. Where she swore she had seen just another thick copse of pines with a carpet of needles beneath, there was now a small gap into which the dirt road gently curved.

It did not at all look like where she had placed her dot on the atlas map -- which had appeared to be moderately close to a little town. That looked decidedly as though she was driving deeper and deeper into the forest.

But there wasn't much to do about that now.

I'm going to be abducted by aliens, she thought to herself. *Or Sasquatch. I'm going to be on the cover of the National Enquirer.*

And she suddenly wasn't sure she cared.

Adjusting her seat again and putting the car in gear, she reluctantly continued following the map, nagged just a bit by a lurking suspicion that she should just turn around and try to retrace her way back to civilization. But looking over her shoulder she realized she had paid so little attention to where she was going, she wasn't sure she could.

With a deep breath and rather intense disgust with herself and her apparent inability to even take a road trip without getting thoroughly lost, she took the turn onto a small road that threatened to quickly deteriorate into little more than a footpath.

Overhead, the clouds grew dense, the shade of green deepening to a murky sludge.

"Arriving at your destination. On the right."

Gabrielle gripped the steering wheel as she bumped and lurched over the rough forest road. As the trees thinned, a building began to come into view; set well back and in the middle of nowhere, it emerged as though from deep, dark shadow.

She felt a chill up her spine. She flicked her gaze to her rear view mirror, her breath catching in her throat as she saw the trees appear to close in behind her, the road vanishing, the sky pressing even farther down upon her.

"What the -- "

She slammed on her brakes, the car skidding on loose rock, the back end swerving just a bit before coming to a stop in a dirt patch at the end of the path.

"Arriving...Recalculating"...

Gabrielle's hands trembled on the wheel, but she snatched the phone out of its holder to silence the manic, ever-repeating female voice that seemed to spew nothing but nonsense.

She sat in the car, the silence falling around her like a shroud -- too silent, it seemed, for such a dense forest -- and she gazed out at the enormous building.

It loomed out of the surrounding trees like a living thing, faded clapboard siding over three stories, railings running along full porches around at least two façades of each story, as though holding the building at the center -- imprisoned.

If it could speak, it would groan, sigh, pop and crack -- in fact,

Gabrielle thought she could hear it doing just that. It was the only sound. No birds. No animals.

Nothing.

Gabrielle tapped her phone, trying to close the map, to get to the home screen, but she fumbled with it, finally noticing that even if she wanted to make a call, she had no bars.

Where the hell was she?

Grabbing her backpack from the passenger side she carefully clicked open the car door, slowly pushing it open, her gaze never leaving the building; afraid that if she glanced away, like a stalking cat, it would lurch forward and be directly in front of her when she found the courage to look again.

Her boots crunched on the gravel beneath her feet, the car door swinging shut clapping loudly in the silence, echoing up into the mountains.

She kept her backpack in front of her like a shield, hugging it -- a child gripping a teddy bear -- and carefully, warily, stepped around the front of the car toward the building.

She knew she should be paralyzed with fear -- alone, lost somewhere in the Vermont woods (at least she thought she was in Vermont), a huge, abandoned building suddenly appearing where her possessed phone GPS told her to go...

But, while she was unsure, something intriguing and curious pulled her forward in spite of her instincts telling her to get in the car, lock the doors and gun it in the opposite direction. It didn't matter where.

Except a glance over her shoulder confirmed that the world did, indeed, seem to have closed in behind her. There was no road, no nothing. Just dense trees, algae green sky, and the building -- what was it anyway? A hotel? A lodge? Can't be an old home, it's too huge, boxy, and imposing.

Another few steps over gravel, then onto a flagstone path toward the front steps, and when she looked up again, Gabrielle saw the front door swing open to reveal a middle-aged woman smiling at her, inviting her in.

The woman was rather nondescript, her clothing simple, plain: brown slacks and sensible shoes, an unadorned shirt -- almost like a man's -- tucked in, sleeves rolled up. Her hair, streaked with gray, but still with some of its original black, pulled back at the sides, the rest hanging long past her shoulders to her waist.

Her face, while beginning to crease slightly with age, remained youthful, clear, friendly, and her smile seemed to pull the tension from Gabrielle's hunched shoulders.

As she approached the front step, she caught movement out of the corner of her eye. Glancing over, she noticed a man on the first-floor porch, standing at the railing, blowing a long stream of cigarette smoke out across the grass. He turned to her and nodded, a small smile lifting one corner of his mouth. His suit was rumpled, as though he'd slept in it, and his tie was undone at the neck, shirt collar open.

He wasn't there when she drove up, was he? Or the woman she then noticed on the third-floor porch, pacing back and forth, tense, distracted, her lips moving swiftly in silent utterances as her heels scuffed across the floorboards like a skittering mouse.

They couldn't have been there just moments ago. She would have noticed. Wouldn't she?

"Come, come," the woman in the door suddenly spoke, startling Gabrielle. "Gonna let loose soon and you'll want to be inside when it does." She flicked her gaze to the thick, green sky, her eyebrows raising, her head tipping toward the dark interior of the building.

Gabrielle made her way up the stairs, each step creaking beneath her boots as though the wood was ready to give way. Five steps and she was on the porch, her pulse a tympani in her ears, her arms still wrapped around her backpack, the woman smiling warm, steady, practiced, her arm outstretched into the entryway of the building, ushering Gabrielle inside.

And as she reached the threshold, her right foot on the porch, her left foot moving forward, her gaze warily on the woman smiling and guiding her in, her phone sprung to life in her hand, and just as both feet touched down inside the door, which swung closed behind her it said,

"Recalculating"

***

Inside the light radiated throughout, warm and inviting, although Gabrielle couldn't see where it was coming from -- no lamps or sconces or overhead lighting. The place just seemed to glow on its own, and the air had a slightly acrid, metallic smell.

The woman at the door gestured gently to Gabrielle's backpack, offering to check it in a booth near the door. Uncertain, but not wanting to cause any trouble, Gabrielle reluctantly relinquished her pack in exchange for a ticket -- the paper old and yellowed, edges peeling and bent from use and reuse, the numbers in red. She slipped it into the back pocket of her jeans. Her phone, she kept in her hands.

Then the woman motioned with a smile and a nod, for her to head in, toward a desk directly in front of her, behind which stood a young man; pale, thin, his suit tailored, but worn, his hair clipped short and slicked back, he smiled as she approached, all the while moving dreamily, as if in water.

Like the woman at the door, he remained quiet save for a "Here you are," as he spun a threadbare book toward her, it's lined pages filled with signatures in black and blue ink, the paper like that of the ticket: yellowed, crumbling at the edges, the fabric cover of the book fraying.

Gabrielle felt as though everything moved slowly, including her thoughts, giving her no time to process what was happening, or consciously acknowledge anything before she found her hand signing her name on the next line on the ledger.

Then he, too, simply gestured toward another doorway -- a large opening with heavy, double wooden doors slid most of the way back into the wall pockets. Through that, Gabrielle saw a kind of café with small tables covered in vintage tablecloths, each with one or two high-back wooden chairs. People milled about, some chatting, other sitting quietly alone, waiters in crisp bow ties and suspenders moving about between them all taking or retrieving teas and martini glasses, coffee mugs, and beer glasses. While clearly, some were conversing, she could hear no sound, save for a faint, distant tinkling of some kind of music.

She glanced back to the man behind the desk, who simply smiled, then back toward the door at the woman, who did the same. She considered the ticket in her back pocket, her gaze flicking to the cubby that held her checked backpack, and took a long, slow breath.

She should just go. Get in her Jeep and find a road, cell phone service...just...leave.

As she leaned toward the door, shifting her weight just a hair toward her right foot, a blinding burst of lightning whitened the room followed by a deafening, rib-rattling crack of thunder. Gabrielle flinched, crouching backward and ducking her head.

When she looked up again out the windowed wall across the café, beyond the rail of the porch outside, the air was dark green, pummeling rain blotting out the view.

Clearly, she wasn't going anywhere now, so focusing straight ahead, she walked toward the café, watching the waiters bustle, people sip from cups or nibble small cakes and muffins, and when she crossed through the doorway,

"Recalculating"

The sound of the room erupted all at once, from deathly silent to blazingly alive. Piano music, a mix of ragtime, swing and something more...modern. Tinkling plates and glasses, chattering conversations and lilting laughter woven through with the occasional shuddering sob all exploded at the same time. Gabrielle whirled around, looking back out the doorway toward the desk, but the young man there had returned to -- well...whatever it was he did behind that desk when no one was signing their name. As she turned again to the cafe, a waiter gently touched her elbow and directed her to a quiet table in the back near an enormous stone fireplace. The opening stood as tall as she and blazed with a roaring fire.

She fell more than sat into the chair, finding it surprisingly comfortable given its stiff, upright design. Without a word, the waiter spun away from her table and disappeared around a corner. Gabrielle sat, taking in the scene around her, trying to fight the cacophonous pummeling of her senses.

An old man appeared at her side, looking weary, worn, his dress casual, comfortable, splotches of oil paint on his trousers and fingertips. He leaned toward her ear whispering, "If you aren't really thinking of staying, don't dawdle. Gather your things and leave before -- "

He was cut off by a young woman -- nearly still a girl -- her hair razored short, her dress and manner harsh, hard, angry. She pushed him roughly out of the way, her smile devious, challenging, daring. "Don't listen to him. It's fine. This place is awesome. Leave all that crap out there," she waved her hand toward the world beyond the windows, "and just let it go. Oh my god, it's...it's just heaven, you know? To forget all the bullshit and just – be..."

Gabrielle shrugged away from them both, sliding into another chair at the table, a chill running up across her back and down her arms.

Glancing around the room, her gaze finally fell on an older woman sitting at the table next to her. She wore a long gypsy skirt and a light blouse, her gray hair in one long braid down her back woven with colorful yarn. Her feet were bare.

Upon catching Gabrielle's eye, she slipped from her chair and into the empty one at Gabrielle's table. Her face showed age, but somehow also held the glow and energy of youth. Whether young or old seemed to depend on how the firelight fell across her face.

"Kind of kicks you in the ass when you walk in, don't it?" The old woman smiled and her eyes actually twinkled.

Gabrielle blinked, held her phone with both hands on the table. "Um...I...what?"

The woman gestured around them. "All this. Gets noisy fast after the easy in."

Gabrielle felt incredibly sleepy. She yawned and rubbed her eyes. "Um...yeah, I -- "

The woman banged her fist on the table. "Wake up! Don't fall asleep. Pay attention. You need to pay attention..."

It startled Gabrielle, who jerked back just as a waiter arrived with a tray, setting down a large mug of black coffee and piece of cinnamon coffee cake.

Gabrielle shook her head and tried to reach out to him. "Oh -- I...I didn't order this..."

The waiter just gazed at her, his eyes so dark they appeared black and smiled, sliding the cake toward her. The rich aroma of the coffee made her heady and she could almost taste the crumbly cinnamon and sugar topping on the cake.

She pulled the mug toward her, laying her phone on the table in front of her, its screen finally dark. Silent. She breathed in the steam -- this was good coffee, she could tell. Expensive, dark roast -- oh this was *good* coffee.

She took a sip and sighed, feeling the tension drain from neck to ankles.

"Yup. They always know what you want, don't they?" The woman broke Gabrielle's coffee reverie.

"What?" Gabrielle asked, mindlessly taking a bite of the coffee cake, which was also insanely delicious.

The woman flicked her head toward all the waiters. "Them. They always know what you want. Kinda nuts. Makes it awful easy to get comfortable, don't it?"

Gabrielle couldn't think, her brain foggy, and she was still so tired. She looked around at the rich, expensive wood trim and carved paneling, and fine linen -- the tired outside hid well the beauty inside. It was nice, warm there by the fire, relaxing -- not a care in the world, good coffee...maybe this stop *was* exactly what she needed.

"I was much like you when I first arrived here." The old woman suddenly spoke, her voice low, quiet.

Gabrielle caught her gaze and felt defensive. "And how is that, do you suppose?"

The woman smiled and breathed deeply, her exhale seeming to send a cool perfume across the room. She pursed her lips in thought. "Oh, tired. Done. But not sure what that meant. Just needing to...find my way..."

Gabrielle remained silent, staring at the old woman, wishing the headiness she felt would clear. She couldn't settle her thoughts, her feelings, nothing.

The woman placed her hand on Gabrielle's arm, drawing her attention close. She motioned to the food and coffee. "Well, this is good. Replenish, refresh. It will clear your head so you can decide. So you can find the strength to -- "

She cut off as a hum filled the room. Gabrielle looked up to see other patrons, many of them appearing soft, filmy, almost ethereal, create an immediate path in the room through which strode an older man, his dark hair to his shoulders, his jaw squared, his eyes and suit a deep, midnight blue -- the latter cut crisply to his stature, the pants slim and fitting -- and a walking stick sharply at his side. He seemed to carry his own shadowy aura with him, as though he was always emerging from some unearthly darkness. He was a walking cliché of every mysterious, unsettling man anyone has ever read about. Gabrielle wanted to laugh but found that while trapped beneath his gaze, she could do nothing but stare.

The buzz in the room dimmed, the conversation lowered, as the man clacked his cane on the floor when he reached the table.

Gabrielle watched the old woman relax back in her seat, her gaze slowly slipping up to meet the stranger's.

"Soteria..." he droned, his voice seeming to carry several tones at once which made Gabrielle dizzy. "Telling your fable of 'arriving just like them'? You know the rules. Guests are to be left to explore the property on their own, uncover what it offers them, and decide if it's too their liking."

The two seemed to be having something of a stare down, the air around them feeling charged and static. Although Gabrielle desperately wanted more of her coffee she kept still, her hands crossed over her phone, her gaze dipping between these two strangers.

"Oh...yes...and you have *never* intervened or made an attempt to sway, have you?"

The man glared at the woman he called Soteria, pulling on his suit jacket, removing wrinkles that weren't there. In fact, the suit sat on him without so much as a crease, or a mark -- not even when he bent his elbow. No matter his movement, the suit remained pristine, as though part of him.

"Only when they seemed they needed some encouragement or nudging..."

"That's not intervening and influencing? Please. Yes, I do know the rules. The rules are that they come here, lost, confused, some on the edge of the unthinkable, some simply adrift and in need of redirection. They may stay as long as they like to figure out what they want, what's gone wrong..." The woman stood, pushing her chair out behind her and Gabrielle was surprised to find she was as tall as the man -- who was quite tall.

"The rules," he drones, his head twisting and nodding, "are that they end up here when they've nowhere else to go. They are here, yes, because they are lost and they need someone to help them find their way. To choose to stay forever lost, if that's what suits them -- "

" -- or to find their way home, Azrael! It is for THEM to choose, and we are free to offer enlightenment to help them. THOSE are the rules!" It was her turn to interrupt him and in so doing the two came nose to nose, the electricity in the room threatening to match the storm outside.

Gabrielle sat frozen, trying to focus her concentration, to place where she might have heard those names, but thinking she couldn't have. She'd never been here before.

Had she?

"Quite right, Soteria. Those are the rules." He glanced down at Gabrielle, his smile crawling across his face like the sun across the horizon at sunrise. Gabrielle's eyes flicked to her coffee and she grabbed the mug, taking a long, deep drink, the rich warmth spreading quickly through her body, comforting her, lulling her anxiousness and unhappiness, all of it beginning to drift peacefully away.

"Recalculating" the voice whispered.

But something nagged at her. Some thought tapped -- a woodpecker -- on the inside of her brain. She had been going somewhere...doing something...what was it?

"Gabrielle," Soteria sat beside her again, a soft, gentle touch on her arm. "The storm is subsiding. That's a good sign...look..."

Gabrielle glanced out the window, noticing the air was less green, the rain down to a drizzle, a small, determined ray of sun fighting through a crack in the cloud cover.

That's right, she was on a road trip. Wanted to find her way...

"Recalculating"

Now Azrael pulled up a chair on the other side of her, straddling it, leaning on the high, curved back, holding the head of his cane, his breath full of cinnamon and cloves. "But the fire is warm and there's nothing wrong with deciding you've had quite enough. There's no shame in wanting some simple peace..." He pushed the coffee cake closer to her. She fiddled with the fork, pushing a piece of crumbled topping around the plate. She felt the heat of the fire at her back so warm, enveloping...

"Recalculating"

Soteria took her hand. "Gabrielle -- in the end, only you can make the decision for yourself but know that I don't believe you are done yet. I believe you had a spark you were chasing that -- "

"No! Unfair! Foul! That is direct intervention!" Azrael leapt to his feet, knocking over his chair, and sending waiters scurrying to corners along with other patrons -- decidedly ethereal and insubstantial now that Gabrielle gave them a solid look, as well as clothed in all different styles and manner. "You may not -- !"

The woman rose as well, squaring off in front of the table, their figures toe-to-toe. "You cannot tell me what I may or may not! You have no power over me!"

A piercing tone cut through the café as Gabrielle sat, confused, afraid. Staring down at her hands as she sipped again at her coffee -- wanting things to just stop, to be quiet, to be alone -- she noticed that her fingers seemed to be growing faint, losing substance, the surface of the mug just barely visible through them.

"Recalculating. Recalculating. Recalculating!"

"What the hell...?!"

Gabrielle jumped up, frantically looking over herself, afraid she was going crazy. She spun in a circle, looked around wide-eyed and panicked to see the man named Azrael smiling, and the woman named Soteria looking at her with sad, questioning eyes.

Azrael stood, his cane positioned directly in front of him, his hands poised atop it, one over the other. "It's okay, Gabrielle. There are many who have decided they'd prefer to stay lost. It's easier. You can be done. Let go, stay...it's that simple..." He gestured around them with one long-fingered hand.

344

Gabrielle felt unbridled panic rising up inside her, the other people in the café now peering toward her, watching, waiting. Some appeared stoic, content, their posture both self-assured and relaxed, but they were also barely corporeal, more otherworldly. Others looked pained, like they didn't want to be there, their bodies physically leaning toward the door, but somehow unable to take the physical step. Their eyes seemed to call to her...*Go.*

Gabrielle still didn't understand it all, but she knew she didn't want to be like the ghostly figures in the café, no matter how serene they appeared. She suddenly remembered she was on a road trip, she just needed to clear her head, take a break, rediscover what she wanted. It was a trip meant to find her footing, ground herself, figure out where she wanted to go next.

To find what she wanted.

She looked around again, backing away from both Azrael and Soteria, while reaching in her back pocket for the ticket stub to her backpack.

She didn't know what she wanted, exactly, wasn't sure answers would be quick, or simple, but she knew she didn't want to be here.

Wherever *here* was.

Shoving her phone in her back pocket and pushing hard against the two figures, forcing the people behind them to part like a current around a rock, she weaved her way through the café and back toward the double door opening and the lobby.

She could feel a dragging behind her, part of her so willing to just grab a table, accept the endless supply of dark coffee and sweets and watch the world go by outside the window in a never-ending cycle of sunshine and storms.

But the rest of her wanted out. Wanted her backpack and her uncertainty -- wanted her upside down life all in a mess, complete with no idea what her next step would be or what was around the next bend.

In the end, that was half the fun, wasn't it?

She nearly threw her ticket at the silent woman manning the front door, and backpack in hand, Gabrielle grabbed the doorknob on the worn, mahogany door she now noticed was carved and inlaid with strange faces and twisted creatures. Feeling the hair rise on her neck, she turned once more to find both Soteria and Azrael standing before the front desk, their figures looming large and imposing, their faces impassive and without expression; they stood firm providing one, last opportunity to weigh her options.

345

But she didn't need it.

"Recalculating"

Pulling hard on the door, it swung open, and without another thought, Gabrielle raced across the overgrown path to her Jeep, skidding across loose gravel, scrambling into the driver's seat and locking the doors behind her.

Tossing her backpack in the back and setting her phone in its caddy, she fumbled for her keys, her heart racing, sweat dripping down her back.

Shoving the keys in place, she started the car, jammed it into gear and forced it forward out of the mud left behind by the storm.

At first, the wheels spun, and she felt the air tighten around her, the woman guarding the door opening it again, stepping out onto the porch to stare at her.

The air grew metallic.

"No, no, no, no..." Gabrielle backed the car up a bit and then tried again, forcing the Jeep forward, perhaps by will alone.

After a few fruitless spins, the wheels finally caught and the car lurched forward, finding solid dirt and gravel. The woman slipped back into the building, the door silently floating closed behind her, as Gabrielle tried to clear her head and find focus.

"Recalculating"

Her phone came to life, yet again, showing a green line directly in front of her, and when Gabrielle looked, the forest ahead split in two, a paved road lined with metal barriers appearing through it. Casting a glance in the rearview mirror, she noticed that direction remained blocked by tall pines and rocky outcroppings.

She inched forward, following the green line, only once glancing in her rearview to see the building suddenly seem once again empty, abandoned, listing, tilting, just an old building falling apart at the seams. No one pacing the porches, no one visible through the windows...

With a deep, steadying breath, she followed the small, paved road through the forest until she came to a major route. Taking her phone, she tapped in her home address and hit 'go'.

She'd had quite enough of this little road trip, and her little, empty house sounded like exactly what she wanted.

The map on the phone configured, zoomed out, then in...

...and a new, fresh green line led her straight to a highway and the road home.

Straight and simple.

Gabrielle smiled, turning left to follow the GPS, the sun blasting through a dissipating cover of clouds.

"Recalculating"

She'd never heard a sweeter sound.

She was going home.

The End

Links:

Website: https://www.melissavolker.com/   (reviews for each book on respective pages)

Facebook: https://www.facebook.com/mvolkerwordphoto

Twitter: https://twitter.com/mdvolker

https://www.amazon.com/MelissaVolker/e/B0037XT4UE/

Cover by Author

The Sea Mither

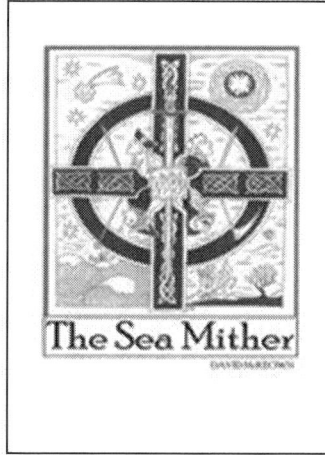

The Sea Mither

David McKeown

I live in Scotland and love to explore the country while looking for inspiration. But it was only while looking into the rich history of folklore, fairy tales and legends of Scotland recently that this story finally came to be written down; a mere ten years after I first had the idea. But when you're a writer, occasionally a story refuses to go away. It will sit like an obstinate house guest at the back of your head waiting for its moment on your computer screen. This one began life as a doomed never-to-be-finished or filmed screenplay. Frustration with the format saw it abandoned only to be revived here as a short story. Of course, distilling a long screenplay with a cast of thousands down to 5000 words was a challenge and it was inevitable much of the story would have to be changed or removed entirely. But in the end I hope I've captured the essence of the original idea - an adventure tale in the tradition of Beowulf, but with a Scottish twist, inspired by the folklore of my country. The one constant is I've left it up to the reader to determine the true nature of the antagonist; just as the people of Orkney did years ago when shaping their wonderful tales in an attempt to make sense of the volatile Scottish weather and understandably creating a few horror stories in the process...

The Sea Mither

The winter mists of my long life have gathered now. The ghosts of my past draw near to witness my passing to what lies beyond. I must do them honour and leave behind my testimony as to the strange and terrible events I witnessed in my youth. So others may learn of it ere the evil should ever return.

***

It was in the Year of our Lord 1743 when I returned home to England from my Grand Tour of Europe to find my younger brother had replaced me in our father's affections. In my long absence my sibling had grown steadfast and strong and become a master of weapons. These qualities made my father very proud. While in his elder son he saw only book-learning and no experience. In many ways I knew this to be true and it was foolish of me to accept the suggestion, made eagerly by my father, that my brother and I should do battle to determine which of us was worthiest of his noble name.

In the great hall of our home he set us against one another. I fought to my full measure and the contest was laborious for us both. But in the end I was humiliated before my ever-loving mother. The lords and ladies of the land, who had gathered to witness the contest, found much amusement in my defeat. In disgust my father sent me away once more. This time to the far north; to lands he held in Scotland at the grace of the King, to "make a man of me"

In the belief my lessons in Europe had prepared me for a position of leadership, my father purchased for me the commission of an officer. I was to be commander of a cavalry brigade. In this role he hoped my newly acquired knowledge of riding and fencing would be put to some use. I bid my mother farewell and took my leave. My heart was heavy at this passing and the road north was long and tiresome with no joy to be found at the end of it. The garrison to which I had been posted was built on a dank and windswept country. The harsh winter weakened my spirits and I soon fell into a deep despair.

It was no surprise to discover the locals cared not for our presence there either. Already there were reports of rebellion. Yet I had not been in this miserable place for long when there arrived a terrible sickness which overwhelmed the nearby townsfolk and their livestock. They gathered at our gates and pleaded for our aid but our commander, a cruel but practical man, ordered all entrances be locked and doubled the guard. Alas, this measure came too late and it was not long before several men of the regiment and every one of our horses fell under the merciless plague. This was terrible to behold. It weakened the bodies of men and beasts alike while a virulent discharge poured ever forth from their countenance.

The garrison was therefore in some disarray on the night of the attack. I was alone in my chamber writing a letter home to my mother when a commotion from outside reached my ears. In haste I gathered up my weapons and hurried out into the affray to find the garrison already ablaze. The screams of men and the reports of wild musket-fire filled my ears. I was scouring the thick smoke in an attempt to determine who had set upon us when a great black shape, flecked with fire, rose up before me. I marvelled at the size of my attacker. In my brief time here I had not beheld any man of this stature among the locals and assumed he must belong to a rebel war band. In alarm I fired my pistol at his bulk. The weapon failed to discharge; or so it seemed to me with no deadly effect upon my enemy. In response he struck me violently across the face with one of his great arms and I fell into oblivion.

It was a bitter morning when I was pulled roughly from the smoking ruins. The rafters of an armoury building had collapsed upon me. Yet I was unharmed save for a bruising of the chest which made it difficult to breathe and a large scar across my cheek where my assailant had struck me the night before. Why he had spared my life I could not tell. But I guessed now I was a captive of the war band.

"There's one still alive here," cried the voice of the man who had raised me out of the ashes. "He must be a skulking coward or a foul tasting fairy."

There followed much harsh laughter at this statement. Being still very proud in my youth the insult stung. But it was soon forgotten when I saw my entire regiment lying dead upon the ground. It was certain they had been butchered by barbarians without honour and I turned to my captors in a fury. They were a rough company of fourteen clansmen appearing to owe allegiance to many different chieftains. Their plaid was varied as were the sprigs in their blue bonnets. Each man carried a basket-hilted sword, a pistol and a short knife or dagger. But among their number was also a thickset grey-bearded man with muscular arms who bore an enormous two-handed claymore upon his back. The weapon extended from his head down the entire length of his body to where it almost pierced the ground. It had been my belief the Scots no longer employed this weapon. It was heavy and cumbersome. But in skilled hands it could remove the heads of two men at once with a single sweep of its great blade.

"Why did you attack us?" I raged at them. "Are you part of the uprisings? You will pay for this outrage."

"No laddie, we played no part in this stramash." It was an elderly Scot who had replied. He boasted only one eye in a head bearing the signs of many past conflicts. "This is the work of the Devil."

"Hush Angus, you old fool," said another. "He's an outsider and should be told nothing of our troubles."

"If you are not responsible for this slaughter," I continued. "Then why are you here? I will not permit the dead to be robbed."

"We have a long chase ahead of us," said a young clansman. "We need supplies. There's plenty of powder here in your coward's hole."

"And what is to become of me now?"

They said nothing in reply to this. But their expressions were hard-hearted and I knew what my fate was to be. My salvation from battle and fire had been brief. They drew their blades and gathered together to restrain me without deference against a post.

"I am the son of an Earl," I told them in desperate fear. "He will pay you handsomely for my safe return." Even as I spoke these words I was not sure of the truth of them. Yet I need not have vexed myself on the matter of my father's love. The clansmen cared nothing for ransom and meant to put me to death.

"You can keep your money, laddie," said the elderly one as he held his dagger to my neck. "We'll leave you hanging for the crows."

It was fortunate there was one among them I took to be a witch. An old crone shrouded in black. "You must not kill this man," she said sternly to them. "His blood will bring ruin to our errand."

"Then what is to be done with him?" they asked.

"He shall accompany us," said the crone with a wicked smile.

The clansmen seemed to take the witch at her word on the matter and let me be, albeit grudgingly. I was much relieved but quickly protested I could not go with them. I was not one of their countrymen and must report this attack to my superiors. I made every pleading I hoped would have some effect on this vulgar company. But they cared nothing for my excuses and ignored me while they raided the wreckage for supplies; showing particular interest in the gunpowder reserves untouched by the flames.

"Prepare yourself as you think best," said the witch to me. "We shall depart soon."

We travelled all that day through the fields and forests. Always we followed the course of the river at the firm insistence of the witch. The clansmen displayed impressive haste and purpose on the journey but refused to speak with me except to ridicule. I was neither their captive nor their comrade. Instead I followed behind them like a loyal dog.

It had come as some surprise to me that I had been permitted to retain my weapons. "You will need them soon enough," they said darkly when we first set out. But they would say no more regarding their errand and grew angry with me when I persisted. Eventually they selected a young man named Duncan to be my constant guard. He cared little for the task and kept me as far from himself as could be permitted. But along with the other clansmen, he appeared cheerful at all times, as if these crude warriors needed nothing more than the companionship of their countrymen. I alone grumbled and was ignored.

When the night fell we made camp in the eaves of a forest. It was only here I learned through stolen scraps of conversation that the witch had appeared without warning at the meeting of the clans. She had come to seek their assistance in combatting an old terror the people of the northern islands had been powerless to resist. And now it had come to the mainland. Indeed many folk had already been slain or had fallen under its great plague. This was a task for great warriors she had said. In particular Dougal who bore the great claymore and knew still how to wield it. Once he had undertaken to go with her the other twelve men had gladly followed. In time they had tracked the horror from its arrival on the eastern shores to where it raged far inland. At last they had come too late to aid the townsfolk and found them already overcome and the British garrison aflame.

I listened to their coarse speech and reckoned some madness must be upon them. But in time the witch, sensing my scepticism, sat with me by the fire and spoke to me of our quarry. On hearing her words to me the clansmen called for hush in the company. They had heard the tale many times before it seemed. Yet they were keen to hear it once more, even if it filled them with a discernible dread.

"It was on a day such as this the fishermen of the islands burned seaweed to make kelp," began the witch. "When night came the stars tumbled in fire from the sky. The seas boiled and a deep thunder rolled around the shores as the great barbarous host rose out of the sea to cut men, women and children down in their beds. There was nothing to be done to protect them. The fortunate few fled to the mainland. In their wrath the demons pursued them and at last came ashore, as they have never done before, to hunt those who evaded them, and in their wake our people sickened and their crops wilted as the great plague was spread."

The men shook and grumbled at the tale but also grew resolute and emboldened by its telling. It was my custom to dismiss such stories as the ramblings of a primitive people; simple fishermen and farmers unable to comprehend the world in which they lived. But the words of this witch lay heavy on my heart. When sleep came my dreams were haunted. I awoke in a fever many times during the long night and gazed upwards at a sky void of stars bar one solitary red pinhole in the veil of night. It shone bright and crimson like an angered flame, a glimpse of a distant hell astray among the heavens, bringing both wonder and terror to my troubled soul.

The following morning they raised me from my slumber by hurling a breakfast of partially-cooked rabbit at my head. Again there was much boorish laughter at my expense and the witch cackled insanely. But not all the men were happy.

"Ach, the Sassenach didn't bolt in the night," Angus wailed. "There might be some man in him after all."

"You've lost the wager," replied a clansman named Ross. He boasted a long, drooping moustache in a vain attempt to conceal his excessively crooked teeth. "Pay up, you old goat."

It seemed they had all gambled on the possibility of my escape. They gathered together in a circle and there was much bellyaching and jeering at the exchange of coin. But following this there was a distinct change in mood towards me and a grudging respect for the simple fact I had remained with them. They tolerated my presence now with good humour and I received many a playful slap on the back. Particularly from those who had benefitted from the wager.

How many days more we travelled I am not certain. The going was hard and we were often footsore. But now I had been taken in as one of their company we spoke often whenever we camped. It was their habit to follow the evening meal with the telling of tall tales and engaging in swordplay. I took much interest in this and regaled them with talk of my fencing lessons undertaken in Europe.

In return they showed me their method of fighting with broadsword or dirk and targe. This exchange of knowledge with them I found fascinating until one night I grew too bold and paid the price for my self-assurance.

Angus was training his son Jamie in the use of the sword they called a claybeg. That evening he was showing the young man how to disarm an opponent using the claw upon the hilt. As I watched them practice it seemed prudent to me to offer them much advice. But Angus was a stubborn man and took offence at my words. Incensed he bade me to demonstrate my knowledge of combat in a fight against him.

"You think you are a clever man with your book-learning and fancy words," he said raising the point of his sword towards me. "Why don't you show me your quality now, Sassenach?"

I objected strongly to this. There was much shame in fighting an old man. But he persisted and in spite of having only one eye he defeated me swiftly and utterly. I was reminded of my disgrace at the hands of my brother and my spirits sank once more. Yet I was not permitted to brood for long. After my defeat at the hands of Angus every clansman claimed the opportunity to display his worth against me. And each night they took turns to beat me in a succession of hard-fought contests. I was never mistreated or suffered much harm but each night I crawled under my blanket bruised and exhausted.

It seemed to me Duncan had less stomach than the others for humiliating me. But his honour demanded he face me nevertheless. We fought one night after we had camped in a forest hollow and once more it looked as if I would be defeated and sent to my sleep in shame. It was in this moment the good Lord granted me the grace of mindfulness and suddenly all things I had learned and experienced in recent times became manifest. I turned the tide of the battle against Duncan and disarmed him to his great surprise. He fell upon his knees as my blade rested near his neck. There was a tense moment of hesitation while the clansmen waited to see what I would do with this chance. At last I dropped my sword to my side and offered my hand to my defeated foe.

The witch and the men cheered as I assisted Duncan in rising to his feet. I was elated in my victory. But even as I took to my bed on the damp ground the matter began to weigh heavily on my mind. I began to doubt myself and while we ran alongside the river the following day I could no longer contain myself and broached the subject directly with Duncan.

"Did you let me beat you?" I asked him.

"No, you needn't fret, Redcoat," he replied. "You fought well and it was a victory well-deserved. You have had a lot of practice recently."

It was at a place where the river met a well-trodden road that we found the dead horses. They lay together in a blackened heap and the air was thick with the buzzing of flies. By the festering of their faces they had perished from the same illness which had befallen my garrison and the townsfolk.

"This is mortasheen," said the witch to me. "It is but one curse of the demon we pursue. It has many more."

Further along this road we saw many cattle also lying lifeless in the fields. Many more in number than the horses we had seen. We smelled smoke and the men fell silent. I saw then the farmhouse nearby was smouldering with flames. There were no signs of life to be seen. But there were many bodies of men and women. A few of them had been consumed by fire but we saw others who had been hacked with swords where they lay; their limbs now lost or taken. They had been gnawed upon as if in a terrible feasting. I imagined such a nightmare befalling my own lands and trembled. I would do what I must to ensure this never came to pass.

There were mists over the hills and forests as we moved on from that terrible place. Not one of the clansmen looked back at the burning farm. They lamented their dead in silence. But when we reached a mountainous country where the river ran through deep valleys they fell suddenly ill and there was much complaining.

"We are getting close," said the witch. "The plague is upon us."

The mist and the weakening of my companions made the crossing of the mountain passes treacherous. Two clansmen lost their footing and fell screaming to their deaths. Dougal almost joined them at the bottom of a crevasse. He was fortunate I caught him by the arm at the last moment when he slipped and fell over the edge. To ascend again he was forced to release the heavy claymore from his back. It tumbled into nothingness and was gone.

Dougal was grateful for my saving of his life but he was much troubled at the loss of his weapon. "That sword was our only hope against them."

"Then we must do without hope," said the witch.

The white mist followed us down from the mountains and lay heavy over the lands beneath. We could not see beyond a dozen paces and stumbled onwards. At last we came to a place where the river ran into the waters of an immeasurable loch. Thick woodland lay about its shores.

"This is the place," said the witch. "I can go no further with you."

"You need not come, Englishman," said Duncan to me as he stripped off his plaid for battle. "This is not your fight."

It was a tempting offer. But thoughts of my garrison and the butchery at the farm came to my mind. "I will come with you," I replied and drew my sword. "If you will have me stand with you."

He looked at me keenly and nodded his approval. Jamie and Angus remained behind with the witch while the rest of us advanced through the trees. The clansmen grew more ill and many vomited. By then the bile was rising in my own gut and a fever was upon me. I thought I could suffer it no longer when Duncan commanded us to stop.

"Knoggelvi," he muttered with distaste and I wondered at the strange name. "There are two of them ahead on watch." He gestured for me to peer into a deep hollow. There I saw two dark hairless shapes squatting and feasting on some dead thing. They appeared manlike in most respects, but not like any man who walks upon the face of this earth. They were tall and broad creatures with long arms that stretched almost to the ground and ended in claw-like hands.

The clansmen fell fearlessly on these foes. They fired a volley from their pistols and plunged forward with swords drawn screaming like men possessed. The demons appeared startled but rose to greet their attackers. They drew their own weapons in turn; long crooked and glistening black broadswords the like of which I had never seen before. Then they howled for battle.

This conflict raged for how long I cannot tell. Many times the creatures were struck with sword and dagger and shot by pistol but never once did they fall. Always they stood defiant. No blood of theirs was ever spilt. Their leathery hides were impenetrable. Or some supernatural power was within them. Yet the clansmen were cut asunder by the great broadswords. The two men to my side were brought down like wheat and I found myself standing alone against one of the demons. He batted away the blows of my slender sabre like they mattered nothing to him and threw me upon the ground. My weapon fell from my hand and landed somewhere unseen amongst the undergrowth.

As the thing advanced towards me with its sword raised high, I saw clearly its aspect for the first time and was filled with unutterable horror. It had a large bald head on its broad shoulders.

Its mouth of sharpened teeth yawned like a bottomless pit and its tongue was black. The skin was nothing more than a thin covering of the palest white and through this I saw blood, black as tar, running through yellow veins. Even from where I lay on the ground the hot breath of the creature was like a flame upon my skin.

In terror I retreated from the monster in hope of avoiding its killing blow. Fortune favoured me and amongst the bracken my hand rested upon the pommel of my sword. I raised myself and swung the weapon towards the creature. Its neck opened like a stuck pig. The wound was not deep but enough to give the demon pause. It dropped its great sword and clutched its neck in astonishment as pitch black blood poured between its fingers.

My spirit bade me to run. Instead I gathered my wits and saw then why the clansmen had valued the claymore so highly. Inspiration dawned upon me and I picked up the creature's sword. It was large and heavy. Indeed it was a trial to raise the strange weapon above my head. Mercifully the downward stroke carried the greater part of my task for me. In one strike the creature fell beheaded.

At this victory a great fire rose up in me and I felt a rage unlike never before. Trembling I watched the head of the demon bounce on the ground like a discarded bauble and lifted the great sword again. "I know how to kill them, I know how to kill them," I muttered to myself over and over again in my delirium. I marched towards where the last of the clansmen struggled with the remaining enemy. They fought bravely but wearily, piercing the demon repeatedly with their knives, their pistols spent and their swords lying broken upon the ground among fallen comrades.

"Do not strike this demon," I commanded them. "Restrain it upon the ground."

It seemed Dougal heard my words and knew my meaning. He swiftly dropped his dagger and seized the demon by one of its long arms. Duncan and the others followed and pulled the demon, struggling and snarling, down to the forest floor. I raised the sword over my head once more. In the eyes of the strange creature I saw it knew the end was near. It opened its wide mouth and uttered a scream like no other heard in the history of the world. The clansmen recoiled in agony at the piercing sound. Still they held fast. I brought the blade down upon the neck of the demon and cleaved its foul head from its body.

We lay panting with exhaustion and grieved for our dead. But our respite was brief. The monster's last scream had summoned its dark clan. Their chieftain was a terrible sight. He brought with him a great storm on his heels and the skies darkened and rain poured. On a horse he sat. The poor animal has been gnawed upon by the demons. Its head was little more than a skull. But somehow it lived on and with its fleshed exposed it was almost as if beast and rider were one foul thing. Larger was the horseman than the others; as though they were mere children spawned from his great bulk. In his head there was one red eye. It shone like the enflamed star I had observed in the night sky. In his right hand he carried a great spear and with his left he commanded his army forward. We turned and ran through the rain and the creatures came after us, bellowing like the roaring of the sea.

There is no greater fear than that of the man who does not know the nature of the strife befallen him. We ran in mortal terror from the fiends. Their onslaught was terrible and they brought down many men. Dougal was cut in twain while he fled from the horseman. Fergus was trampled under the hooves of the horse and his body crushed flat. Ross and Colum were overtaken by the hoard and hacked to pieces to be feasted upon where they fell.

It was only by God's good grace that Duncan and I came at last to the river where the witch still stood. I saw the two clansmen who had remained behind had gathered near the water great bales of kindling from the forest. The demons hurried past these and paid them no mind. Yet they stopped in wailing despair when they reached the flowing water. I knew then our attack had been but bait to goad the creatures out in number. Now only Duncan and I remained from the men who had entered the forest. We crossed the water and fell exhausted at the feet of the witch. The old crone rose to greet our pursuers, stretched herself to her full height and threw her arms wide at their approach.

"I am The Mither O' The Sea," she cried aloud. "I bind you here between fire and water. Too long you have brought your plague to our fair land. You shall spread it no further."

Now no longer did she seem old and withered. To my eyes she was a girl, young and beautiful. There had been a light hidden within her only now revealed to us. The demons recoiled with horror and the clansmen hidden in the trees saw their moment and fired their muskets. The kegs of gunpowder taken from the garrison and concealed within the bales exploded and many demons were killed outright. The forest caught afire and the horse reared in fear and threw its rider. He fell upon the ground and cursed the witch as the smoke obscured everything and I lost sight of him and his wicked kind.

When the reek had passed there was nothing left of the demons but smoke and ashes. The husk of the horseman remained. I watched his charred body drift downriver. In time he would pass unto the sea to be bound in the depths of the great ocean. But the witch was nowhere to be seen. The storm had ended and the sun was shining. The warmer weather had arrived at last and we felt blessed like newborn men.

"You did well, laddie," said Duncan.

"The witch has gone. What will become of me now?"

"You need not worry, Redcoat. You will be returned to your people and we will part in peace. For this moment at least. We may meet again soon enough."

In truth it was a heavy undertaking to depart from him and the remainder of the company. We set out for a nearby village and here I was furnished with a horse to travel to the nearest British garrison. In the months following my return my body healed but my mind was never at rest. I looked in earnest to the day of my journey home to see my mother again and confront my father and my brother. I would have words with them ere the matter of my inheritance was finished.

***

Now winter of the foulest kind has come for me. It is a time of brittle bones and fading memories. But I remember Duncan well. In the long years since we parted I have often sat by my hearth, upon which the black broadsword now rests, and wondered what became of him and the others. I pray they did not meet their fates on that terrible battlefield so soon after our journey. It pleases me to believe they lived to be old men content with their lives, as I have been. But I also pray I have been a good husband, a kind father and a worthy master to my people. If this be true then I can take my rightful place in the Kingdom of the Lord. Otherwise I fear I may meet the red-eyed horseman once more.

The End

Follow David on Twitter @davidmckeown28

Cover by Author.

The Owl and the Dove

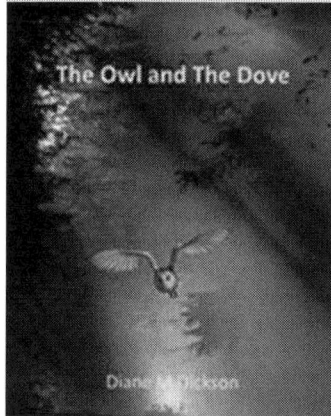

Diane Dickson

The owl knows about evil.

It rides in the night and goodness is the only defence. When goodness prevails, as it must, tragedy results. Where then, does evil go? The owl knows where, but so does the dove and in the tears of the dove is hope.

***

The sound of the owl woke him, it had woken him often and as before he lay for a long moment waiting. Yes, there it came again through the darkness. He knew how it came, he had envisaged it, tangible, winding and twisting between the huge limbs of the old trees. And then, once it gained the open field rising, sweeping and speeding over the stubble towards his window.

His bare feet found the rough boards, and bony toes carried him forward to the window, over the ledge and across the tiles of the lower roof. The old tree was as a staircase so familiar were the branches and the notches on the bark. Soft earth kissed the skin on his soles as he landed, gentle as a baby mouse, between the twisted roots.

He didn't wait and he didn't need to look. The owl had called and the house would be sleeping. His sister curled under her coverlet, a soft fist crushed against her infant face, and the long lashes like spider legs laid against the flawless skin of her cheek.

Mother would be, by now, in a drunken stupor. He had heard her earlier snores rattling thin walls, and the guttural grunts as she shifted her bulk across the sagging springs of the bed.

Now he was away, he picked up speed, his legs flashing in the moonlight, the tail of his nightshirt flapping against young, sturdy thighs. Faster and yet faster over the grass and the roadway and the meadow. Still the owl called to him, the night enfolded him and the mystery formed and reformed filling the world and carrying him away and into the magic.

The light was dim through the glassless window and there, up in the rafter, eyes were watching. It didn't call again; its job was ended for this time and so the owl stared down in silence on the scene. The boy opened the trunk hidden against a wall and dressed in the shabby garments.

In the damp darkness he waited. The only noise was his breathing, slightly laboured now after the run to the barn, but slowing as he regained his wind. The night crackled with tension and he felt the desire deepen and then it came, a tread on the gravel in the yard.

A low whistle sounded and he slid like a cat to the door of the barn. A horse with muffled hoofs stood in the darkened corner by the stone wall, alongside was the man. His cloak shifted and billowed in the small wind and the buckles on belt and boots glinted silver in the night.

As the long face turned, eyes glinted with red fire under a fringe darker than a raven's wing. Approaching he smiled at the boy, a sinister smile filled with promise and lust and knowing. The boy felt the strangeness come upon him now, he felt the swell of his gums as the fangs shifted and he felt the stirring and the need for blood calling and he raised his head and he roared the call of the vampire and the cry of the wolf.

The man mounted and then, eyes agleam, he leaned and grasped the small hand hauling him onto the haunches behind the saddle. Leaning into the hard body of the rider the boy savoured the thrill and the fear and the wonder. They rode out onto the moor and on to the town. To the alleys and the doorways, and to the blood.

The owl knew that in the stable yard there would be a freshly killed rabbit or a rat. Reward. It knew also evil was abroad tonight and so, flying swift and sure it swooped on the still warm corpse and then regained the rafters to turn inwards, and to tear with talon, and beak, at the soft fur. It savoured the flesh and left the evil of the world of men, to the world of men.

For the bird the flesh and the blood were sustenance but for the riders on the dark road there must be more, much more. Yes, there would be flesh, there would be blood but the flesh must be living tissue, soft and yielding. The blood must pulse and flow singing with life and still more, there must be skin, white and fragrant and hair soft as thistle down. Hair cascading in great waves over a fragile neck and cloaking slender shoulders. Most though, above all else, there must be fear driving the breath into desperate gasps and sparking in terrified eyes. The fear would spark the lust and the lust was the reason to ride.

The boy knew there was much to learn, he had only begun his apprenticeship. As the stallion's great haunches flexed and pulled under his behind he leaned into the man and felt the muscles knotting and twisting with the rise and fall of the canter. He closed his eyes. No harm would befall him he knew and he let his mind take him back.

The road had been dark on that other night, with the moon sailing between gusty clouds and the great limbs of the forest trees reaching and bending towards him. Back then he was afraid of the dark, and the night wind, and the scudding clouds obscuring the moonlight, leaving him floundering on the ink black highway. He did well to be afraid.

He heard the muffled hoofbeats through the darkness and scuttled to where he believed the side of the road would be, into the cover of the gulley. It was useless to try and hide from this rider, but the boy didn't know it yet as he shuffled crab wise into the underbrush.

The horse slowed from the gallop into canter and eventually to a walk and the boy understood he was discovered. The rider leapt to the sod and stood silent and watchful in the moonshine. The boy had never known anyone so still. As he watched the figure, immobile, merging with the surrounding dark only the glint of water in the eyes and the dullest gleam of belt buckles bore witness. The child had stilled his breathing and now, with his lungs screaming for oxygen and his head swimming he knew he must act.

Taking in a huge breath he leapt from the ditch onto the road and ran, his legs pumping and his arms flailing in terror and panic away from the figure of the man and the great horse snorting and shuffling. It was hopeless, he was a small boy nothing more, he had a small boy's body and the man was tall and strong and reached to fetch him in with barely a step forward.

Before there was time to think or twist or writhe in the grip, before there was time for a guardian angel to sweep down in mercy, and before there was time to cry out, the man bent over the child. As the moon showed for a moment there was the flash of a smile, a dreadful rictus, the stench of decay and then, oh then, the whirl of the stars as the heavens retreated and the horror took over his blood, and his heart, and his very soul. The boy was captured and the future was lost.

Now, he opened his eyes and left the reverie as the horse slowed, and the man turned in the saddle, his face a gleaming skull against the murk.

"Tonight boy, tonight it is to be your night. Tonight, you will take your own whore." The youngster gasped. Till now he had waited outside and then at the end when it was almost over the man had called him in. He had sated his lust with leftovers and the lifeless seeping, which only served to inflame his need and make him hungrier for the next time. He thrilled to the thought, now, tonight he would know the passion and the power.

Seven times the owl had brought him to the stable and seven times they had taken the road into the small town. He knew they would wheel round the market square and over the bridge and so avoid passing the church and they would clatter across the flagstones in the inn yard. The horse would be taken by a stable lad, cooled and watered and readied for the pre-dawn ride back to the moor.

The man's gloved fist hammered on the door.

"Ah tis you my lord."

"Madam, must I stand here till you regain your senses or will you bid me enter."

"Sorry, sire. So sorry, please come in."

"The boy is here. Tonight, he will take a room of his own."

The fat old woman's eyes shone with fear and with hatred, but she stepped aside and dragged the door further open.

"Ah, young sir of course come in, come in." With a new found swagger to his bearing he stepped over the threshold, his nerves afire, and his brain in a fever of anticipation.

As they took the stairs a door in the passage opened and a young girl peered through the cracks. She moaned as she watched the man and boy walk to the room at the end of the hallway and she resolved it could happen no more, not again, not for all the gold in Christendom, and not even at the very forfeit of her own life. She would act now, tonight.

Terror will oftentimes birth a coward, but tonight it spawned a heroin. Sally hoisted her petticoats and tucking them tight in her drawers she shinned down the drainpipe. Fleet-foot over the slick cobbles she made for the old church and hammered on the great door.

"Father, Father you must come. Evil is in the house, terrible evil. Bring the crucifix and the holy water." And the priest threw on his garments and ran to the altar. The great cross was all but too heavy for him and only the passion in his heart gave him the strength to hold it fast. He ran back with the young whore to the inn and up the stairs to the top floor where the darkest of deeds sullied the very air.

She pointed quaking fingers at the old wooden door and he threw it back with a cry. Holding the holy relic before him he entered the room, all too late. The body of the young woman on the bed was as pale as a moth in the moonlight. The scarlet punctures on the skin of her neck spoke of the manner of her death, and the billowing casements told of the means of escape.

The cry was up, all over town lanterns and flares blazed. Shouts echoed and rebounded up the alleys and the passages as the fugitives ran through the darkness to the stables and for the horse.

Suddenly the boy tumbled with a shriek into the filth of the street, his leg was twisted and his agonised cries overwhelmed even the baying of the mob. A bone white splinter stuck through the young skin. Blood trickled from the skinny limb and into the gutter. The man stayed his progress for a moment and their eyes locked beam to beam and the youngster raised an arm. Taking the slender hand in his for a moment a tear shuddered on his lower eyelid, then with a screech like that of the devil himself the master turned and ran on to the stable, to the horse and flight.

The boy struggled to rise but the fracture and the bleeding, the terror on him now, was overwhelming. With a groan he fell back as the mob rounded the corner of the building. The priest rushed forward with the huge crucifix offered before him as a sword. Desperate prayers split the night and his tears when he saw the child writhing on the ground blinded his gentle eyes.

"Now Father, you must do it now. Sally urged him forward, pulling and pushing with all her strength. "Father for the sake of his immortal soul, do it now."

The priest raised the great cross and with a cry that echoed through all eternity, and a sob which bought him his place in heaven, he thrust it downward and saved the boy.

As the scream echoed through the alley and the roof tops, so the soul of the child was found and as a white dove it flew. It fled from the evil through the sacred night and it found the old farmhouse and it paused. It rested a moment beside the open window and shed a glow of holy light above the sleeping girl child. A tear as pure as the rain and as precious as a heartbeat fell and blessed the innocence and then, it was gone.

The owl called into the night and the sound flew across the field and over the meadow and it found an open window and in a shabby room a boy was raised from slumber and as he heard it again, the cry of the owl, he threw aside his coverlet and crossed the wooden boards.

The End

Links:

Diane Dickson
https://dianemdickson.wordpress.com/

https://www.amazon.com/Diane-Dickson/e/B001KC8S2E

Visit Amazon.com's Diane Dickson Page and shop for all Diane Dickson books and other Diane Dickson related products (DVD, CDs, Apparel). Check out pictures, bibliography, biography and community discussions about Diane Dickson)

Cover by Author.

The Soul of Nemach and the Manhattan Murders

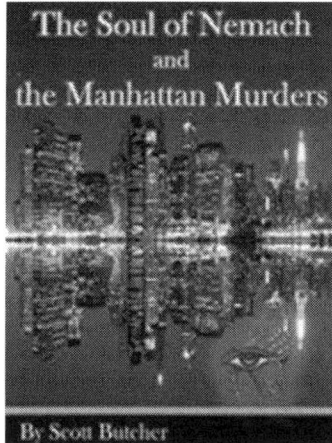

Scott Butcher

Scott Butcher is a Canadian/Australian author. Born in Australia to Canadian parents, Scott spent much of his youth between the two countries. He settled in Australia for a while, but in search of new adventure, after over 30 years in Australia, he returned to Canada in 2009 with his wife and three children.

In this story, people die every day, and when unlikeable people go, nobody looks too closely, except maybe for Nemach. For him no loss is insignificant. Problem is, Nemach's not alive himself, he died centuries ago, though his spirit was cursed to never find rest while his descendants still roamed the Earth.

Andrea needs help, people around her are dying in bizarre, if not suspicious, circumstances. If she's lucky, she may be a descendent of Nemach, and if not, she probably won't survive.

***

Martinis and Tears

Andrea stirred her martini and wondered when, and if, she'd ever be able to afford another round like the one she was currently contemplating. The pickle looked lonely, she'd have to order another shortly. Her severance pay would provide for at least one night of self-indulgence.

"Note to self, being fired ensures mandatory alcohol intake," she sighed.

Somewhere in the background the Piano Man started playing – it was very down and out-on-your-luck Manhattan appropriate.

It was still early, only 4 pm. Andrea had a whole evening of liquid inebriation to look forward to – as a means of killing her insecurities. With any luck, some hot looking dude would hit on her and give her a reason to live again. Hopefully he'd have money. Having money would be a good thing. No such luck right now though, there was hardly anyone else in the bar. Of course, that would change in about an hour. Maybe she should eat, by 5 pm she would probably have downed four or five martinis, and that one olive wouldn't be nearly so lonely to look at. Being totally legless wouldn't be a good option if she wanted to get laid by a rich, exciting, young male.

Andrea fingered the edge of the box that held the contents of her once work desk – it was a bit of a giveaway. Maybe she should put it on the floor and hide her desperation. Or, maybe she should leave it on the bar as an advert for self-same, she might pick up a few more potential suitors that way. Was the 'I've just been fired' look 'in'?

In the end the box went to the floor, but that one really annoying piece from the box stayed on the bar.

"This is total bullshit. I need another drink. Waiter!"

"I'd normally pay for that, but it seems I'm joining you." It was Rodney.

"Oh Rod, I'm so sorry. I hadn't realised that this was happening to anyone else."

"So am I. Seven others, as it happens. We're the first round. Apparently, more will follow." Rod propped his own box of desk goods up on the bar, then looked over at the one object that Andrea had left there… to hate on.

"Soooo, that's what he 'gave' you, is it?" He used air apostrophises for 'gave'. "What's its story?"

"You first, what did he give you?" Andrea took the bait, realising there was another story to be had.

"What will it be, Miss?" The bar tender interrupted.

"Another of the same," Rodney offered, "put it on my tab. I'll have a straight up Crown Royal rye. "

"Thanks for that Rod, I don't have a lot of reserves to rely on."

"Perks of having a family with money, I guess. Though this still sucks, and big time."

"Yeah, I get that, totally," Andrea smiled. "So what's your object of mirth?"

Rodney rummaged through his box, and pulled out what Andrea recognised to be a Chinese puzzle.

"This," he said. "I've had it on my desk for ages, it was missed in some inventory or other. No one knows who it actually belongs to. I could never work it out."

"The puzzle, or the ownership?" Andrea asked.

"Either," he answered. "Infuriating, I've never been good at puzzles. Dillan said I could keep it as my farewell present, the Dickhead. I'd much rather have left it behind. And yours?"

"Ah," Andrea replied. "This... is the reason I was fired." Andrea looked fixedly at the object.

"But what is it?" Rodney prompted.

"Oh, well, it's a bit humiliating really. I authenticated this object from Lauren Bacall's estate."

"What, you mean the real Lauren Bacall? The Humphrey Bogart, Lauren Bacall?"

"One in the same, Rodney. One in the same."

"It looks like, well it looks like the Maltese Falcon."

"Yeah, but it isn't. Everyone thought it would be, and that it would be worth millions. But it isn't. It's real."

"What do you mean it's real?" Rodney asked. "If it's real, doesn't that mean it is the Maltese Falcon?"

"No. It's real in that it is an ancient Egyptian image of Horus, probably from the end of the 18th dynasty. So it's more than three thousand years old."

"*Pawh.*"

"What? Anyway," Andrea continued, "it's ancient, it's not a Hollywood prop, how could an ancient Egyptian relic be a Hollywood prop? There were several props used as the Maltese Falcon, but this couldn't be one of them, I mean, everyone would know if a real relic were used as the Falcon, wouldn't they?"

"Hmm, yeah, I see what you mean. Hundreds of thousands s of dollars in potential auctioneer's commission gone. Still, hardly your fault, you did your job and authenticated the piece. If you'd got it wrong the corporation could have been sued for millions. Well done to you for doing the job properly."

"Dillan didn't see it that way."

"What? Really? Oh, that drop kick is an absolute dick head, no doubt about it. So he gave you the falcon, on the way out? That was a real asshole of a move on his part."

Andrea just nodded trying to hold back the tears as she eyed off the alabaster bird that had lost her, her job.

"Still, it is a relic, is it actually worth anything?"

"Well, yeah, it's probably worth a good five thousand dollars." Andrea perked up as that thought came into her mind. And Dillan had given it to her, she actually had a receipt. "I can pay the rent with that, and then some."

"Well that's not so bad. It was still a dick move by Dillan to fire you for doing your job properly, but five thousand dollars is nothing to sneeze at. This next round is on you." Rodney downed his rye slapping the empty glass on the bar. "Time for another."

Plotting Murder

Carson joined them for a time, his own box of goods beneath his feet, but concern about his family drove him to the subway after just the two rounds. He had a wife, three kids ...and no job... to worry about. Carson had been given the pieces of an antique plate he had dropped three years earlier. It was another real dick move by Dillan.

Andrea and Rodney watched him leave.

"I'd like to kill Dillan, really." Rodney's hand had gone a bit white around his glass.

"How would you do it?" Andrea asked him. "I'd like to handcuff him down, take his clothes off, and slowly skin him alive."

Rodney turned to Andrea and laughed. "You're not going to get that out of me easily." He turned to Andrea with a wry smile on this face.

"Who else got fired today? And why? Why now, I thought the auction house was going fine. That everything was on the up?"

"Humph, yeah fine, three years of losses after 2008, I think they finally broke back from the losses late last year. The down turn was a bad time. Dillan's dad kept us all on, even when he probably shouldn't have, but he kept it going and turned it around. Apparently, that wasn't good enough for Dillan when he took over.

Pity his dad died, nice old guy, I had a lot of time for him. He was old school, and knew how to look after his employees. Dillan is... something else."

Andrea took a sip of her martini. "I really do need to have something to eat. I don't think I'll be able to stand up in a moment."

"Do you want to grab a table? I could do with a bit of food as well."

Andrea shrugged. It was a date, an 'we've been fired together so let's get wasted with good food and drink date'. "Sure so long as you're paying."

Rodney smiled. "Why not, I'm the one with money, you only have a bird to rely on."

Andrea grabbed her 'bird' as they began moving to one of the bar booths. Rodney was good enough to pick up her box with his own, which was just as well, because at that stage Andrea wasn't sure she would have made it up from leaning over to get it.

A twenty something in a short black skirt showed them to their table and gave them each a menu.

"I feel like fish and chips."

"Really?" Rodney asked. "Let's go upmarket, mummy and daddy are paying, we could go oysters and lobster?" He winked at her.

"I'll see your oysters, but I'll sit on the cod and chips for the mains. I need something to absorb the alcohol."

"Humph, you seem to be doing okay, I'll go for the lobster. I've had it here before and they do a good job of it. Another drink? I'm moving to a white wine to go with the seafood."

"I'll take a glass of red, I'm allergic to the sulphurs they put in whites."

"Oh, you rebel you. Okay, a bottle of each it is."

"A bottle of each? Steady on there boy, I've already had my fill of martinis."

"Hey, it'll be there if you want it. And there's water on the table too. You don't have to drink the whole bottle. Live a little, indulge in the waste, after all, it's not every day you get fired."

Andrea smiled. Why not? He was right. They'd been fired! What the shit. Tonight was a night of indulgence. A waiter took their orders and soon enough there were two bottles in front of them.

"I haven't let loose like this in ages."

"Humph, all work and no play, huh. I know you worked most weekends."

"Well... I loved my job."

"It sucks, doesn't it?"

"Yeah, but hey, how were you going to off him?"

"Off who?" And Rodney seemed genuinely surprised.

"Dillan, of course."

"Oh, that, well… cleverly, of course, no spur of the moment stuff for me. It would have to look like an accident. Let's see. The building is old, and the elevator doesn't work well. The basement has flooded a few times. I bet I could set it up so that the elevator just sinks down to below the lobby slowly sinking into a sub-basement full of water. He'd drown like the rat he is."

Andrea palled, the basement did flood, and the elevator had malfunctioned more times than she cared to imagine. It had even been known to overshoot the lobby from time to time. It was all totally plausible. Andrea had another sip of her wine, as she considered clever little Rodney in other ways.

The World Turns Strangely

"Oh, my head."

"Sorry, Andrea, I have to rush, I have an interview in an hour, and I have to get home, have a shower and change."

"Really? You have an interview already?"

"What can I say, financial advisors are always in demand in the city. Just got the text message. Sorry, I can't let this opportunity slide, it's almost too good to be true." He pecked her on the cheek as he slide out from beneath the sheets they had shared. "I'll call you tonight if you like."

Andrea's eyes popped open. "Yeah. Yeah, sure." Truth be it known, Andrea had no idea what to think, or what she wanted, but 'yes' seemed to be the response that left her the best options.

"Well, that seemed enthusiastic."

"Sorry, hung over, lost my job yesterday, had sex with this gorgeous guy last night, who's leaving me for his new job when I have no prospects of my own. It's a lot to take in."

"Yeah, I guess so," Rodney commented as he pulled on his trousers. "I'll call you anyway."

"Yeah, let me know how it goes, we can celebrate with another dinner if you want?" the question mark in her voice was implied.

Andrea slipped back to sleep as the door closed behind her bedtime guest.

***

Several hours later, Andrea awoke to the sound of her mobile tone, looking at the phone there were three missed calls.

"Oh shit." She pulled the phone toward her and hit the answer button. "Andrea here."

"Why aren't you at work?" It was an oddly familiar male voice on the other end of the phone.

"Who are you?" Andrea asked.

"Who am I? I'm the guy whose rung three times already to find out why you're not here authenticating the items from this Italian sale that's happening next week."

"Chris? Chris, your cousin fired me yesterday, I don't work for you anymore."

"Like hell you don't. I'm in charge now, Dillan is out. You get your cute little hiney in here and get to work."

"What? I don't understand. What happened to Dillan?" The slight slur to her words may have underlined that.

"Oh, you've been drowning your sorrows." Was that amusement Andrea heard over the phone? "Well take a couple of hours, get yourself some coffee and have a shower. You're hired back with no loss of benefits, but I want you back here this afternoon. Dillan had an accident yesterday evening. He left early after firing everyone, only the elevator malfunctioned, it took him right down to the sub-basement, and it was flooded. He drowned. I'm in charge of the auction house now, and I need everyone back onboard doing what they're best at doing. So, see you in a couple of hours."

Andrea just stared at her phone screen trying to take in what she had just heard. Her eyes hurt, it was far too early, her mouth felt like a cesspit and... had her lover from last night just killed their boss? She couldn't remember exactly, but she was pretty sure that Dillan had died exactly as Rodney had said he'd like to kill him. That couldn't be a coincidence could it?

"I wouldn't think so."

"What?"

"I wouldn't think it was a coincidence."

Andrea's eyes went wide. Who had just spoken to her?

"No need to fear Andrea. It is I, Nemach, an accursed servant of Pharaoh, you are a descendent of mine, or so you must be to be able to hear my thoughts."

Andrea lay on her bed. She hadn't really heard that, had she? No, her mind was playing tricks on her.

"I assure you, I am no trick. I am very real."

Andrea pulled the sheets up over her still naked breasts wondering where this stranger who seemed to be in her apartment might be. "Hey, come out. Where are you?" she yelled out to her two rooms.

"I'm right here on your bedside table. I've been here all night."

Andrea looked to her left where the statuette of the God Horus sat looking down at her.

"No, it couldn't be."

"It would be so much easier if you accepted it was. My Ka is contained in this statue, it has been so for many thousands of years."

Gathering the sheets around her as she continued to stare at the statue, Andrea pulled herself up inching toward the bathroom.

"Nothing to say? You're just going to ignore me, are you?"

The young woman scuttled away to the small bathroom, and the sound of retching soon emanated from the toilet bowl. *"Oh, well. I guess so. I'll just leave you to it then."*

***

Andrea was worried that she'd lost her mind, the rest of the day went by in a blur of coffee and gossip. It all seemed so surreal. Everyone was in shock, Andrea more so than the others.

"You're not really here, Andrea."

"Sorry, Gale. What did you say?"

"You're not really here. Your mind is somewhere else, you just mis-catalogued that vase."

"Humph, so I have." Andrea's eraser went down to remove the offending numbers. "Far too much has happened."

"Yes, Dillan firing all those people, and then ending up dead. It's like karma was out to get him. We could hear his shouts from the bottom of the shaft. Some of the men tried to get him out, but that old metal cage that the elevator car is made from is of good quality 19th century steel. There was nothing they could do."

"There were still people here when it happened?"

"It was just on five, there are always people who stay back later than that."

But, but that didn't make sense at all.

"Do you know where Rodney is, Gale?"

"Why your mind is all over the place isn't it Honey, but no, I haven't seen Rodney today, I'm pretty sure he's not here. Why do you ask?"

"Ummm, I need a financial decision, it might be better to eBay this vase. It's old, but it's not worth very much."

"Oh, well, I think you'd have to ask Chris where Rodney is, he's the one that got in touch with everyone who was fired to make sure they came back in. And if you can't find Rodney, Chris can give you an answer."

Andrea nodded as she gathered herself up to make her way to Chris' office. A second later she was knocking on an open door – strange it had always been closed with Dillan, and even before that when Dillan's dad had been at the helm. Was this the beginning of a new policy? An open door policy?

"Chris, can you spare a moment?"

"Sure, how are you coping through those blood shot eyes of yours?" he smirked from his desk.

"Really? My eyes are blood shot? Say you're joking, that would be terrible if they are."

"Well, not blood shot maybe, but certainly a little bleary. What can I do for you?"

"I'm looking for Rodney. I need to ask him a question about a borderline appraisal." It wasn't even a lie, all the best lies aren't.

"Can't help you there, I'm afraid. Rodney's not coming back, he picked up another job. Apparently it was a big step up moneywise. I couldn't offer him anything like it. Can I help in some way?"

Andrea's mind was mentally tripping over. "Umm, I have a vase, it's old, but I think it's borderline to auction, it could just go on e-Bay."

"Well, put it aside for now. If there's anything else in that category we'll bundle them together into one lot, that'll make it worthwhile, otherwise we'll eBay it."

That made sense, Chris knew the business. It was strange that Dillan had been in charge at all, he had no love of antiques. Chris did. It probably all came down to being the owner's son rather than a slightly more distant cousin.

The question of what to do with the vase was answered, but there were other questions that were pressing on Andrea's mind, and only Rodney could answer those. She would have to wait until after hours to give Rodney a call and get the low down.

The Return of Nemach

As Andrea unlocked the door to her apartment, her eyes immediately went to the statuette of Horus, which she could just see through the still open door of her bedroom. Her mind must have been playing tricks on her, after all she'd consumed her own weight in alcohol the previous evening. She'd never had anywhere near as much as that before, and... never again. She hesitated though, waiting to see if there would be any strange words coming into her mind, but no, nothing. She had imagined it after all. That was reassuring, she would have to stay away from booze. No more binges like last evening.

Entering the apartment and locking the door behind her, she pressed the contact number for Rodney out on her phone. But the phone rang out to his answering service. "Rodney, call me please, something has happened. I need to speak to you."

"May I ask if it has to do with the murder?"

The phone fell to the ground, and Andrea froze.

"Tut, tut my dear, really, you should trust your own senses. I am very real indeed."

Andrea edged toward the door of her bedroom. "But... you're a bird."

"Really? I was under the impression that my Ka resided in a statue of the God Horus. Hardly 'a bird' as you so describe me."

"Yes, I... I know that."

"Mmm, I noticed as much when you did the appraisal of me. By the way, I'm early 18th dynasty , from the reign of the great pharaoh Thutmose the III."

"Oh, so not later 18th dynasty?"

"No, but you were close. Mind you, it was really very disappointing not to be recognised for my great role as the Maltese Falcon, I mean, anyone who checked the movie should have been able to see that I was there. Coerced by my friend Humphrey, but there none-the-less."

"Humphrey, Humphrey Bogart?"

"One and the same, my dear. Not only a great actor, but a stalwart figure who risked his life in the fight against evil and injustice, something that has not been revealed with the passage of time, and is now, rather sadly, probably only known to myself."

In spite of herself Andrea was intrigued by the conversation she was convinced she was only having with her own inner self, seeing as she was strongly of the opinion that she had gone quite mad.

"Now my dear, back to this murder – why are you trying to contact

the main suspect? That may not be the wisest of moves if you wish to remain in the land of the living."

"What? Oh, Rodney couldn't have done it."

"Oh, your midnight tryst? Quite entertaining it was – I understand the predilection with popcorn that modern people have, but alas I cannot partake. Your bedtime performance was admirable. I think there were a few pointers I could provide that would lead to improvement, but you did very well. That being said, you cannot rely on the passions of a lover to keep you safe if he is a murderer. Too many graves are filled with people who have made that mistake."

"Huh! What? No, Rodney couldn't have done it, he was with me when Dillan died. It had to just be some sort of freaky accident. Maybe Rodney's clairvoyant, or sees the future, or something. I'm moving you out of my bedroom though, you can live in the kitchen until I can sell you. This is just too freaky, having some old guy whose all in my head leering at me and rating me on my sex technique is all a bit much. I need to see a shrink and quickly."

"I'm afraid that will not help, you should probably save your money. Besides, I am well prepared to act as a psychologist, having once belonged to Carl Jung himself. By the way, he would have been quite intrigued by your theory regarding Rodney. Though of course, it's rather obviously inaccurate."

"Huh, you knew Carl Jung? And what do you mean it's inaccurate? Rodney was with me, he couldn't have done it. He just somehow pulled Dillan's means of death cosmically from somewhere."

"Or, the murderer told him how he or she was going to do it. And yes, I knew Carl Jung, I think he entered the field of psychiatry because of me. He was also worried that he had gone mad, but through many philosophical discussions, he learned to cope with my presence, and went on to found the field of modern day psychology while also putting forward his rather fascinating theories on synchronicity."

Andrea was silent for a moment. "That actually makes sense."

"Hmm, Synchronicity?"

"No, I think you're right. Someone else must have spoken to Rodney."

"Yes, I often make sense, the gods have cursed me with a mind of logic, but it can be useful sometimes. You should continue your efforts to contact your lover. It is rather imperative now"

"He hasn't answered any of his texts, or anything else."

"I should be plainer, the murderer may decide to cover his tracks. Rodney's life may be in danger, and if he mentions to the murderer

that he spoke to you, your life may also be in jeopardy."

"Oh! I have to get hold of Rodney."

"You have to get hold of Rodney. A taxi to his place of residence is not an inappropriate approach, and given the circumstance, it is not at all a sign of desperation from a lover of the night before."

Andrea's eyes had gone very wide. "I'll go right now."

"Andrea?"

"Yes."

"I have lived a very long time and I have learnt that there are many reasons for killing someone. However, if Rodney is not alive, I know we're dealing with a psychotic killer."

"And if he's alive?"

"Well, that is an entirely different circumstance, in that case it could well be a one off, if I understand the situation with this Dillan correctly, it could be considered something akin to a beaten wife who rises up to kill her abusive husband. In some times and places such a thing would be thought of as a justifiable homicide, though perhaps not in this time and place. Certainly there would be little chance the killer would reoffend."

A blur of possibilities ran behind Andrea's eyes as she slipped out the front door.

Grappa and Sorrow

Rodney lived in the Village, Greenwich Village. The cab ride there was uneventful for Andrea, except that she chewed the nails of several fingers away – a nervous habit she thought she had rid herself of years ago. Stepping out of the cab onto the sidewalk opposite her lover's brown stone, a building she was familiar with because of Rodney's predilection for after work cocktail parties, a familiar figure could be seen just getting out of a cab on the opposite side of the street.

"Rodney!" Andrea called out. A deeply felt relief flooded her now that she knew that Rodney wasn't dead somewhere, his body hidden never to be found. He was very much alive and well.

The figure looked across the way, and waved, before heading her way. "Andrea. Was my performance so spectacular that you couldn't wait for more?"

Andrea rolled her eyes as they stood on the street corner talking to each other. "You didn't answer any of your calls or texts?"

"A new job, it would have been poor form to spend my time

texting while I was learning the ropes, so I turned the bloody thing off. Horrible things cell phones anyway. Society is better off without them, your being here is an example of that, if the phone had been on and I had answered you might not be here now. Why don't you come upstairs and we'll have a quick dinner together?"

"You didn't want to come back? Chris said he tried to make you an offer to return."

Rodney stood there a second. "Come back? It was Chris who got me the contact for the new job. What's there to come back to anyway, didn't Dillan fire us? I'm pretty sure he did."

"Haven't you heard? Dillan's dead, Chris is in charge now, he hired all of us back, it's – rather bizarrely – life as usual back in Manhattan."

"Dillan's dead? How did that happen?"

Andrea explained the circumstances, and as she did, Rodney's face flushed white.

"That's... that's how I described it."

"Yes, but you were with me when it happened. Who else did you mention this to?"

"Well, no one really, just you. Oh, but it wasn't my idea. I think I need a drink, let's go up to my apartment."

"Sure, I need to sell that Egyptian statue too, it's freaking me out, I know you're familiar with potential buyers in the area. You can help me get rid of it."

As they spoke. Rodney turned and stepped out onto the street, but as he did so, a delivery truck swept his body away right before Andrea's eyes. The truck didn't even slow as the lifeless corpse slide from the vehicles front and fell beneath its wheels almost thirty yards away. There were screams as people ran toward the body, but there was nothing they could do, and the truck was quickly gone, almost as though it had never been there at all. In shock, Andrea watched as the scene unfolded around the body that lay down the street, then turned her head back to stare at the pair of shoes that had been left behind on the normally quiet roadway where a second before a living Rodney had invited her up to his home.

*****

Andrea plopped herself down on her lounge, a straight vodka in hand. As her Eastern European father had taught her, she downed the shot in one motion, her unsteady hands aided by the familiar quickness of the motion. That would take the edge off, she poured a glass of a good Bulgarian grappa that she had grown somewhat fond of over the years. Normally she would sip it while having an oily salad that would coat her gut, limiting the alcohol intake, but not tonight.

"I'm sorry, I take it that all did not go well."

Andrea shook her head, it was all she could do to keep the tears at bay.

"Can I ask what exactly transpired?"

Andrea broke down in a sob, "I was going to sell you. Rodney was going to help me, I knew he would. He was there one minute, and then... and then just gone the next."

The ancient Egyptian waited patiently, as Andrea's sobs turned to a flood of tears, then many minutes later to a dull nothing. As she calmed, he patiently, and sympathetically, coaxed more details about the death of Rodney from her, and about Andrea's last conversation with him. Then finally, he became silent.

The quiet was eventually too much for Andrea. "Nemach, Nemach are you still there?" Andrea wiped her arm across her tear stained face as she spoke.

"Very much so, my dear, very much so. I have just been ruminating over the possibilities."

"And they are?"

"Well, I think it is highly likely that it was your new boss, Chris who killed Dillan, he had motive: with Dillan out of the way he has become the new owner of the company. As someone highly familiar with the building he had means, and it is strange that he provided Rodney with a new job rather than taking him back into the auction house. It's almost as if he wanted to get him out of the way. Then there's the fact that Rodney confided in you that the means of Dillan's death was not his own invention, but someone else's."

Andrea nodded her head in agreement, it all made perfect sense.

"Of course, there is absolutely no evidence at this stage, all of this is simply conjecture on my part. And then... well, then we have the question of Rodney's death. Was it a tragic accident, or was it premeditated? The timing tends toward the latter, but again there is no evidence of foul doing. Perhaps if the police can find the truck some evidence may arise, but for now there is nothing."

"Nothing," Andrea repeated emptily.

"So, we are left with the question of whether Chris is a high level psychopathic murderer, one who quite cleverly removes those who are

in his way. Or... is he simply a one off killer, someone who would be no further danger to anyone else."

Andrea's head swung around to the statue. Nemach was right, there was no evidence either way, the very likeable Chris could be either, but there was nothing to go to the police with, it was all just supposition and suspicion. Andrea knew in her heart that Nemach was right, she was sure that Chris was a murderer, but was he a psychopath? She still had to work with Chris, leaving now would only lead to suspicions on his part, and she didn't want that. The little man in the statue was incredibly astute – if a bit of a perve... he could live in the kitchen, it was clear that she needed him to help figure this thing out, preferably, without ending up dead herself.

"I don't think I'll be selling you after all."

"Why thank you, my dear, I've grown quiet fond of you too."

The End

As well as *the 'Soul Nemach and the Burbank Adventure'*, Scott has written some children's books: *'The Fairly Stillwart Chronicles'* and *An Eagle's Heart'*. Both of these have been published by Morning Rain Publishing (see https://morningrainpublishing.com/). These books are also available through Scott's website at. http://www.scottiesbooks.com/

In addition to these, Scott is also writing 'The Dark Witch' series, under the pen-name Tabitha Scott.
Check the first one at

Evil Doing - https://www.amazon.com/Dark-Witch-Time-Evil-Doing-ebook/dp/B01N53KQP5/

https://www.facebook.com/scott.butcher.37

http://www.scottiesbooks.com/

Cover by Author.

Dhampir Twin Powers Activate

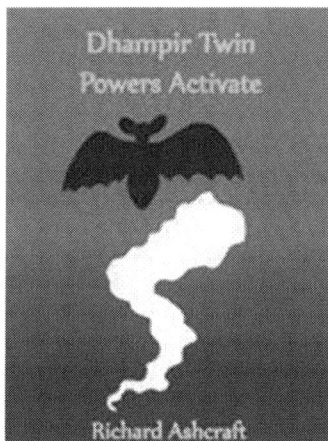

Richard Ashcraft

Louisiana-born Richard Wayne Ashcraft lived in Australia and Singapore in the 1970s because his father was an oil engineer during the Oil Crisis. As a result, he was exposed to many cultures and their supernatural stories. As an adult back in America, he sold four prose stories to IF-X Comics. He also posted on Amazon Kindle his collection of short sci-fi tales called Superhuman Interest Stories.

His story, Dhampir Twin Powers Activate, was oddly inspired by both the Wonder Twins and the old horror movie Son of Dracula. He first saw Count Alucard turn into a bat and mist in Adelaide. So he gave the Dhampir Twins those abilities. The boy thinks he has the greater power since he can fly anywhere as a bat. But even though the girl can barely levitate as a mist, she knows how to make the best of a "weaker" power. Enjoy.

***

Gale Rogers woke up sweating in the middle of the night. The sixteen-year-old girl should have been freezing. She had the fan blowing on her, and the air conditioner was on.

Gale put on her bathrobe to cover up her soaking nightgown. She left the fan on so it would blow-dry her wet pillowcases and sheets. Then she walked into the kitchen to get some cool water.

In the dim light she saw her twin brother coming out of his bedroom. He was covering his ears.

"Boyd, what's wrong?"

He grimaced in pain. "Shut up, shut up, shut up!"

"How dare you—"

But he cried out in pain before she could say anything more.

"Don't talk!" he said quietly and desperately. "My hearing has gone berserk! I can hear Mr. Joyce snoring next door!"

"What?" Gale said way too loudly. Boyd yelled in pain and fell to his knees.

Gale ran to their mother's bedroom. She saw the light come on under the door. Then Joan Rogers came out while she put on a robe.

"What's wrong?" Joan demanded.

"Turn off the light!" Boyd yelled as he covered his eyes. "It hurts my eyes!" Then he groaned as he covered his ears. "OW! My ears!"

"Oh, my God!" Joan said. Then she looked at Gale more closely. "You're sweating all over."

"You gotta take us to the hospital!" Gale said as she held back her tears. "Something is very wrong with us!"

Joan rushed to the cell phone by the sofa. Gale stopped her.

"Mom, we can't afford an ambulance!"

"I'm not calling an ambulance," Joan whispered. "I'm calling Uncle Fred."

"Uncle Fred? What for?"

"You'll see," Joan said as she sat down and speed dialed. "Hello, Fred. It's Joan. I'm so sorry to wake you up this late at night, but it's finally happened."

"What finally happened?" Gale asked.

"Shhh," Joan said to her. "Boyd is sensitive to light and sound. And Gale is sweating like a pig."

"Mom! You didn't have to tell him that!"

"Shut up, shut up, shut up!" Boyd repeated in pain.

"Shhh," Joan said to her kids. Then she became silent while she listened to Fred.

Boyd sat up in shock and looked at Joan.

"I'm not turning into a bat!"

Gale gaped at him in bewilderment.

"Yes, you are, dear," Joan replied calmly. "Now be quiet."

She held the phone closer to Boyd. They all heard Fred's voice.

"Boyd, I command you to completely turn into a bat!"

"What the—"

Gale never got to say hell. She stopped talking when she saw Boyd quickly transform into a bat.

"Thanks, Fred," Joan said nonchalantly. "I'll take over from here. Now go back to sleep. Good night."

"M-M-M-M-Mommmm!" Gale stammered as she stared at the bat. It flapped its wings and squealed.

Joan looked at Gale. "Just relax, dear, and turn into mist."

"Turn into—"

Gale never got to finish her sentence.

Because just then she transformed into mist.

Joan smiled with pride.

"That's my girl. Now I want you both to change back to your human forms. Just concentrate, and it will happen."

The bat turned into Boyd lying on the floor. The mist turned into Gale one foot off of the ground. She fell to the floor, and she nearly hit her head on the coffee table.

"Oh, no!" Joan said as she got off the sofa. "Are you two all right?"

"We are now!" Gale said as she stood up.

"Don't sh—" Boyd started to say in protest.

Then he smiled as he stood up.

"Hey! Your voices don't hurt my ears anymore! And the light in Mom's bedroom doesn't hurt my eyes!"

He approached them while Joan turned on the lamp near the couch.

"And I'm not sweating anymore!" Gale said as she shivered in the air conditioning. "Mom, what happened to us?"

"Sit down, and I'll explain everything!"

The twins sat on the sofa, and Joan sat on the chair closest to them.

"Boyd, the reason you were sensitive to light and sound was because you were changing into a bat against your will."

"If I hadn't seen my wings and claws, I never would have believed it."

"Gale, the reason you were sweating was because you were turning into mist against your will."

"But I don't understand, Mom. Why would that make me sweat so much?

"Because the water in your body started overheating. Water

385

turns into vapor because of heat. Then the vapor turns into mist when it cools down. You just never got to the cool part."

Joan looked at both of her children.

"Now let me explain about Uncle Fred. He has the power to control animals. So he commanded Boyd to turn completely into a bat. And when you saw him do that, you were able to accept the fact that you could become mist. That's why I called him."

Joan took their hands and smiled. "Now don't you two worry about a thing. This happens to people like you when they first gain their powers."

"People like us?" Boyd repeated.

"When they first gain their powers?" Gale added.

"What are we, Mom? Mutants?" he asked.

"No, dear," Joan said matter-of-factly. "You two are dhampirs."

"Damn what?" Boyd said in confusion.

"What are dhampirs?" Gale asked.

"They are the offspring of a vampire and a human being," Joan said.

"Vampire?" the twins yelled in horror.

"A vampire can turn into a bat!" Boyd said as he looked at Gale in panic.

"And he can also turn into a mist!" Gale said back to him.

"You're not vampires, dear," Joan said calmly. "You don't drink blood, and you don't fall asleep during the daytime. You two are dhampirs. On your father's side."

"Daddy was a vampire?" Gale asked.

"No, dear," Joan said while she tried to keep her cool. "He was also a dhampir. And so is Uncle Fred."

Joan sighed as she forced herself to continue.

"Now please bear with me. I'm going to tell you a very long story that goes back to the Crucifixion of Jesus Christ."

"Jesus Christ?" the twins said before they gaped at her.

"Please say that name with much more reverence," Joan said with a motherly look of disapproval. "Yes, He did exist. You two are proof of that."

"Mom, are you saying that we..." Boyd began.

"We are descended from..." Gale added.

"NO!" Joan said quickly. Then she calmed down and sighed. "A Roman centurion named Longinus used his lance to pierce the side of Jesus. Which resulted in the Savior's holy blood and water flowing into the soldier's eyes. The liquids cured him of his blindness.

Because of this miracle, Longinus converted to Christianity.

"However, a soldier just doesn't leave the centurions. So Longinus tried to sneak away in the dead of night. But another soldier found him, and they fought with their spears and shields. Somehow Longinus ran his spear through the soldier's body. That soldier's name was Enloch. He died, but he came back to life as a vampire the next night."

"Why did he turn into a vampire?" Boyd asked.

"Because the spear became cursed when it violated the body of Jesus. So anyone who was evil and was killed by it became an anti-Christ figure. Or what we call a vampire.

"You both read *Dracula* in school. He and Jesus both came back from the dead. But while Jesus was the symbolic Lamb of God, Dracula could become a wolf, which preyed on lambs. Jesus calmed the seas while Dracula could create thunderstorms. Jesus could walk on water while Dracula could travel in his mist form. Jesus offers His blood to His followers. Dracula drank people's blood, sometimes in his bat form. So basically, Dracula's powers were blasphemies of the miracles of Jesus. That's all."

"That's all?" Gale said in disbelief to Boyd. "That's all, she says."

"Anyway, Enloch became the real-life Dracula," Joan added.

Then she looked away in awkward embarrassment.

"And your ancestor."

"WHAAAAAT?" the twins said in astonishment.

"It's true. Enloch lived hundreds of years. And while he drank the blood of thousands, none of his victims ever turned into vampires. Because only the spear of Longinus could do that. However, Enloch could mate with human women. The few who survived their pregnancies bore him many, *many* dhampirs. But the dhampirs did not inherit all of his vampire powers. They only inherited one."

"Like turning into a bat or mist," Gale added.

"Yes, dear. And the dhampirs also had children, and they inherited one vampire power as well. Some used their powers for good, a few for evil, and many never used their powers at all. The few evil dhampirs were killed in the Crusades and the Spanish Inquisition. So were the good dhampirs who used their powers in public."

"Oh, that's encouraging," Boyd said dryly.

"Mom, what are the...powers...that dhampirs have?" Gale asked with some hesitation.

"Well, bat shape and mist form, of course. And they also can turn into a wolf. Your Uncle Fred can control the meaner animals like bats, owls, wolves, bugs, and such."

"Meaner animals?" Boyd said in disgust.

"Sorry, dear. Some dhampirs have superhuman strength. Others can control the weather. Some are immortal if they drink blood."

Gale said, "EWWWW!" while Boyd shuddered.

"Your father used his power of mesmerism on the people of Autumn Falls. He made it the perfect small town this side of Mayberry."

"What?" Boyd said in surprise.

"Daddy could hypnotize people into doing what he wanted them to do?" Gale asked in shock.

"He did," Joan said with a knowing grin. "That was the best dhampir power. Because you could get anything that you wanted. And Cleveland wanted you two to live in the best place possible."

"By turning everyone else into his slaves?" Boyd said scowling.

"I wouldn't say that," Joan replied. "But you have to admit that you two have lived the good life here."

"Did Dad ever use his mesmerism on us?" Boyd asked.

"Uhhhhh," Joan said in embarrassment.

"MOMMMM!" Boyd yelled.

"MOTH-ERRRR!" Gale screamed.

"We wanted you two to be straight-A students. And grow up to be well-adjusted adults. So sue us."

The twins glared at Joan for several long seconds.

"Next question. And stop looking at me like that."

"Do you think Daddy was killed by another dhampir?" Gale asked with a sad expression.

"No, dear," Joan said with a sigh. "I'm sure his car crash was caused by his flat tire. We were going to replace the tires the next day, but he had to get that damn phone call from his police flunky that night."

"Police flunky?" Boyd repeated.

"Sorry. Poor choice of words."

"Wait," Gale said. "You told us that Daddy picked Uncle Fred up because his car broke down in the middle of nowhere. Was that a lie?"

Joan nodded her head.

"The police had just brought in an insane man they thought was a serial killer. Cleveland calmed him down, and he confessed to kidnapping a college coed. The police found her barely alive in a basement and saved her life."

"So she's alive today because of Dad's hypnosis?" Boyd said.

"Yes, dear."

"Oh, my God!" Gale said as she looked at Boyd. "We owe Uncle Fred a big apology!"

"Oh, no, you're right! We really tore into him after Dad's funeral!"

"Oh, Mother! We're really sorry that we did that!"

"Yeah! We didn't know the real story!"

"And that's because Fred and I lied to you," Joan said. "We couldn't tell you the real story. So Fred came up with the lie. And he was prepared for your reaction. Still, an apology would be nice."

Gale waited for Joan to apologize for lying to her and Boyd.

But *that* wasn't going to happen.

Instead, Boyd changed the uncomfortable subject.

"You said Enloch was the real-life Dracula. What happened to him?"

"He grew tired of being immortal, dear. All of his loved ones died while he remained young. Plus, he was always on the go. When you're eternally young, you can only stay in one place for just so long. Otherwise, the townspeople become suspicious after awhile.

"So Enloch decided to kill himself. And since Catholics knew that confession was good for the soul, he decided to write down all of his sins in an effort to go to heaven. He wrote for many nights, and he wrote over a hundred pages."

"Talk about the ultimate suicide note," Boyd said.

"Then Enloch mailed his confession to the Church of Ireland, which he thought was a Catholic house of worship. But in reality it belonged to a Protestant sect. One that Bram Stoker belonged to."

"Bram Stoker?" Boyd said. "He wrote *Dracula*."

"I don't know how Stoker wound up with Enloch's confession. Maybe he stole it. Maybe he found it in the trash. Enloch did ramble on senselessly while he was writing. So I can't blame the minister for throwing it away. In any event, the confession inspired Stoker to write *Dracula*."

"Mom, did you ever read the confession?" Gale asked.

Joan shook her head.

"No, but your father did at his family reunion. One of his hypnotic relatives used his power on Stoker and learned the whole story. Then he made Stoker give up Enloch's confession. Now that you both have your powers, you'll get to read it at the next reunion. At least you'll read the translated version."

"I can't wait," Boyd said.

Gale couldn't tell if he was joking or not.

"So now you know everything, kids. And I'm giving you both permission to use your powers all night long. Chances are you two won't be able to sleep, so why not? I'll even let you skip school tomorrow."

"You are?" Gale said excitedly.

"Mom, I love you!" Boyd yelled.

They got off the sofa and hugged her at the same time.

"As much as I'm enjoying this, let go!"

So for the rest of the night, Boyd the bat flew outdoors and used his echolocation sonar.

And Gale the mist moved her vapors under closed doors, through keyholes, and between the small cracks in locked windows.

It only took them a few hours to completely master their new powers.

Joan was so proud.

And so was Cleveland.

***

Life soon became easier for the twins. Once in a blue moon Gale would start sweating again, and Boyd would be sensitive to light and sound.

But when those things happened in public, they simply excused themselves to the nearest bathroom. They changed into a bat or mist in private. A minute or so later, they resumed their human forms, and all was well again.

And eventually the forced changes became things of the past.

Boyd loved to fly in his bat form, and he would take every opportunity to become the winged creature.

So he let Gale drive their shared car home from school with his backpack in the back seat.

Because while his clothes did change shape with him, his backpack, books, and tablet did not.

Gale loved having the extra opportunities to drive, but she was jealous that Boyd was having all the fun.

She could barely levitate in her mist form while her twin could fly anyplace that he wanted.

At least she could turn her menstrual blood into mist. So her time of the month had virtually disappeared.

And that saved her a small fortune since she didn't have to buy tampons anymore.

***

Gale turned the corner to her house.

Then she saw Boyd flagging her down.

He also motioned for her to keep quiet by putting his finger to his lips.

She parked next to him, and he quietly got into the car.

"What's wrong?" she asked quietly.

"I was flying to our house when I heard Mom talking to somebody else!"

"Boyd, you shouldn't eavesdrop on Mother. That's not nice."

"I didn't mean to eavesdrop! You know how sensitive my ears are when I'm a bat! And never mind that! It's a good thing I heard Mom because somebody has her mesmerized right now!"

"Mesmerized? There's a vampire in our house?"

"A dhampir is in our house, yes! And he ordered Mom to spike our Cooler Colas with roofies!"

"Oh, my God!"

"What are we going to do? We might resist his mesmerism in our non-human forms, but we don't know that for sure! And he can make us surrender by threatening to make Mom kill herself! And even if he doesn't do that, a bat and a mist are powerless to stop him!"

Gale smiled knowingly.

"Speak for yourself, little brother."

***

The mist drifted through the crack in Gale's window. Then it descended to the floor and made its way to the hallway.

"Where are they?" she heard an annoyed man say.

"I don't know," her mother said in a monotone voice.

The mist stayed close to the floor as it moved toward the kitchen. Joan was sitting next to a bearded, middle-aged man at the table.

"Maybe you should call them," he said impatiently.

"Yes, sir," Joan said like a robot and reached for her cell phone.

While the man watched her speed dial a number, Gale took her chance, became human again, yelled at the top of her lungs, and ran into the man. His chair tipped over, and she landed on top of him.

Then Gale turned back into mist and forced her vapors into the man's mouth and nostrils. All the while, she had only one thought on her magical mind:

"Keep him from breathing! Keep him from breathing!"

And Gale's misty body did just that. It prevented him from inhaling and exhaling the air in his lungs by forming a thick and foggy layer in his throat.

She could hear him choking.

Then Gale heard her mother come out of her trance.

"Where am I? I'm home? But I should be at work!"

Then Joan looked at the choking man.

"What the hell?" she said as she got off of her chair. "Who are you? And what are you doing on the floor?"

Then she became concerned.

"Oh, my God! You're choking!"

Joan grabbed her cell phone and was about to dial 911 when Boyd flung open the front door.

"It's all right, Mom! Gale's got everything under control!"

"Boyd? What's going on here?"

Boyd answered as he closed and locked the door.

"He's a dhampir, Mom! He controlled your mind so you would spike our colas with drugs! He must have wanted to kidnap us!"

"Good Lord Almighty!" Joan said in a near faint. She sat back down again while Boyd quickly approached her.

"But Gale is choking him from the inside out! She became a mist inside his throat!"

"Oh, is that all?" Joan said sarcastically.

"How did this guy know about us?" Boyd said as he looked at the man.

"There are some evil dhampirs out there, son," Joan said with a sigh. "Who knew about your father's power. They must have known that you kids would gain your powers eventually. And according to one legend, an immortal can gain the powers of other dhampirs by drinking their blood."

"Oh, is that all?" Boyd said sarcastically as he glared at her. "Why are we just hearing about this now?"

"Because I hoped that it was just a legend," she said sheepishly. "And it would never happen to you two."

"I see," Boyd said grimly. "But there's one thing I don't understand."

"One thing?" Joan said dryly.

"Uncle Fred controlled me by talking over the phone. So how come this guy didn't use the phone to control Gale and me? And you?"

"Oh, that!" Joan said with authority, but in a funny manner. "Mesmerizing dhampirs can control their victims only if they make eye contact. Animal-controlling dhampirs use mental telepathy. Uncle Fred didn't need to talk to you when you first became a bat. He just told you to turn into a bat for Gale's benefit. So she would be inspired to become a mist. Understand?"

"Not one damn bit."

"That doesn't matter now. What are we going to do with...*him?*"

Boyd looked at his mother.

They both knew the answer to that question.

***

When the bearded man stopped moving, Joan checked his pulse.

Then she said, "You can come out now, Gale! He's dead!"

The mist flew out of the man's mouth and nostrils. Then it turned into Gale, and she looked down at the corpse with a stunned expression.

"Whoa! Wow!"

"Dear, are you all right?" Joan said as she got up and put her arm around Gale's shoulder.

"I'm okay. It's just that...Whoa! Wow! I gotta sit down!"

Gale did that while Joan turned to Boyd.

"Cover him with a blanket while I get your sister some water."

"Uhhhhh, ohhhhh, okaaaaay!" Boyd said as he went to the hall closet.

I'll cover his body! he thought. But I'm not touching him!

"Now don't you worry, dear," Joan said to her daughter as she got out three glasses from the cabinet. "I'll call Uncle Fred, and he'll get rid of...*the uninvited guest!* And I'm sure he'll be very discreet about it."

"He's done this thing before?"

Joan began filling up the glasses with the cold water coming out of the refrigerator.

"We're going to find out. Now just sit back and relax."

"Mom, I covered him up!" Boyd said as he put the fallen chair upright again.

"Good boy. Now sit down, and let's have something to drink while we think."

Boyd sat down as Joan filled the last glass. Then she gave the twins a glass each. And eventually she sat down with her glass.

Nobody said anything for a full minute. They also avoided eye contact.

Then Boyd looked at the covered-up corpse and said, "And here I thought I had the better super-power. How did you think of doing...that?"

"Yes, dear," Joan said. "How did you know that would work?"

"I saw the Hollow moving its molecules into Cole's body through his nose and mouth," Gale replied a little too calmly.

"The Hollow?" Boyd repeated.

"Who's Cole?" Joan asked.

"He's Phoebe's demon boyfriend on the *Charmed* TV show. But the Hollow is much more evil and can possess people's bodies with its essence."

"We gotta start watching *Charmed* now," Boyd said half-sarcastically, half-seriously.

"I didn't know if my plan would work though," Gale added. "So if I had to, I would have turned back into my human form while inside his body."

"EWWWWW!" Boyd and Joan said in disgust.

Gale glared at them.

"Oh, like you two could have stopped him," she said before taking a sip.

The End

Richard Ashcraft's book, *"Superhuman Interest Stories",* can be found here: https://www.amazon.com/Superhuman-Interest-Stories-Richard-Ashcraft-ebook/dp/B01728IHX4/

https://www.goodreads.com/book/show/27265506-superhuman-interest-stories?ac=1&from_search=true

https://bookoutantiques.info/2401351-superhuman-interest-stories-by-richard-ashcraft.html/

http://bookrest.insuperhuman-interest-stories/2239810.html

Cover by Jeremy Khan.

The Sentinel

Oliver Pratt

I was born in the early eighties, and I grew up wearing colorful lycra turtlenecks - until the day grunge (it's music) saved me.

Like many, I was bullied in high school, so, like many, I started drinking and vandalizing innocent mailboxes. Luckily, I eventually made some friends. With them, I kept drinking but found less violent hobbies (jigsaw puzzles, going to the zoo, and so on).

I always liked to write. At first, I wrote in French. Later, I still wrote in French, but better. Now, I'm giving it a shot in another language, because I've always liked challenges (once, I stopped eating baguettes for a whole week!).

My main novel is about pirates, because my story about a kid finding out he was a wizard was stolen before I even started it.

The Knight in this story of the Sentinal was walking through the plains of my mind since I was 15 or so (a *few* years ago). For some reason, he never found the way to a page until now. And considering how hard it was to wrap his story up in a roughly satisfying way, I think he had his reasons.

***

The Knight awoke with a jolt. On instinct, his hand seized his warhammer seconds before he sat up straight again in his saddle.

Around him, the silence of the night blended into the plains' quietude.

Ahead, for as far as the eye could see, there was nothing but the tall white grass, gently swaying despite the stillness of the air, heavy and dead as that of a tomb.

Behind, straight as an arrow until the horizon, nothing but the path he had opened through the plains, showing the way back. The way toward renouncement and cowardice.

Above, spreading in all directions, nothing but the purple sky. The pale-blue moon was shining silently, lonely pearl in an empty case. Cradled in the shimmering embrace of its ring, she was gently mocking his quest.

The Knight looked away. The moon could laugh all she wanted; the Gate was over there. And guarding it, the Sentinel was waiting.

His fingers relaxed over the smooth leather covering his heavy weapon's handle. He leaned down to pet the muscular neck of his horse. Under his palm, he could feel the mare's warmth, the sweat in her hair, the hard pulse of her blood. She exhaled a soft, mournful neigh. Her hooves were crushing the grass on an ever slowing tempo, more and more heavily. She would not be able to push forward much longer.

Yet, forward they pushed.

Straight ahead the Knight went, pressing his mount until her breath became heavier than the weight of her hooves on the white grass.

Straight ahead the Knight carried on, guiding his mare through the never-ending night long after she exhaled her last breath.

Straight ahead the Knight persisted, riding the bones of a long-dead horse across the white grass plains toward the Gate.

And when the bones crumbled underneath him, when they turned to dust to be carried away by an imperceptible breeze, the Knight grabbed his hammer and began to walk.

The ground was uneven and tricky, but he walked, never stumbling on steady feet.

The white grass was tall and sharp, but he walked, oblivious to the cuts on his hands.

His pack was cumbersome and heavy, but he walked, enduring the weight of precise preparation.

The plains couldn't be infinite. The night couldn't be endless. His quest couldn't be vain. His resolve would not waver. One step after another, under the vast purple sky and the mocking moon, the Knight was getting closer to the Gate.

Eventually, the grass started to shrink. Like a foamy white sea, it withdrew, slowly freeing the Knight's thighs. Then his knees. Then his calves. He finally emerged from the plains, crossing ponds of scrawny turf and banks of dry orange ashes.

The Knight stopped, laid his burden on the ground, let his hammer go. Standing on the blurry line between a sea of grass and a desert of dust, he smiled. Far ahead, where sky battled ground to dominate the horizon, something had interposed. It was only a thin grey line, a stroke of hope, but it was there.

The Knight picked his hammer up, gathered his pack, and strode onward.

The grey line became a grey strip, running from one side of the world to the other—a ribbon growing wider, pulling earth and the heavens further apart with each step. It grew wider and the shape of turrets arose. It grew wider and the turrets became towers. It grew wider and the towers showed crenels. The ribbon turned into a wall.

The great wall the Gods built.

The Rampart.

And in the Rampart, would be the Gate. And guarding the Gate, would wait the Sentinel.

The wall slowly pushed the sky away and, after ages, there was nothing left in the horizon other than light rubble stones. Yet, the Knight walked for another eternity before his slightly trembling hand touched any of them. The smallest one was as tall as he was, the biggest as large as a barn. They piled up to the sky, each one inset in the next without any mortar.

The Knight had reached the End of the World, the frontier between the human realms and the Beyond that no mortal ever saw. The legends, bards' songs and witches' tales, were all true. The Rampart was there, right under his palm. And somewhere in the Great Wall, he would find the Gate.

But where should he go? On the left, the sand washed up against the impassible stones. On the right, the immutable barrier gave birth to the orange desert. Mirrored images of confusion and doubt. Going back was inconceivable. The Knight was trapped. Facing a stone wall, he was stuck between the wall of his own determination and the wall of his own indecision.

Left or right? Two options so similar he felt like a mother asked to give up one of her twins.

Should chance decide the outcome of his quest?

No! It couldn't be! Not after all the sacrifices!

The Knight screamed through the silent night and threw his hammer against the wall. The booming sound echoed into the vast emptiness. The Rampart stood impassive, unmarked. The Knight fell on his knees as if to pray. But the Gods wouldn't listen; they were the ones to have built the wall keeping him from his destiny. Perhaps would it be easier to rest his head on the sand and go to sleep, dream about the Beyond he would never see, and never wake up again.

A sudden gust of wind blew away the dark thoughts clouding the Knight's judgement. He went too far, for too long. The cost had been too high.

Another draft carried a hint of smoke in the air. The Knight stood again

He faced the wind, but it died on his face, not to pick up again. Did he imagine it? Was he losing all sanity? Was it a sign or some cruel joke from playful Gods?

For all answer, a star blinked at him in the distance, right next to the stone frontier. It has been very furtive, but the knight got the sign he needed. So he began to walk again.

The star came back, only to disappear again, playing with the Knight's sanity.

The star came back once more, a little longer, taunting, teasing, a tenuous light like a siren's chant.

The star came back again, and this time, stayed for good.

Twinkling right above the sand, it became a guide toward a sacred goal. Unmoving fabric of the sky, it became a lighthouse for an already wrecked ship. Competing with the ringed moon through the never-ending night, it became a shining thread inside a maze made of void.

So the Knight answered its call, and strode onward.

The star was low on the horizon, dancing on the edge of the world, dancing like flames. The wind picked up and the acrid scent of burning wood came back.

Not a star; a bonfire. The Sentinel's bonfire.

The end of the Knight's quest was nigh.

A man was sitting in front of the flames, his face hidden under the hood of his coat.

He sat still as the Knight came closer and closer to his destiny. He sat still as the Knight laid down his pack. He sat still as the Knight grabbed his heavy warhammer in both hand.

Next to the man, a huge sword was waiting in the dust, glinting in the dancing light. In the flames, a skull, white still, was burning among bones of all size. Fair warnings. But the Knight wouldn't walk away. He had reached the Gate.

It was immense and beautiful. The gold of its intricate, divinely crafted bars seemed to mimic the ever changing convolutions of the flames. The dark wood of the gigantic panels sang along with glints of red and white.

The Gate. And behind, the Beyond never seen by any man. Yet.

The man lifted his head up. His eyes showed surprise in the middle of a face torn by anger.

The knight gripped his hammer tighter, ready to fight, and asked: "Are you the Sentinel?"

The man never answered. He stood up. Fast. Sword already in hands. The wide blade, as tall as the man weaving it, seemed to shine. The combat started.

The silence shattered, clash of steel filling the never-ending night. The blade crashed into the hammer. The hammer smashed into the blade. The weapons sang their song of fury, their song of clamor, their song of death. And the combatants danced, drawing their choregraphy in the dust.

Many times, the Sentinel nearly cut the Knight's leg, or his arm, or his head. Many times, the Knight nearly crushed the Sentinel's ribs, or his hip, or his shoulder. But neither one nor the other seemed able to get the upper hand. For eons, they kept fighting under the gaze of a mocking moon and the contempt of oblivious Gods.

Fate finally put an end to the dance. Or maybe it was luck. Or maybe one of the Gods took pity on the Knight. The sentinels foot slipped in the dust. For a second, he lowered his immense sword. More than enough for the Knight to strike the deadly blow. He threw his hammer across the Sentinel's face, crushing bones, spraying blood all over. The Sentinel fell on his knees. The wreckage of his face hit the ground. His body twitched once. Twice. Thrice. And that was it.

The Sentinel was dead. The Gate was at hand, now undefended. But the Knight needed to catch his breathe, to relax every muscles of his body, to enjoy such a victory.

The Gate wasn't going anywhere.

Hunger came, so the Knight ate. From his pack, he ate the stale bread and the dry meat. He ate the stone hard cheese and the dry fruits and the nuts. He devoured it all at once, never satiating his starvation. So he turned to the Sentinel's body. He took his cloak for himself, he took his immense sword to replace his hammer, and when he got him naked, he started to cook him.

The Knight took the strength of the Sentinel's muscles. He took the bravery of his heart. He took the virility of his genitals. He took the knowledge of his brain. He took everything from the Sentinel and watched his bones burn in the fire that was a star once.

And for the first time since he set foot on the white grass plains, fatigue fell on the Knight. It proved itself greater adversary than the Sentinel. The Knight closed his eyes and surrendered to sleep.

Under the mocking moon shining in the purple sky, the Knight slept.

Facing the bones of the Sentinel, burning among those of less worthy opponents, the Knight slept.

Back to the magnificent Gate to the Beyond, unknown to mortals, the Knight slept.

When he opened his eyes again, someone was standing in front of him.

A woman, clad in chainmail from head to toe. Her axe shone, reflecting the flames.

Her voice rang in the endless night:

"Are you the Sentinel?"

The End

Most of my stories are yet to be published (or written), but you'll find some of my work in English on Wattpad:

Puerto Seguro is a pirate story, some kind of dark, fun, and mature Pirates of the Caribbean but without Johnny Depp.

Vlad's blog is my very mature, very harsh recess. I use Vlad's vampiric voice to blow off some steam and spit on bad best selling novels including baseball playing, shining vampires.

Oliver's (not so) original miscellany is where I stuff all my short stories and my opinion on very important matters such as: are semicolons from hell?

https://www.wattpad.com/user/PedanticAndGrumpy

Cover by Author.

On Wings of Night

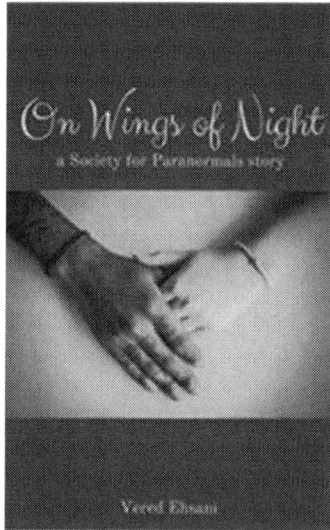

Vered Ehsani

When the mysterious Mr. Tiberius Elkhart arrives in the small town of Nairobi, Lilly is convinced she's met the man of her dreams. But Tiberius has a dangerous secret: he's an African shapeshifter wanted by the Society for Paranormals. This is a short story from the Society for Paranormals series in which Jane Austen meets Lara Croft in colonial Africa.

***

"You've been too long among savages, Lilly," Mama shrilled as she dodged a goat. "Put on your gloves. This may be East Africa but we will uphold the standards of Queen Victoria."

"Yes, Mama," I muttered, twirling a finger through one of my dark curls.

We were standing on the rickety platform of the Nairobi Train Station alongside peddlers, porters and traders. Unfazed by the heat and dust, the goat sniffed at my long dress before trotting away through the crowd.

"And don't slouch," Mama said, waving her lavender-scented handkerchief.

"But I'm tired, Mama," I said, not caring if I sounded as whiney as my cousin Beatrice Knight accused me of being.

"And unmarried," she retorted, scowling as if it were my fault we'd moved to some horrible African colony. "This may be your only opportunity to secure a decent match."

"The Governor's sons will probably be ugly," I grumbled.

Even if they were disgusting as toads and with less fashion sense, Mama would insist I attach myself to one of them. Beatrice glanced at me, disdain obvious in the tilt of her eyebrows and the narrowing of her yellowish eyes. I resisted the urge to stick my tongue out at her.

Mr. Evans the stationmaster stood nearby, notable for his thick glasses, thin hair and pink complexion. Beside Mr. Evans was a young African man looking very uncomfortable in military band regalia and a snare drum hanging from his neck.

"We must not allow them to become distracted," Mama warned me. "We must not risk our futures."

There was no further time to reflect on how distractible the new Governor's sons would be, for a shrill whistle warned us of the impending arrival. The crowd shuffled and shifted closer to the tracks.

The moment arrived in a huff of steam and a squeal of metal on metal. It was clear from which carriage the Governor would be alighting. While the rest of the train was a soot-covered, scratched and dented collection of metal hobnobbed together, his carriage's surfaces were shiny and clean, the inside plush with heavy curtains and thick cushions.

"Here we go," Mama whispered, her eyes glittering. She pushed me ahead.

Mr. Evans elbowed the young man beside him. "J-James," he said with a stutter. "Now. P-p-play now."

Biting his lower lip in concentration, James massacred a drumming solo. To the accompaniment of the drum, several humans spilled out of the Governor's carriage in a tangle of shouts, hurrahs and various limbs.

"George and Henry, you rascals," a strident voice cut through the commotion. A box-shaped woman with frizzy gray hair pulled apart two young boys and a younger girl.

"Oh look, Lilly," Beatrice whispered, "just wait a few years and you'll have the choice of two young lords. Until then, you can offer to babysit them."

"You're horrid," I whispered back.

Mama scowled but motion caught my eye. I swiveled to face the carriage entrance and stared at a man with magnificent posture and an attractive countenance. His dark suit fit him perfectly, emphasizing his slim yet firm build, his solid shoulders and his graceful movements.

"Nurse Manton, perhaps we should place these miscreants back on the train and return them to London," the man spoke in a warm voice.

"Indeed, Mr. Elkhart sir," Nurse Manton said.

"My, oh my," I breathed out.

Mr. Elkhart's cherubic lips widened into a radiant smile as he assisted Nurse Manton in sorting out the children. His dark brown eyes twinkled, and his black hair swished across his forehead.

"What is he, a well-dressed stable boy?" Mama sniffed. "Such a tan. He's ruined his skin working in his Lordship's fields."

He was darker than any Englishman I knew, and more handsome as well. "Not at all," I said in his defense even as I wondered at his unusual skin coloring. "He must be a lord's son who spends his time in the south by the beach, or perhaps sailing along the Riviera."

More commotion ensued, and a couple descended the carriage. Mr. Elkhart straightened up. "Sir, m'lady, let me assist."

Mr. Evans stepped forward, after waving at the drummer to cease his racket, and said, "Lord Hardinge, Lady Hardinge, welcome to Her Majesty's p-p-protectorate of East Africa." He ended the formal statement with a hand flourish and a deep bow.

"A lord and lady," Mama gushed.

Lord Hardinge nodded at Mr. Evans. "Most kind of you," he said in a polished, educated accent. He was a tall, slim man of fair complexion and kind eyes. "Please let me introduce my ward who has recently become my business partner, Mr. Tiberius Elkhart."

Mr. Evans bowed again, sweating so profusely that little drops splattered onto the splintered wood of the platform.

"Did he say his ward? And business partner?" Mama demanded. I was too engrossed in admiring Mr. Elkhart to respond. Sniffing, Mama pushed past Mr. Evens who in turn stumbled back and nearly sent the drummer flying off the platform. "What a marvelous coincidence. My daughter, niece and I came down only to deliver a letter. Mr. Evans, an introduction, if you please."

"Ah, y-yes," Mr. Evans stuttered, wiping a handkerchief across his brow. "May I introduce Mrs. Steward, and her daughters?"

"Daughter," Mama corrected, her smile fixed wide and welcoming. "And my niece."

Beatrice and I exchanged a glance, both of us united in our wish for my mother to observe silence. Sadly, she was not so inclined. "Your travels must have exhausted you, Lady Hardinge," she gushed. "Such a rough trip."

Lady Hardinge smiled and beneath her fashionable hat and layers of lace and dust, she was passingly pretty. "Well, I am somewhat fatigued," Lady Hardinge admitted, "but would be grateful for some company. Would you care to join us for tea? It would provide me some relief after our trip."

A thrill of delight tingled along my limbs, for no sooner had Lady Hardinge extended the invitation, the glorious Mr. Elkhart glanced at me and held my gaze for a moment longer than was strictly necessary. My cheeks heated, and I turned my head aside.

Having witnessed this interaction, Mama's smile widened as she readily accepted the invitation with a rapidity that bordered on ill-mannered. For once, I didn't mind.

TIBERIUS

Of all the foul luck.

The escape from England, orchestrated by my faithful guardian Lord Hardinge, had been a success. The Society for Paranormals hadn't registered my existence, and now they never would. Or so we'd hoped. In such a remote part of the British Empire, surely I could be safe from the gossip of London and the devious hand of the Society. Safe and welcomed. From the moment we disembarked, the land of my mother embraced me with its chaotic joy and warmth.

But now...

Schooling my features to reflect nothing more than a mild interest in the conversation, I studied our guests. Mrs. Steward and her daughter seemed innocent enough, although the mother complained at regular intervals as the covered wagon jolted along the rough, unpaved road leading to our new home. The daughter was pleasant in appearance. In other circumstances, I might have allowed myself to be distracted by her sky-blue eyes and her dark hair that curled in charming fashion around her pretty features.

Seated across from me, she bestowed sufficient smiles to indicate she'd be receptive to my attentions.

Instead, I focused my study on the niece, my suspicions increasing by the minute. Her yellowish eyes gave her away: like me, she was not what she appeared to be; she was not entirely human. But was she here on behalf of the Society? And if so, for what purpose?

Before I could develop a line of indirect questions with which to quiz Miss Knight, Miss Steward interrupted my thoughts. "Mr. Elkhart, do you plan to take up permanent residency with Lord and Lady Hardinge?"

Resisting the urge to growl, I forced a smile and replied, "As they raised me as their son, I would say my stay will be an extended one."

The young lady's face reddened. "Oh, I don't mean to pry…"

My smile softened, and I waved a hand. "Be at peace, Miss Steward. Due to his travels, my father requested his best friend to care for me during my school years."

I didn't offer any explanation for my father's need to travel constantly. What could I tell them without startling the humans amongst us? That my father was a vampire, hunted by the Society? Or that my Swahili mother, now deceased, had been an African shape-shifter? I wasn't sure which heritage — African or paranormal — they would find more scandalous. A familiar bitterness oozed through me.

"Where's your father now?" Miss Steward asked.

"He's based in Java," I answered her, the sharpness of my tone causing her to flinch. My hands clenched tighter but I didn't apologize. Instead I turned to Miss Knight and said, "I hope you don't mind my observing what fascinating eyes you have."

"Most kind of you, Mr. Elkhart," she said.

Leaning back against the cushioned boarding of the wagon, I removed a cigarette from a packet and lit it. Tendrils of smoke swirled about as I continued my inquiries. "And what brings you to East Africa, Miss Knight?"

Both young ladies frowned at me. Miss Knight said, "Like you, I live with my legal guardians, both my parents having died some years ago."

"Yes, the Andersons," Miss Steward added. "Perhaps you heard the story? Mama said it was a terribly violent accident which left their only child destitute and dependent on the charity of relatives."

"The Andersons, you say," I said, my shoulders tensing.

407

"You know of my parents?" Miss Knight asked, her eyes narrowing.

"I've heard of them," I said, swallowing against the tightness in my throat. One of my suspicions was confirmed: Miss Knight wasn't human.

I changed the conversation to one which encouraged the participation of our fellow travelers. Yet my attention was divided as I pondered what I should do with a witch who was most likely in the employment of my greatest enemy, the Society for Paranormals.

LILLY

The Hardinge home was an impressive stone structure, a small mansion really. In all ways it was superior to the poorly constructed buildings in which most Nairobi residents (ourselves included) suffered. Housestaff had already unpacked the family's possessions which had been sent in advance.

"What a delightful abode," Mama gushed, her double chins wobbling.

Nurse Manton ushered the young Hardinge children to their nursery while we were escorted to a charming room lined with bookshelves. A large Persian carpet covered much of the stone floor. We settled on the plush paisley sofas and were soon served tea and pastries. Beatrice and Lord Hardinge, seated next to one another, began an earnest conversation about medieval weaponry.

I sat away from them as I had no inclination to join such a conversation. Even more fortuitous, Mr. Elkhart lounged in a chair next to my sofa. His gaze was unfocused, his countenance distant.

"Where are you, Mr. Elkhart?" I dared to ask, breaking his reverie.

Startled, he turned to me, his eyes gentle and inquisitive. Smiling, he shook his head. "It's of no consequence. There is a small matter to which I must attend but it can wait."

Silence settled between us. Mama glanced at me, her eyes widening with a meaning that was too obvious. Sighing, I toyed with my gloves and struggled for a topic upon which we could converse. His tanned features inspired me to ask, "Have you been to Africa before?"

His gaze sharpened as did his tone. "Why do you ask?"

I leaned away from the sudden intensity that gleamed from his dark eyes. At that moment, he didn't look like an English gentleman but rather something wilder, almost savage. "No particular reason," I hastened to reassure him. "You seem to have an exotic history, what with your father in Java and you here."

The words tumbled out in a chaotic gush. To my own ears, I sounded frivolous and inconsequential, yet I couldn't stop.

The tension in Mr. Elkhart's features eased away as he bestowed on me the slightest of smiles. "Exotic is one way to describe it."

Before he could elaborate, Lady Hardinge passed between us, saying, "We're going for a turn in the gardens. Would you care to join us?"

Mama's glare made it clear I had little choice in the matter. To my surprise, Mr. Elkhart also accepted the invitation. The two women strolled ahead of us, far enough to be discreet and close enough to chaperon us. Mr. Elkhart however remained silent. There was only the crunch of dry grass underfoot to mark our passage. The call of birds and insects and the occasional distant bellow of an elephant filled in the gaps.

After several minutes of this intolerable quiet between us, I ventured, "Lady Hardinge has her work cut out for her. African soil seems only to grow the wildest of trees and the strongest of weeds. And whatever survives the heat and dust is devoured by zebras and trampled by elephants."

Chuckling, Mr. Elkhart said, "So no rose gardens then."

"Perish the thought," I said, smiling at the refined features turned toward me. "It will only serve to attract every insect and herbivore in the land."

Perhaps fatigued with his previous silence, he continued to converse, asking me about my life in London and my hobbies. A pleasant time ensued as we strolled through the grounds. Upon returning to the house, Mr. Elkhart paused at the front door, placing a hand on my arm to stop me. A buzzing energy surged from that point of contact.

Peering down at me, he said, "My guardians intend to hold a party next week. I do hope to see you there."

I had to constrain the urge to reach out and stroke back the lock of black hair that had fallen across his forehead. "Of course," I breathed, my voice quivering. As we entered the house, I wondered how I would endure a whole week before we met again.

TIBERIUS

The telegram crunched in my fist, its damning message confirming my suspicions. Yet being proven right was no consolation. Lurking in my room upstairs, I heard the guests begin to arrive, their idle chatter floating through my window on a flower-scented breeze. Further afield, a hyena cackled, mocking my despair.

"I'm not a murderer," I whispered. "But I have to do something."

Gritting my teeth, I tore up the telegram into little yellow flakes and tossed it into the small fire. The thin paper flared briefly in the flames, the rough stone walls around me reflecting the glow.

Pacing the room, my thoughts turned to Miss Steward. A sweet, innocent human, she knew nothing of my world. Perhaps that was her attraction. I snorted, imagining her horror if she should ever learn the truth.

As for Miss Knight...

Brushing specs of dust from my dinner jacket, I straightened up and breathed through my tension. With something resembling a smile on my lips, I strode downstairs. I didn't have to wait long.

"Mr. Elkhart," Miss Steward said as she and her mother entered the reception area and curtsied. "A pleasure to see you again."

"Likewise," I murmured, bowing to her as I held her delicate hand in mine, smiling as I recalled the coincidental meetings we'd enjoyed over the past week.

My gaze slid over her shoulder, and my throat constricted as I observed Miss Knight lingering near the entrance. "Forgive me," I said to Miss Steward, "but there is a small matter to which I must attend. Please go through to the patio. I'll join you shortly."

Ignoring her pout, I hurried past her. Every step away from her was a reluctant one. I focused instead on my quarry.

"Miss Knight," I said, hoping the witch wouldn't notice the quaver in my voice. "We didn't have an opportunity to enjoy each other's stories the last time we met. I hope to remedy that situation."

I clasped her proffered hand and bowed over it as I studied her reaction: surprise, delight but no suspicion.

Escorting her in the opposite direction of Miss Steward, I led her into the half-wild garden, distracting her with trivial details of my life.

"Fascinating," she murmured when I recounted how I'd traveled the world with my father as a young child.

"Indeed," I said, glancing casually behind us. We had passed out of sight of the other guests, a large Angel Trumpet screening us. I breathed in the sweet perfume of the poisonous, bell-shaped flowers, allowing the change to occur. My canines began to lengthen.

Perhaps Miss Knight wasn't as oblivious as I'd hoped. She glanced at me, her eyes widening. "Come, Mr. Elkhart, I insist we return before I'm bitten by these horrid mosquitos."

"What do you see, Miss Knight?" I asked, my voice lower, thicker, as I gave up the struggle to stay human.

I didn't hear her response as my bones snapped. My back arched against the pain that zapped down my spine as two giant bat wings sprouted from below my shoulder blades. The wings unfurled above me. My hands and feet enlarged and curled into scaly claws; my ears elongated; my face pushed outward into a snout; and my skin vanished beneath a coating of short, dark fur. In the moment it took her to take three stumbling steps away from me, I had transformed into my Popobawa form.

As she turned to run, the predator in me — the monster I kept leashed in the dark — stretched out of the shadows and filled my mind. In one movement, I launched myself at the woman, clutched her in my claws and flung myself into the night. The whistling of my flight and the thump of my wings drowned out her scream. The human part of me cringed while the Popobawa savored her fear.

I flew toward the hills near the small town. The savannah changed into forest. Too soon, I tilted my wings and began to descend toward a steep slope embedded with mossy boulders wrapped in thick vines. I swept into the gaping mouth of a cave, illuminated by two storm lanterns. Once inside, I deposited a crumpled Miss Knight and shifted into my human form.

Miss Knight scrambled away from me and collapsed upon a small boulder, her breathing ragged. "You're a Popobawa," she gasped, a hand over her heart. "The Bat Winged One. My gardener told me about your kind. You're a shape-shifting demon."

A demon. That was all I was to her. Would Miss Steward have the same sentiments?

I covered up my inadvertent flinch by brushing at my dinner jacket.

"Well, what do you have to say for yourself?" she demanded with bravado, even as her limbs shook.

Acid churned in my stomach, and I reminded myself I was doing this to protect my family. "I was hoping to ask you that very question," I said, keeping my voice gentle.

"What do you mean?" she asked.

"Please, let's not play these games," I said, weariness creeping into my limbs and my heart. "Did the Society send you here?"

411

"No. But how do you know…?" she began.

"I'm well acquainted with the Society for Paranormals," I said while slowly approaching her. I sat on a rocky outcrop nearby.

Frowning, she replied, "I'm here because the Stewards abandoned London due to a series of disastrous investments."

Leaning my elbows on my knees, I studied the woman before me. The words of the telegram replayed in my thoughts: *Miss Knight top paranormal investigator for Society. Use extreme caution.*

The accusation and disgust in her eyes caused me to look away. Scuffing a shoe against the rubble scattered across the rocky floor, I asked, "But you do work for the Society."

She shrugged. "They've asked me to observe and report. Our knowledge of African paranormals is scanty at best."

This time, I couldn't disguise my shudder. After all the Hardinge family had sacrificed to take me far away from the clutches of the Society, it hadn't been far enough. If the Society wanted information about African paranormals… I was a prime target.

I studied Miss Knight. "You do seem innocent of malicious intent."

"So I hope that means I'm free to go," she said. "Or are you planning on feeding me to the local fauna?"

Tipping my head to the side, I smiled. "It had crossed my mind."

"Charming," she said. Hesitating, she continued, "For a moment, I thought you were the one attacking the girls, and that I was the next victim."

"What girls?" I asked, my thoughts spinning to Miss Steward.

Shrugging, she said, "Young women are being targeted by an evil spirit. I believe the creature is seeking the right one for possession. In the process, it kills the ones it rejects."

I snarled at the implication. "You believed I was the killer."

She had the decency to blush but insisted, "Well, you are a demon."

"I would never hurt her… them," I hissed, my teeth barred even as my heart's pounding filled my ears. Was Miss Steward safe at the party?

Nodding, Miss Knight kept her eyes averted, studying one of the storm lanterns. "No, I suppose not," she said. "Shall we return to the party?"

My shoulders slouching, I rose. "I'm sorry, Miss Knight, I truly am, but I shall be returning alone." Straightening up, I gestured to a corner of the cave. "I've left ample provisions for you to ensure a somewhat comfortable stay."

"And then?"

I half-smiled at her refusal to beg or give way to tears. "A ship departs for England. I'll prepare a letter on your behalf for the Stewards, to explain your sudden absence." Walking to the cave opening, I stood on the edge and stared down, silently telling myself this was the right thing to do even as sweat slicked over my hands. "I will ensure you are on that boat. And if you are foolish enough to return, I will consider more permanent measures."

"But why?"

"My guardian brought us here to escape the reach of the Society, a reach that separated my parents and forced my father into permanent exile." I glanced back at Miss Knight, the Society's lead investigator. "We'll not tolerate their presence over here, not after all the sacrifices that we've made."

With that, I flung myself off the ledge. A breath later, my wings of night carried me over the trees and away.

LILLY

"Make sure to extract that proposal tonight," Mama hissed.

The flush in my cheeks had nothing to do with the warm evening. "Mama, really," I huffed, glancing about. No one seemed to have overheard.

"Don't *Mama* me, young lady," Mama said, her jowls wobbling. "Such men don't fall out of the trees with the bananas and monkeys, you know."

She sniffed into a lavender-scented handkerchief as she glared at a nearby acacia tree. "You've seen each other on a few occasions now, during which you completely captured his attention. What more could you want? I only had one conversation with your father before we were betrothed, and look how well that turned out."

"Yes, indeed," I muttered just as Mr. Elkhart appeared on the patio.

Mama dug her elbow into my side. "How handsome he is, Lilly, and how fashionably dressed. Go on, child."

She continued providing advice, but I didn't hear the rest of it. Mr. Elkhart strolled through the crowd, his every movement strong and graceful, his dark eyes fixed on me, a smile brightening his features. Only when he was standing before me did I notice the nervous twitch of his hands.

"Well, I'm going for a drink then," Mama said as she waddled away, pinching my arm as she did.

The flush in my cheeks deepened, and it was all I could do to keep my chin up. "Is everything all right?" I asked.

"It was a small pest control issue," he replied.

I sighed at the warm depth of his voice. "That's lovely."

His eyebrows rose. "I'm glad you think so. Shall we take a turn in the garden?"

It didn't matter there was hardly a garden, only untidy grass, thorn trees and wild bushes inhabited by all manner of nasty insects and noisy birds. Just being with him transformed the savage landscape into a paradise. Stepping off the patio, we meandered along a dusty path and circumambulated the house.

Of what we spoke I couldn't say. The melodic tones of his voice obliterated the need to understand anything but this: he and I walked arm in arm. Every time I glanced up, I found his warm gaze meeting mine. Eventually words ceased, leaving only the tread of our shoes against the rustling grass.

"Miss Steward," he finally spoke as he stepped into my path and stood before me with an unearthly stillness.

"Yes," I whispered, hardly able to breathe as he grasped my pale, shivering hands in his firm, dark ones.

"Surely you must be aware of my sentiments toward you," he murmured. When I remained mute, he chewed his lower lip. "At least, I hope you are, and that you might return my affections."

The skin of my hands tingled, distracting me. My lungs could barely draw enough air, and a lightheadedness threatened to overwhelm me. "Yes," I said, the word strangled by the constriction in my throat.

As if he suffered from the same affliction, he coughed and continued, "I would like to discuss the matter with your parents. But before I do, I wish to have your approval."

"Oh," I said.

His finely arched eyebrows rose in silent inquiry.

"Oh!" I gushed. "Yes. Yes, of course."

His posture relaxed, and he smiled. "Sweet lady, you've made me the happiest man. I can only now hope your parents will grant us consent."

Only when he raised my hands to his lips did I realize this wasn't a dream. "They will," I reassured him, imagining Mama's reaction. "It will all be marvelous. Won't Beatrice be amazed when I tell her." I half-turned toward the patio where guests mingled and chatted, the murmur of their conversations intertwining with the buzzing of insects.

"I... I didn't think you and your cousin were very close," Mr. Elkhart said. Something in his tone caused me to spin around. His eyebrows scrunched over his straight nose, and he was again biting his lower lip.

"Well, we did grow up together," I said, marveling at the rapidity of his changing moods. "She's like a sister to me. I couldn't imagine a wedding without her presence." I stopped babbling, unsure why I was praising Beatrice to him. "Whatever is the matter, Mr. Elkhart? You've paled."

Shaking his head, he tightened his grip on my hands. "Think nothing of it. It's the emotions of this momentous evening. I must leave you but I will pass by your home tomorrow evening to meet with your parents."

"Where are you going now?" I demanded, sulking at the prospect of his departure. Hadn't he just returned from attending to some task?

"An errand," he said.

"Another one?"

Sighing, he nodded. "It's somewhat urgent, otherwise I would never leave your side."

Thus mollified, I allowed him to escort me to the patio, after which he disappeared.

TIBERIUS

Like a sister.

Snarling, I spread my wings across the night, the speed of my passage creating a fierce wind around me. Fiercer still were my bitter thoughts. Why had I imagined I could break apart Miss Steward's family? Would her sister-like cousin forgive me? As I visualized myself on my knees, begging the paranormal investigator to return to the party with me, a growl rumbled through my chest. What would I do if she refused or threatened to tell the Stewards my secret?

It didn't matter: by the time I returned to the cave, Miss Knight was gone.

How she'd managed to scale the cliff below the cave was beyond me. Hissing, I flew low over the treetops, skimming across the thick, interwoven branches. Even with my keen night vision and sense of smell, I couldn't trace her whereabouts. Hoping none of the carnivorous forest creatures had devoured her, I at last abandoned the search and returned to the Hardinge mansion.

The next day was a torment. Every time the front door opened, I expected either news of Miss Knight's messy demise or the arrival of a constable coming to arrest me. By evening, I couldn't leave the house fast enough, and arrived at the Steward residence promptly after supper. Standing next to a beaming Miss Steward, I turned my attention to her parents, breathed deeply and stuttered my request.

"Oh, oh, oh! What delightful news, what happy times, what joy, what rapture, what a delight!" Mrs. Steward shrieked before collapsing into a chair.

Mr. Steward was less susceptible to such theatrics and extended a hand to me. "Congratulations, my fine fellow," he said. "You've brought us great joy and removed from my shoulders a tedious burden."

"Mr. Steward," Mrs. Steward snapped.

"Oh, I wasn't referring to our daughter being tedious or a burden," Mr. Steward hastily amended. "Rather, I was recalling our shared concern over the lack of suitable prospects for her."

Mrs. Steward huffed, her eyes narrowed.

My grin was wide enough to cause my cheeks to ache, but I didn't stop smiling until a movement caught my attention. Her face pale, Miss Knight entered the room and muttered a barely civil greeting to me before joining the family around the coffee table.

While Mrs. Steward pressed her daughter for details on my proposal, I couldn't stop staring at Miss Knight. How had she survived? And why hadn't she told the Stewards of her misadventures?

After a few moments, Miss Knight asked, "Lemon water, anyone?" Sounding out of breath, she moved to a table across the room.

"Let me assist you," I offered and joined her, my hands clenched as I wondered how to thank her for her discretion.

Before I could apologize for stranding her in the cave, she glared at me and whispered, "What's wrong with you?"

"What?" I asked.

Huffing, she said, "Why should I allow your relationship with my cousin to continue?"

My throat constricted. Would she reveal my secret? How would Miss Steward look upon me if she knew the truth?

"Not to mention your plan to toss me onto the next outbound

ship."

"At least I wasn't planning on tossing you into the ocean," I pointed out before adding, "You need not worry about my plans now. How could I inflict such harm on the family that will soon be mine?"

"Hardly reassuring," she muttered. "Lilly will find out eventually, you know. I'm sure the news will horrify her."

I forced a chuckle even as my breath hitched. "Let's hope she can forgive me then." Pausing, I lowered my voice further. "What news of the evil spirit? Have there been more murders?"

Miss Knight glanced at the happy party. Mrs. Steward was describing in detail how the wedding plans should proceed. "No. But if I'm correct on this matter, and I usually am, we don't have much time. It will soon seek out another victim."

Only then did I realize she was staring at her cousin, my fiancee. My chest constricted.

"Let me assist you," I said, the joy of a few moments ago overtaken by a quaking in my limbs.

She turned her yellow gaze to me and studied my countenance as if seeking to verify my intentions. Whatever she saw must have satisfied her, for she said, "Very well. I'm meeting someone later this evening who can help trap the spirit. Until then, could you flap around this house when everyone's asleep? I've been keeping guard over Lilly but while I'm away..."

"Consider it done," I breathed out before forcing a smile. "Who better to guard against a demon than another demon?"

"Indeed," she said. As she turned to leave, she glanced over her shoulder and said, "Don't think I'm finished with you."

"Do with me as you must," I said, "but protect Miss Steward."

"I intend to," she retorted.

LILLY

Not surprising, I couldn't sleep. What a marvelous evening it had been! Eventually, I abandoned my bed and went outside to walk off my energy around the large tree overshadowing the courtyard. Leafy branches rustled against each other. A sweet perfume drifted on a breeze from the Angel Trumpets near the outhouse. A night bird fluttered overhead but when I gazed up, I could see only stars.

"Mrs. Lilly Elkhart," I murmured, meandering toward the Angel Trumpets. "How lovely."

"Yes," a voice hissed by my ear.

Spinning about, I saw only our small, stone house and the large tree looming over it.

"Who's there," I whispered.

"Your new master," came the reply before my head thrummed with pain, and darkness overwhelmed me.

TIBERIUS

If my giant bat form could smile, it would have. Floating above the house, I watched Miss Steward exit the building and wander closer to the outhouse. My pointed ears detected every sweet word, and my heart cherished every one of them. Only when she glanced upward did I swerve out of sight, allowing her privacy as I watched for any sign of threat.

Moments passed. Only the creak and shiver of branches, mingled with the occasional call of a hyena or lion, filled the silence.

The silence.

Where was the crunch of her shoes against the soil, or the rustle of her housecoat across the tops of the grass? Despite the risk of being seen, I flew over the courtyard, hovering just above the tree branches.

Miss Steward wasn't there.

I glided closer to the outhouse and the Angel Trumpets. Their perfume blocked out all other scents but my hearing was unaffected.

She was gone.

Shrieking, I flapped higher and flew ever-larger concentric circles around the house. Nothing stirred.

Only when my flight took me over the forest did I notice a flutter of clothing. Miss Steward was staggering toward the cave-riddled cliff as if intoxicated, alternatively whimpering and growling. Then she disappeared.

Flying further ahead, I found an opening in the trees where I could descend and shift into human form. Cursing every lost moment, I ran back to where I'd last seen her. Thorns snagged at my dinner jacket, vines slapped at my face, and thick roots tried to trip me. When I reached the spot where she had been, I spun around, searching for any indication of her fate as my heartbeat thundered in my ears.

A faint glow lured me through the bramble to the entrance of a shallow cave. I slipped to the side of the opening and peered around.

A small fire crackled, washing the cave walls with a watery orange. A human form leaped toward the flames, its head flopping. It was Miss Steward. Her eyes rolled about, white replacing color, and her jaw hung slack. Drool slathered around her mouth. Her hands tugged at her filthy housecoat.

Whatever demon inhabited her body hissed and snarled, "Submit."

The voice altered slightly, and she whined, "No, please stop." Her eyes rolled forward to reveal contracted pupils.

"Miss Steward, my love, it's me," I said, stepping into the cave. "Fight it."

Miss Steward shook her head from side to side, tangled curls whipping about her. "Leave," she ordered in a garbled voice even as her eyes widened with fear, a plea shining out to me.

"You're hurting her," I said, my teeth gritting.

"She's mine," the creature replied, a maniacal grin distorting Miss Steward's face.

Growling, I said, "A demon to fight a demon." Forgoing caution, I welcomed the shift. In a rush of energy that left every nerve and limb tingling, I snapped into my Popobawa form. The demon inhabiting Miss Steward shrieked as I towered above, my wings wide, my talons clicking and scratching against stone. I snarled, hardly noticing when the demon vacated its victim and vanished, leaving Miss Steward to collapse onto the floor.

As I loomed over her, she gazed up at me and screamed.

"It's all right, Miss Steward, you're safe," I said but only snorting, hissing and growling echoed through the cave.

I flapped my wings and shuffled backward. The human part of my mind thought, 'Leave her. Let her believe the forest is home to giant bats.'

Oh, the temptation. But Miss Knight had been correct: eventually my wife would learn the truth.

No sooner had I come to my decision than I shifted again. With a crack of bones, a snap of skin and a flutter of wings, I stood before Miss Steward in my human form.

"Forgive me," I spluttered as I sank to my knees.

"You..." It came out more as a gasp. Her lips quivered, her cheeks paled, as she stared at me.

"I'm so sorry I deceived you." Closing my eyes, I sighed, accepting the truth of her rejection. At least she was safe. Miss Knight would take care of the demon, and Miss Steward would find another love.

Choking on the thought and unable to look at her, I said, "We haven't announced our engagement, so there is no need to explain your reasons for ending the relationship. And…"

"What are you saying, Mr. Elkhart?" Miss Steward interrupted, her voice strained.

"Well, you'll be canceling the wedding, I presume," I said, daring to glance up.

"You presume too much," she said with a sniff.

She sorted out her housecoat, disentangling her legs from its folds as she attempted to stand. My mouth gaped open as she waved a hand at me. Leaping up, I strode over, took her hand and helped her stand.

Shivering, Miss Steward crossed her arms over her chest, gazed at me and whispered, "My mind is rather addled at the moment but… Did you really just turn into a bat?"

Gulping, I nodded.

"I thought as much." Inhaling deeply and peering into my eyes, she asked, "You're not a vampire, are you? Because I have no intention of spending my days in a coffin."

"No, I'm not," I said, wondering when she would come to her senses, scream and run away.

Shrugging, she lowered her arms and said, "Well, then, I see no reason why the wedding can't proceed, for my feelings haven't shifted." Pausing, she tilted her head to one side. "Even if you can."

Clutching her soft, slender hands in mine, I raised them to my lips. Inhaling deeply, I savored her perfume, her beauty, her forgiving heart while words of gratitude and endearment swirled through my mind. Before I could think, do or say anything, she frowned at me. My smile and my heart both faltered. She'd realized her mistake. I braced myself for the end of my happiness.

Wagging a finger at me, she said, "I hope you don't expect me to live in a cave."

So saying, she stood on her tiptoes and raised her lips to mine, thus ending one conversation and starting an entirely different one.

The End

Vered Ehsani lives in Kenya with her family and various other animals. Pick up two free books and a photo album of Victorian Nairobi by visiting http://veredehsani.co.za/free-books/

Cover by Author.

Reap

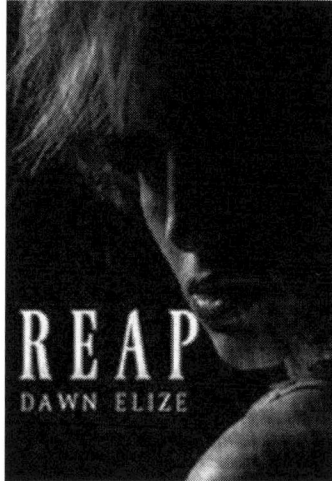

Dawn Elize

Dawn Elize's first love was reading, and writing soon came after, when the power of words overtook her mind, creating beautiful characters. When she's not buried in a book, she can be found exploring the world and helping with animals.

Reap is a tale of what happens when Death dies.

***

Death was gone.

The shrieking cries of the souls had ripped apart the barrier around Leith, hauling him awake. He went into the Abyss; a resting place, and the world between the humans and the next. Once a peaceful passageway, it had now become flooded with suffering souls, clawing around for a sense of peace.

A new Death was needed.

Being a messenger from the beginning of time, Leith had found the last Death, and now his time had come again. The soul had to be perfectly cursed. A daunting task to do because all souls were purified upon birth.

***

Below, in the human world, Rei was staring at his uneaten meal, head bowed, clenching his fists on his lap as his father mocked him. Cursed him for being born and not his dead twin brother. Cursed him for making his mother suffer in agony.

Unable to bear it any longer, the boy jumped to his feet, the chair skidding back with a loud screech, silencing them. His shoulders shaking, he spun around and bolted from the house, slamming the door behind him.

He stomped around the dim alleyway, the flickering lampposts casting his lurking shadow above him. As he kicked aside the garbage with each stride, he rounded another alley, the stone walls protruding high above him, blocking out the sight of the darkening sky. That was when he caught sight of the figure standing a few meters from him.

It was a dying man.

He clutched the stone wall, his body shaking as his dark eyes locked on Rei. A large, bloody stain on the front of his white shirt gave away his impending death. As the man slowly slumped to the littered ground, he reached out his hand to Rei, his mouth open as he tried desperately to whisper a plea for help.

Rei's hand latched on his own thumping chest, a ringing sound vibrating in his ears as he took a step back. He couldn't be here. He ran.

He had bolted back to his house, his heart pounding, not willing to look back or to stop. Slamming the door to his room, he slid to the floor, avoiding everyone as he buried his head in his hands, trying to hold back his broken sobs. He had watched someone's life pass away in front of his eyes. Something that would haunt him for years.

Sadly, it wouldn't be the last death. Fifteen years later, he had witnessed ten dead people. He had found them all unexpectedly, either coming home from work or when going to get groceries. He couldn't help any of them as terror gripped him, always making him run for his own life.

The only form of happiness he ever had in his life was his girlfriend, Eve. She had become the love of his life and the only one who ever truly believed in him. He hadn't gotten the courage to tell her about the deaths he witnessed, but she seemed to understand and comfort him when he had nightmares or when the guilt robbed him of any sane thought.

The day of their second anniversary, he had returned to the apartment and found her waiting at the dining table, a whole meal cooked and ready. His stomach had growled at the smell as he hugged the life out of her.

"Where would you be if it wasn't for me?" she asked, smiling.

That might have been the last smile he saw on her face. They argued after that about his family, making her storm out of the door. He had buried his hands in his hair, massaging his throbbing temples. She wanted him to make peace with his family. He couldn't.

Forty minutes later, he received a call. He fell to the floor, his heart crying as he threw up the food. He knew she was dead. It was an accident. One he didn't witness. One that was even more painful.

She was gone.

It was always the same. Tragedy after tragedy. Over again. How much more did he have to suffer? When could he get happiness? He got on his knees and bent his head, his words breaking out into sobs as he cried desperately for her to make it out alive. That she would beat the fate surrounding him.

***

Rei's eyes felt heavy as they flickered open, staring at a white wall. His head throbbed as if he had gotten hit with bricks. Confusion muddled his senses as he sat up, trying to understand where he was. Had he gotten drunk and passed out somewhere?

An old man was standing in front of him. He had a resigned look on his face, experience engraved through the slight wrinkles and the curve of his lips. His gray hair was styled backward, adding a touch of elegance as his black eyes studied him.

"Where am I?" Rei croaked out, as he stood up.

It was a white room, with no furniture. Only marble white walls. He rubbed his temples, unable to remember how he ended up here. A chilling shiver ran down his spine, fear making his body tense up. There was something *wrong* with the place.

"Rei Wilt," the man spoke. "I'm Leith. You are dead."
Dead.

He stumbled back, clutching his chest. Terror gripped him as his hands trembled. "What?" he gasped out.

The old man clasped his hands, hardening his expression. "Death is another part of life. Do not be afraid. Your human memories will fade. You were a cursed child. A fate that makes you qualified for a job."

Rei was stunned in disbelief. "A job?" he stammered out, aghast.

"Yes, there is a need for a new Death. A grim reaper," he said, in a steady voice. "We need a pure, cursed soul, which is yours."

Rei stared at him in frozen shock, unable to speak.

"You shouldn't be surprised. Death has followed you everywhere. This is your fate, Rei, should you choose it to be. You are fit for this task."

Rei's memories were slowly returning. He recalled the only person he truly cared about. A hollow feeling clawed at his chest. "Eve? Can I see her? Is she dead?" he broke out.

Leith shook his head, his eyes falling. "She is dead, sadly. You also cannot visit the dead. However, since the old Death is gone, Eve's soul remains in the Abyss, waiting to be reaped and guided to the afterlife. She is suffering. You can end it if you become Death."

She was dead and in pain. Two things he never wanted for the love of his life. "Please," he begged, his body trembling. "Give her peace. I'll do anything," he croaked.

Could he become Death? The creature of nightmares. His nightmares, ever since it had followed him. Was this his curse?

Sensing his thoughts, Leith exhaled. "Death is not what you make it out to be. It is not something you escape. It is within all humans and it makes up who you are. Do not be afraid to embrace it."

Rei pondered his words. There was a gnawing feeling in his chest, fear creeping through his veins. He realized this room, this atmosphere—it was meant to calm him. To ease him into being Death. Leith was observing him, so Rei tried to conceal his worry.

"Come," Leith said, turning sideways to reveal a door. "We shall go see Eve."

Rei's eyes widened at his words but he trailed behind Leith as he walked through the door. He shot a quick glance at the old man, observing him. He seemed human but a twisting feeling in his stomach knew he was not. There was a bitter taste in his mouth. His life had come to this. Dying and becoming Death.

When they had passed through the door, there was darkness all around for a moment. Rei's feet felt lighter, as if he was floating, unable to find a steady grounding. Suddenly, there was a burst of light. He squeezed his eyes shut, raising his hands in front of his face.

Hesitantly, he peeked through his fingers, seeing a glow of light from all around, small orbs lighting up. Some red, some white, some dark blue.

"These are the souls," Leith spoke, standing beside him. "They are trapped here until Death guides them onward." He paused, gesturing to an orb. "That is Eve."

The air was knocked out of Rei's lungs and he struggled to breathe. Eve's hue was vibrant, dark blue, blinding his vision. He could sense Eve's soul crying out in pain; a scream that made him clench in agony. The sensation of terror rippled through him.

"How can I help her?" he cried out to Leith.

"You have to become Death. It is a challenge. A tough one. Are you ready to take it on?"

In his desperation, Rei nodded, willing to do whatever it took. Eve would not suffer—that was a promise he made to himself. Leith guided him towards the door again. However, this time they didn't go back to the room. They were back on Earth.

They were standing between two skyscrapers, in a chaotic city that was buzzing with noise; somewhere he had never been before. Across the street, Rei made out the outline of a man leaning against the back of an old building, his head thrown back. He turned to Leith who had entwined his hands, watching.

"Is he the one dying? What do I do?" Rei asked.

"No, he's not the one." He gestured with his head to the edge of the building. A boy crept out of the shadows, watching the man with wide eyes. Rei's body jolted. "You need to touch him. Guide him. It will come naturally to you."

Rei's mouth fell, a heavy breath escaping him. The boy looked about seven years old—he was too young. How could he kill him for something so unfair?

The boy moved a step closer to the struggling man. The man, spotting him, took out a gun from his pocket. And shot him. The loud noise rattled Rei's eardrums as he watched the boy fall to the floor, his hand outstretched as the last message that he came in peace.

Rei clutched his forehead with trembling hands. He couldn't do it. He couldn't watch anymore. Letting out an agonized yell, he spun around, running away. Stopping at the side of a building, he slid to the floor, his head aching as his ears rang, the sound of the gun replaying over again.

Leith appeared beside him, taking in the sight of the broken man. "Death is not the end. It is painless. It is a soothing calm to the misery. But, it is also a new beginning. Death leads to another life. You should not feel terrible for granting that to another being. The boy's time had come and his soul needs to move on."

Rei spoke in a cracked tone, "What about those you leave behind, then?"

"They will move on from the loss. That is a part of life, and it is the way the world works."

"What happened to the old Death?" he asked, wishing he didn't have to do this.

"He has moved on and joined the souls. It must have been his time."

Death had died. What an irony, Rei thought. Now, it was his job. He thought of Eve; her vivid blue soul aching away in pain. The boy's soul must have joined with her. Suffering. It wasn't right. Standing up, he braced his shoulders, knowing what to do.

Leith watched him as he began walking back to where the boy was. Bending, his face scrunched up in pain, his hand reached out slowly and closed the boy's dead eyes. The soul—white and pure—had come back from the abyss, hovering over its body. The moment Rei's touch connected with the boy's, the soul vanished.

***

Rei was back at the white, marble room as he stared at the walls. The boy's soul was in peace. It had moved on. To a better place. The soul had used Rei as a guide or a portal, bouncing off him towards another world. The boy was terrified at first, but then a sense of calm had descended on him, spreading through his body.

"Why did you pick me to be Death? I thought being Death was a curse for doing badly in life?" Rei asked, his head spinning with too many thoughts.

Leith let out a weary sigh, his shoulders aging. "You may not have killed anyone else, but you did kill someone. Yourself."

Rei stiffened. "I—I committed suicide?"

"That is the fate of a cursed soul. I had found five of you. None of them could pull through. It isn't over yet. Death isn't easy, but it is a part of life," he said.

"I'm Life?"

"You are as much Life as you are Death."

Rei became quiet, acknowledging the truth behind his words. He hadn't done much when he was living; perhaps he could do better now that he was Death.

"I want to help Eve," he said, resolve in his tone. "I'm ready."

Leith observed Rei, sensing a new-found strength brewing within him. He had understood the truth and was ready to take on the heavy duty. He would make the old Death—Jakob—proud. He was ready.

***

Walking forward, the door appeared again as Leith gestured for Rei to follow him. They were back in the room with the souls. Rei immediately spotted Eve's soul as he reached out a hand, unconsciously craving her presence.

But, on touching her soul, she let out an agonizing scream, ripping his heart apart. He took a step back, his chest heaving as Eve stopped the moment he let go. Leith placed a hand on his arm, trying to calm him down.

"It happens when the soul has been here too long," he said. "Touch it again and connect."

"No," Rei shook his head, taking another step back. "No, she's in pain. I bring her pain. She's suffering because of me. I—I can't do this."

Helplessness tearing him apart, he spun around, bolting from the room. Running like he always had. Instead of being back in the white marble room, he was back on Earth. Back to where he had lived a terrible life.

***

He wandered through the familiar alleyways, eventually ending up in front of his family house. A place he hadn't been to in years. He could hear crying inside. Were they really mourning his death? He couldn't think straight; his stomach shifting uneasily as his body tensed up. He walked away, down the same road he had witnessed his first murder. A place he had never visited again.

His throat swelled up as his fingers trembled. No-one could see him but his emotions were bursting. Reaching the same alley, his chest tightened as he blew out a misty breath, the vivid image of the bleeding man appearing behind his closed eyes.

Instead, there was a teenage girl.

She looked to be around fifteen years old as she sat slumped on the filthy floor, crying loudly, her face buried in her hands. The same agonizing scream which Eve let out burst through his eardrums again as if this girl's soul was the one doing so. Rei took a step closer to her. She couldn't see him anyway.

Suddenly, she took out a gun from her pocket. Rei's heart pounded as his head spun. *No.* With trembling hands, the girl placed the gun next to her head, releasing loud, broken breaths as tears ran down her dirty cheeks.

Helplessness overpowered him as Rei pushed forward, reaching out to stop her. It was a pointless gesture as she released the gun, her eyes now gazing at him, dead. She was gone.

Immediately, he sensed her soul as it began to form, pieces of screams and pain merging together. Tears slid down Rei's cheeks as he gazed at the body. He wished he could have prevented it. Suicide was not the right way to die. He knew it better than anybody else.

When the soul had fully merged, Rei reached out and guided her. Showing her another world. Letting her go. He had taken on the role of Death. He would not let Death go to waste, just like Life.

***

Suddenly, Leith appeared beside him. He gazed at the body and looked at the last essence of the soul. Their eyes held each other's as Leith took in Rei's change of heart.

"Are you ready?" he asked, quietly.

Rei nodded. "I am."

Leith's face broke into a smile. "That's good to hear. I was worried for a moment, but something about your soul was meant to be. Come, now, let's finish the job."

"Wait," Rei said, his eyes focused intently on the girl's body. An idea occurred to him. "I want to stop these. Suicides. It can be prevented."

Leith shook his head adamantly, his eyebrows tensing. "That is the human's choice. You have no control over these deaths. How could you possibly prevent it?"

Rei reached out his hand, placing it over his chest. "I felt it. Her scream right before she died."

"You did?" Leith asked, eyes widening. That had never happened before.

He nodded, a solemn expression appearing in his eyes. A surge of power rippled through Rei, wrapping its arms around him. It was warm, enchanting his soul, spreading throughout his body. Leith gazed at him in awe.

"I know what to do. You said I was Death but also Life. When a suicide happens next, I shall be there. As Life. And I shall stop it. They will live until their rightful time," he announced.

***

"And that is how Rei came to be Death. A different one. There were many Deaths I have met. One which wanted a scythe to reap souls, one which wanted to look like a monster because he felt so within. But, Rei was the only one so far who used his abilities the way he has. He was a great soul," Leith said, smiling at the young man.

The man, Hano, remembered a distant memory. "It was he who saved me before, wasn't it?"

Leith nodded. "It was him who chose you. He lived long enough to pick the next heir of Death. A rightful one."

Hano gazed around the colorful marble room. "But what happened afterward with Eve? Where did Rei go?"

Leith smiled. "He returned here and he sent Eve to beyond. Just like he did with all the other souls. Now, he has joined them among the stars. Still guiding the way for those lost in the darkness."

The End

For more stories by Dawn, follow her on:

Watt pad - DoveReign

Check out her Instagram and Twitter @DoveReign

Cover by Author.

Second Chance

Seb Jenkins

Seb Jenkins is a 20-year-old student from Bedfordshire, England. His recent works are described as dark, gritty, and atmospheric which he attributes to a lifetime of immersing himself in endless horror books and gore-fuelled TV shows/films. When he isn't writing, you can find him banging his head slowly against a brick wall, or desperately trying to think of that best-selling idea he came up with at 3am last night.

As of 2015, Seb is currently attending the University of Kent to study journalism and hopes to carve a career out of his passion for writing.

In this story, what happens when your life is taken from you? Is there really an after life? Once you die, is there any way back? After her brutal murder, Tara Mulligan finds out the hard way, and somehow must find her way back home.

***

Prologue

Second chances are rare. Not everyone can trust enough to give them, and not everyone is smart enough to take them.

Sometimes people who don't deserve them have one dropped into their lap, while those who crave one sit in silence.

What if someone, somewhere was watching out for those who really need one, for those who deserve one, for those with nothing left. What if?

***

Tara Mulligan's hands plunged into the soapy water beneath, her fingers immediately engulfed by the cascading icebergs of bubbles. Her vision of the sharp knives and pointed forks lurking below was clouded, as was her awareness of what fatal events lay but minutes away.

A few metres back, hovering beside the sofa, Tara watched herself in awe. Such a mundane task of washing up became a wondrous event, just for those few seconds. It was life; pure and simple life. They do say that a near-death experience makes you appreciate the little things, even gives you a whole new outlook on life. Well, Tara now knew exactly what that meant as she gazed upon her past self.

For this was the night that Tara died.

The Planned Proposal

Tara pinged her yellow rubber gloves back towards the sink with a satisfying snap, before spinning around and sliding back into her room. Her socks glided softly across the wooden floor of her apartment, coming to a halt perfectly in front of her wardrobe.

She was in extremely high spirits, her underlying nerves temporarily halted by the half bottle of wine sloshing around in her stomach. A solitary blue dress was draped carefully over a hanger, the silk edges curving down like calm waves on an evening sea. She slipped into the expensive fabric, taking enjoyment from the way it perfectly fit her body as she zipped up the back. She gave her hips a little shimmy to ensure that the material had just enough give, before slipping into a pair of matching heels.

"Shit!" she cursed, clip-clopping her way across the room to her bedside drawer and retrieving a small black box.

Tara held it delicately in her hand, as if the slightest movement could crush it. She ran her fingers across the seam and flipped the lid open, revealing a simple but elegant gold ring.

The band glistened under her bedroom light, just about illuminating a winding calligraphed inscription on the inside of the ring.

'Be happy- Mum'

Her boyfriend's mother had insisted upon the inscription as part of her blessing when she'd approved of the proposal. She had known that she had little time left after fighting cancer for years, and this was her way of being there on her son's wedding day.

She actually passed away only two weeks after Tara had gone to see her.

They had been very similar women in truth, both unwilling to conform to stereotypes or what was expected of them. She had been thrilled when Tara had informed her of her unconventional proposal plans.

Tara clicked the box shut and deposited it safely within her handbag just as three loud knocks echoed around the apartment.

She took one deep breath before striding towards the door, her heels clicking on the hard wood floor. She'd told her boyfriend to be here at seven, but knowing how early he always was, she made sure to be ready half an hour before.

She'd also made sure to clean her little apartment as best she could for the occasion, making a change from the usual life of squalor.

"Coming!" Tara called as she slid back the chain. "I knew you wouldn't be able to keep to my timings!"

However, as the door swung open, Tara wasn't greeted by her loving boyfriend, but instead a hooded stranger.

"Can I help you?" she asked confusedly.

"I'm sure you can," the man growled, planting a strong arm on the door and forcing his way in.

Tara went to scream but found her mouth muffled by a large gloved hand before even a peep could escape. Her muffled cries died in the evening air, as the stranger slammed the door shut behind him.

"I want all your money and jewellery in the next minute, and maybe, just maybe I won't hurt you," he whispered into her ear.

His warm breath spread across her face like a cloud of foul stench, engulfing her in a frozen state of shock.

"Is that clear?" he clarified, running a hand along her arm.

Tara nodded, her eyes stretched wide with uncontrollable fear.

"And you promise not to scream?"

Tara nodded again, calming herself down as best she could as the hand was removed from her face.

"HELP! SOMEONE HELP ME PLEASE!" she screamed, planting a powerful right hook onto the bridge of the stranger's nose as she did so.

Mrs. Faversham in the apartment below had gone on holiday a few days before, and Tara resided on the top floor of the block.

No-one could hear her. No-one would come.

"Little bitch!" he seethed, bundling her to the floor and shoving his hand forcefully back over her mouth, taming her screams into whimpers.

Tara cursed her pride, part of her was screaming to give him what he wanted, but the other half was determined not to roll over. She was stronger than this.

The man snatched up her fallen handbag and rifled through it as fast as he could, very aware of the fact that Tara's screams could have alerted any number of people.

"What have we got here?" he smiled, withdrawing the ring box and flicking it open. "Looks like this would have set you back a pretty penny!"

Tara tensed every muscle in her body, thrashing her limbs around as much as she could to free herself, but her body was pinned to floor.

Her throat was already hoarse with screamed protests, all of which went unheard, masked by the gloved muffler.

"You're lucky this is the only thing you're losing," the man spat as he released Tara and fled back towards the door.

"NOOO!" Tara yelled, planting a hand around his ankle and yanking him back.

"Get the hell off me, you little bitch!"

"Please, not that, anything but that!"

Tara stumbled to her feet, desperately trying to retrieve the box, but to no avail. She cracked a sharp slap across the man's face before pummelling his chest with her fists and tearing the hood from his face.

His eyes were dark, his pupils and irises almost one merging shade of black. His shaggy brown hair dropped over his face and a thin scar ran up the left side of his face.

"You did this," he said simply, as he withdrew a blade from his waistband and drove it deeply into her stomach, before he wrenched the door open and escaped into the night

Tara crumpled to the floor, her hands clasped around the wound, desperately trying to stem the tidal wave of crimson pouring onto the blue of her dress.

Her eyes, once wide with panic, began to flicker shut as she faded into the welcoming arms of death.

Second Chance

Tara's eyes opened once more, with blinding white light flooding her very existence. It flowed through her body, intertwined with her muscles, and took control of her very bones. Once the light cleared, Tara's body was rising through the air as she stared down upon her own lifeless corpse.

A pool of blood had now framed her body, flowing into the cracks between the wooden floorboards as it trickled around the entire room.

Her eyes were wide open, but dead, of that there was no question. Any trace of life had flooded out that gaping wound, leaving behind only an empty vessel.

She couldn't help but think about her boyfriend. He would surely arrive any minute now to find the love of his life dead, sprawled across the floor. Of all the happy memories, she would leave a legacy of hurt and pain.

Tara had little time to dwell further on this thought as her body began to rise once more, through the ceiling, above the apartment block, rising faster and faster. The world whirred past her as she sped through the air, the people, cars and buildings soon becoming mere dots as she crashed through the clouds.

Then there was nothing. The world was replaced by light, pure white light.

"Hello Tara," a mysterious ethereal voice spoke softly.

Tara turned to face her host, her mind flooded with confusion and anxiety, "Hello? W-where am I?"

"You are nowhere," the voice continued.

A small, almost spherical, cloud floated down gracefully, stopping just in front of Tara's face.

"What do you mean n-nowhere? I have to be somewhere!" Tara stammered.

"You are between reality and...what comes after. You are nowhere."

"Then why am I here? Am I...dead?"

"Death is a fate set in stone, yours is still to be decided."

Tara was more confused than ever, "What does that mean?"

"Your life was stolen from you, your death was not by design."

"So what?" Tara scoffed. "That happens every single day."

"And every single day those who have lost are given a second chance," the cloud explained.

"What do you mean a second chance?"

"If you wish, you will be sent back to live your time again. You will appear in spirit form fiveinutes before your death, the rest is up to you."

"Spirit form? So, like a ghost?"

"Indeed."

"But, I won't be able to touch anything, how can I stop him without being able to touch him?" Tara asked.

"You will take the form of a spirit, but a spirit can always bond with a physical body, as long as the body is willing."

"So, I have to convince my former self to let my current self join bodies, making one future self? This is fucking crazy! What if I fail?"

"Then you shall embrace death, just as everyone else does."

"Then what? Does this mean there is an afterlife?"

"What's beyond is unclear."

"What the hell does that mean?" Tara demanded.

"What's beyond is unclear."

Tara grumbled under her breath before finally exclaiming, "Okay, I'm ready."

"Then you shall commence your second chance. Good luck."

And with that, Tara's eyes were once again filled with blinding light.

***

Tara Mulligan's hands plunged into the soapy water beneath, her fingers immediately engulfed by the cascading icebergs of bubbles. Her vision of the sharp knives and pointed forks lurking below was clouded, as was her awareness of what fatal events lay but minutes away.

A few metres back, hovering beside the sofa, Tara watched

herself in awe. Such a mundane task of washing up became a wondrous event, just for those few seconds. It was life; pure and simple life. They do say that a near-death experience makes you appreciate the little things, even gives you a whole new outlook on life. Well, Tara now knew exactly what that meant as she gazed upon her past self.

Tara glanced down at her spirit form which was clearly recognisable as a human figure, but beyond that all features were removed. She shone a bright shade of blue and hovered a few inches off the ground.

She knew she only had five minutes, no time to think things over any more. She'd just have to think as she went.

"Tara-" she began.

Her past self jumped out her skin, snatching up a knife from within the bubbles and spinning on her heels.

"Who's there?" she screamed, dropping the knife as soon as she spotted the ghost-like figure haunting her living room.

"Tara, don't panic. You are in danger, you have to listen to me!"

Her past self backed away, stumbling against the counters as she went, desperately trying to stay on her feet.

"W-w-what are you?" she stammered.

"I am you, a future you, and you have to listen to me!"

Past Tara screamed and continued to back away before making a sharp dart towards the front door.

"Your favourite colour is indigo!"

Her past self stopped, for a moment.

"Your father was called Steve, your Mother was Sarah. You grew up in London, you went to Victoria Grammar School, your childhood best friend was Kimberly Westfield!" Tara blurted.

Her past self turned back slowly.

"How do you know that stuff? What the hell are you?"

"I told you, I am you, from the future, and you are in danger!"

"No, no, no. Anyone could know that stuff, you could find that out anywhere. What is this, some kind of joke? Is this a projection? Is this you Danny?" she called out to the room.

"This is not a joke! I swear to you!"

"Oh okay, so you're my future self, right? I've always wondered what the future is like, are there flying cars?" her past self mocked, now clearly confident that it was a hoax.

"You have a ring in your desk drawer!" Tara yelled.

The smile vanished from her past self's face. "What did you just say?"

"*An engagement ring. You have an engagement ring in your top drawer, you're proposing tonight.*"

"How do you know that?" her past self probed. "Danny, did you find the ring?"

"*This isn't Danny for fuck's sake! This is me...you! We are the same person, please, we don't have much time!*"

"What's my favourite food?"

"*What?*"

"Well, if you are who you say you are, what's my favourite food?"

"*Your dad's lasagne.*"

Her past self stiffened up slightly before asking another question. "What was my first car?"

"*A purple Fiat Punto, second hand, with one long scratch down the right-hand side. You knocked one of the mirrors off on a trip to Manchester and had it replaced with a bright yellow one.*"

Past Tara's face went blank, still unable to process the reality of the situation. The only logical explanation was that this was a joke, but she was starting to believe that comforting idea less and less.

"Imaginary friend," she demanded.

"*Jimmy. He was a pet lion cub you had when you were five. He could talk and you went on adventures every day in your room. He had a red collar, with a blue tag.*"

"What the fuck is this? Danny! Danny come out now! This isn't funny anymore! I don't know how you know all this but I want it to stop now."

"*Tara, there is no Danny, this is real. I know it's hard to understand, but you have to listen to me. If you don't, in two minutes, you end up lying on that floor, in a pool of your own blood!*"

"I-I die?"

"*Yes, you die. A man tried to rob you, you fight back and he stabs you. I'm sorry.*"

"I don't believe you! Danny stop this now!" her past self sobbed, striding forward and throwing a hand through the glowing blue figure.

It was cold, freezing cold, and she couldn't just feel it in her hand. She felt it in her heart. As if they were connected somehow. She pulled her hand back out, staring up at the figure in shock and confusion.

"*You're pregnant.*"

"W-what did you say?"

"Six weeks gone. You're planning on telling Danny tonight, after you propose."

"How could you know that? I haven't told a soul, only I kno-"

"Only you know. Exactly. And I know because I am you, please, trust me."

Something in her past self's eyes changed. The fear and shock had disappeared, replaced by hope. She finally believed it, there were no other explanations.

"Once you remove the impossible, whatever remains, however improbable, must be the truth."

"My favourite quote," past Tara smiled.

"Now please, listen to me, he'll be here any moment."

"What do I have to do?" past Tara asked, throwing every inch of trust she had at this glowing blue woman floating in her apartment.

"We have to bond somehow. You have to accept me into your body, then we can live out a second chance together," Tara explained.

Her past self screwed up her face, "Bond? How the hell do I accept you?"

"I'm not sure, just shut your eyes and think it over and over?"

"Glad to see that we don't get a lot smarter in the future," past Tara smirked.

Tara laughed, "Good luck."

"You too."

They both shut their eyes and pictured their souls and bodies bonding, over and over again. At first nothing happened, but then, just as a knock at the door echoed through the room, Tara began to move.

Her spirit form floated towards her past body, completely out of her control, until it was mapped exactly on top. A blinding white light shone for a moment as the bodies rose into the air together and joined as one.

Tara fell to the ground in a heap. It was over, it was done. She stared upon her skin and clothes as if they were alien to her after living as a spirit. A second knock brought her mind crashing back down to earth.

Behind that door was her murderer, the one who had started all of this. The merging of soul and body had finished, she had done as she was told, she could easily hide behind the safety of the chained door and wait it out. But then what would happen? Maybe Danny would show up and face the same fate she had, or the stranger would move on to target someone completely different.

Despite surviving, Tara could never live with herself if she just let him leave. She snatched up a knife and a nearby rolling pin before darting towards the door, unlocking the chain and tearing it open.

"Can I help you?" she asked, before plunging the knife into the man's shoulder blade and cracking the wooden rolling pin into his temple.

Before even a yelp could escape his mouth, the man crashed down on the floor in a heap, knocked out cold.

Tara pulled out her mobile and dialled 999, just before her eyes were once again blinded by a powerful white light.

***

"You did well, Tara," the cloud figure exclaimed.

"What happens now?" Tara asked.

"You will be returned to your life to continue it as you please."

"But I won't remember any of this, right?"

"Why do you say that?"

"Well, I figured since I've never heard of this second chance deal, there's some kind of memory wipe involved?"

"You are a bright woman, Tara. I'm afraid this is true, any knowledge of the spirit world or the afterlife cannot be common fact among the living."

"I understand," Tara smiled warmly. "Thank you."

Epilogue

"What? Are you joking? Of course I will!" Danny screamed.

Tara gasped, "Seriously?"

"Yes, you idiot! Now get up and come here!" he yelled.

Tara jumped up from her position on one knee and flew into his tight embrace. Tears rolled down both of their cheeks as they stood there together, almost as if their souls and bodies had become one.

"Oh, and Danny, there's one more thing," Tara whispered into his ear. "You're going to be a Daddy."

***

Sometimes people who deserve a second chance are rewarded with one. Sometimes, those who take away other people's chances are punished.

What if someone up there is watching out and doing their part? What if?

The End

Where to find Seb:

Website: https://www.sebjenkins.co.uk/

Wattpad: https://www.wattpad.com/user/SebJenkins

Facebook: https://www.facebook.com/sebjenkins96

Amazon: https://www.amazon.co.uk/Life-After-Death-Seb-Jenkins-ebook/dp/B06XJR5HQ5/

Goodreads: https://www.goodreads.com/author/show/16585589.Seb_Jenkins

Cover by Celin Chen.

Aletheia's Truth

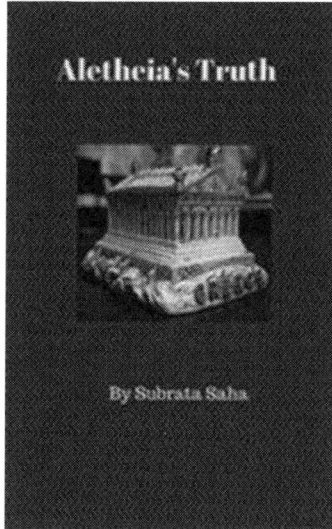

Subrata Saha

Subrata Saha is a writer and lives with her family in London. She had written a few books and is part of a writer group and has run book clubs. She is a keen reader and writing is her passion. She mainly loves creative fiction.

Short summary of Aletheia's Truth story

A young girl in Ancient Delphi has been pledged to the great God Apollo to be the next Oracle of Delphi. However she believes she is meant to be a healer at the Temple of Artemis at Ephesus. Will she defy Apollo and follow her own truth path?

Chapter 1

Aletheia looked out of her window and felt the warm summer breeze touch her face. She gazed out over the rugged terrain and looked over the bay of Mount Parnassus. The sky was a blue hue, and the sun shone overhead.

Aletheia sighed. She was wearing a simple gown of blue and her hair was braided up into the latest Grecian style, with gold bands to hold it in place. She was indeed very beautiful with dark brown hair and sea green eyes.

She was in deep thought over her destiny and her life. Thoughts that went beyond this world to the next. Thoughts that haunted her psyche every day and wanting to know the truth. The truth of who she actually was and where her path lay.

Having grown up in a rich, wealthy merchant's home, she was a humble, obedient daughter. This befitted her background and rank in Grecian society. She was close to both her parents.

When her mother was pregnant with her, she had a dream of the mythical Goddess Aletheia the Goddess of Truth. Aletheia loved her name and was proud to bear the name of a very beautiful Goddess.

Aletheia knew all about the mythical story of this Goddess. The Goddess was not as high ranking as the other Greek gods, but it was believed she was the daughter of Zeus. A virgin, who lived apparently at the bottom of a well because of her elusiveness. Other stories said she lived in the wilderness because untruths had now spread through human society. She may have been created by Prometheus from clay. Prometheus was then summoned by Zeus, and Dolos (the Gods apprentice and known as Trickery), used Prometheus's absence to fashion another replica clay piece of the Goddess. Unfortunately, the clay ran out, and he could not complete the Goddess's feet. Prometheus returned, and Dolos sat in his seat very much afraid. Prometheus was very impressed by Dolos's artistic skills and wanted to take credit not only for his sculpture but for Dolos's sculpture as well. Both the sculptures of the Goddesses were baked in a kiln and when they were finished Prometheus gave them life. The real Goddess Aletheia (Truth) walked with measured steps, but her twin Falsehood stayed where she was. Hence Truth would always prevail.

Our Aletheia stood looking out the window. Would her truth prevail like that of her Goddess 's namesake? She did not know the answer to that question as yet.

There was a knock on the door, and Aletheia snapped out of her daydream.

"Yes come in," she said. The wooden door opened and her father came into the room

"Aletheia, how are you doing my child?" her father asked her gently.

"I am fine, Father," said Aletheia.

Her father Aetios was one of the most prosperous men in Delphi. He had built a good business from the olive trade. Her brother Alcides would inherit the business one day and was already proving to be a willing apprentice in his father's trade.

They lived in a comfortable Greek home that kept them cool in the summer months.

Her father's house was build of stone, centred around a courtyard. The roof was tiled and two stories high. There was a kitchen, rooms for bathing, a dining area and a sitting area. The house was guarded by a strong gate. They had a few servants and guard dogs and horses.

"Are you looking forward to seeing Pythia tomorrow Aletheia?" asked her father.

"I don't know, Father," said Aletheia truthfully.

"It will be such an honor. You are after all her successor. You have been chosen since your birth. The Pythia predicted it," said Aetios.

"I wish I could have chosen my own destiny, Father. Not have it chosen for me."

Aetios looked at his daughter with empathy. "Aletheia, I thank the Gods for my beautiful family and the good prosperity that we enjoy. But you don't get something for nothing. You have been promised to the great Apollo, and we must honor that promise."

"I understand what you mean, Father, but I don't have the gift of foresight," said Aletheia.

"Once your initiation begins, you will have no problems with that. Trust in Pythia and trust in Apollo," said her father firmly.

Chapter 2

That night Aletheia tossed and turned in her bed. She was sweating profusely and felt her chest tightening. She was having a dream, and the palms of her hands were burning.

In her dream, she felt a force was leading her up some steps, through the stone columns into the inner sanctum of Apollo's temple. She tried desperately not to go in, but the force around her was stronger than her own will.

She felt like she was floating towards the inner womb of the temple, and then she heard them. They were hissing, and when she saw them, she gave out a silent scream. There were thousands and thousands of snakes, slithering over one another. They were green, yellow and red in colour and she realised that the Apollo Temple was truly the House of Snakes. She then looked up, and instead of seeing the statue of the great Apollo, she saw the God himself.

The real Apollo looked so handsome. He had no beard and looked young with long hair. He was not holding his lyre or bow or arrow as he usually did. He stared at her with a piercing look that went straight to her soul. This God had slain the Python in the inner sanctum of this temple with his bow and arrow for vengeance. Python had tried to prevent his mother, Leto from giving birth to Apollo and his twin sister Artemis. For that, Apollo took to his revenge. The Temple of Apollo was built on the dead remains of the Python, and the Pythia became the Oracle of Delphi who channelled Apollo's messages in phrases. Was Apollo going to kill her for doubting the path he'd chosen for her?

Aletheia woke up and realised she was safe in her home. Everything was quiet. She could hear the street dogs barking, but there was nothing to be afraid of - yet. Once she realised this, she lay back into her soft pillows.

***

The morning was bright as Aletheia, and her family made their way into the heart of the city of Delphi. Today was a celebration day, as the Pythia was going to announce her predictions to the people of Delphi and the world. Her own family was very excited by this prospect and today she would be presented to the priestess.

As her family's horse cart moved towards the temple, Aletheia had a good look at her birthplace.

Delphi really was the centre of the world. The "bellybutton" of the world. Aletheia knew the legend of the "omphalos" well. Zeus was said to send out two eagles to the ends of the world. He was looking for the centre of the world. The two eagles crossed at the middle of the earth, and that centre was Delphi. Zeus then sent a stone from heaven, and it landed in Delphi and became the "omphalos" which meant the "navel of the world." It was now housed in the Temple of Apollo.

As they passed the main entrance to Delphi, Aletheia observed how her city was constructed. Built into the hillside, the buildings were mostly made of local material, like limestone. Since the God Zeus "blessed" the city, people from the known world came to visit and left gifts, mostly in the form of magnificent statues lining the route to Apollo's temple. It was a sight to behold! Each statue or sculpture was a dedication to the country that created it.

There were only two dedications that enthralled Aletheia; The Serpent Column and the great statue of the God Apollo. The Serpent Column was erected to commemorate the Greeks who had fought and defeated the Persians at the Battle of Plataea. Made of three bronze snakes coiled together, it reached twenty-six feet in height! The three heads of the snakes did not look at each other but seemed to be hissing in different directions. On their heads laid the golden tripod glinting in the morning sun.

The marble statue of the God Apollo, standing proudly on his plinth and holding what seemed like his bow. He was naked except for his robe that partially covered some of his modesty. He has just fired an arrow from his quiver, and he has just killed the Python. Aletheia remembered her dream of Apollo from the previous night and shivered.

There were some important buildings in Delphi. There were a number of Treasuries that housed offerings to Apollo. These were called votive offerings and could be mostly of statues and precious jewellery. They would signify some sort of victory. Aletheia felt she too would be an "offering" to the God soon.

There was The Stoa. A beautiful colonnade of solid columns, with a roof next to the main Athenian treasury and the polygonal wall. One could walk here and feel the cool breeze in the evenings, and it was a gathering place for Delphi businesses.

Overlooking the city was The Theatre with steps going up the mountainside. From the theatre, one could see the whole of The Temple of Apollo and Delphi. It was a real bird's eye view. Aletheia and her family had seen many plays at the theatre of Greek tragedies, and they were usually held when the Pythian Games began. Voices carried very clearly in this place of creative art. Aletheia loved the arts, but she loved the healing arts more.

During the Pythian Games, the Gymnasium was used by the youth of Delphi. They competed in the main Stadium of Delphi and The Hippodrome. The stadium came alive and was a place for many athletic games.

Delphi also had famous athletic statues. There were the statues of the brothers Kleobis and Biton, who pulled their mother's cart without horses to the sanctuary of Hera. People were really impressed, and the brother's mother asked for a gift from Hera for this. As soon as they entered the temple, the brothers fell into a deep sleep. They died at the height of their fame... to be remembered forever.

The Charioteer of Delphi stood proudly in bronze holding the reigns of his chariot and guiding his horse. Chariots were another mode of transport in Delphi. Aletheia looked at his lifelike eyes and smiled. It would have been nice to have had a husband that looked so handsome, but she could not marry or ever have a family of her own.

She would be "married to Apollo" just like the slaves who had carved and left their inscriptions to Apollo on the polygonal wall. They too were pledged to Apollo. Aletheia felt she should carve her name into the wall as well.

Chapter 3

They eventually stopped in front of The Great Apollo Temple.

There was a long wait to see the Pythia. The queue was long, and Aetios had decided that his family should have something to eat and take shelter from the midday sun. They found a place in the shade and so did their horses and servants in attendance.

It was good to rest because it gave Aletheia a pause for reflection. Her younger brother Alcides came up and sat himself down with some bread and a glass of mead.

"You look far away, Aletheia. This should be a very happy and honourable day in your life. You are going to be the successor of the Oracle of Delphi. You are going to help so many people and will be so famous. Your name will spread far and wide in Greece," said Alcides.

He carried on, "I can't wait to start my training in the Gymnasium. I will be the finest chariot racer of the Pythian Games next year. I will win the races and the glories that go with it."

"Stop boasting! All you can think of is fame", said Aletheia. "I don't want to go through this initiation. I don't want to be the next Oracle of Delphi. I would not be very good at predicting the future. In fact, I think I would make it up as I went along and so many people will be hanging on to my every word. What if I get it wrong? It's such responsibility!! I know I am destined for another path."

Her brother looked at her thoughtfully. "You still have the gift of healing in your hands. You still feel the heat. I have seen how you healed our horses, dogs and other pets. You can still be the Oracle of Delphi and do that."

"No I can't!" said Aletheia. "I just want to run away to Ephesus. I want to be at Artemis temple. Not here in Delphi. I feel I am meant to be a healer in Ephesus, at the Artemis Temple there. I could learn all about the healing arts there."

"Ephesus has a great library," said Alcides.

"Yes it does," said Aletheia. "Yet, Apollo the God of Healing wants me here at Delphi as an Oracle."

"Father says we owe Apollo a lot for our prosperity and fortune. We have to give a gift in return," said Alcides.

"You mean me. Don't I have a say in the matter?"

"The Gods rule our lives, Aletheia. We are at their whim and pleasure. Best not to anger them. Imagine what could happen if their anger fell on us."

Their mother Lydia came up to them with more food. Aletheia stood up.

"Mother you must speak to Father. I don't want to do this. I don't want to see the Pythia. I don't want to be her successor."

"That's enough! Alcides, go and see how your father's doing," said her mother. Her brother left.

"We have had this conversation a number of times, and you will do as you are told. I did not raise disobedient children. Do you really want to anger Apollo? Do you want his wrath to fall on us? Please, Aletheia, be reasonable. It's a dream come true that you have been chosen. As a mother, I could wish for no more."

With that Aletheia went silent. It was their turn to enter the Temple of Apollo. In time, this could be her home forever.

***

Apollo, the God of healing, son of Zeus and Leto and twin brother of Artemis. He is God of music, poetry, art, oracles, archery, plague, medicine, sun, light and knowledge. A very important God no less.

He had slain the Python and each night rode a chariot of horses at immense speed to bring the sun into the sky and light the day.

Hermes his brother had made a lyre from a tortoise shell after eating one of Apollo's treasured cows, and Apollo carried the lyre everywhere. Music was in Apollo's blood.

Apollo had also given the gift of prophecy to Cassandra, the Oracle of Troy for a kiss. She had predicted the downfall of Troy and was very upset. Seeing her upset, Apollo added to his gift. He could not take the gift away. Cassandra would be able to see the future, but

449

no one would believe her! Cassandra had warned her people about the wooden horse, but the Trojans were too busy celebrating the Greeks retreat and brought the horse into the city. The horse was full of Greek soldiers, who then at the dead of night let the city gates open and the Greek army destroyed Troy and brought Helen of Troy back to her husband.

Artemis was just as famous as her brother Apollo. She rode a chariot of stags across the sky and brought in the evening. She is the Goddess of Hunting, and her bow and arrow were made of silver. Like her brother Apollo, she could inflict plague and death, but she could also heal. She protected children and baby animals.

She had vowed never to marry and did not like her space intruded upon. A very strong and independent Goddess. Actaeon was slain by his own dogs after he had seen Artemis bathing with her attendants in a stream. She had turned him into a deer by splashing water on him, and his dogs took him to his death.

It seemed she had been infatuated with the God Orion and this made Apollo angry. He wanted to protect his sister's maidenhead and keep her vow. He sent a scorpion, Scorpius, to kill Orion. Artemis then had him made into a constellation of stars so that he would live forever.

What would Apollo do to Aletheia if she defied him was anyone's guess.

As Aletheia entered the temple, she made a silent prayer to Artemis. Artemis was the only one who could help her change her destiny. Together with Artemis, she was sure she had chosen her destiny as healer and not of the next Pythia.

Chapter 4

The Apollo Temple was a mighty structure and the centre of Delphi itself. Built of stone, it had more than fifteen columns. It was a sight to behold!

Aletheia looked at the statement carved into the temple, "Know Thyself" and she suddenly recalled the philosopher Socrates' sayings.

"An unexamined life is not worth living."

"To move the world, we must move ourselves."

"Be as you wish to be seen."

"The secret of change is to focus all of your energy not on fighting the old but building the new."

"To find yourself, think for yourself."

"The mind is everything. What you think, you become."

"Why should we pay so much attention to what the majority thinks."

"I shall never fear or avoid things of which I do not know."

Finally, the words came again, "To find yourself, think for yourself."

Aletheia's father had encouraged her and her brother to study, and she was grateful for that. She felt it was important to be literate. Now the words of Socrates came into her mind in a swirling mass of meaning and words. She admired Socrates greatly. In fact, she had hoped to study all the great Greek philosophers of the day at the Celsus library in Ephesus.

She looked at the carving again. "Know Thyself", and that was the moment her mind finally achieved some clarity. She had to find a way to escape.

They made their way into the temple, and it looked busy. Other priests and priestesses lived here with the Pythia. Aletheia could smell a fragrance in the air, and it felt very misty inside the temple. The Pythia had now seen the rest of her petitioners that morning, and Aletheia and family were the last. A priest summoned them to the adyton, a very sacred place and where the Pythia sat. Aletheia was relieved that today they did not have to make an offering of a sacrificial goat to the Pythia. Well, she was the "offering" herself!

The priest then said, "Only Aetios and his daughter Aletheia may enter the Oracle's presence. She says that she and Apollo are very pleased to see you both."

Aletheia's mother and brother were to stay behind. The two them followed the priest into the inner centre of the adyton

***

Aletheia saw the Oracle of Delphi, and she felt she had entered another world.

This Oracle of Delphi was in her fifties, and she was the most powerful and famous woman in the known world. A direct channel to the God Apollo herself and blessed by the Gods. People of the known world of every background, including emperors, came to see her. Aletheia could sense the weight of responsibility that the Oracle of Delphi had to shoulder.

The Pythia signified both Aetios and Aletheia to come forward with their laurel leaves as gifts. She sat on a bronze tripod and steam rose from cracks on the ground beneath her. She had dark hair tied back, and her hair was covered. She wore a simple gown and looked very mystical, or slightly mad?

The Pythia then spoke to Aletheia, "Well, we finally meet. The last time I saw you, you were just a baby. You have grown into a beautiful, virginal woman. I believe you are chaste and honourable. I am so glad you are here today to accept your destiny. I am going to teach you everything that I know and Apollo will be our guide. You are truly blessed that Apollo, son of Zeus has chosen you. Do you have anything to say?"

Aletheia looked at this woman who she hardly knew and felt the energy drain from her. She felt the dead slain python under her feet, was sucking the energy out of her. The whole temple was so warm.

She looked at omphalos at the right of the oracle. It was said the Python was under there.

"Are you ready to accept your training and initiation?" asked the Pythia.

"Yes," she said. "I want to know all about the initiation, and I need some air. It's very warm in here with all these fumes."

"Of course, my child," said Pythia. "Come with me, I shall take you to the Castellian spring and explain in some detail what your training will involve."

Aletheia glanced at her father. "Go with her, Aletheia. I will wait for you here with the priest."

She left her father's side and followed the Pythia.

They made their way to the Castellian holy spring, and the Pythia told her what was involved in the initiation of her successor. She would teach Aletheia how to make predictions, but there was a procedure involved. The Oracle gave prophecies during the nine warmest months of the year. During winter, Apollo would stay with his half-brother, Dionysus. Apollo would then return in Spring, and the oracle had to undergo purification rites.

On the seventh day of each month, she would bathe in the Castellian spring, where Aletheia was now. She would be led by the priest wearing a purple veil and then wash herself in the spring and hence be purified. She would then drink the holy waters of the Cassotis, and the priests would chant verses. Then she would be presented to the people. At all times, she must present a chaste public persona for the rest of her life.

Then the Oracle said, "Aletheia, you have such a beautiful name, meaning "truth." And the Oracle of Delphi always predicts the truth."

"Really?" said Aletheia. "I heard sometimes they got it wrong on a few occasions!"

"We are never wrong, my dear. It's not our problem how petitioners translate our message. They draw their own conclusions," replied the Oracle. "Now we need to decide when your training will begin, and this temple will be your new home for the rest of your life."

Aletheia thought quickly. "May I come after the Pythia Games? I just want to spend a little more time with my family. It will be a huge transition for us."

"Of course," replied the oracle. "Now let us return to the adyton."

Aletheia began to pray to Artemis for her escape. The Pythia games would buy her much needed time.

Chapter 5

Apollo and his twin sister, Artemis, met at the beautiful Tholos of Delphi, a sanctuary of their half-sister Athena. Apollo and Artemis have decided to call a truce and prepare a neutral meeting ground for their talk.

The Tholos itself was circular in structure with columns and a vaulted ceiling. The carving and decorations were visually pleasing to the eye. There Apollo and Artemis stood facing each other, while torches burned in their holders in the walls providing light.

Apollo started to speak, "Artemis, dear sweet sister. I do not wish to bargain the mere mortal Aletheia's soul with you. I want her to be the next Oracle. My Oracle! She will be mine, and I will be her master."

Artemis replied, "Brother you are infatuated with her. The Gods have given her the gift of hands-on healing. She is mine. I want her at my healing temple in Ephesus, and there she can balance the four humors in my followers and make sure they have perfect health. She will learn about the healing arts at my temple and pass new knowledge for generations to come. She would be a huge asset."

Apollo then said, "But as the Oracle, she will be gifted with the power of foresight. She will be the most powerful woman in the known world".

Artemis then looked at her brother, "We both are patrons of the healing arts. You know she does not seek fame or power. She wants to serve and heal. Please give her that chance."

Apollo looked at her thoughtfully. "Fine. I will set a test. I will send a plague to Ephesus, and if Aletheia cures the people of Ephesus, I will lay down my claim for her. If she fails, she stays at Delphi for the rest of her life."

Artemis looked at her brother. "Agreed. Its good of you to set this test brother. Aletheia will fully understand her healing abilities and her true path after she passes this test."

"You have a lot of confidence in her sister," said Apollo.

"That I do!" replied Artemis, with a smile on her lips.

In Delphi, Aletheia dreamt of the beautiful Goddess Artemis. She told her of her meeting with her brother Apollo. She told her about the test and that a certain person would bring her to Ephesus. She was to pack food and light clothes for the journey. The person would come for her during the Pythian Games to be held within a week. Aletheia needed to be ready and waiting.

Aletheia woke from her dream with hope in her heart. She would soon "Know thyself" whether she was to be an oracle or healer.

She quickly got out of bed and started to make plans for the journey ahead.

Chapter 6

The Pythia Games were the highlight of Delphi. They were held in Apollo's honour every four years, and it was Aletheia's brother Alcides dream to become a charioteer racer at the games.

By his father Zeus's orders, after slaying the Python, who was a creature of Mother Earth and Mother Gaia, Apollo had to pay a debt. He did so by creating the Pythia games.

Today was celebration day, and Aletheia and her family were not going to miss it. Aletheia especially wanted to be at the games to make sure she did not miss Artemis's devotee who would take her to Ephesus. Aletheia had prepared some clothes and food for the journey, which she had secretly hidden in her room for her escape.

They were seated in the Delphi Theatre watching a play. Surprisingly it was all about Apollo's life and him killing the Python! Aletheia was impressed by the acting and costumes the actors wore. The other good reason for coming to the games was to listen to news of the known world. Delphi was a place of gathering and information sharing.

As the play continued, Aletheia heard two men talking behind her. From their conversation, the men had only visited Ephesus a week ago, and an unknown deadly plague had hit the city. The healers, priests and priestesses were doing their best to help the citizens with this affliction. Aletheia's hands began to warm up. They had a greenish glow about them, and very quickly she hid her hands under her cloak. She certainly did not want spectators looking at her hands. Only her brother knew of her "gift."

It would soon be time for the opening of the Pythia games, so the family had luncheon, and they made their way to the Stadium.

"It will be wonderful when your brother competes," said her mother, Lydia.

"Yes, he can't wait," replied Aletheia.

"I will miss you when you start your training at the temple," said her mother.

"I won't be that far away, mother," said Aletheia with a sad smile. For all she knew and hoped for was that Ephesus would be her new home. But she would miss her family. She had truly prayed that Apollo would spare her family misfortune because of her defiant stance against the Gods. How dare they rule and demand humans for this, that and the other. And if mortals did refuse, they would pay the ultimate price! They had no free will.

***

The games were about to begin. First, there was the opening ceremony that included a hymn addressed to Apollo. Then, songs would be sung with a reed pipe and a kithara (an old Greek string instrument). There would be face painting and acting. The creative arts brought a spark to the beginning of the games.

When the games started, Aletheia cheered at every event... be it wrestling, boxing, or pentathlon.

The equestrian events were held at the Hippodrome. There was chariot racing, harness racing, racing a chariot with two or four horses and racing a horse without a chariot. Her brother wanted to learn all of these charioteer skills.

The winners of the Pythian Games would win a spray of laurel leaves, which were sacred to the God Apollo and which he wore on his head.

As Aletheia's mind was diverted to the chariot races, she suddenly remembered the bronze statue of the chariot racer known as Heniokhos. She then had a sudden impulse to go and see the

455

statue.

"Father and Mother, I will have to leave you for a moment. I just need to use the latrines," said Aletheia.

"Take Alcides with you," said her father.

She and her brother were making their way to the public latrines, and then Aletheia did a detour.

"What's going on?" asked her brother. "Where are you going, Aletheia?"

"Be quiet and follow me," she said.

They finally made their way and stood in front of the bronze statue. Just like last time, Aletheia looked into his lifelike eyes and then she heard the message, "Midnight tonight, wait behind your home. Make sure you are packed. Artemis had decreed that I am to take you to Ephesus tonight. The city is in turmoil with the plague of Apollo. It is hoped you can heal the citizens." Then the voice disappeared.

Her brother had heard every word too. "You are going to go tonight, Ally?"

"Yes," said Aletheia. "I will tell you everything, but you must not breathe a word to anyone. If you do, you will feel the wrath of Artemis and Apollo combined. Understood?"

"You know I will not say anything, Aletheia," replied Alcides. "How could you think that?"

Chapter 7

That night she waited with bated breath outside her home. It was dark, and everyone was asleep. They had all gone to bed happy and drunk, with fond memories of the Pythia games.

Tomorrow it would all begin again, but Aletheia would be long gone. It was very quiet and the midnight moon was high in the sky and shone on Alethea's beautiful face. She was nervous. She knew her brother would not betray her, but she was nervous about the "test" ahead. If she passed it, she hoped Apollo would finally let her go to follow her true path as a healer of Ephesus and not the Oracle of Delphi.

As she waited, she heard something coming from the East of Delphi. When she looked hard enough in the twilight, she saw a figure, and it sounded like grinding metal coming in her direction. It was a chariot but no ordinary chariot. Then she realised it was the bronze charioteer.

Eventually, he reached Aletheia. He and his bronze horse looked

456

lifelike, and it was a very eerie sight.

"Are you ready, my, lady? I am your escort. Please get into the chariot," said Heniokhos.

She felt her heart thudding against her chest. Her palms were sweaty and heating up again. She had to travel with this strange devotee of Artemis, but she had resolved to let go of her fear.

Aletheia got in, and then the chariot began to move. When it moved, it moved very fast. It was like time had disappeared and she felt a vague awareness of traveling over mountains, rivers and seas. At times, she felt like she was traveling in the air or maybe in the starry night sky itself.

When she did awake, they were finally at their destination:- The Artemis Healing temple in Ephesus and waiting for them was the Priestess of the temple to greet them.

Aletheia got down from the bronze chariot and walked up to the Priestess.

"You knew I was coming?" asked Aletheia.

"Of course. Goddess Artemis told me so in a vision. Apollo's curse has struck this city. The Gods that create can also destroy. You are only one who can end this nightmare and calamity that has struck the city. This plague that strikes my people has no name and no cure."

"I will do all I can to help, Mother Priestess," said Aletheia.

"You have to prove that you can you use your gift to Apollo, or he will wipe out this great city."

"I know it's my test. If I do not pass, then I am Apollo's prisoner forever. Please show me where the sick are."

They made their way into the heart of the temple, and Aletheia saw so much suffering. The people of Ephesus were lying helplessly on the floor with fever, sickness, and sweat. The healers and other priests and priestesses did everything they could to help the victims. They provided food, damping down the patients and used a variety of herbs to no avail. They were doing their best to balance the four humors in the patients, and it was heartbreaking to watch.

Aletheia thought, One day Apollo, you and the Gods of Olympus will disappear. How can you inflict such suffering and rewards at the same time! You treat mortals like a chess game in the heavens.

Aletheia turned to the High Priestess. "Please bring me lukewarm water to wash my hands and then bring me the citizens affected by the plague one by one. I will set up my healing chamber here."

"Do you wish not to rest, my lady? You have travelled a long way," said the Priestess.

"I am fine. We need to hurry. We don't have much time."

Once the healing chamber was set up, Aletheia closed her eyes and said to herself, "Know thyself, Aletheia. You can do this." Then all Socrates words came to her mind:

"An unexamined life is not worth living."

"To move the world, we must move ourselves."

"Be as you wish to be seen."

"The secret of change is to focus all of your energy, not on fighting the old, but building the new."

"To find yourself, think for yourself."

"Why should we pay so much attention to what the majority thinks?"

"I shall never fear or avoid things of which I do not know."

And then, "The mind is everything. What you think you become."

And, Aletheia healed and cured the people of Ephesus.

Ephesus had much jubilation after that.

***

One week later, Aletheia was at the Apollo Temple in Delphi before the Pythia. Her family were also in attendance. The whole of the Grecian world had known how Aletheia had removed the terrible plague in Ephesus. She was now a famous healer.

The people of Delphi, her family, and the Oracle of Delphi were impressed, and applauded her for what she had achieved. The High Priestess at the Artemis temple in Ephesus, her attendants, and the people of Ephesus were more than grateful.

Then the Oracle of Delphi delivered a message to Aletheia from Apollo.

"You have passed the task I laid out to you. You may go to Ephesus and be a healer for my sister Artemis at her temple there. I now release you from your family's pledge to me. You have proved yourself worthy."

"Thank you, Apollo, for finally letting me follow my own truth and path. I take my leave of you," said Aletheia.

With that, Aletheia saw all the yellow and brown hissing snakes fade away in an instant inside the Temple of Apollo. She saw Artemis and Apollo smiling at her and felt empowered at that very moment.

The End

Links:

subratawriting.blogspot.com

My writersblogg page. http://www.amazon.co.uk/Little-Lost-Baby-Beluga-Whale/dp/1605941794

My first published book. A children's picture book

https://www.smashwords.com/books/view/724171

My first poetry e-book.I am a member of Pinners Writers Group and Society for Authors. I did help form two bookclubs in the past Shepherds Bush Booktalk and Sunday Bookclub which ran its course.

Cover by Author.

Charon

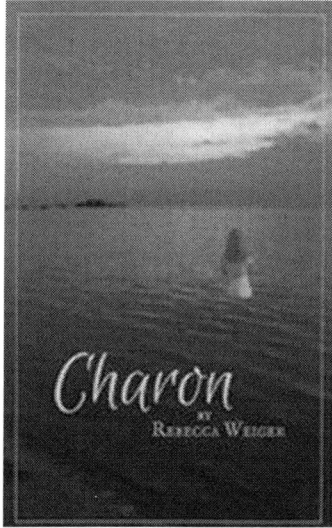

Rebecca Weiger

Rebecca Weiger is an aspiring writer from the very south of southern Sweden. She likes to think her pale complexion comes from being Scandinavian, but if she's being honest with herself, she knows the hours spent behind a book or a laptop (which she may or may not have named Mr. Bingley) might be the true cause.

She started writing almost a decade ago, but CHARON is one of her very first short stories. It invites you aboard the boat of the mythological ferryman of souls, and tells the tale of how a red-haired girl manages to give him his first glimpse of life above the Underworld.

Cassian Raines knew that days were numbered.

Centuries upon the rivers of the Underworld had not taught him much about mortal life—after all, he was only ever allowed to witness the very end of it—but if there was one thing he'd learnt, it

461

was that death was a ticking time bomb not even the deftest of hands could defuse. It was a universal expiration date, a set count of heartbeats; it was a lighthouse horn and it never failed to bring his lonely ferry to shore.

Cassian had never considered himself a sentimental man—in fact, he hardly considered himself a man at all—but he sometimes dreamt of gaining a proper glimpse at the world his boat travelled. He dreamt of birthing cries and birthday songs, of chests racking with laughter and eyes tearing up with something more mirthful than sobs. He knew every noise that grief could make, but still, he dreamt of anything and everything that could sound more beautiful than the word *goodbye*.

Human life was not an hourglass for him to gaze at, though. It was a countdown, and Cassian's only task was to hear the last grain of sand hit the bottom. The conclusive thud steered his ferry with more conviction than his age-old oar.

It was guiding him now, too, as he made his quiet way across Hudson Bay.

If he'd been a petty creature, Cassian would've likened himself to a galley slave, sentenced to row his own prison boat through eternity after eternity. He preferred to go by other adjectives, though, even if they did happen to start on the same human letter. Principled by nature, patient through effort and—above all—punctual by choice.

Judging by the outline of a figure on the docks he was approaching, it seemed the very last word was in danger of being scratched off his resume.

Decade upon decade had left Cassian with an endless record of passengers, ranging from the smallest of high-spirited children to the wisest of the elderly. The girl waiting on land seemed no different from any of them, except for the very fact that she was *waiting*.

As if she'd known he was coming for her.

Cassian let the movement of his oar still, leaving the boat at a leisurely pace and consequently buying himself more time to observe the soul he was about to invite onboard. She was sitting on the very edge of the docks, long legs dangling above the surface of the water and head bent as she watched her restless feet. At least, that's where Cassian assumed her gaze was focused. It was hard to tell with a yard of space separating them and a curtain of fiery hair shielding her face.

It didn't part until the rocking waves gave his silent approach away.

He quietly counted the emotions as they flitted across the girl's features, ticking them off the checklist he'd accumulated over the years. He'd encountered mortal feelings frequently enough to know their man-made names, but he couldn't pinpoint the one that eventually settled on this new passenger's face. There was no anger clinging to a pair of furrowed eyebrows, no sorrow dancing in fresh teardrops.

There were just two blue eyes, curious and solemn and completely inscrutable. The pale lips lingering a few inches below had no problem with clarity, though.

"You're late," they announced.

The words pricked at Cassian's pride, but he halted his defense and focused on stopping the boat. The girl narrowed her eyes, either at his silence or at the sound of his oar scraping across the rocks and pebbles hiding below the surface, but she didn't push her point further. Instead, she began fiddling with something, twirling it over and around her fingers. The glimmer of gold flashing every now and then quickly identified it as his *obol*.

"I was told to give you this," she said.

Her voice was softer than the meaning of her words. Cassian wasn't the prying kind, though, so he didn't ask how she'd come to know the importance of his coin. He just stretched out his hand and waited for the familiar weight on his palm.

The girl's fingers closed around the golden object.

"That's it?" she asked.

Cassian leaned against his oar, ready to wait her out. The girl seemed just as ready to wait for an answer, though, so he finally said, "Payment is simple."

Something changed in the mortal's expression. The corners of her eyes crinkled; the corners of her mouth lifted. Cassian had never seen a smile quite as lively. He doubted he'd seen a proper smile at all.

"He speaks," the girl said, still flashing him that toothy expression. "I was starting to worry there was no face beneath that hood."

Cassian shifted his weight and glanced at his feet, seeking a break from the spotlight of those blue eyes. When he looked up again, her lips were no longer grinning and her gaze was unreadable.

"You know," she said, leaning forward, "you're not the Charon I

463

expected." A second smile made an even briefer appearance than the first. "I'm willing to bet there's a tusked mouth or a crooked nose you're trying to hide, though."

The words made little sense to Cassian, so he made little effort to answer them. Instead, he straightened his back and murmured, "It's time to go."

The girl cocked her head to the side, still staring, even though Cassian knew there was little for her to focus on but the shade his hooded cloak was casting.

"You don't want to know my name."

The lilt of her voice added a natural question mark to the statement, but Cassian only shook his head in response. Her name wouldn't give him a glimpse at the life she was leaving behind; it would only add to the weight of her passage. The boat was already full of those invisible tombstones.

"Why not?" the girl asked, sounding just as young as the roundness of her cheeks would suggest. Her eyes seemed positively ancient in comparison.

"I need your coin," Cassian answered, "not your name."

His hand was still waiting. He caught the girl glancing between it and the object in her own grip. Finally, she let the *obol* slip from her fingers.

Cassian withdrew his hand, but he couldn't withdraw his boat without his passenger onboard. Arguments and persuasion and manipulation—they were all foreign forces to him. So, instead, he just waited to see if his patience could coax the girl out of her stubborn pose.

It took her a heavy sigh or two, but she finally slid off the docks. The boat jostled with the impact of her landing—harshly enough that Cassian considered telling her to be gentle—but the girl seemed unfazed. She claimed a spot at once, even though every part of her seemed ready to continue the battle. The arms folded across her chest looked the most troubling.

"It's Lila, by the way," she said from her new seat. She was no longer looking at him. "Lila Hayward."

Lila. Lila Hayward.

Cassian reined in his sigh, shouldered the weight of her soul, and set the boat in motion.

***

The dark waters of Acheron rippled with the steady movements of the ferry.

A quiet hour had already passed—an hour during which the girl had simply run her fingers through the waves and hummed foreign melodies under her breath. For some reason, her abrupt lack of questions was more unsettling than the brief opposition she'd posed on the docks. It amplified something within her, something far darker than the bottomless river they were crossing.

Cassian wasn't sure how death had chosen to claim her, but he could sense the answer in those quiet exhales of hers. He didn't quite know how to break a silence he'd wished for, though. He had a feeling it would go against his principles.

"You're awfully quiet for a guide."

The girl had to be more bloodhound than human. Cassian couldn't tell if she'd sensed his lingering gaze or if he'd voiced his thoughts out loud, but he did know that she was staring unflinchingly at him.

Waiting for a response. Again.

"Ferryman," he answered. He didn't know why he bothered; the specificity of his title had seldom concerned him. There was something about the girl, though—perhaps it was the way her button nose seemed to be sniffing for a way under his dark skin.

"*Ferryman*," she echoed, one ginger eyebrow arched. "So you *do* care about something."

Cassian glanced at the edge of the boat, at the very side the girl was leaning against, but he didn't want to voice the affection he harbored for his wooden vehicle. Still, his grip on the oar tightened instinctively as the girl's pale hands skimmed the surface of his ferry.

It was his home, his shelter, his legacy—and she was leaving her fingerprints all over it.

"What did you name her?"

Another name; another weight.

"Nothing," Cassian said. He didn't realize he'd been glaring at the girl's dancing fingers until they suddenly stilled. Softening his voice and diverting his gaze, he repeated, "Nothing."

There was a prolonged moment of silence.

"Is that a sensitive topic?" the girl finally asked.

Cassian rowed quietly, thinking of an answer. It wasn't his pride that her words had stabbed at this time. It was something deeper within him, something as nameless as the boat he was manoeuvring.

If he'd been mortal, he suspected he would've called it his heart.

"You've got a lot of questions," he settled on saying.

The girl leaned back in her seat. "Can you blame me for being curious?"

He might've, but he didn't get the chance to.

"This might be everyday business for you," his red-haired passenger continued, clearly not stopping for a breath, "but I was only planning on making one of these journeys. *And* I was planning on making the most of it."

One of her eyelids shut for a second. Cassian frowned at the strange tic.

"It's a wink," the girl said in response, "not an insult." She wasn't quite smiling, but she was shaking her head as if *he* was the strangest one onboard. "You know, you could learn to loosen up a bit, Charon."

Cassian tried focusing on his oar, but the repetition of his false name left him feeling unsettled. Perhaps it was because Lila had offered hers so stubbornly; perhaps it was because she was the first to call him by any name at all.

"It's Cassian," he admitted quietly.

Lila froze for a full second, mouth slightly parted. There was something hiding in the forget-me-not blue of her gaze, something Cassian had witnessed more than once. Fear—mortal and lively and so fleeting that it was gone a moment later when her face scrunched up. Something that sounded remarkably like a cackle left her lips.

Laughter.

There was a sense of otherworldliness lingering there, a sense of life tying the girl to a place far brighter than his aquatic home. Cassian almost wished for the strange sound to last, if only to memorize the human emotion, but the chortles quickly ceased and turned into full-fleshed words.

"If you're about to tell me I'm in the wrong boat..."

She seemed nearly breathless—from fear or amusement, Cassian could not tell. Her shoulders relaxed when he shook his head, though, so he took it as a sign to answer her more thoroughly.

"Do you know how many humans pass away every minute?" he asked. A moment later, he realized the first question he'd ever posed had been an unethical one.

Lila didn't even flinch, though. "You'd need the whole of Titanic to escort them," she answered.

Cassian didn't laugh, and it was not only because laughter didn't

466

live in the muscles of his face. Still, the girl smiled up at him—a crooked, half-hearted smile. He'd never realized quite how many nuances a grin could bear.

"How strange," Lila said. "I would've pegged you to have a morbid sense of humor."

Her questions—though unfamiliar to him—made sense. Her assumptions and knowledge of him didn't.

"How do you know my name?" Cassian couldn't help but ask. His second question came out just as harshly as the first, but it was already filling the cold air between them, too far away from his lips to take back.

"Clearly, I didn't," Lila answered. Her left eyelid was doing its forced fluttering again. A wink—that's what she'd called it.

"You knew the name Charon."

Lila spun a few strands of red hair around her right index finger, twirling the tendrils around and around like she'd played with the *obol* before. Her questions had come out like spitfire, but she seemed to be chewing on her answers.

"My dad used to have a book on Greek mythology," she finally said. Her gaze had been studying his cloak, but it turned towards the river, as if it could spot her father or his book of myths there. "I would always sneak it out of his office when I thought he wasn't watching," Lila continued. "When I moved out, he bought me my own copy."

Cassian stared at her—or rather at the words she'd just expelled. He'd never expected to glean such a clear glimpse at life through three short sentences.

"I think you're supposed to move that."

The return of Lila's voice startled him out of his reverie. He realized he'd been clutching the oar, keeping it halfway out of the water. Lowering his gaze yet again, he continued rowing, all the while remembering the image of a red-haired girl and her father's worn book.

"There are more of you." Lila was speaking again. "That's what you were trying to say before, wasn't it?"

Cassian nodded.

"But you're still taking me to…"

Another nod.

"Are you ever going to take off that hood?"

The oar froze again. From the safety of his cloak, Cassian peered down at his nosy passenger. She still had her hair wrapped around

467

her finger, but the rest of her was free—free and so passionately curious it was nearly impossible not to get blindsided.

Nearly.

"You're too curious for your own good," Cassian said.

Lila didn't seem offended. Without missing a beat, she replied, "What if I told you curiosity killed me?"

Though he knew the possible causes of death—though he *knew* that curiosity was an innocent sin and nothing more—Cassian found himself asking, "Did it?"

"No," Lila said, practically chuckling the word. The laughter died in her eyes even before her mouth had stopped producing the sound. "It was another word starting with *c.*"

The confession was another glimpse, but it wasn't as bright as the previous one. Cassian rowed silently for a minute or two, considering the appropriate payment for such an uncomfortable truth. He only knew the cost of his ferry, though.

That, and the fact that Lila seemed more interested in answers than sympathy.

With hesitant fingers, Cassian lifted his free hand to the top of his hood. The material was worn and familiar, but he was so used to tugging the fabric further over his head that the reversed movement felt strange. The silky sheet slithered down the back of his skull and huddled around his neck.

Lila's neutral expression felt heavier against his skin.

"Well," she said after a moment's observation, "it seems my book was wrong about your tusks, too."

When she smiled this time, Cassian felt his lips attempt to mirror the emotion.

***

The remaining part of their journey was meant to consist of arching river bends, sharp rocks and dreadfully slow minutes. Instead, the boat rocked with Lila's laughter and time was filled with her anecdotes. Strange and unfamiliar as they were, they told Cassian more about life above the Underworld than his previous centuries ever had.

There was a part of his mind that knew he was endangering his second most trusted, self-proclaimed adjective. It knew that he had a certain role in the universe, just as it knew that this role did not include getting to know the soul in his small ferry. Whenever Lila's eyes shone with something other than tears, though—whenever she smiled without a hint of sorrow or laughed without restraint—Cassian found himself shoving yet another one of his principles over the edge of his boat.

He'd blamed the lack of his hood at first—blamed it, and wondered if it had been a shackle to keep more than his identity at bay. By the time the tenth question had left him, however, he'd realized he'd always held the key to his curiosity.

He'd just doubted there'd be someone willing to answer him.

"It must get tiring," Lila was saying, half hanging over the boat's edge again. Her hand wasn't touching the water, though—in fact, she hadn't touched it in a long time. Perhaps she could sense its otherworldliness much like Cassian could sense hers.

"What?" he asked.

"The rowing." She stretched out of her pose, looking more feline than human for just a moment. "The ferrying. The silence."

They were past the worst of the bends—past the real danger of capsizing—so Cassian claimed the seat opposite Lila's and laid his oar across his lap. His muscles were aching, but he wasn't about to admit that.

"I find that silence is underrated," he said instead.

Lila's eyes turned skyward for a second. "I bet you think questions are highly overrated, too."

A few hours ago, he might've. But now... "No."

The smile that graced Lila's face was the gentlest one so far. She rested her elbows on her knees and leaned forward, minimizing the distance between them.

"So," she said, "ask me another one."

Cassian contemplated leaning away from the blue of her eyes or the quietly demanding tone of her voice, but he felt himself leaning in, too.

Just an inch.

"Did you ever fear it?" he asked.

The morbid truth of his words—though slightly less blunt than before—didn't make Lila back down. She gazed at him thoughtfully, as if the answer to his question was waiting in the expression his face wore for him.

Finally, she murmured, "No." There was a pause, and then she was further away, staring out at the waters again, even as she added, "What's the point in fearing the inevitable?"

The question was a moment of breathless déjà vu. Cassian could remember the day he'd come to the same conclusion as his red-haired passenger, the day he'd realized that death wasn't something to be feared, but rather something to be expected. The thought had been his companion for so long that he'd come to find it comforting, but as he gazed at the fiery girl in front of him, he realized he'd never fully understood the finality of death before this moment.

Lila Hayward hadn't feared him or death or the Underworld, but they'd all come to claim her.

Lila Hayward had stepped onboard his ferry, and she was never going back to her father's book on Greek mythology or her mother's walnut bread or her sister's sarcastic sense of humor.

Lila Hayward was dead, and she'd offered him the last glimpses of the life she was leaving behind.

"Get out."

The words left him quietly, so quietly that he wasn't sure Lila had heard them until she turned back to face him. Her blue eyes were blinking at him.

He wouldn't forget them.

"What?" she asked.

"You heard me." Cassian nodded towards the dark waters. They weren't forgiving, but they *would* forgive him this one mortal mistake. "Get out."

"Cassian…"

"There are more things to see," he said. "There are more books and myths to read, more birthday candles to blow out, more—"

"Cassian."

The sound of his name didn't halt his unusually hurried voice, but the soft touch on his hand did. Glancing down, he only had time to observe the contrast of their skin tones before Lila was speaking again.

"There's no return policy," she said. "Just as there shouldn't be. I made peace with this long before your boat came to shore." She smiled softly. "Believe it or not, but I'm storing more than morbid jokes and questions in here."

Her free hand knocked against her temple. The other one was still clutching Cassian's.

"Besides," she continued, "I never did like swimming. I thought I'd feel like Ariel, but I always ended up looking like a drowned rat."

Cassian understood all of the words except for one. "Ariel?"

Lila laughed a little, the sound as sudden as the feeling of her second hand encircling his. In that moment, she was the sun locked in the shape of a human, radiant and warm and bright. Cassian couldn't hold her gaze.

"When you come back," Lila said, "I'll tell you all about her."

The words made Cassian pause, even though he knew he should've gone back to rowing by now. For centuries, the mortal world had been one harbor, the gates of the Underworld had been another and the waters in between had been his makeshift home. He'd never known the feeling of having someone waiting for him— waiting for more than just a silent ferry, that is.

He could get used to it.

"You better hope I don't rat you out." Lila's voice brought his gaze back to her. "A ferryman trying to convince his passengers to swim back to shore? You'd start a riot."

"A riot?"

She shook her head at him, and he could almost hear those four words again.

When you come back…

Cassian Raines still knew that days were numbered. But as he approached the shores of the Underworld for what could've easily been the millionth time, he realized there was a new countdown beginning at the end of every life.

Each mortal deadline would bring him back to this fire-haired, warm hearted soul.

The End

You can find more of Rebecca's work at the following link:

Wattpad link: https://www.wattpad.com/user/reaweiger

Cover by Author.

Afterword

Please tell all your friends about the One Million Project and our aims for charity, both in raising money and highlighting worthy causes. Sharing, tweeting, face-booking, blogging and recommending the collection will help us achieve our goal of raising £1,000,000 for cancer research, and combatting homelessness.

If you liked the stories in this book, please check out some of the writers other work and drop by the OMP website to comment and chat.

http://www.theonemillionproject.com/

Twitter - @JayGreenfield

Books available on Amazon in the series

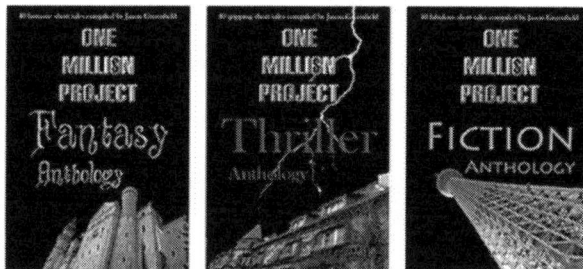

Thank you for reading the OMP Fantasy Anthology. If you enjoyed it, please go to the Amazon page and leave a review. As you can see, we have two other books in the series for your consideration available on Amazon.

24769828R00273

Printed in Poland
by Amazon Fulfillment
Poland Sp. z o.o., Wrocław